RANDOM
HOUSE

LARGE
PRINT

# THE GOOD PILOT
# PETER WOODHOUSE

# THE GOOD PILOT
# PETER WOODHOUSE

Alexander McCall Smith

RANDOM HOUSE
LARGE PRINT

All rights reserved.
Published in the United States of America
by Random House Large Print in association
with Pantheon Books, a division of
Penguin Random House LLC, New York.

Cover design and illustration by Iain McIntosh

The Library of Congress has established a
Cataloging-in-Publication record for this title.

ISBN: 978-0-5256-3457-7

www.penguinrandomhouse.com/
large-print-format-books

FIRST LARGE PRINT EDITION

Printed in the United States of America

10   9   8   7   6   5   4   3   2   1

This Large Print edition published in accord with the
standards of the N.A.V.H.

THIS BOOK IS FOR
**Michael and Angela Clarke**

# ONE
# TINNED PEACHES

The farmer taught her to avoid blisters by spitting on her hands.

He looked at her in that sideways manner of his, and she noticed that his nose had veins just visible under the skin, forked and meandering, like tiny rivulets marked on a map. She knew that she should not stare at his nose; she had been taught by her aunt that she should never pay attention to any obvious physical feature. **People come in different shapes and sizes,** Annie said. **Don't make it awkward for them.**

She wrested her gaze away from the farmer's nose and looked into his eyes, wondering what age he was. She was nineteen—twenty in a couple of months—and it was still difficult for her to judge the age of those even a decade older than she was. He was in his late fifties somewhere, she thought. His eyes, she noticed, were grey, and clear too; they were those of one who was used to the open, to wind and weather, to open spaces. They were a countryman's eyes, accustomed to looking at things that were really important: sheep, cattle, the ploughed earth—things that a farmer saw, and understood. She spotted these things; she may not have had much formal education—she had left school at sixteen, as many did—but she saw things that other people failed to see, and she understood them. They said at school that she could have gone much further, as she was of above average intelligence—a "thoughtful, articulate girl," the principal had written; "the sort of talent this country wastes so carelessly." University, even, had been a possibility, but there had not been much money, and she had found the thought of going away was daunting.

"Spit on your hands, Val," he said. "Like this, see."

He spat on his right hand first, then the left. "Then you rub them together," he continued. "Not too much, mind, or it won't work. You try now. You show me."

She smiled, and looked down at her hands. They were already dirty from salvaging hessian sacks in one of the barns to stack them ready for use—nothing was wasted these days, old string, rusty nails, scraps of wood—everything could be put to some use. Her hands were still soft, though, and he had noticed.

"You don't mind if I call you Val?" asked the farmer. "It would be a bit of a mouthful to call you Miss . . ." He trailed away, looking momentarily embarrassed.

"Eliot. Miss Eliot. No, Val is who I am."

"And you should call me Archie. Full name Archibald, of course, but nobody ever used that—apart from my mother. Mothers usually call their sons by their proper names. I knew a lad at school who was called Skinny by everybody—he was that thin—but his mother always called him Terence." He shook his head at the memory. "Not much of a name, Terence, if you ask me. A town name, I'd say."

She laughed. "My aunt sometimes calls me Valerie. Same thing, I suppose." She paused. "So I should spit on my hands when I'm picking things?"

"Yes, if you like. But mostly when you're using a spade. The handle can be hard on your hands. I've seen young lads get blisters the size of a half-crown from spades."

She promised to be careful, and to remember to do as he said. There was so much to learn: she had been on the farm for only three days, and she had already learned eighteen things. She had written them all down in her land girl's diary, each one numbered, with its explanation written in pencil. Eighteen new pieces of information as to how to work the land; about how to be a farmer.

They had been standing in the yard, directly outside the larger of the two barns. Now the farmer suggested that if she came to the farmhouse kitchen he would make tea for both of them. She should take a break every four hours, he said. "Take fifteen minutes to get your breath back. It's more efficient that way—at least in the long run. A tired man . . . sorry, a tired girl too . . . gets less done than one who's well rested. I've always said that. I told young Phil that. He was one for working all hours, but I told him not to."

He had mentioned Phil on the first day. He had explained that he was his nephew, the son of his older brother, who had helped him on the farm for almost a year, and had gone off to join the army two months earlier. "He saw through Hitler," he said. "Even when he was a nipper, fourteen, fifteen, he said 'Hitler's trouble.' And he was right, wasn't he? Spot on. Look where we are now. Hitler sitting in all those countries—France, Holland, them places—and if it hadn't been for the Yanks coming in we'd be on our knees, begging for mercy."

He had welcomed her, because with Phil gone he would not have been able to cope. The farm was not a large one—eighty-five acres—but it was intensively cultivated and it would have been too much for him to manage by himself. That was where the Women's Land Army came in: they said they would send him one of their land girls, and they sent her, riding on her bicycle from the village six miles away. She lived there with her aunt Annie, the local postmistress. Archie knew Annie slightly, as the local postmistress was friendly with everybody. He must have seen Val about the place, too, but had not noticed her. He did not pay much attention to women and girls; he was a shy man, who had never married, and tended to feel awkward in female company. But he liked Val; on that very first day he had decided that here was a well-brought-up girl who knew her manners and was not going to be afraid of hard work. She would earn her two pounds four shillings a week, he thought. It was a decent wage if you did not have to give up some of it for board and lodging—and he assumed she did not have to pay Annie for lodging, although she probably contributed something for her food. She might even be able to save—if she stayed the course, which he had a feeling she would do. If they had sent him somebody from town, it could be a very different story. He knew somebody who had been allocated a land girl from London and she barely knew that milk came from cows; there was no work in her, he had been told, just complaints about mud and requests for time off every other day. He would not have a girl like that about the place; he would refuse, and they couldn't make him take her, even with their powers to tell you to do this and that, as if the Ministry of Agriculture knew how to run a farm.

"So, Val Eliot," he said as he poured her mug of tea. "Tell me a little more about yourself. Where are your mum and dad?" He immediately regretted the question. He should not have asked her that, and he became flustered.

He was relieved that she did not seem

upset. "My dad went to Australia," she said. "That was twelve years ago, when I was seven. My mum died five years ago."

Well, at least she was not an orphan; that would have made his question all the more tactless. "I'm sorry about your mum," he said.

"My aunt is her sister," said Val. "She took me in. My dad sends money, sometimes, or did until last year, when I turned eighteen. But my aunt was all right with that. She says that my dad isn't a bad man; he's just not the sort to settle down. He moved around in Australia. He's a roofer. They have a lot of tin roofs out there." She paused. "You want to see a photograph of them? Of my mum and dad?"

He nodded, and she crossed the kitchen to the peg where he had told her she could hang the jacket and scarf she wore when cycling from the village. She took out a purse, and extracted from it a small photograph. The photograph had been posted onto a card for protection.

"That's them," she said. "Before he left for Australia."

He looked at the picture of the man and

woman standing outside a shop front. They were holding hands, dressed in their Sunday best, the man with one of those stiff, uncomfortable collars, the woman with a blouse that buttoned up to her neck.

"She has a kind face," he said. "I like her smile."

"My aunt says that my mum always smiled. All the time. She said that even when she felt low about something, she still smiled."

"That's the attitude," said Archie. "No use being down in the dumps. That never makes anything any easier."

"I think that too," she said.

Archie looked at her with admiration. If he had ever had a daughter, she would be something like this girl, he thought. That fellow who went off to Australia—he didn't deserve a daughter like this.

She was still working at six, when Archie told her she could stop.

"You should be getting home now," he said. "Lots of light still, but you'll be needing your tea."

She stood up, brushing the earth from her fingers. She had been weeding a line of cabbages and her knees and her back were sore from the bending.

"I don't have a watch," she said. "It broke."

He smiled. "No need for watches on a farm. There's the sun. It comes up and you know that's morning. Goes down and you know it's night. Simple, really."

He walked back with her towards the farmhouse. While she collected her scarf and coat, he made his way into a shed and emerged with a basket.

"I've got three eggs here for you," he said. "Fresh today. The hens are laying well. I think they like you."

She had fed the hens that morning, and they had pecked and fluttered about her feet, desperate for the grain; silly creatures, she thought, with their fussing and clucking about nothing very much. Now she peered into the basket; he had wrapped each egg in a twist of newspaper, but she could see they were of a generous size. The ration was one egg a week for each person, and here were three.

"You're very kind," she said, taking the basket. "I'll bring the basket back tomorrow."

He nodded. "You say hello to your aunt from me."

"I shall."

"And ride carefully down that lane. Those trucks from the base sometimes come this way and they don't know how to drive, half of them."

"I'll be careful."

It took her forty minutes to reach the village. There were no cars—not a single one—and no trucks. This was deep England, far away from any big town, a self-contained world of secret, hedge-marked fields and short distances. Wheeling her bicycle into the back yard, she leaned it against the wall of the shed. Then she went inside, the eggs her trophy, proudly held before her.

Annie kissed her. "Clever girl," she said. "You must be working hard for him to treat you to those."

"He's a kind man, Auntie."

Annie agreed. "Everyone speaks highly of Archie Wilkinson." She began to unwrap the eggs. "They say he wanted to get married but never did. Too much work to do. Never got away from that farm of his." She paused.

"It could still happen, of course. But look at these eggs: lovely brown shells. Look."

Val examined one of the eggs. "Made so perfectly, aren't they? So smooth."

"One each," said Annie. "Coddled? A coddled egg is hard to beat."

Val nodded. "Is Willy in yet?"

Willy was a relative—a distant connection by marriage—who had been staying with Annie for the last year. He was working on the land, too, although the farm to which he had been sent, a farm that belonged to a man called Ted Butters, was further away, and by all accounts very different from Archie's place. Not that they heard much about it from Willy, who was not very bright and forgot things easily. He was two years older than Val and had never been able to have a proper job. He had come to live with Annie when he had been sent to work on the farm, which was more or less all he could do.

"There's no danger of the army coming for Willy," Annie had observed. "Poor boy, but at least he's not going to have to put on a uniform. He'd never cope with army life."

Val got on well with Willy—it would be

hard not to. She liked his openness, and his innocent, generous smile. "He's very gentle," she said to a friend who enquired about the rather ungainly young man she had seen coming out of the post office. "Willy wouldn't hurt a fly. But there's not much he can do, really. He can pick potatoes and things like that, and precious little else."

Now Annie said, "Willy will like this egg. He loves eggs, doesn't he? I bet that farmer up there will not be giving him much. Mean piece of work."

Half an hour later they sat down at the kitchen table. Annie served the coddled eggs with pieces of bread on which she had scraped a thin layer of dripping.

"This is a real feast," said Val.

Willy beamed with pleasure. "I like eggs," he said. "Always have."

Val washed up, with the wireless on in the background. She listened to the announcer with his grave, clipped voice. Bad news given in measured tones could even sound reassuring. Willy, of course, only half grasped what was happening. "The desert's very dry," he remarked. "Where do they get the water for the tanks?"

"Oases," said Annie. It suddenly occurred to her that he might be thinking of water tanks, rather than armoured tanks. "But don't you worry about that, Willy."

"That's where camels go," he said. "That's so, isn't it? Them oases have wells and palm trees that give you those things, those nuts."

"Dates," said Val.

"The Americans are here, anyway," said Willy. "I saw some. Big fellows. They had one of those jeeps."

Val gazed out of the window. She did not mind the fact that her life was like this, with not very much going on; with Willy saying these odd, unconnected things, and her aunt with her knitting; but sometimes you wondered—you could not help yourself—you wondered whether it would be like this forever.

Ted Butters' farm, where Willy was now working, was large enough to be quite profitable, but was badly run. Ted was a mean-spirited man, and lazy too. A glance at a farmer's fields will tell you all you need to know about his character: a well-kept farm, with fences in good order and well-cared-for livestock, is a sign of a hard-working farmer who understands the notion of stewardship. Badly drained fields, rank grazing land on which weeds have gained the upper hand, a farmyard littered with malfunctioning machinery; these all betray the presence of a farmer who has given up, or who drinks, or who simply does not know what he is doing. People knew what Ted Butters was like, and it was only a matter of time, some thought, before he was dealt with by the local War Agricultural Executive Committee. It would sort him out, they said; it would put him off the land and let somebody else take over.

The committees had been given wide powers. They could order unproductive land to be ploughed up; they could tell farmers what crops to grow; and, if defied or disobeyed, they could order the offender to quit his farm. Such powers were justified by the emergency of the moment: the country needed food, and every square inch of ground would have to be used—and used well—if the land were to yield crops to its capacity. Nobody could argue with that.

Ted Butters was exactly the sort of farmer who might be expected to fall foul of the local War Ag committee. And he would have done so, were it not for the fact that in spite of his sloppiness and the dereliction of his land, he managed—against all the odds—to produce good harvests. And perhaps even more important, there was something between him and the chairman of the committee. The chairman would listen to rumblings about Ted but would never comment on what he heard. Nor would he act. "Ted has something over him," people whispered. "He owes Ted money, I shouldn't wonder."

"Unfair, isn't it? Others get booted out of their farms and Ted gets away with it."

"One of these days they'll catch up with him, so they will."

"Don't hold your breath."

The worst consequence of Ted Butters' negligence was the state of his livestock. His farm was mostly arable land, but he kept a few animals because his father had always kept them and Ted could not be bothered to do anything differently from his father. These animals included two cows, a flock of just under thirty sheep, and two dogs.

"You any good with animals?" Ted asked Willy when he first arrived, brought to the farm by a Ministry of Agriculture official. The official remained silent; he was watching. He had not thought that Willy would be up to this job, but he had been overruled.

Willy nodded enthusiastically. "God loves them," he said.

Ted looked at him. "Cows? You know how to milk a cow?"

Again, Willy nodded. "You pull . . . you pull those things. The milk comes out. It goes into the bucket."

"Bright lad, this," whispered the official.

Ted had accepted him grudgingly, but he had his suspicions. "You'd think they'd send me a couple of those girls," he remarked. "Those land girls. Do they send them my way? None of it. I get the dolt. Maybe he's somebody's eyes and ears—who knows?"

Willy was keen. He was taught to milk the cows and gradually mastered the technique. He was good at muck-spreading— pitching the manure from the cart over the fields, spreading it with his fork, indifferent to the stench.

"That stuff's good for plants," he said to Annie. "They grow like crazy."

"I can imagine it, Willy," said Annie. "You're learning so much, aren't you?"

"Could be," said Willy.

Willy was in charge of bringing the cows in for milking but did not have much to do with the sheep because the sheepdog would not listen to him if he tried to give commands.

"The dog senses that he doesn't know what he's doing," confided the farmer when the committee came to inspect the farm.

"You're doing a good deed, keeping that boy," said the chairman.

Ted shrugged. He had regarded Willy as a nuisance, but now he was satisfied that the young man was harmless—and was useful enough, in his way. "He doesn't seem to know very much," he said. "But he knows how to pull weeds and he's handy enough with a bale of hay. Can't complain, I suppose, though some places have got three, even four, land girls. Why not me? The government think there's something wrong with me?"

Willy noticed things. For all that his conversation followed its own idiosyncratic path, for all that he would turn away in the middle of an exchange and start doing something else, he could see what was going on. He noticed the occasional visits of the two men who drove up to the farm in a small green van, loaded boxes, and then drove away again without going into the farmhouse. He knew that the boxes contained chickens that Ted had slaughtered in one of the barns amidst great squawking and clouds of feathers. He knew that meat was precious and that you could not buy chickens off the ration. But the farmer had said to him, right at the beginning, "Anything you see around here, my boy, you keep to yourself, understand? No poking your nose into things that

don't concern you." And he had accompanied this with a gesture that Willy correctly
interpreted as somehow threatening him, a
wringing motion, as if he were strangling a
chicken.

Ted need not have worried about Willy's
reporting anything of that; the young man
was not interested in such matters. But what
did interest him was the condition of the animals, even if he had no idea that anything
could be done about it. He noticed that the
cows were lame; somebody had explained
to him that hooves needed to be trimmed,
and if this were not done regularly, could
be painful for the animal. He pointed this
out to Ted, who was indifferent. "They can
walk, can't they? Nothing wrong with those
cows."

Willy was responsible for the feeding of
the two sheepdogs, Border collies, who were
housed in a small shed at the back of the
barn. These dogs were mother and son, Ted
having put the mother to a dog owned by
another farmer down in Somerset. He had
done so to sell the puppies, of which there
were four; good prices would be paid for a

good-looking sheepdog, and he disposed of three of them within a few hours at the local market. He kept the fourth, because the mother was getting on and he would need a dog to train up to take her place.

Willy wondered why the dogs got no meat, but were given a plain porridge topped up with a few unidentifiable kitchen scraps. It was the sort of food one gave to pigs, he thought, rather than dogs. Why not give the dogs rabbit? There were enough of those on the farm, and Ted could easily shoot a few for the dogs' pot. It was unkind, he thought, to deny a dog meat and to keep it tethered for days on end, as Ted did, in that darkened shed.

The dogs liked Willy and whimpered as he bent down to stroke them.

"You poor fellows," he said, allowing them to lick him on the arms, on the face. "Some-day things will get better for you. When the war's over, maybe. Maybe then."

He watched Ted as he tried to train the younger dog. He used a stick, a branch he cut from the patch of willows near his pond, and he wielded this with a vicious determination. He beat the mother dog, too, who cowered when he approached, scraping the ground with her belly, rolling over in the classic canine pose of submission, her legs cycling in the air as if to defend herself from impending blows.

"Bite him, bite him," muttered Willy under his breath.

He told Annie about this. "Ted Butters beats the dogs," he said.

She raised an eyebrow. "Oh yes? When they do something wrong?"

Willy shook his head. "Just for being dogs. He beats them because they're dogs."

Annie looked at him. He had an odd turn of phrase, that boy, she thought; sometimes he said things that made you stop and think. "For no reason?" She shook her head. "He's not a very nice man, that Ted Butters. Never was."

"With a stick," said Willy.

Annie sighed. It was too small a wrong to make a fuss about, and nobody would interfere with the way a farmer treated his dogs. For most people, that was the farmer's business. "Lots of people are unkind to dogs, Willy." She paused. "He doesn't lay a finger on you, does he?" You had to be careful; Willy was not much more than a boy, really, and there were some men who had to be watched when it came to boys.

Willy looked at her blankly. "Me?"

"He doesn't beat you? Or anything?"

He laughed. "No, I said that he beats the dogs, not me. He beats them."

Val had overheard this conversation. She had been sitting in a corner of the kitchen with a magazine. There was very little to read, because of the paper shortages, but she had obtained this from a friend on the promise that she would give it back. It had pictures of the king and queen inspecting a house that had been bombed. They were not worried about bombs, said the report. They carried on with their duties in spite of everything that Hitler could throw at them.

She looked up. "I hate people who mistreat dogs," she said. "That man . . ."

"They should run away," said Willy. "Dogs can run away, I think."

Val turned a page of the magazine. "Sometimes they do," she said.

Willy was watching her. He knew that Val would be kind to dogs. They would love her, those dogs at the farm; they would lick her just as they licked him. They would appreciate somebody like Val.

The new planes arrived one morning, all coming from the same direction, dropping down below the trees just before they landed, seeming to disappear into the countryside. But even after they disappeared they could be heard, their throaty growl rising up into the sky, before this eventually died away and silence ensued. She said to Archie, "One flew right over me. Like an eagle swooping down. Big thing. Almost knocked me off the bike."

"American planes," he said. "They never told us, but they're going to be staying at the base. They were cutting the grass on the airfield. I saw that going on and thought they might be expecting visitors. They're setting up their own base, right next to ours."

"All the way from America," said Val.

Archie nodded. "And a good thing too. Give Goering something to think about, I'm sure. Old Fatty with his blue uniform."

There were not many planes, and their flying patterns seemed erratic. A fighter base would have had constant comings and goings, but this sent out no more than a flight or two a day, aircraft that Archie identified as Mosquitoes, but in U.S. Air Force livery.

"I know we're not meant to talk about it," he said to Val, "but I heard down at the pub that they're reconnaissance people. They fly off and take photographs of what Jerry's up to. Railway lines, factories—stuff like that."

She spoke in mock admonishment. "Careless talk costs—"

He stopped her. "I'm only saying what I heard."

"Well, we'll see."

She got on with her work, which that day was weeding a field of carrots. She used a hoe to begin with, but damaged so many of the carrot-tops that she laid it aside and began to do the task by hand. The field was not a big one, but ploughed and sown it had produced what seemed to Val to be a sea of carrot-tops. Archie had said she could take her time—that the task would normally have kept three or four people busy—but her slow progress was an affront to her own sense of urgency. It was as if the fate of air battles fought far away was somehow dependent on her ability to clear the carrot field of weeds;

she thought of the weeds as enemies—each one plucked and tossed aside was another Nazi dealt with.

Her back started to trouble her, and there were other muscles, too, that she was only just discovering. There was a crick in her neck that brought on a vague ache somewhere at the back of her head. She stood up and stretched, trying to loosen and unknot her aching muscles. She thought: **What if this war goes on indefinitely?** She had not learned much history at school, but she had heard of the Hundred Years' War. If it had happened before, then surely it could happen again: her children, if she ever had any, could be weeding this carrot field for year after year before passing it on to their own children.

She mentioned this to Archie. "There was a hundred years' war once, you know. A long time ago, but it lasted for a hundred years."

Archie set her mind at rest. "A hundred years? No, more like a hundred days. Jerry won't stand a chance now that the Americans are here. A hundred days should do it, I'm reckoning."

"But the Germans still—"

He did not let her finish. "They're no match," he said. "There are these American factories, see, turning out hundreds of planes a day. Hundreds. Rolling them out."

"I hope you're right."

An American serviceman came to the farm to ask about eggs. He arrived in a jeep, being driven too fast, with a younger man who remained at the wheel and did not get out. This younger man had an angry skin, pitted and red; he looked barely eighteen, and he avoided eye contact. He was one of those people, Val thought, who was probably always unhappy to be where he was. There were people like that. They were both dressed in uniform of some sort, or working clothes, perhaps, as it seemed very casual.

The older man said that he was from the base. "We're looking for more eggs," he said. "We get a lot of our rations centrally, but not enough eggs."

Archie scratched his head. "I could speak to the hens."

The man laughed. "Sure, speak to the hens. Any chance?"

Archie looked over in the direction of the

hen coop. "I could get a few more chickens. If I did, I could do maybe four or five dozen a week. Depends on the hens, though."

"Every little helps," said the man. "Can you deliver to the base?"

"I can send the girl," said Archie.

Val glared at him, but then she smiled at the man. "I can bring them," she said. "On my bike."

The man smiled. "That's mighty helpful of you, m'am."

Val thought it was better to be **m'am** than **the girl.** She hoped that Archie noticed. Afterwards, when the jeep had gone, she remarked to Archie, "They have good manners, those Americans."

Archie nodded. "Yes, but they speak all peculiar."

"They probably think we do," said Val.

Archie looked surprised. "Us? No, we speak English as it's meant to be spoken. It's them that's got it wrong."

A week later she made the first delivery. The base was about eight miles away, and it took her a good hour to reach it on her bicycle, three dozen eggs safely stored in the handlebar basket. They had warned the sentries of her arrival and she was waved through after the eggs had been inspected.

"Nice," said the sentry, and added, "For the officers, I bet."

He directed her to an office, a Nissen hut with a large sign on its front. It was a scene of busyness: men were milling about; planes lined the edge of the runway; a mechanic stood on the wings of one and shouted to another man below.

A thin man in civilian clothes asked her what she wanted. She explained that the eggs were for Sergeant Lisowski; it was the name of the man who had come to the farm, and she stumbled over it. But the thin man knew who it was. "Cookhouse," he said. "I'll call him."

A figure emerged from the door. He was walking somewhere purposively, but stopped, and turned his head. He looked at Val.

"Something good in there?" he asked, gesturing to the basket.

She was shy. He was wearing a uniform and there was something unusual about him. She glanced at his face. It was the eyes, which were blue, and the regularity of the features, perhaps, and the way he seemed to be smiling at her without really smiling.

"Eggs," she said. "Eggs from the farm. They're for Sergeant Lis . . ." Again she stumbled over the name.

He grinned. "Lisowski?"

"Yes."

Something made her want to prolong the conversation. She reached for one of the small cardboard boxes in which the eggs were stored. She took it out and prised open the lid. He peered into it, and as he did so, the box slipped out of her hand and fell to the ground.

He reached forward in an attempt to catch it as it fell, but he was too late. Hitting the ground with a dull thud, the box disgorged several of its eggs. Val gasped, and instinctively bent down to retrieve them, upsetting her bicycle as she did so. Slowly, but irretrievably, the bicycle toppled over, tipping out the remaining two boxes of eggs.

"Oh, no . . ."

She wanted to cry, and almost did. She felt flustered and embarrassed. They were all broken, she thought; every one of them. Eggshell lay on the ground covered with slippery, translucent white. Streaks of rich yellow yolk mixed with the viscous white and with grit on the ground below.

His face registered his dismay. "Oh my, this isn't so good."

She looked up at him—they were both crouched down in an attempt to fix the unfixable.

"Could be worse," he said, straightening up. "Eggs are just eggs, after all."

She started to pick up her fallen bicycle, but he was there before her. "There," he said. "I'll get you something to wipe your hands."

"I don't need anything," she said, and then, lest she sound churlish, "Thank you anyway. I'm all right."

"Pity about the eggs," he said. "Do you want me to square it with Lisowski?"

She shook her head in her confusion.

"I guess I should introduce myself," he said. "My name's Mike."

"I'm Val."

He nodded, and then glanced at his watch. "You're from round here?"

She told him about the farm.

"I've probably flown right over your place," he said.

"Probably."

"I hope I didn't give you a fright."

She told him she was accustomed to planes.

He looked at his watch again. "I could give you a ride home," he said. "I come off duty in twenty minutes. I could take you—and your bike—back to the farm."

She wanted to spend more time with him; she did not want the acquaintance to end. She felt something unfamiliar in her stomach: a lightness. She looked down at the ground. "You don't mind?"

He shook his head. He was smiling now and she saw that there was a dimple in each cheek—perfectly placed. It was a boyish face, clean-cut, the features regular. There was an openness about it, too, that gave it a strong sense of innocence. She thought he was probably a bit older than she was—perhaps mid-twenties—but it was hard to tell. She had heard people say that Americans looked younger than British people;

a friend had told her it was because of the food they ate—"buckets of ice cream and corn on the cob and such things."

He was telling her he did not mind. "It would be a pleasure. We can take a jeep—official, you see, on the grounds that we need to replace a few eggs. Your bike can go on the back."

Annie said to Willy, "Now, Willy, you're going to have to take your shirt off."

Willy looked resentful. "Don't like taking my clothes off. Not with women around."

"It's just your shirt, Willy. And if you think we haven't seen men's chests before, then you don't know very much about anything."

He hesitated, and then began to unbutton the shirt. Annie looked away in a gesture to his modesty.

"Turn around," she said.

Holding the shirt in front of him, he turned his back to her, and she gasped.

"That devil," she exclaimed.

"He only hit me once," said Willy.

She reached forward and put a finger on the weal. He gave a start.

"That hurts, doesn't it?"

"It's not bad. I told you: he only hit me once, and I don't want any fuss."

She walked round to his front and took his hands in hers. "What with, Willy? What did he hit you with?"

"He had a sort of whip. Those fellows who walk with the hounds carry them. I've seen them."

She drew in her breath. "You can do a lot of damage with those things." She paused, and returned to her examination of the weal. "I don't think the skin's broken."

"I told you, it's not a big thing."

"Put your shirt back on. But I'm going to watch that—I'll look at it again tomorrow, and if needs be we'll get Nurse Simpson."

"I don't need to see her."

"I'll be the judge of that, Willy." Her manner had become stern. "Do as I say now."

He put his shirt back on, buttoning it right up to the collar.

"I'm not having him raising a hand to you," said Annie. "You're a grown lad, Willy—you're not . . . you're not some boy." She paused. "Why did he do it? What was it all about?"

Willy bit his lip. When he answered, his tone was reluctant. "He was beating one of the dogs."

She stared at him. "And you tried to stop him?"

It took him a while to answer, but finally he said, "They'd killed one of the chickens. Dogs do that. They don't know any better."

She frowned. "So what did you do, Willy?"

He sniffed. "I grabbed the whip from him. I hit him with it—I wanted him to see what it felt like. Even if you're a dog—"

She stopped him. "You mean you struck him first?"

He stared at the ground. "Maybe. But he was beating the dog and she had done nothing to deserve it."

"Other than killing a chicken . . ."

He pouted. "It's in their nature. I said, that's what dogs do."

She nodded. "You're right. And you shouldn't beat an animal—it's not right."

"No, it isn't."

She reached out for his hand, and held it gently in hers. "The problem is, Willy, that you started this fight, you know. You struck him, and he'll just say that he was defending himself. You know how these things work, don't you?" She suspected he did not.

He looked confused.

"If you hit somebody, he can hit you back?"

Annie sighed. "I think we should leave it, Willy. I was going to go to Bill Edwards about this . . ." Bill Edwards was the village policeman, brought back out of retirement because of the war; too tired to exert authority, he relied on friendship to police his patch. "But now I think I shouldn't."

"No, you shouldn't. I told you I didn't want any fuss."

"But you promise me that you won't provoke that man again. You promise me that?"

He crossed his heart—a childish gesture, but one that signalled to her that he had understood.

"Good boy," she said.

Later that night, when Willy had gone to bed, Annie talked to Val about what had happened. She expressed the concern that the young man's lack of judgement could cause difficulties. "Any sensible person would have known not to interfere in something like that," she said. "Farmers and their dogs—you stay out of it, even if it's hard to do. And a man like Ted Butters . . ." She shook her head. "You don't go laying into him."

Val felt she had to smile. "I don't suppose you do."

"Willy has a strong sense of right and wrong," Annie continued.

"Even if he hasn't much sense about anything else," said Val.

Annie looked disapproving. "He does his best," she said.

Val decided to change the subject. "I'm going out tomorrow night," she said.

"With the other land girls?" There was a group of five land girls billeted in a big house on the edge of the village.

"Yes," said Val. "We've been invited to a dance."

Annie took up her knitting. She had been working on a sweater for weeks and was frustrated at not finishing it. "Very nice. RAF?"

"The Americans," said Val.

Annie smiled. "They say they have tinned peaches. Have you heard that too?"

Val had not. "Nylons, some say. And chocolate."

"I don't think men should give girls nylons," said Annie. "Chocolate is one thing, but nylons . . ."

"If I see any tinned peaches," Val promised, "I'll bring some back for you."

Annie laid down her knitting and closed her eyes. There was a look on her face that was half longing, half ecstasy. "Just imagine—a bowl of tinned peaches with a drop of cream. Just imagine it."

"You never know," said Val.

Annie opened her eyes. "Don't be too late. Will they be bringing you back home with the others?"

"They will," said Val. "They have a lorry. It's ever so bumpy, travelling in the back of it, but they'll bring us right to the door."

It was not a large dance. She, like the others, had been to larger ones at an RAF base twenty miles away, but what made the difference here was the catering. The U.S. Air Force may have been looking around for extra supplies of fresh eggs, but there was no shortage of anything else. Two trestle tables, laid with red gingham tablecloths, were laid out with things that had long since disappeared from the shelves of British groceries, or had never been there in the first place.

And there were tinned peaches, but in bowls now, and she could not think of a way to get some back to her aunt. She could wrap one in a handkerchief, perhaps, but without its syrup it would not be the same, and it would stain her dress anyway. So she thought of her aunt as she helped herself to three peach halves, savouring their sheer deliciousness and wondering how one might describe the taste and the sensation accurately. There was the sweetness, of course, but there was something else—a slight roughness on the tongue that gave them their characteristic texture. Or perhaps she should not mention them at all, but simply say that the food was good, and leave her aunt to imagine the rest.

She looked out for Mike, who had driven her home after the egg incident, but although there were only twenty or so officers there she did not see him. She felt a pang of disappointment: she had assumed that he had been behind her invitation, and now she was not sure. Perhaps she had been too quick to imagine that there was something there when there really was not. Perhaps she was just another young woman to him, nothing more than that—the girl who rode over with the eggs and clumsily dropped them all over the place. Perhaps he felt sorry for her. Americans were rich—they had so much—and the British were so poor now, scrabbling around for enough food to eat, counting every round of ammunition, every drop of fuel. She thought: **What do we look like to them?** Poor cousins who were exhausted by a long fight against the local bully and must now be helped to finish something they could never have completed by themselves.

After the guests had been there for ten minutes, he arrived with another two officers. He was in uniform, as a few of the men were, the others being in civilian clothes. He made straight for her, and briefly took her hand, in what could have been a handshake or could have been something else. He held it, though, and only dropped it when he went to get a drink for both of them, and as she watched him cross the floor towards the bar she thought, with pleasure, that she had been right—he had invited her. It was him.

They had organised a small band—two saxophones, a trombone, and a percussionist. This quartet now struck up, although people were still helping themselves to plates of food and were not ready to dance. She sat with him on a small sofa that had been put along the side of the room and sipped at her drink, conscious that her dress, of which she had been proud until then, was almost dowdy by comparison with what some of the other women had managed to produce.

But he said, "I like that," and gestured to the dress. "It's pretty."

She lowered her eyes. She was not sure whether she should say that she liked his uniform. There were so many bewildering uniforms now and a compliment directed at a uniform could seem flat, or even sarcastic.

She struggled to think of something to say and ended up asking where he was from.

"The United States of America," he replied, and laughed.

This helped. "Oh, I know that."

His eyes were bright, as if he were amused by something. "Just making sure."

"But where in America? It's a big place, isn't it?"

"A place called Muncie, Indiana. It's not right in the middle, but it's heading that way. Mid-West, we call it. You heard of Chicago?"

She gave him a look of mock reproach.

"Of course I've heard of Chicago." She was trying to think where Chicago was. Was it near Los Angeles?

"Well, Muncie, Indiana, isn't all that far from Chicago—a few hundred miles. Chicago's there . . ." He jabbed at a point in the air. "And Muncie's down here." He made another jab.

"I see."

"It's not a very big town," he continued. "But we've got some great things going on. You know those glass jars for preserving fruit? You know them?"

She nodded, although she thought the glass jars he was referring to must be much bigger and better than the ones her aunt used for making jam in the blackberry season.

"We make those in Muncie," he said. "Invented there. Those famous jars. There's the Ball glassworks. You heard of them over here—the Ball family?"

She had not.

"They're generous folks," he continued. "They helped build a college, and a hospital. My mother knew one of the sisters from that family—not very well, but she knew her. She lived in a big mansion near the river, and you know what? She believed in fairies. She was real keen on fairies. She had a whole library of books about them and pictures on the wall and so on. Fairies flying around, sitting on bushes, doing everything really. I guess she was hoping to see one herself some time, but she never did, poor lady."

She was wide-eyed. This was a world so far from her own. Glassworks. Mansions beside a river.

Mike took a sip from his glass of beer. "We're nothing to do with the glass business," he said. "My dad runs a dry goods store. We sell clothes, but most other things too. Sewing machines, some kitchen stuff."

She asked him what he had been doing before the war. "I was at college in Indianapolis," he said. "I was studying engineering. They wanted me to finish that first, but two of my friends were enlisting and I thought that if they were going then so should I. You could say that Uncle Sam called." He took another sip of his beer. "But I'll go back after all this is over. It won't be long now."

She seized at this. People clutched at everything—any scrap of comfort they encountered. Rumours abounded: there were new weapons, on our side; the Germans were running out of oil; their own people were rioting because they were even more short of food than we were; somebody was planning to shoot Hitler and the war would come to an end that way. Every fresh story gave a few moments of comfort before being discounted.

"It's not going to be long?" she asked.

He seemed so confident. "No. We're hitting them hard—and your boys are too. That's my job, you see. We fly those planes over and take photographs, so we know what's going on. We're a reconnaissance unit."

She had a slight sense of being made party to information that she should not know, and she changed the subject. "That tune the band's playing—do you know what it is?"

He listened. "'Speaking of Heaven,'" he said. "Glenn Miller played it. At least, that's what I think it is."

"I'm bad at songs. I like them, of course, but I get them mixed up."

"I find I remember the words," he said. "It's not much use, of course, because I can't sing. But they stick somewhere up there." He tapped his forehead. "**Speaking of heaven, once I found an angel** . . . and then I forget what comes after that."

She glanced at him. She had been too shy to look at him properly. She lowered her gaze to the glass in her hand. This could not be happening, but it was. And that, they said, was how it always happened: you were not expecting it; and then it happened, and you were in love. Just like that. She thought that was why they used the expression **falling in love,** because it was sudden, and unexpected, as a fall is, and it was very much the same feeling, of sudden powerlessness as gravity took hold of you, as love does; love and gravity were very similar: equally strong, equally irresistible.

Over the two weeks that followed, he saw her eight times: twice when she went to the base to deliver the eggs, and on other occasions when he managed to get a few hours away from the base in the evenings and came to the house in the village. As an officer, he was allowed to be away from the base when not on duty, and his evenings were free, as photographic units rarely flew at night. Annie liked him, and would tactfully leave them alone in the small sitting room, on the pretext that she had to go out and Willy would have to accompany her. Willy was bemused, but was won over by a book that Mike gave him on the identification of American planes.

"He's nice, that American pilot," he said. And then, with un-feigned interest, "Do you really like him, Val? Are you sweet on him?"

"I really like him, Willy. He's kind, isn't he?"

"Is he from Texas?"

She smiled. "No, he's from a place called Muncie, Indiana. It sounds like a really nice place. He's shown me some photographs."

He had a camera and what seemed to her to be an unlimited supply of film. He developed this in the same darkroom they used for their reconnaissance shots, and he said there was no cost involved. "I get the film cheap and the chemicals are there anyway, so I slip mine through when the guys finish with the spools from the planes. Nobody minds."

He was generous with his time. He took a portrait photograph of Annie, who dressed especially carefully for the sitting, wearing her best dress, a dress she had not worn for fifteen years: a silk shift in the flapper style. "It makes me look ridiculous," she said. "Mutton dressed up as lamb."

"You could never look ridiculous," he said.

Val liked that. Mike knew what to say, she thought. They said the Americans had good manners, and they were right. Those things they said about Americans boasting and smoking cigars was all invention, she thought. People were jealous because they had tinned peaches and lots of fuel and because they did not look hungry, the way so many English people did.

He took a photograph of Willy in his suit, which was too small for him and pinched about the chest and shoulders. Willy was pleased with the result and framed it, placing it on the chest of drawers in his room. Val wanted to tell him that people did not put up photographs of themselves—it would be considered odd to do so—but then realised that perhaps it was not so odd if you had nobody else to display. And Willy had nobody, unless you counted her and Annie:

there were no girlfriends—he was too shy for that—and she knew that the other young men from the village, although kind enough, laughed at him behind his back.

Mike did not. He said, "It's a shame that Willy can't get to the States. He's a hard worker, and he could get somewhere in Indianapolis. We have a big plant there that makes medicines. You ever heard of Colonel Eli Lilly?"

"Is he at the base?" Val asked.

Mike laughed. "No, he was a colonel in the Civil War. He came back from the South and started making medicines back home. They built it up and now there's a big place that has hundreds of people working for it. Chemists, doctors even. But there are jobs for all sorts of people. Drivers. Guys who work on the machinery—the tubes and vats and things like that."

"I'm not sure if Willy . . ."

"Maybe not. But if he met a nice girl who could take care of him, he could get by just fine."

She looked at him and knew, at that moment, that if he asked her to marry him, she would accept without hesitation. Muncie,

Indiana, was a long way away, and there would be things about it that would be strange to her, but that would not matter if Mike was with her. And that was all she wanted: to be with him.

On one occasion, when he was unable to get away from the base, he sent a card to her, delivered by an airman. She opened it in her bedroom, her hands shaking. It was in his handwriting: **To my sweetheart,** it said. **The sweetest girl in England. From Mike, the guy who thinks of her every minute of those longs hours of flying. Every minute.**

She slipped it under her pillow and, that night, waking up in the small hours, she took it out, switched on her light, and read it again and again before she tucked it back under the pillow and dropped off to sleep smiling.

It was on a Saturday evening that Willy brought the dog back to the house. Willy worked all day on Saturday—Sunday was his only day off—but he came back on this occasion slightly earlier than usual. Annie was listening to the wireless and Val was cooking when he came into the kitchen and announced that there was something outside he wanted them to see. Annie asked if it could wait—her programme had twenty minutes to run—but Willy said that it would be best if they came right away.

The dog was in the small garden behind the post office, tied to a leg of the wooden bench on which Annie sat in fine weather.

Annie exchanged glances with Val, who rolled her eyes. "Whose dog is this, Willy?" she asked. She thought that she already knew the answer, but asked the question anyway.

"It's one of the dogs from the farm. He's the young one. His mother is the one he uses for the sheep."

Annie nodded. "I thought as much. And why is he here, Willy?"

Willy said nothing for a while, but then he burst out with his explanation. It was a torrent of words, a rambling imprecation.

"He beat him this morning. I saw him. He told me to mind my own business, but he hit him with a stick because he'd been barking. So I've brought him here. I knew you wouldn't mind—and please say it'll be all right. Butters went off somewhere with one of his pals and I was there by myself, so I untied him and brought him here. I left a note for him on the kitchen table. I said, **Your dog's run away and I don't know where he is.** I said that I'd look for him and bring him back if I saw him, but I won't. So can he stay here, Auntie? Please. He wants to stay—I can tell he does. I'll feed him and he'll be no trouble."

He drew breath once he had finished and looked at her imploringly. Annie bent down to pat the dog's head. He whimpered, and tried to lick her hand.

"You see," said Willy. "He likes you already."

She straightened up. "We can't have a dog, Willy. You're out all day long and I'm

busy in the post office. I can't take him in
there. You know that."

"He'd be no trouble. He's not a noisy dog.
He's very quiet."

Val moved forward. "He could come to
Archie's farm. He used to have a dog. He
said something the other day about missing
him."

Annie frowned. "You'd have to ask him
first."

"I'll take him with me on Monday and see
what he says. Will he run alongside a bike?"

Willy told them that this was how he had
brought him home. "He's got strong legs.
You tie a bit of string to his collar and he'll
run beside the bike for miles. Give him a
rest now and then, but otherwise he's fine."
He looked at Annie. "So, can he stay until
then—just two nights?"

Annie sighed. "One more mouth to feed,
I suppose. But we can't turn him out." She
bent down to pat the dog once more. "Has
he got a name?"

"Peter Woodhouse," said Willy.

Val laughed. "Peter Woodhouse? That's a
grand name for a dog."

Willy looked defensive. "That's what's written on the side of his kennel. It's on one of the boards. It says Peter Woodhouse."

Annie burst out laughing. "Woodhouses were a firm of removers. They used to pack people's furniture in crates. Peter Wood-house. That's where it comes from—it's an old Woodhouse crate. That's what his ken-nel is made of."

"Well, that's what I call him anyway," said Willy. "And he answers to it. You try."

"Dogs answer to anything," said Val. "If you called out Winston Churchill, I bet he'd answer."

"It's a good name for him," said Annie. "Let him be Peter Woodhouse."

Permission was given, and the dog spent the night on an old rug under the kitchen table. In the morning, he awoke the house-hold by scratching at the door, and it was Annie who took him out into the garden. Then she fed him with a bowl of porridge mixed with a small amount of chicken's liver that a friend had given her.

"It's going to be a new life for you, Peter Woodhouse," she said. "Your war's over now."

. . .

Archie took it in his stride. He was standing in the doorway of one of the barns when he saw her ride down the track with the dog trotting beside her.

"So, you got yourself a dog," he said as she drew up and dismounted in front of him.

She leaned her bike against the wall of the barn. "My cousin rescued him," she said. "He was being mistreated."

"Nice-looking animal," said Archie. "Reminds me a bit of my last dog."

Val took advantage of this. "Then you wouldn't mind if he stayed here?" she said. "He's had a miserable time."

"Hold on," said Archie. "I didn't say I wanted a dog."

"No, but he wants you. Look at the way he's gazing up at you. Look at that. He thinks the world of you already, I'm sure he does."

She could see that it was working. Archie was ruffling the fur around the dog's neck.

"You're a good fellow, are you?" he said. "A good watchdog? Bark at any ne'er-do-wells who come around the place, will you?"

This was her chance. She knew that farmers were worried by theft. For people in towns, worn down by queues for rations that seemed to get smaller and smaller, the temptation to help themselves to a chicken or a duck was sometimes just too great. "He's good at that," said Val. "You know how Mrs. Carter lost ten of her chickens the other night? They traced them from the feathers. They were on the ground, all the way down to that army camp. Right into the barrack room where the lads who stole them were living. They would have caught them red-handed, if they hadn't already sold the chickens."

"Heard about it," said Archie. "A bad business."

"Well, Peter Woodhouse wouldn't let that happen."

Archie looked puzzled. "Peter Woodhouse?"

"That's his name," said Val. "It's a pretty unusual name for a dog, but it suits him somehow."

Archie sucked in his cheeks. "He'd need to be fed."

"Rabbits," said Val quickly. "Teach me how to shoot and I'll get them myself."

"I'll do it," said Archie. "I can fix him up with a rabbit. Last him a week, a rabbit will."

She realised now that she had won.

"I'll find something for his kennel," she said. "A box, perhaps . . ."

Archie had already thought of that. "There's an old wooden crate in the barn. It's got something in it, but I'll clear it out. That'll do fine."

On impulse, she turned round and kissed the farmer on the cheek. He looked flustered.

"Sorry," she said. "It's just that you're so kind and I thought I might give you a kiss. It's really from Peter Woodhouse, not from me."

"Nothing wrong with a dog's kiss," said Archie gruffly. "My old dog used to kiss me when I let him loose each morning. He jumped up and was all over me. Great wet kisses all over my face. Never did me any harm."

They looked for the wooden crate together, and Val watched as Archie cut a door in the front and nailed planks together to make a roof, over which he pinned sacking to provide protection against rain. Then they moved the crate into position near the kitchen door—the best place for a dog to be, Archie said, "so that he doesn't feel left out."

She had been putting off the moment

when she would tell him where the dog came from. But now, with Peter Woodhouse introduced to his kennel and already lying down on the sacking bedding inside—the long run from the village had caught up with him—she broached the subject.

"My cousin Willy gave him to me," said Val. "He took him from his last owner. He beat him."

Archie was not paying much attention. "Oh yes?" he said vaguely.

"He was one of Ted Butters' dogs."

This brought a reaction. "He belonged to Ted Butters? Over at Craig Hill?"

Val nodded. "Willy works over there. He says he treats his dogs terribly. Beats them. That's why he took this one away from him."

For a while, Archie was silent. Then he asked, "Does Butters know?"

"No, he doesn't."

Archie stroked his jaw. "There's no need for him to know," he muttered. "Can't stand people who treat dogs badly. Never could."

Val felt relieved. "He'll assume he strayed. Dogs do that."

Archie agreed. "Keep it to yourself," he said. "If nobody knows, Butters won't ever find out. That man! Disgrace to farming, he is."

Val knew then that she had an ally, and Peter Woodhouse, who had been at the mercy of a bully and a tyrant, now had two allies too. It was like the war, she thought: small countries who had been bullied had discovered there were big friends willing to fight for them. It was enough to make any-body believe that there was such a thing as justice—somewhere in the inner workings of the world, in the mechanisms of human affairs, there was justice.

The dog settled in quickly. At lunchtime on that first day, Val left her work cleaning out the hen houses to check up on him in the yard. He greeted her effusively, and she untied him to let him explore his new sur-roundings. Archie called her in for lunch—he had heated a pot of leek soup—and from the kitchen window they both watched Peter Woodhouse running around the farmyard, sniffing at everything and getting to know his new home.

"I've got some stew for him," said Archie. "I'll call him in."

He went to the door and shouted the dog's

name. Peter Woodhouse hesitated, uncertain what to do—a call in the past might have been the prelude to a beating, but he sensed now that things were different, and he came trotting over to the kitchen door. Rewarded with a large bowl of stew, which he wolfed down with all the urgency with which dogs attack their meals, he was allowed to join them in the kitchen. There he wasted no time in finding a spot near the wood-fired cooking range, stretched himself out, and was soon half asleep. One eye remained fractionally open, though, in the way that dogs will have it when they are keen to keep at least some sort of watch on what is happening around them.

"The thing to remember," reflected Archie, "is that these creatures are pack animals. Understand that, and you understand a dog."

"They need a leader," said Val.

"Yes, they need a leader. And that's why they put up with people who are unworthy of them—like that Ted Butters. He's the man in charge, you see, and they just accept it. You never get dogs arguing about that sort of thing. Even dogs over in them

communist countries. They don't go around
having revolutions and what-not."

Val laughed. She had begun to see a dimension to Archie that she had been unaware of at the beginning, when she had first
started working on his farm. He was just a
farmer then—a taciturn middle-aged man
who liked things done in a particular way
and seemed to be content enough with his
own company; but slowly he had revealed
his sense of humour and his kindness, and
she was heartened by both.

Mike said, "I guess you're my girl now." He blushed. "I find it kind of hard to say these things, but you know what I mean."

They were sitting in the pub in the village. There were few people there: a couple of the girls from the land girl house, waiting for some young men from the RAF base; two farm hands, still in working clothes, their trousers tied with binding twine just above the ankles; a lonely-looking man in a sports jacket and tie, reading the racing page of the paper. Val and Mike were far enough away from anybody to be able to talk without lowering their voices, and to hold hands without attracting attention.

She looked down at the floor, and then up again, to meet his gaze. She liked to see him blushing; it was a curious, boyish thing—almost a matter of manners.

"I'm happy with that," she said. "I like being your girl."

He squeezed her hand. "When all this is over . . ."

She sighed. "We say that all the time, don't

we? **When this is over** . . . But somehow I wonder whether it ever will be, or whether it will just go on and on and we'll . . ."

He interrupted her. "It'll be over, and then I'll take you back to the States with me. Would you like that?"

She felt her heart beating. Willy had asked her that morning whether Mike had proposed to her yet. He had said, "He'll want you to marry him, I bet. Any time now, he'll ask you."

She had told him not to be ridiculous, but his words had thrilled her. Of course she had thought about it—any girl going out with a man at least thought about the possibility, unless, of course, she was purely out for a good time; for tinned peaches, as her aunt would say. And there were girls like that; girls who were out to get what they could without any thought as to the man's feelings.

Now he was talking about her going to America, and how could that be seen as anything but a proposal?

"What would I do in America?" she asked. She knew that she sounded teasing; she did not intend it, but she did.

He hesitated for a few moments before answering. "I'd look after you."

"We'd go to Muncie, Indiana?"

He squeezed her hand again. "Anywhere you want. We could go out west if you liked. Los Angeles, maybe. I could get a job there, now that I have this experience of aerial photography."

She wished that he would ask her directly. Why could he not just say, **Will you marry me?** She would say yes to that question. It was what she wanted.

"I wouldn't mind going to America," she said.

He leaned over towards her and planted a gentle kiss on her cheek. One of the land girls, still waiting for their RAF boyfriends, noticed, and flashed a smile of encouragement.

"Then we're engaged," he said. It was not a question; it was a statement of fact, and she nodded her assent. She did not say anything, although she tried. It was too difficult for her because she found herself not thinking of him, or even of herself, but of her mother and of how she would have approved of him; she had approved of everything her daughter did, right from the beginning. She had never thought her daughter anything less than wonderful.

She realised that he had said something about a ring. "I'm sorry, I was thinking."

It seemed as if he understood. "Of course. It's a big thing, isn't it—getting engaged and then getting married."

**Getting married . . .** She closed her eyes.

He said, "There's a guy at the base can get hold of rings from the States. He knows somebody in the business. He can order them."

"That would be lovely." It was all she could think of to say.

"I need to know the size of your finger. He has a card, this guy, and you put your finger into the hole that fits. Then you know the right size."

She laughed at the thought. "You Americans think of everything, don't you?"

But now a shadow passed over her face, and he saw it. He asked gently if something was wrong. "You don't have to say yes, you know. The last thing I'd want to do is to make you say yes. You know that, don't you?"

She reassured him that she had said yes freely, and that she meant it. She did not reveal to him, though, what her thoughts had been, because they had been of the path of danger into which he flew every day, or almost every day. She had seen a plane limping home, a trail of smoke—not wide, but visible—issuing from an engine. Even if they were just taking photographs, they were flying over the heads of people who would be trying to bring them down, and who from time to time—probably rather often—succeeded in doing so. There were legions of young women who had become engaged to men who were risking their lives in this way and had learned that the game of dice their menfolk played had gone against them. One of the land girls on another farm was in this position; Val had seen her, and she had been tearful. One of the other girls had whispered the explanation: her fiancé of two weeks had been shot down somewhere and now she had been notified officially that he was dead.

"I don't want to lose you," she said.

He laughed. "Nobody's going to take me away from you. Nobody." And then, with an expression of mock bravado, "Let them try!"

It suddenly occurred to her that there were young women on the other side thinking the same thing about their men, and their men would be saying the same words back to them. It was the men who started it, she thought. Left to women, it would not work out this way; they would ground the planes that took their lovers from them; they, and the mothers, would put a stop to war.

That was a thought that Annie had often expressed, but no sooner had she done so than she had admitted that men were needed to fight evil. "Hitler wouldn't listen to us women," she said. "There's only one thing that Hitler understands."

Mike was looking at his watch. She did not dare ask him whether there was a mission that day; she assumed there was.

"I have to get back to the base," he said. He looked at her. "I'll be thinking of you tonight. I have to go out with a bomber tonight. They're short of men."

Her heart gave a leap. Not all bombers came back; everyone knew that. They were lumbering and defenceless, people said, and the men who flew them simply had to grit their teeth, do their job, and hope that they dodged the flak thrown up at them.

"You must be really careful."

"Yes. Of course I will. In and out. Back to base."

"And I'll be thinking of you too. Always. All the time."

He put his fingers to her lips. "Promise?"

She moved his fingers gently, and placed them where she imagined her heart was. "Promise."

"I ain't going back," said Willy. "I don't care if they shoot me—I ain't going back there."

Annie attempted to calm him. She had seen how he could get worked up, and she knew it could end with him in tears, sobbing his heart out over something that any normal young man would treat as minor.

"Hush, Willy. Hush. Nobody's going to shoot you." She glanced at Val, who rolled her eyes.

"They don't shoot people who leave their jobs," said Val.

Willy stared at her, his bottom lip quivering. "This is wartime. It's different in wartime. They can shoot you if you disobey."

"That's in the army," said Val. "And only if you run away from the enemy."

"And not any longer," added Annie. "That was in the first war—at the Somme and places like that. The army's more civilised now. They don't shoot their own men." She was not sure about that; she thought they probably did, but she was not going to give Willy yet another thing to worry about.

Willy looked unconvinced. "Anyway, I don't care. They can't make me go back to Ted Butters' place."

They were standing in the kitchen. Willy had just returned from work early—usually he arrived half an hour or so after Val, but he had come in before that, his hair dishevelled and his expression agitated. Now, Annie suggested they all sit down at the kitchen table and Willy could tell them exactly what had happened.

"So just calm down," said Annie. "Calm down and tell us what went wrong. From the beginning."

"I went to work on his farm," said Willy. "I started four months ago. He told me —"

Annie reached out to put her hand on his arm. "No, Willy, not that beginning. From today, this morning. What happened today that made you come back early?"

"It was the rats," said Willy. "Them rats in his haystack. They made a big nest like they always do. Pa rat, Ma rat, and all their nippers."

"Kittens," supplied Val. "They call the little rats kittens. They have litters, same as cats do."

"I knew they were there," Willy continued. "They weren't doing any harm. He didn't have to kill them."

Annie sighed. "Farmers do, Willy. They kill rats because they eat food that's meant for livestock. And if the farmer grows grain, too—oats and barley and so on—rats love that for their tea."

"Auntie's right," said Val. "Archie lays poison for rats. He says they steal his eggs. And they do—I've seen eggs broken by rats. You can see the tooth marks."

"These rats were doing none of that," persisted Willy. "They were minding their own business. They weren't in the barn." He paused. "And I wanted to take one of them. A rat can be a friendly creature—same as a small dog, they say."

This brought a response from Annie. "I'm not having rats around here," she warned. "Not for anything. Nasty creatures, with those long tails of theirs, and their teeth."

Willy ignored this. "He hit them with a shovel," he said. "All of them—the whole family."

Annie exchanged a concerned glance with Val. "You didn't—"

He cut her short. "I didn't hit him, if that's what you're worried about. But I told him what I thought of him."

Annie breathed a sigh of relief. "Well, he probably knew that already."

Willy smiled. There was a sly satisfaction in his look. "He didn't like it, he didn't. I told him that he didn't deserve to have any animals. I told him that his dog hadn't run away: I'd taken him. He didn't like that neither."

Val frowned. "You told him you'd taken Peter Woodhouse? Did you tell him where he is, Willy?"

Willy did not seem to appreciate the gravity of the situation. "I told him he had a much better home over at Archie Wilkinson's place."

Val suppressed a cry of dismay. "Oh, Willy . . ."

"He didn't like that," crowed Willy. "You should have seen his face. He went all purple. Ted Butters gets purple when he gets cross." He sniffed. "He said I should go and not bother to come back. I told him I didn't want to come back, but what about the money he owed me? A full week's wages.

He said I could do what I like but he'd never pay me. He said if I didn't clear off he'd fetch his shotgun."

Annie glanced again at Val, and shook her head slightly. "You can't be blamed, Willy. You should never have been sent to that man in the first place. You're well away from him."

He seemed reassured. "They'll find me some other place?"

"Of course they will," said Annie. "There are plenty of farms needing somebody."

"And the army won't take me?"

"No, the army won't take you. They told you that, remember? They said that you were better working on a farm." She paused, once more glancing conspiratorially at Val. "You know what I reckon, Willy? I think that if they told Mr. Churchill himself about the work you do on the land, he'd say **Well done, William Birks.** That's what he'd say, Willy. Mr. Churchill himself."

He rubbed his hands together with pleasure. "It's what I do best. It's what I do best to help win the war."

Annie was soothing. "Of course it is, Willy. And now, why don't you go and have a bath before I serve your tea. There's a clean shirt in your cupboard—I ironed it this morning. You put that on."

Once Willy had left the kitchen, Val shook her head in disbelief. "I can't believe he doesn't understand. It's so basic. He told that Ted Butters to his face where Peter Woodhouse is. Now what?"

Annie sighed. "You tell Archie tomorrow that he has to find somewhere safe for the dog. There'll be plenty of time. Ted Butters won't do anything this evening. So put the dog some place where he'll not be found. Let the whole thing blow over."

"But what if it doesn't?"

"It will—it'll blow over. Ted Butters is too busy with his black market activities to spend time making a fuss over a dog."

"Black market?"

"He sells chickens. Sometimes a pig. He sells to that Martin Crowhurst and his friends. They'll be caught one day."

Val told her aunt that one of the men at the base had been caught stealing the Americans' supplies and selling them on the black market. He was going to prison.

"Best place for Ted Butters," said Annie.

.   .   .

The following morning Val arrived at the farm half an hour earlier than usual. Archie was still at the kitchen table, nursing a large mug of tea and reading a farming leaflet. She knocked at the kitchen window and was invited in.

"Has something happened?" he asked.

"Nothing. Well, something has, I suppose. Ted Butters knows that Peter Woodhouse is here."

Archie raised an eyebrow. He did not seem overly concerned. "How did he work that out?"

She told him, stressing that Willy was not entirely responsible for his actions. "He understands some things," she said. "But he doesn't always work things out the same as you and I do."

"So I see," said Archie. "But no use crying over spilt milk."

"No." She paused. "What do you think Ted Butters will do?"

Archie shrugged. "He might come round here. If he does, I'll tell him the dog has voted with his feet. I'll tell him there'll be no taking him back."

She was concerned that the other farmer might create trouble. Archie nodded. "Yes, there's always that, I suppose. But I'll deal with any trouble he makes. He has a foul temper on him, that man, but I've dealt with the likes of him before."

She was reassured. "So we do nothing?"

"We carry on," said Archie. "Isn't that what they're always telling us—the government, that is? Carry on, they say. Well, that's what we'll do." He swigged the rest of his tea and then rose from the table. "We've got half a field of cabbages to get in while this weather holds, my girl. Let's not waste any time."

They went to work. At eleven in the morning, they stopped for a short break, and that was when they saw Bill Edwards coming up the farm track on his ancient black bicycle. The policeman waved to them and then parked his bike against a hedge at the bottom of the cabbage field. Picking his way around the side of the field he came to join them.

"Well, Bill?" said Archie. "You looking for a German spy or something? Nobody round here, I'm afraid."

The policeman smiled. "You checked your hayloft recently, Archie? It's a great place for a German spy to hide up."

"I'll do as you say, Bill," said Archie.

The policeman cleared his throat. He was still sweating from the ride up from the village, and now he wiped his brow with a large red handkerchief. "Actually, Archie," he began, "it's a tricky one. I've had a visit from Ted Butters. You know him?"

"Of course I do," said Archie. "Not that I'd describe him as a friend."

"There's a lot would say that," said the policeman. "I keep out of these scraps, obviously, but I hear what people are saying— and thinking, too, sometimes—and I know who's popular and who isn't. Not that I'm saying anything about it, mind."

Archie nodded. "Of course not."

"Anyway," continued the policeman, "Ted Butters comes round to see me first thing this morning and lays a complaint that you've stolen his dog. He says it's worth six pounds, being a highly trained sheepdog."

"A good dog's not cheap," said Archie.

Bill Edwards looked embarrassed. "You can't turn a blind eye to the taking of a dog worth six pounds," he said. "That's the same thing as stealing a horse. Just as valuable."

"I suppose so," said Archie. "But nobody's stolen that Butters' dog. He mistreated it, by the way; he beat it something terrible. A dog won't stand for that, you know; a dog will try to get away."

Bill Edwards pursed his lips. "A dog doesn't run away by itself. Dogs stay. I've had dogs myself."

"Some dogs do," insisted Archie. "It all depends on the dog."

Bill fiddled with the policeman's helmet he was holding. "You wouldn't happen to have this dog on your farm, would you, Archie? I'm asking you directly, see, as a friend, so to speak."

Archie hesitated, but then he gave his response. "It's here, Bill, because the poor creature was being beaten to death up at Butters' place. We couldn't stand by."

The policeman's embarrassment deepened. "A farmer's dog's different, Archie. You know that. It's part of the farm equipment, so to speak. You can't take it off him."

"I'm not disputing that, Bill," said Archie. "But there's the dog to think of here. A dog's not like other . . . bits of property. A dog's different."

The policeman shifted his weight from foot to foot. "I don't want to make a fuss about this, Archie, but if a complaint's been made . . ." He gave the farmer an imploring look. "Of course, if the dog were to go somewhere else for a while, then I could truthfully inform Butters that there's no dog here. I'll come back officially tomorrow—this is an unofficial visit, you'll understand—and there'll be no dog and that'll be the end of it as far as I'm concerned."

Archie smiled. "You're a good man, Bill," he said. "We'll make sure there's no dog for . . . for your official visit."

They watched him ride down the road back towards the village.

"That's the way a policeman should behave," said Archie. "There's always a solution if you're prepared to be flexible."

If they could manage it, the time Mike and Val had together, precious hours snatched between the claims of flying and working on the farm, was spent away from others. Wartime was a period of constant sharing with people you did not know—in bomb shelters, in overcrowded public transport, in the endless queueing for almost everything. To be alone with another, to talk without fear of being overheard, seemed at times to be an impossible, only dimly remembered luxury, almost an act of selfishness.

After completing a spell of intensive duties, he was given two days' leave. He wanted to go away—to drive off with her in a car lent by one of the other pilots—but it was a busy time on the farm and she felt unable to ask for two full days off. One day at the most, she said, would be all that she could manage.

He said that in wartime you had to take what you could get. The weather was fine and they could take a picnic; he would still get the use of the car and they could go wherever she suggested.

"I know a place," she said. "There's a river, and a bank that will be ideal for a picnic. Sometimes people swim there, but most of the time there's nobody."

He said, "I have some . . ."

"Tinned peaches?"

He laughed. "Yes."

Tinned peaches had become a private joke, because she had told him about Annie's craving for them and he had already supplied a few tins for her. "What's it with you people and tinned peaches?" he asked. "Tinned peaches are just . . ." He shrugged his shoulders. "Just tinned peaches."

"I know that. But there's something about . . ."

"Something about tinned peaches?"

She smiled. She loved him so much; she was sure of it now. Love came to you on the coat-tails of such small things—conversations about tinned peaches, looks exchanged at odd moments, the way that the other person glanced up at the sky, or scratched his head, or said something about the weather.

"Yes," she said. "Maybe it's because we could never get them. You really want the things you can't get, don't you?"

He kissed her. They were standing outside the post office and there were people about, but she did not mind. Some people did not like the way the Americans flirted with the local girls, but most did not feel that way. And if those who did not like it should choose to talk, what difference did it make? People disapproved of the things they had themselves missed; Annie had pointed that out to her once and she realized that it was quite true. "If somebody shakes their head and tut-tuts," she said, "you can be sure it's because they wanted to do whatever they're shaking their head and tut-tutting over."

"So," he said. "Tinned peaches. And what else?"

She thought for a moment. "Sandwiches. A picnic isn't a picnic without sandwiches."

"What sort?"

She answered without hesitation. "Oh, ham, I'd say. And egg. And maybe cucumber." She paused. "Yes, cucumber. That's what Annie gives the vicar when he calls round: cucumber sandwiches. The vicar tucks into a whole plate of them—and eats the lot. Every one of them."

"I suppose it's part of his job," said Mike. "I think that you have to eat things in some jobs. We have a congressman back in Indiana who's really fat. He said something in the newspaper about how it all came from his job—visiting folks' houses and having to eat their cookies and cakes or they won't vote for you. It's tough."

Val smiled vaguely; she was thinking of their picnic. "I don't think we've got any ham . . ."

"Leave it to me," said Mike.

"We've got plenty of eggs," said Val, brightening. "And cress. We grow that."

"Then that's our picnic fixed," said Mike.

He leaned forward and kissed her again. As he did so, she thought: **Don't fly ever again. Stay with me. We'll run away together. Anywhere. Anywhere. The war can get on with itself—it doesn't need us.** But she knew that was wrong, even as the thought came to her. This was their war and they had to see it through. He flew a plane and she dug potatoes and carrots: two different ways of fighting the same war.

.  .  .

They found the place by the river, but only after taking a few wrong turnings and having to reverse down impossibly narrow lanes, bounded by out-of-control hedgerows. With people being too busy growing food, there was little time for the luxury of hedge-trimming, and here and there unbridled growth from either side met above a road, making a tunnel, a green womb of dappled light and startled birds. At length Val saw a road she recognized and they found the lay-by where the car could be left. From there, a path followed the edge of a field of ripening wheat down towards a copse of willow trees and the river bank.

She remembered the spot from when she had last been there, just after the war had started. She had come with three other young women, cycling over from the village, a journey of almost ten miles. It had been a hot day, and they had swum in the river, just beneath the lip of a weir, allowing the cooling water to cascade over them like a shower. Then they had lain in the sun, waiting for their bedraggled hair to dry, with one of them keeping watch in case any of the boys from the village should arrive. There was a story—and nobody knew if it was true— about how boys would steal the clothes off swimmers and then hide in the bushes to witness the commotion.

She pointed to a spot shaded by one of the willows, and he laid down the rug he had brought from the car. They embraced.

She said, "I don't want you to go."

He touched her forehead lightly. "I don't want to go either. But I can't . . ." He shrugged. What was the word? Desert? There had been a deserter at the base, a young man from Kentucky who had travelled to London and been picked up by the military police in a bar, drunk and in the company of a woman he had met on the streets of Soho. He had been sent back to the States and to prison.

She sighed, and took his hand in hers. "No, I know you have to do what you're doing. And I wouldn't want to marry a coward."

He looked at her, and wondered whether people who did not go up in planes, who did not face enemy fighters and flak, knew what that particular terror was like. Of course, you could not allow yourself to think about it, and certainly not to talk about it. You had to behave as if you felt none of it, as if you didn't care what happened, while all the time it was always there within you—a cold, hard knot of fear that settled in your stomach and could make you want to retch; only retching solved nothing because the fear would soon return.

She sensed his doubt over what she had said. "Of course, I wouldn't call people cowards if they simply couldn't take it. I know how difficult it must be."

He lay back on the rug, looking up at the sky. "I've not met any cowards," he said. "Not one. I've met people who have cried their eyes out because of everything—sitting there crying their eyes out because . . . well, I guess because they don't want to die, or because they're thinking about the guy they shot down, or something like that. I've met them, but I've never met a coward."

"No," she said. "I'm sure you haven't. I shouldn't have said it."

"No, you can say it, because there is such a thing, and because I can think of times when I've been a coward."

She stared at him. She wished she had never mentioned the word.

"Can I tell you about it?" he asked.

She nodded her head.

"Because," he went on, "I've been thinking about this . . . this thing a lot recently. I don't know why." He paused. "Maybe it's just that when you know that at any moment . . ." He stopped himself. You did not discuss that possibility—especially with your girl.

Of course, she knew what the unspoken words would have been. She looked into his eyes. "Yes," she began, and then trailed off.

"Anyway," he continued, "I've been thinking of something I did when I was a boy—something I'm ashamed of."

She tried to make light of it. "Who hasn't done things they're ashamed of—lots and lots of things—when they were young? Who?"

He shrugged. "Maybe no one."

"Well, there you are."

"Except I can't get this out of my mind. I say to myself, you were just a kid, it was a long time ago, and I wait for that to work. But it doesn't."

At first, she said nothing; she was thinking now of how committing to a joint future brought two pasts together. She realised that she had not given much thought to what marriage meant—how could you think about such things when the world was topsy-turvy with conflict? You could not. But now she thought: **I'm taking on another person's memories, another person's family, another person's life.** Love obscured all of that because if it did not, then nobody would marry at all, and there had to be marriage, didn't there, if people wanted to continue, have children, keep everything going . . .

"I shouldn't bother you with all this," he said. "There are other things to talk about."

She reassured him. "No, you should, because I want you to talk to me. We shouldn't have any—"

"Secrets?" he interjected, smiling. "Isn't that what they say? You don't have any secrets from the person you're going to marry?"

She chided him. "I'm being serious."

He thought for a moment. "Okay."

Val waited. Somewhere in the distance there was a shout, answered by another—

boys playing along the river. A cuckoo calling. A breeze in the leaves of the trees. The vague sound that heat made.

"There was a kid at school," Mike said. "He was called Jimmy Clark. We called him Stan—after Stan Laurel, because he looked a bit like him, and walked like him too. We laughed at him—everybody laughed at him. He was, well, sort of uncoordinated. Clumsy. You know that sort of kid?"

Val thought of a girl she had known at school who was always losing things and getting into trouble as a result. She nodded.

"This guy, this Jimmy Clark, didn't have many friends. In fact, he probably had none. He used to ask people if they would be his friend—he asked me once, I remember—and although people didn't exactly say no, they never really hung around with him. People were kind of embarrassed, if you see what I mean."

"Children are like that, aren't they?"

"Yes, but this went on all the way through high school."

She sighed. "I suppose that's the way it goes."

"He admired me," said Mike. "I was on the football team. I guess I found it easy to make friends."

"He looked up to you?"

"Yes, I think so." Mike paused. "He asked me to go to his place and see this model railway set-up his dad had made. His father was one of these railway enthusiasts who collect model trains—engines, track, the lot. They make a big thing of it. And Mr. Clark had made this whole system, it seemed—tunnels, the works."

"You saw it?"

Mike shook his head. "No. I said I was too busy, because . . ." He faltered before continuing. "I didn't want people to think that I was friendly with Jimmy Clark, who was a real loser who still played with trains."

She looked at him, and saw pain in his eyes. But it was such a little thing, she thought; such a little thing. And her heart went out to him: that he should fret over a small unkindness of childhood. He should not; no, she was proud that he should care about something that all of us must have done at some time or other because we were young and thoughtless. "You shouldn't blame yourself for that," she said. "It wasn't such a big thing."

"I haven't told you what happened."

She caught her breath.

"I heard that he enlisted. After I joined the air force, I heard that Jimmy Clark enlisted in the army. He was put into the dental corps. He helped the dentist, I suppose. You know, with the instruments and the mouthwash and so on."

Val said that she thought that must have been important. "You always need dentists, even when there's a war going on."

"Of course," agreed Mike. "Of course it was important. Toothache's toothache. We've got a dentist at the base."

"So that's what happened to him?"

Mike looked away. "Until he was killed, yes."

She closed her eyes. It was the way wartime stories ended.

"He was somewhere in the Pacific. I heard from my aunt, who reads everything in the local paper and sends me cuttings. She sent me the report. There was a picture of Jimmy, and the article just said that he'd been killed on active duty. There was a picture of his mom and dad too. The report quoted them. They said how proud they were of their son. Then the paper said that he would be much missed by his friends."

Val reached out to take his hand. "Oh, Mike," she whispered.

"Missed by his friends . . . me?" He turned back to face her. "You see how I feel?"

"Yes, of course I do. But you shouldn't dwell on this. You didn't know."

"Didn't know that he was going to go off and get himself killed? In the dental corps? No, of course I didn't, but I don't think that made me feel any better. I could have been his friend. I could have gone to his place to see that damn railtrack. I could have done **something.** But I didn't."

"But it's the war that makes everything, well, rather worse. It's not you, Mike. It's the war."

He shook his head. "It makes me think that you should never not say what you need to say."

"No."

"So, I love you, Val. I love you so much."

She made an effort at cheerfulness. "What

will our house be like? Our house in Muncie, Indiana?"

He smiled. "Really neat."

"With a garden?"

"Yes. A garden. Trees. Flowers in the summer. Anything you like."

"And a car?"

He laughed. "Of course. I'll teach you how to drive. Our roads are much straighter than yours. Wider too."

"So I won't hit anything?"

"Not if you drive straight."

They ate their sandwiches. They walked along the river bank to where the boys they had heard earlier on were swimming. They had a dog in the water with them, and the dog was fetching sticks.

"Could we take a dog with us to America?" she asked.

He looked doubtful. "I don't think so. I don't think you can take a dog." He looked at her fondly. "You shouldn't worry too much about dogs. Dogs have their own lives, you know."

She knew that. "But their lives get all tangled up with ours," she said.

He agreed. "It's what they want, I think."

"Even in our wars?"

He had not thought about that, but she was right, he decided.

They turned back. One of the boys shouted from the water. "Good luck, mister! Kill the Germans, mister!"

"They're just boys," said Val.

When Bill Edwards had gone, Archie said to Val, "Can you take that dog back to your aunt's place, just for the time being? A week or two—maybe a bit longer."

Val thought about this. Annie had a kind heart, but her situation was awkward. Everybody went to the post office from time to time—including Ted Butters. Ted's cousin, Alice, lived a couple of houses away. She and Ted were on good terms, and she would probably recognise the dog easily enough. They could not risk that now that Bill Edwards was involved.

"It would be better for him to go somewhere else," she said. "You know how it is in the village. People talk—even in wartime, they talk."

Archie understood. "You're right: he must go somewhere else." He looked at her enquiringly. "Any ideas?"

Suddenly it came to her. "Yes," she said. "Mike will take him."

"Your fellow?"

"My fiancé now. Yes. He likes dogs, and

he said that somebody at the base had a dog but it ran away."

Archie looked unconvinced. "An air force base is no place for a dog. All that noise. All that coming and going."

"It won't be for long," said Val. "And think of the attention he'll get—and the food."

Archie had to admit the food would be better. "They have steaks down there," he said. "They have steaks the size of which you wouldn't dream of. A dog could get the trimmings and do very well out of them."

Val smiled. "He'd be well fed. The Americans look after their own."

Archie shrugged. "If he'll take him, that's the answer." He paused. "We could drive him there in the van. I've got a drop of petrol."

They went out into the yard. Peter Woodhouse was in his kennel, tied to the wire run that allowed him a certain measure of freedom. He leapt up at Val and licked her hands and arms enthusiastically, reaching her face and covering it with slobbering kisses.

"He knows," she said. "He knows that we're planning some-thing for him."

They drove to the base, taking with them

the delivery of eggs that would get them past the guard. Val was known there now, not because of the engagement, which was unofficial, but as a supplier of eggs. Sergeant Lisowski had told the guardroom that she could come and go as she pleased, and she had never encountered any difficulty in getting past the front gate. Now, on this visit, there were a few more questions as Archie was asked who he was, but they were soon waved through.

Because Val did not know whether Mike would be there, she spoke to Sergeant Lisowski.

"The lieutenant's on a mission," he said. "Just left."

She explained about Peter Woodhouse, without mentioning the real reason why refuge was needed. "We can't look after him right now," she said. "I wondered if Mike could take him."

Sergeant Lisowski looked down at the dog. "I love dogs," he said. "We had wiener dogs back in Pittsburgh. Three of them. They're great dogs. Small bodies, big hearts."

"This is a sheepdog," said Val. "They're not like . . . what did you call them?"

"Wiener dogs. You call them sausage dogs over here," said Sergeant Lisowski. "They're German, but they're not Nazis."

Archie laughed. "Dogs don't know about these things," he said.

Sergeant Lisowski looked momentarily surprised. "I guess they don't." He bent down to pat Peter Woodhouse. "I can take care of this dog, even if the lieutenant doesn't want him. Maybe we can look after him together."

"I'd like that," said Val.

Sergeant Lisowski took the lead they had attached to Peter Woodhouse's collar. The dog looked up at him, and then at Val and Archie; he was clearly confused. Val saw that, and her face fell.

"They know when we're abandoning them," she said. "They can tell."

"He's not being abandoned," said Archie. "I would never abandon a dog."

"No," said Val. "I'm sorry. We're handing him over temporarily."

"Temporarily," agreed Sergeant Lisowski. "Everything's temporary these days, isn't it? Life itself. Temporary."

. . .

It was ten days before she saw Mike again. She had a message, though, left with her aunt at the post office, delivered from the base. It was a short note to tell her that Peter Woodhouse was doing fine. **They call him Woody here,** he wrote. **The base commander has taken a shine to him and says he can be on pay and rations as a mascot. So Uncle Sam is paying for him now! One of the men has gotten hold of a collar from somewhere—a swell new collar with his name burned into the leather. It suits him just fine.** And then he ended with the private fondness that made her heart skip. She loved this man; it was as simple as that. This was a good, kind man who would take on somebody else's dog, and was so gentle in everything he did; a gentle boy in the middle of the great machinery of war.

She told Archie about the note, and he seemed pleased. Bill Edwards had called round at the farmhouse on his official visit while Val had been in one of the fields. She had not seen him, but Archie told her how Bill had made much of looking around the barn and noting things down in that notebook of his. "He showed me what he had written," he said. "He wrote: **Inspected barn: no dog of the description. Inspected farmyard: no dog of the description.**"

Archie laughed. "I said to him: 'Bill, this is a bit of play-acting, ain't it?' and he shook his head and said, 'Archie, I never told any lies in my whole police career and I'm not going to start now. I can show that Ted Butters my notebook and tell him, face-to-face, that his dog was not at your farm. I can tell him I looked. And all of that will be God's truth—every word of it.'"

Val smiled. "It's better not to lie. And you don't want policemen who lie, do you?"

"If we have that," said Archie, "if we have lying policemen and all that, then what's the point of this war, I ask you?"

She looked at him. She was thinking of Mike, and of what he was doing. Why was he here? He was risking his life every day—or however often it was that he went on those missions—because he had been told to do it. It was a long way from Muncie, Indiana, but he had come because it was his duty.

Archie had more to say. "I wonder if they'll

take Peter Woodhouse up in their planes. He said he was going to be a mascot. They won't take him with them, will they? For good luck?"

Val said she thought this unlikely. "A plane is no place for a dog. Dogs don't like planes."

This tickled Archie. "Dogs don't like planes? Who told you that, young Val? You ever put a dog in a plane?"

She blushed. "Stands to reason, doesn't it? Dogs don't like loud noises."

Archie disagreed. "Peter Woodhouse hopped up smartly enough on Henry Field's tractor. Remember? When he brought it round, Peter was up there like a rat up a drainpipe. He didn't mind the noise. Wanted to be part of what was going on."

"Tractors and planes are different," said Val. "I don't think dogs like planes. I just think that—I've got no proof."

Mike took her to the local pub when he had his next pass.

"We've been busy," he said. "Your boys have been pounding the Germans and we've been taking pictures of it all." He shook his head. "They won't be able to take much more of this now that we've landed in France. We'll just push on and on until we get to Berlin."

"I want it to end," she said.

"So does everybody. Germans, too, I imagine. They're people, after all."

"But Hitler's their fault."

"Sure, he's their fault." He was silent for a few moments. Then he said, "Woody is doing just fine. When do you want him back?"

She had not thought about this, but she explained their concern about Ted Butters. "Someone might tell him again," she said. "We probably need to leave it a little while yet."

Mike seemed pleased. "He fits in well. He obeys orders, you see. Some dogs wouldn't. Sergeant Lisowski had those little dachshunds back in Pittsburgh."

"He told us."

"Yes, well, he says that his dogs would never obey orders. He said they'd be court-martialled pretty quickly."

She moved her knee, so that it was touching his under the table. There were fewer opportunities for physical closeness than they would have liked. A war was a public time; private moments were difficult, although people took what chances they could.

Mike took a sip from his glass. He had forced himself to drink the warm beer that had so surprised him at the beginning; now he liked it. "He came with us last time," he said. "You know that? He came in the plane."

She was wide-eyed. "Over there? Over . . . wherever it is you go?"

He nodded. "He whined and whined and the major eventually said, **Okay, you guys can take him with you.** That was all, and he was great in the plane. We took an old flying jacket for him to lie on and he lay there all through the mission. I held him when we made it back to the base so that he wouldn't get thrown around if it was a rough landing."

"As your mascot?"

"Yeah. A mascot. For good luck."

She asked him whether they would take him again. He replied that they would. "Once you start doing something for good luck, you can't stop it just like that. That's bad luck. So you keep on doing it."

She told Archie the next day. "They're taking Peter Woodhouse up in their planes. He's flying with them."

Archie did not express surprise. "They're quite the boys," he said. "All those air force people are—ours, theirs—they're all the same."

The colonel sent his clerk to fetch Mike from the officers' mess. It was a summons that everybody dreaded: bad news from home was usually delivered by the colonel himself, who did not believe in delegating unpleasant duties to subordinates. And he did it well, because he was sympathetic— some said the most sympathetic colonel in the U.S. Air Force. That was not the same thing as being soft, they said; he could be as tough as a situation demanded, but he felt for his men and he understood how difficult this war was for so many of them: farm boys who should have been driving tractors rather than flying planes and being killed in Europe.

Mike saluted, and waited for the worst.

"I haven't called you in for bad news," the colonel said quickly. "Nothing like that."

Mike relaxed. He grinned. "That's a relief, sir."

The colonel indicated for him to sit down. "Nor is there any problem with your flying. Nothing but good reports."

"I do my best, sir."

The colonel looked past him, over his shoulder, to where the flag fluttered in the afternoon breeze. A wireless was playing somewhere, and then it was switched off.

"This mascot you guys have taken on— what's his name again?"

Mike smiled. "Peter Woodhouse, sir. He had that name when we took him. We're looking after him for my girl, but he's somehow stayed on."

"No objection to that," said the colonel. "Nice dog. I had setters back in Maine. Irish setters. You know those dogs?"

"I've seen them, sir."

The colonel looked back into the room. "My daddy swore by them. He said you couldn't get a smarter dog in this world than an Irish setter. He bred them, you know, and won all the prizes at the dog shows. When he died I took over his dogs. Four of them. One very old one who never got over his death—pined, you see, pined away to nothing. Had to shoot him eventually because he was just skin and bone and it hurt him too much to walk. A great dog, though."

Mike nodded. "My grandfather had a

coon dog on his farm. Nothing special. He was the greediest dog you ever met."

The colonel laughed. "Dogs are always hungry. You show me a dog that's not hungry and I'll tell you you've got yourself a cat by mistake."

Mike looked at his hands: the colonel had not invited him into his office to talk about the merits of different breeds of dogs.

"This dog of yours—I know he's been up in the planes." He looked at Mike over the top of his rimless spectacles, but he was smiling as he spoke. "Don't ever think I don't know what's going on."

Mike nodded. "I'd never say that, sir."

The colonel sat back in his chair. "He likes it?"

"He seems to, sir. He likes being with us. You know how dogs like going in cars and trucks? It's like that. He thinks it's a truck, I guess."

The colonel laughed. "Well, I suppose it feels the same." He paused. "And he doesn't get in the way?"

"Never, sir. Just lies there. Tries to stand up when we land but soon lies down again."

The colonel laughed again. "All right. It's

going to have to stop, though. You won't
have heard, but I'm being sent down to London for two months. My job here is going to
be done by Colonel Harold Mortensen. He's
not the easiest man in the air force and . . .
well, I'm just making sure that everything is
regular before I leave. I don't want him telling anybody that I let people get away with
things."

Mike said that he understood.

"So, after next Monday, this . . . what's
his name again?"

"Peter Woodhouse."

"This Peter Woodhouse is grounded."

Mike inclined his head in acceptance.
"But we can keep him here on the base?"

The colonel made an expansive gesture.
"Sure, you can do that. And he can carry on
flying until Monday—if he wants."

Mike grinned. "I think he probably will
want to," he said.

The colonel looked at his watch. "That's
it, Rogers. Leave the door open on your way
out. This heat—we're not used to it over
here."

. . .

Mike passed on the news to his crew and to Sergeant Lisowski, who had taken on responsibility for feeding Peter Woodhouse. They were to fly a mission the next morning, leaving shortly after five, and Mike had the dog's rug brought over to his room so that he could sleep there that night rather than in his kennel behind the cookhouse. It was raining in the morning, but the cloud had lifted by the time they took off, and the sun was already bright on the rooftops of the village when Mike looked down on it. He saw the post office and he thought of Val, wondering whether he should have asked her to be outside, looking up as he flew over her. He had never done that before, and thought that he probably never would. It would be bad luck to do that; doing anything out of the ordinary could tempt providence when the odds were stacked so dangerously against you.

England was a carpet of green beneath them. He saw Cambridge, a smudge of grey lanced by a silver strip: the morning sun was on the river, sending up a shard of light. Then came the blue expanse of the North

Sea and, beyond that, the coast of the Netherlands, with its covering of thin mist. Once they were above that, it was mostly water down below, dykes and polders confusing the transition between the sea and the land behind the sea.

His navigator was usually accurate. He knew by dead reckoning where they were and how long it would take them to get to where they wanted to be. But he could also find railway lines and church spires and roads just by looking, reading the landscape below as easily as if it were a map. He now said, "Half an hour, and we'll be there."

They were to photograph Arnhem, which was heavily defended by the occupying Germans. Their pictures would show the position of fortifications and their strength. They had to go over their target quickly, hoping that the anti-aircraft guns would not spot a single plane coming from an unexpected quarter. Conditions were right: a cloudless sky stretched off to the east while the land below was bathed in light. Mike looked up, as he often did before the final approach. He said a prayer, the words a vague jumble of propitiation. There was **God** and **sorry** and **return;** there was **Val** and **mother** and **home.**

On the deck, Peter Woodhouse was half asleep, half awake. The navigator leaned down and stroked his head, and Peter Woodhouse looked up, licked his hand. Mike half turned to see this, and smiled.

The navigator slipped his fingers under the collar that they had put on the dog, to check that it was not too tight. He believed that dogs swelled up at altitude and that could make the collar uncomfortable. It needed no adjustment. He looked at the inscription that he had painstakingly burned into the leather with a heated nail, the dots making up the words **Peter Woodhouse, U.S. Air Force, Dog First Class** and giving the name of their base. He was proud of that; it was Peter's identity disc, the token of his membership and service.

Mike pointed to something off their wing: small puffs of smoke appearing in the sky before dissipating quickly, like the birth and rapid death of tiny clouds.

Archie explained to Val that there were always more potatoes than one imagined, and that you had to dig deep enough to find them. "You probably know that," he said. "Everyone knows about potatoes."

She did. Annie grew potatoes in the post office garden at the back of the house; where once there had been flowers, vegetables now grew. She had taken out the roses she loved so much and turned some of the ground over to leeks and potatoes, and the Jerusalem artichokes that were now colonising most of the rest. The grocer bought the surplus of those, or exchanged them for beans, of which there sometimes seemed to be too many.

It was hot work. Val had found a hat—a battered straw hat that belonged to Annie but had not been worn for years. It provided some protection, but she felt the rays of the August sun beating down on her back and shoulders. Mike liked her complexion; he said it was paler and softer than that of most girls back home, and he would not want her to burn. She looked about her: a small clump of alders along the edge of the field would give some shade, and she could take her break there.

She was thinking of him. It was only ten days ago that they had become physically intimate. She had thought of that moment again and again and was in awe of its significance. It had changed everything for her. She had given herself to him; she was his. Nothing would ever be the same again; nothing. Annie had sensed it. She had said, "Be careful—that's all I'm going to say to you: be careful." Val had looked away, avoiding her aunt's gaze, but then had turned to her and Annie had put her arms around her and said, "He's made his promise to you—it's all right. It's different for engaged couples, which is what you are. It's allowed, especially in wartime."

**Especially in wartime:** she knew what that meant, and it made her heart a cold stone within her. The rules were different in wartime because people knew that they could lose each other so easily; everyone was in harm's way, not just those who flew or fought on the ground or at sea. Civilians died in their thousands, bombed in their homes at night, crushed to death by falling masonry, burned in the firestorms of shattered cities.

She tried not to think of that; you couldn't, because if you did you would cry or scream and just make it hard for everybody else. So you worked. You did what you were asked to do, which in her case was to dig potatoes out of the earth and pile them on hessian sacks for Archie to come and collect with a handcart that looked as if it belonged in an agricultural museum.

She took lunch early, when Archie called her into the house. He had made apple juice from his own apples, using his precious sugar to sweeten it, as he knew she had a sweet tooth. Then they listened to the news together: much was said about Montgomery's 21st Army Group. "He won't hang about," said Archie. "He'll tell the men what he wants them to do, and they'll do it. I read that in the papers. They said that Monty always speaks to his men, all the time. That's why they'd do anything for him."

He told her to wait until half past two before going out again. "It won't be so hot then," he said. "And those potatoes are going nowhere." He said she could take some home. "Just one bag, but your aunt will appreciate them, I think, unless she has too many of her own."

"She has some," Val said. "But she won't turn down more. We'll give you some artichokes."

"Blow you up, them artichokes," said Archie, rubbing his stomach.

She worked until half past four, and then took another break, lying on the grass under the alders, looking up at the sky. Mike had told her that they were on a training course for three days, so he would not be up there, up in that dizzy, echoing blue. She blew a kiss up at the sky, that he might collect it when he was next up there; she would tell him it would be waiting for him.

And then she heard Archie calling her. She stood up, dusting her overalls. She looked towards the other side of the field, where the path came up from the farmyard, and she saw Archie, half concealed by the hedge, but now coming into full sight. There was a man with him, a man in uniform, and she thought for a moment that it was Mike. But then, as they approached, she saw that it was Sergeant Lisowski.

She knew immediately from Archie's expression. She closed her eyes. She dug her nails into the palms of her hands. She made herself think of something else; oddly, of her bicycle, which had had a flat tyre on the way home the day before. She saw herself fixing it, dipping the tube into a bowl of water until the tell-tale line of bubbles revealed where the hole was. She asked herself: **Why am I thinking about this when Sergeant Lisowski is coming to speak to me and I know what he's going to say?**

The sergeant supported her on the way back to the farmhouse. Archie walked behind them, awkwardly, unsure what to say. She asked Sergeant Lisowski to repeat what he had said—three times. He told her patiently. He said the plane had not returned. He said that even before it was due to return there had been a message from the RAF. One of their planes had been in the area and had seen a Mosquito go down, an engine on fire. They had not spotted any parachutes and they had seen fire on the ground. They had to assume that the plane had been lost, with both its crew.

She insisted on riding home. They tried to dissuade her, but she brushed them aside and set off, her eyes full of stinging tears. Sergeant Lisowski followed her in his jeep, keeping a discreet distance, but close enough to rescue her when she rode into a ditch and fell off, grazing her right forearm. He loaded the bicycle into the jeep, securing it with a rope. Then he drove her home and delivered her to Annie, who put her hands to her eyes and said, "Oh, my God, I knew it, I knew it."

The colonel came to the post office the next day. His manner was grave, and he spoke to Annie for twenty minutes after he had said what he had to say to Val. He told Annie, "He was a fine young man. He was popular at the base and he was a good flier. It's going to be hard on his family—and on this young lady, too, of course."

He then spoke about how wretched war was and how even he had hoped that he would end his air force career without ever seeing the men under his command losing their lives. "But it was not to be. And so I've found out what it is like to send young men off to their deaths. I now know."

Annie said, "We have to do this. We have to see it through, even if we didn't start it."

"You're right," said the colonel. "But does that make it any easier? I'm not sure that it does."

Before he left, the colonel remembered there was something else he had to say. He spoke to Annie about this, because Val had gone to her room, sobbing, and he did not think it would be wise to impart more bad news to her.

"I'm told that the dog we've had as a mascot came from your niece. I'm told it had been her dog."

"Not quite," said Annie. "But we'll find somewhere for him now that Mike—"

The colonel interrupted her. "That won't be necessary, m'am. I'm sorry, but the dog was with them on the plane. If you could break that news to your niece, I'd be obliged. I'm very sorry. The men liked that dog."

Willy said to her, "Have you got a photograph of him?"

She stared at him. He had been avoiding

her, and at first this had hurt her. But then she came to realise that this was how many people reacted: they did not know what to say and so they kept out of your way. Willy was like that, she thought. Of course he's sorry, of course he knows what I'm feeling, but he has never been in a position like this before and nobody has taught him how to behave. She wanted to say to him, "Willy, all you have to do is show me that you know I'm unhappy, that's all. Hold me when I cry. And cry yourself, if you want to, because you liked him, too, and you must feel sad as well."

"Yes, of course I've got a photograph. I took it on his birthday. Remember? He came round here and Auntie made a cake."

He nodded. "I remember that. But I was wondering if you had two photographs. A spare one, see. One you could let me have."

She caught her breath, and nodded. Silently, she fetched it from the drawer and brought it to him. He examined it, holding it reverentially. "I'll have to cut a bit off— round the edges here." He drew an imaginary line. "So that it'll fit in my frame, you see."

She wanted to kiss him, but he always blushed when Annie tried that, and so she simply reached out and patted his arm. "He liked you a lot, Willy. He said once that it was a pity you couldn't go to Indianapolis. You know that place he talked about? He said you'd do well there."

He was surprised. "Me? Do well?"

"Yes. Of course. He knew you were a hard worker. He said hard workers did well in America."

Willy beamed with pleasure. He looked down at the photograph. "I'll put it in my frame when it's the right size. I'll have his photo in my room. When I wake up in the morning, I'll see that he's all right up there. Like Jesus."

She bit her lip. "That's right, Willy."

Later that day she went to the base to deliver eggs. Archie had said that he would do it, or he could get the neighbour's boy to go, because he was keen to earn a bit of money, but she insisted. "Brave girl," he muttered as he watched her ride down the lane. When she arrived at the base, the young man with angry skin was on sentry duty. He seemed embarrassed and muttered something she did not hear as he let her in. Another man went past on a motorbike, slowed down, and waved to her before moving off again.

Sergeant Lisowski met her at the cookhouse door. He said, "I could come and collect these, you know."

She shook her head. "I want to bring them." She paused. "There's been no news, has there?"

He hesitated. "No, not really. But . . ."

She searched his face for a sign.

He was trying not to give false hope. "When there isn't a definite report, then we assume the worst. But there have been cases—plenty of cases—of people surviving and being taken prisoner. We usually hear one way or another. The Red Cross do their best. We haven't heard on this occasion."

She weighed his words. **Usually . . . this occasion . . . plenty of cases.**

"They could have survived?"

He was being very careful. "It's possible, because . . ."

She waited.

"Because the RAF guys who saw the fire

might have been looking at something else. A bonfire, perhaps. There are plenty of reasons for a fire."

There were, she thought. There were plenty of reasons for a fire.

"So I shouldn't give up hope?" Her voice was small.

Again she watched. She would be able to tell if he really meant there was a possibility, or whether he was trying to be kind.

It took him some time to answer. Then he said, "I'd say you could have a tiny bit of hope. A glimmer. But not much more than that."

She mounted her bicycle. She felt that her life was beginning again. She saw a bird, a thrush, watching her from a hedgerow, its tiny head moving jerkily, as birds' heads will do. She shouted at it in sheer exuberant joy.

They descended rapidly when the first engine was hit, and the other one quickly overheated. He was surprised at his own calm as he went through all the procedures they had been taught. He did everything in the correct sequence, his only miscalculation being that he might be able to save the plane. By taking it down, he lost the altitude that they needed to bail out, and then it was too late. He still had control of the aircraft, but insufficient power to do anything but attempt a crash landing. He thought, **This is where I'm going to die. Right here, in Holland, and on this day, in five minutes or so. My last five minutes.**

The navigator pointed beyond the starboard wing. It was wooded terrain, but there were some fields, and one had opened up in that direction. He struggled with the controls; the plane was sluggish, but eventually responded to his coaxing and turned in the direction he wanted.

There were saplings, an incipient forest of them, and they hit the plane like tiny whips.

Then there was the earth, and the thump and bucking of the undercarriage on rough ground. The plane reared up, shuddered; settled again. Then the wheels hit a ditch traversing the field and they slewed off first to the left and then to the right. Something hit his shoulder a glancing blow, and then, miraculously, they stopped moving. His only thought was that both of them were alive and must leave the plane as soon as they could. He smelled fuel.

There was a whimpering at his knee. They had both forgotten about Peter Woodhouse and he was there, unsteady on his feet, looking up first at Mike and then at the navigator.

They wriggled free of their restraining belts.

"There's blood on your face," said Mike. "All over."

The navigator reached up tentatively. "Something hit my nose," he said. "I think it's broken."

"Get out. We must get out. You first—I'll pass you the dog."

They scrambled out, together with Peter Woodhouse. He tried to lick the blood off the navigator's face, but was pushed roughly away. Now they stood and surveyed the plane from a safe distance. One of the wings had cracked and was at an odd angle to the fuselage. Both propellers were bent, one blade dug into the ground by the engine's dying efforts.

Mike looked at the navigator. He wanted to hug him, just because he was another human being and they were both alive. That was the miracle. But not wanting blood on his flying jacket, he confined himself to saying, "I'm glad you're alive."

"I wasn't planning to die," said the navigator, his voice pinched and nasal from his injury.

"We need to get away from the wreckage," said Mike. "People will have seen it going down."

People had, but only two men hunting in the nearby forest. They heard it first, and then, when they got closer, they saw the wreckage. They were hunting discreetly, because they could not be caught with a firearm, but they had to take the risk because food was scarce. It was not as bad in the eastern provinces as it was in the west, because food was still getting through. But there was not much.

The two men came to the edge of the forest and then stood still. They waited for the two airmen to see them, which they did after a couple of minutes. Then they beckoned to them.

Mike hesitated. "One of them is carrying a gun," he said.

"But they're not in uniform," said the navigator.

Mike made up his mind. "Let's risk it," he said. "Come on."

They began to walk over towards the hunters, who started to advance towards them. The one who had been carrying the gun had slung it over his shoulder.

"Americans?" he shouted.

"Yes," Mike shouted back. "American."

They approached each other gingerly. On seeing the blood on the navigator's face, one of the men reached into his pocket and passed him a handkerchief to press to his nose. Then the other one, who was fair-haired and taller than his companion, said, "You must come with us." He spoke slowly, but his English seemed good enough.

They looked at Peter Woodhouse in astonishment.

"Where did you find this dog?" the fair-haired man asked.

"He was with us," answered Mike. "Crew."

The fair-haired man translated this into Dutch, and his companion shook his head in mock disbelief.

"We were shot down," said Mike.

The man laughed. "I had worked that out," he said. Then he added, "Probably by the Germans." He laughed again. Then he turned serious, and indicated they should hurry.

"They'll be searching for you," he said. "We have to get you as far away from here as we can. Can you run, or at least walk faster than this?"

They set off. There was a path through the forest that they followed until they reached a narrow unpaved road. They did not follow this, but crossed it to reach another field in which again there was a track. Eventually they came to a farmyard; the man who spoke English said it was a friendly house.

"They will hide you," he said. "Then we'll get you away this evening." He looked at the navigator; he was clearly concerned. "We can find a doctor, if you like. Not today, but in a day or two. He could look at your nose."

"I think it's broken," said the navigator.

"I broke mine when I was a boy," said the man, pointing to the bridge of his nose. "See? It's not straight. But I can tell you something—women like a man with a broken nose."

He gestured to Peter Woodhouse. "We won't need to hide him. He can stay in the yard." Then he added, "Dogs are innocent, aren't they? This isn't their war."

The fair-haired man was called Mees; the other man was Pauel. It was Mees who did the talking when the farmer appeared. There was a low, murmured conversation in Dutch, accompanied by anxious looks in the direction of the two airmen. The farmer pointed to Peter Woodhouse and asked a question; Mees shrugged and made a gesture of helplessness. Peter Woodhouse, who seemed completely unharmed by the crash landing, looked about him with interest, sniffing the farmyard scents.

The farmer came over to Mike, took his hand, and shook it.

"He says that there is a place in his barn where you will be safe," said Mees. "He says that we must try to get you out tonight, if possible. The Germans are everywhere in the area and they will be conducting searches once your plane is found."

Mike said that he understood. "We don't want to put anyone at risk."

Mees replied that they were used to risk; they had lived with it for four years, but now they could see the prospect of liberation and they could take a few more risks. "We're no longer on our own. The Canadians are not too far away. The Americans and the British too. It won't be too long now."

The farmer started to become concerned. He tapped his watch and then pointed at the barn. Mees said that they should go with the farmer; he would show them what to do, even if he could not tell them. He and Pauel would try to be back that night— "with people who can help you"—but they could not guarantee it.

They did come, though, just before midnight. Mees was there, but not Pauel, and there were two other men, who spoke no English and whose names weren't given. They took the two airmen from the barn and led them to a river bank. Peter Woodhouse was secured to a lead that Mees had brought, and he trotted along uncomplainingly beside Mike. On the edge of the river a small rowing boat was tied up beneath a spreading willow, and they were told to climb into it. The two unnamed men rowed; Mees sat in the stern, occasionally whispering something to the rowers.

An hour later they drew up where the river flowed into what seemed to be a small town. Bundled out of the boat, they were taken to a nearby house and led immediately upstairs and into a sparsely furnished attic. There were two rolls of bedding on the floor and a chair with a stub of candle. Peter Woodhouse was not taken upstairs, but was held in the kitchen by one of the men who had done the rowing. A few items of clothing had been left by the bedding, including a fresh shirt for the navigator, whose clothes had been stained with blood from his face; his nose had stopped bleeding by now.

"Your dog will be looked after by one of these people," explained Mees. "This is not the place for him."

They were left to go to bed. They used the candle for long enough to take off their flying boots and their jackets. They were both close to exhaustion, and Mike summoned just enough energy to blow out the candle before sleep claimed him.

The occupants of the house were an elderly man, Henrik, his son and daughter-in-law, and a ten-year-old boy named Dirk. Dirk brought them their evening meal on most days, and sometimes stayed until they had finished so he could take the plates away. He spoke no English, but occasionally addressed them in Dutch, apparently asking questions to which no answer could be given. Their diet was spartan: potatoes dressed with a thin meat or fish gruel; onions and cabbage; helpings of an oaten porridge that barely covered the bottom of the plate. They realised, though, that every scrap of this fare was taken from somebody else's table: the country was not far from starvation and the feeding of two extra mouths tested resources even further.

At least once a day Peter Woodhouse was brought up to spend half an hour or so with them in the attic. He seemed pleased to be reunited with them, wagging his tail and whining with pleasure in spite of the gloom of their attic hideaway. Mike could tell that the dog was losing weight, and he would save a scrap here and there from his own meagre rations to give to him when he came up.

Henrik, the owner of the house, took them downstairs to spend part of each morning in a small living room immediately below the attic. He spoke a few words of English and for the rest could make himself understood through an elaborate and idiosyncratic sign language. In this language, the Germans were signified by the puffing up of cheeks and the furrowing of the brow, to produce an impression of ire and menace.

They should keep away from the window, he indicated, although they could look out if they stood well back. Not that there was much to see, as the street outside was a quiet one. On several occasions, though, they saw a small German patrol—never more than five or six men—making its way down the street. They watched these passing men with fascination. These were the enemy, the cause of all this—their being in Europe in the first place, the danger they had been subjected to, their crash landing, their virtual imprisonment in an attic. And far away, of course, they knew far more serious things were happening, all brought about by these ordinary men in grey marching down the street of a small Dutch town, flesh and blood like them, no doubt with lives from which they themselves had been taken; yet the enemy, nonetheless.

Mees told them what was being done on their behalf. "It's too dangerous at the moment, but we'll try to get you back to your people. They aren't too far away now, and it may be safer just to keep you here until they arrive. We'll see."

Mike understood. "But every day we're here means more danger for these people." He gestured towards the floors below. "They would be shot if we were found."

Mees nodded. "Yes, but this is as safe as anywhere else—possibly safer. Those soldiers you may have seen out of the window stay just a few yards away, you know. They've taken over the school round the corner. They're your neighbours, and it wouldn't occur to them that anybody's hiding a stone's throw away, under their own shadow." He smiled. "And anyway, Henrik looks after their building for them. Why would they search his house?"

Mike was incredulous. "He works for the Germans?"

Mees laughed. "What better cover?"

There was something else that was troubling both Mike and the navigator. It preyed on their minds that people might think them dead. They both knew what people at the base would have thought when their aircraft did not return: they themselves had thought exactly that of those who had not come back. **Missing in action: presumed dead.** The bleak conclusion was usually true, and that, surely, was what people would be thinking of them. Mike thought of Val and of what they would have said to her. He knew that they frowned on giving people false hope—that this only led to a postponement of grief. He concluded that there would have been little encouragement for her.

If only a message could somehow get

through; not much of a message—just one word would do: **alive.** He asked Mees whether he could contact someone. "Just to tell them we're alive. A few words, that's all."

"We've done what we can," said Mees. "It's been our practice all along. But we're short of a wireless operator at the moment, and so we've used the Red Cross. We haven't been able to talk to them directly, but we've tried to send a message. They may have received it or they may not."

"And you have nothing for us? Nothing back?"

Mees shook his head sadly. "In these conditions, people often have to work in the dark. We work as cells—we've done that from the beginning. That means that information doesn't travel easily."

Mike felt that he had fallen into a world of darkness. There was the gloomy attic, with its tiny skylight that let in a shaft of light no wider than a man's hand; there was the room below, in which no lamp ever shone; there was the street onto which they were sometimes allowed to gaze, which was dark because of its narrowness; there was the whole continent that was plunged into such blackness at night because of curfews and blackouts and lack of streetlights. And alongside this all-embracing physical darkness there was a spiritual blanket that smothered all sense of joy and optimism. It was night, and although people talked of dawn, risked their lives to bring that moment forward, in so many places it was still the darkest of hours.

When Val asked for time off to go to the doctor the following day, Archie told her she could take the whole morning.

"Or, if you want, you can have the whole day," he said. "You deserve it. Not much going on round here."

That was not true. Val knew there was a long list of tasks that had to be done before the end of August, and that Archie was just trying to be kind to her. He had been over-solicitous ever since **that day,** which was the way she referred to the day of Mike's disappearance. She had eventually told him that she did not need special treatment, that there were plenty of people in the same position, and that she wanted to carry on doing her share irrespective of what had happened. She heard the expression **young widow**—there were plenty of those—and thought, **That is what I am.** But not quite: young widows had a status that she did not have; they were looked after with payments and pensions; they had their husband's name to hold on to; there was a whole world of officialdom to show support for them. She had none of that: she was just somebody who had lost her fiancé. People felt sorry for women in that position, but that was all there was to it. They thought **bad luck,** but then they went on to think of all the other things that engaged their sympathy, and for most that was a lengthy list.

"I don't need the whole day," she said. "I can see him in the morning. They said ten o'clock. Then I could get over here by twelve."

"If that's what you want." He paused, looking at her with undisguised curiosity. "You're not sickening for something? This is hard work you're doing—I wouldn't want it to get to be too much."

She held his stare. "I can do the work," she said quietly.

She wished that he would leave it there, but he continued. "Because if you're sickening— after what happened, of course—nobody would blame you, you know. Folks know about what happened."

"Archie," she said patiently, "it's all right. There's nothing wrong with me."

He started to ask, "Then why . . ." but stopped himself. Women's problems, of course. **How stupid of me,** he thought. **Women have these problems, and I go and ask this poor girl.**

Blushing, he turned away. "I'll see you tomorrow," he said. "Whatever time you turn up."

The doctor's surgery was in a small town seven miles away from the village. There was a bus that left just before nine, but on a summer's morning it was no hardship to catch it after she had eaten breakfast with Annie and Willy.

"Why are you going to the doctor?" asked Willy. "You not well, or something?"

Annie looked at him. "Mind your own business, Willy," she said.

"A check-up," said Val. "You should go, too, Willy. The doctor listens to your heart, and—"

"Nothing wrong with my heart," said Willy.

Val spread jam thickly on her toast. There

would be no more butter for two days: they had used their ration and must do without, unless Willy could get hold of some from his new farm; he brought home milk and cream quite regularly. One of the other land girls worked on a dairy farm and was never short of butter; people said that she got it from the cowman in return for favours, but they always said things like that. She pointed a finger at Willy. "How do you know? There's something called a heart murmur, although you can't hear it yourself. The doctor listens . . ."

"Oh, I know all about that," said Willy. "He listens with one of them things . . ."

"Stethoscopes," said Annie. "And you'd better catch that bus, Val. Ten minutes."

They had told her to be there by nine-thirty, and the doctor would try to see her before ten. He was running late—a small boy had a bad cut on a finger that had to be stitched—but eventually she was taken in by the nurse, who sat in as chaperone. The nurse had a magazine with her, and read it discreetly in the corner until it was time for Val to be examined.

The doctor asked how long it was.

"Three weeks," she said.

The nurse looked up from her magazine, but dropped her eyes again.

"And you're usually regular?"

She nodded. "But I feel a bit different. I don't know how to put it, but I feel different. Sort of light."

The doctor was making a note. "Morning sickness usually starts about six weeks after you first miss," he said.

She could see the nurse looking at her. She wondered whether such people looked for a ring on the finger. Or did they take the view that it was none of their business—which it wasn't, in her view.

The doctor cleared his throat. "I'd like to examine you," he said. "But remember, it's too early to know with any certainty. It'll become clear enough in time." He put the cap back on his pen, screwing it on with elaborate care while he asked the next question. "And the father?"

She felt the nurse's eyes boring into her. "I'm engaged," she said. "He's my fiancé."

The doctor relaxed. He glanced across

the room at the nurse. "Well, that's not too bad, is it? The date of the wedding can be brought forward—if necessary." He allowed himself a smile.

Her heart was pounding. "But he's dead," she said. "The U.S. Air Force. He flew a Mosquito." She had begun to come to terms with his death. Her earlier hope—slender at the best of times—had grown weaker with each day. She was beginning to mourn.

The doctor's face fell. "My dear young lady, I'm so sorry."

She looked down at the floor. She did not want to cry in front of these people, but it was hard. She had cried and cried so much that she thought she had used up what tears there were, yet it seemed there were still more to shed.

The nurse stood up. She crossed the room and put an arm about her shoulder. She had a small handkerchief in her hand, and offered this to her.

"All these brave young men," said the doctor. "We're losing all these brave young men. Our men. Americans. New Zealanders. Canadians. All of them." He shook his head. "And there doesn't seem to be an end to it."

The nurse spoke. "It'll come."

"Yes, nurse," said the doctor. "You may be right, but in the meantime, it still goes on." He rose to his feet. "I'll examine Miss Eliot now."

She had to wait more than an hour for a bus back to the village. There was a small bus shelter, stale and dank, and she sat there thinking of what she would do. The doctor had said that there was a place they had used, a place near Cheltenham, that took girls in her position. "Not exactly the same position as yours," he said. "You're an engaged woman—or you were—which is almost the same as being married. Some of those girls don't have that advantage; some of them younger than you."

"Fifteen," said the nurse.

"Yes, fifteen. But they do what's necessary. They take them in and let them have the baby. Then the babies are placed."

She drew in her breath. "Placed?"

"For adoption," said the doctor. "There are other places, of course—some of them run by nuns. They look after you well, although some of the nuns, I believe, can be a bit on the severe side."

"Don't go to the nuns," said the nurse. "Stay away from them. You're not RC, are you? No, well, best to go somewhere else."

"The almoner at the hospital can help," said the doctor. "We have a very good woman there, Mrs. Knight. She's probably the best person to advise you."

Now, sitting in the bus shelter, she imagined herself going off to one of those places. She would have to go early if people were not to notice. She could tell them she was going to another farm—somewhere further away—and that she would not be coming back for some time. Would she have to tell the Land Army people? They must know about these things, because she could not be the first land girl to be in this position. They may have their own place, for all she knew, where they sent girls who got themselves into trouble.

She would have to tell Annie—if she did not already know. No, she must know; she must. She had been able to work out what was going on and had said that it was all right with her. She had said that, hadn't she? She had said, **It's different in wartime,** and she had been right. She probably knew that there was always a chance of this sort of thing happening. She must know that, being a postmistress and seeing all the things that postmistresses saw.

In the event, Annie did know. She had not said anything about Val's going to the doctor, because there would be only one reason why she needed to do that. A fit young woman like her—strong as an ox, with all that farm work—eating a good, healthy diet with those extra eggs and the milk that Willy brought back, cream sometimes; you would be healthy with all that and being nineteen, too, twenty next month.

She called Annie out of the post office. There was nobody in at the time, and Annie came back to the kitchen to talk to her. "Well," she said. "Is everything all right?"

She did not answer immediately, and Annie came towards her. She took her in her arms. "Dearie, you know that I love you very much. If this is what has happened, it's because of the war—everything's because of the war." Annie paused. "What did he say? Did he say that you are?"

She nodded her head. "But he can't say definitely yet. He says I should go back in a few weeks."

Annie patted her gently, as one would a child. "Dearie, that's all right. I'll look after you—and the baby. You mustn't worry."

She told Annie about the almoner at the hospital, who was apparently the person to go to for advice. Annie shook her head. "That Mrs. Knight is a gossip. I wouldn't tell her what time it was unless I didn't mind the whole world knowing. We'll find somebody else."

Val thought of something. "We'll have to tell Willy," she said. "Eventually. He'll . . . well, he'll see, won't he?"

"All in good time," said Annie. "No sense in getting Willy upset over anything just yet."

She considered this. "No," she said. "I want to tell him earlier rather than later. It'll give him time to get used to it. You know how he is. He doesn't always understand things at first."

She started to cry, and Annie held her to

her. Neither said anything for a few minutes. Then Annie said, "You're a good girl, Val. You've done everything right. You've worked hard. You made a good man happy. You've got nothing to be ashamed of—nothing at all."

He was a **Feldwebel,** a corporal, and was the second most senior soldier in the small unit posted in the town. The most senior was an **Oberfeldwebel,** a thin-faced man from Hamburg whom none of the men liked, and who was both lazy and unpredictable. The **Feldwebel** was called Karl Dietrich, but was known, for some reason, as Ubi. He was from Berlin and had recently turned twenty-two.

Ubi hated the war. He had joined up at seventeen under pressure from a threatening youth leader, who said he would denounce him for disloyalty if he failed to enlist. His father had tried to dissuade him, but he had been away when Ubi made the decision and on his return it was too late. He himself, a union leader, was already under suspicion and any suggestion that he had stopped his son from serving would have resulted in his arrest. Ubi had hated every moment of his training and had seriously considered desertion, but had been warned of the consequences by a close friend, a fellow infantryman, who had had the misfortune to have been detailed to serve in a firing squad.

The friend had said, "I'll never forget it. Never. I was sick over my rifle, over my boots, over everything."

His posting to Holland had saved him from being sent to the east, and once he was there the army seemed largely to have forgotten about him, to his great relief. He served in a number of small occupying garrisons, this last one being an ideal post for him because nothing much happened. There were regular searches, of course, and the occasional arrest. But for the most part they left the Dutch to get on with their lives provided they did nothing overt. They knew they were hiding people—all sorts of people, apparently—but in his view that was their business. The people they were hiding were small fry: undocumented foreigners, criminals on the run from somewhere, Jews. Ubi had nothing against Jews and could not understand the obsession of people like the **Oberfeldwebel,** who ranted about the bankers he said had brought Germany to her knees before their machinations had been exposed.

The only drawback to this posting, he felt, was the **Oberfeldwebel** himself. The locals were far too passive a bunch to do anything hostile, such as mount an ambush or blow something up; he rather liked them, with their slow, rather rustic ways and their guttural speech. He had even learned their language, since he had a good ear for these things, and it relieved the monotony to be able to talk to people in the street. If you spoke to them in Dutch, some of them could be quite friendly, although you always had those looks from others. The looks were hard to define: if they had been accompanied by a hostile gesture, then you could arrest the offender, but if they just looked it was harder to do anything about it.

"If anybody spits at you," advised the **Oberfeldwebel,** "bring him in. Spit is a weapon, especially in the mouth of a Dutchman. He'll regret it."

The **Oberfeldwebel**'s laziness at least meant that Ubi and his men were able to get on with their duties as they saw fit, which was with a lack of enthusiasm and a discretion that ensured they encountered little trouble. They made sure that their patrols were on the periphery of their allotted territory, so that neighbouring commanders should see them and assume a high level of activity on their part. This worked, and no attempts were made to relocate them to more hazardous posts. With any luck, Ubi thought, they might spend the rest of the war exactly where they were. How the war would end was something he did not care to dwell upon: when first he joined up he had assumed the invincibility of Germany; then had come North Africa and Italy and now the landings in Normandy. Germany would make peace, he hoped, and everyone could go home honourably; or, and this he feared was more likely, they would be hounded and pursued to the end. That man was mad, with all his ranting and raving, and his disastrous foray into the mud and snow of the Ukraine; he would carry on with his delusions until the Russians and Americans overran him and Germany ceased to exist. He dreamed of Russian soldiers—

vague, shadowy figures who looked at him from encircling darkness and then slipped away, vanished, when he tried to confront them. In his dreams, death came as a wakening up, and he found himself coming to, sweating and uncomfortable, in his shared room with the shape of the two other men under their blankets a few feet away, enduring, for all he knew, their own nocturnal demons.

Ubi had got to know Henrik, who was in their building several times a day, attending to blocked drains and matters of that sort. He was paid for two hours of work a day, but he seemed to spend more time than that there, which suited the men as he would also make coffee, bake bread, and keep the kitchen neat and tidy for the **Oberfeldwebel,** who, in spite of his laziness, was particular about cleanliness.

When Ubi called at Henrik's house eight days after the arrival of Mike and the navigator, Henrik assumed that the visit had something to do with his duties at the garrison building. He had started to paint one of the barrack rooms, as the Germans had somehow got hold of several tins of paint—stolen them, he imagined—and he had started but not finished the job the previous day.

Henrik knew that the two airmen were in the attic and that they were careful about making no noise, and so he was not too concerned. But then he remembered something: Peter Woodhouse was sleeping on the mat in front of the kitchen range and it was into the kitchen that he had invited Ubi.

It was too late to do anything—Ubi had seen the dog.

"So, Henrik, you have a dog. You never told me that."

Henrik tried to smile. "Oh, that dog. He belongs to a friend . . . a friend who's ill and can't look after him."

Ubi nodded. "That's why it's useful to have friends," he said. "They can help you out when you're in a spot."

"Very true," said Henrik. "Keep your friends happy—you never know when you'll need them."

Ubi crossed the room to stand over Peter Woodhouse. Then he bent down to stroke the dog's coat. "He looks a bit thin," he said.

"But then I suppose these are hard times for dogs as well as people."

"He likes fish," said Henrik hurriedly. "I catch fish for him from time to time. It's fine, as long as I take all the bones out."

"Bones," said Ubi. "Have you ever tried eating pike? Those bones they have! Like arrowheads."

"Good flesh, though," said Henrik. He was watching Ubi as he stroked Peter Woodhouse. He saw the collar, and he turned cold inside. The collar: the most basic mistake imaginable, and they had made it. With all their care, with all their insistence on anonymity and silence and doing things by night—in spite of all that, they had forgotten his collar.

Ubi was looking at the collar now, squinting to read the words burned into the leather. This, thought Henrik, is how death comes: through a little thing, in slow motion, while people are having dinner and walking in the street and the wildfowl on the river are drifting with the stream; this is how death comes.

Ubi read the name. "Peter Woodhouse,"

he said. "How do you people spell Peter, Henrik? Isn't it with an i—**Pieter**?"

He twisted the collar round so that he could see the rest of the inscription. At first he said nothing, then he said, "An American dog! Well, that's unusual, isn't it?"

Henrik had been thinking. "Oh, somebody gave that collar to my friend. He got hold of it in Amsterdam. It must be a leftover from something—heaven knows what. But it fits him, and so we've left it on."

Ubi was looking at him with a strange expression. Henrik swallowed. If he were handed over to the Gestapo, would he be able to bear the torture? He doubted it: younger, stronger men than he gave in, within minutes sometimes. Anything to end the pain, they said.

Ubi came back across the room so that he was now standing close to Henrik.

"I believe I should search your house, Henrik," he said. "We haven't searched you yet, have we?"

Henrik shook his head mutely.

"And why should we?" continued Ubi. "What need is there to search our friends?"

Henrik said nothing. He saw that Ubi had his pistol on his belt. He could hit him over the head or push him down the stairs or something, he thought; but no, he could not. Ubi was well built and would over-power him effortlessly, even without having to shoot him.

"Shall we go upstairs?" asked Ubi. "There's obviously nothing down here—apart from our friend over there."

He had no alternative but to accompany Ubi up the stairs. He waited while Ubi looked in the three rooms on the floor above, open-ing cupboards and glancing under beds.

"I'm sure I'll find nothing," Ubi said. "This is just a formality, Henrik."

He looked up at the ceiling. He noticed the small stepladder left against the wall.

"An attic?" he asked.

"Yes," said Henrik, raising his voice. "An attic."

Ubi frowned. "Why so loud, Henrik?" He looked up at the ceiling. Then he fixed Henrik with a stare. **He knows. He knows.**

Ubi pointed to the trapdoor. Then he leaned close to Henrik and whispered, "Guests, Henrik?"

Henrik froze. He opened his mouth to say something, but he could not find the breath, or the words.

Ubi continued to whisper. "Listen very carefully, Henrik, my friend. I can do one of two things: I can fire my pistol through the window, which will alert the garrison and they'll be here in less than a minute, or—and this is what I'd much prefer—you invite your guests to come down and say hello in the proper manner." He paused. "That keeps all this just between ourselves."

Henrik made his decision. Reaching for the stepladder, he placed it underneath the trapdoor and climbed its few steps to the top. Then he pushed the trapdoor open and called out in his limited English, "Come, now."

They complied.

Ubi looked at the two men standing before him. He had drawn his pistol, and they were looking at it nervously. He turned to Henrik and asked him who the men were.

"American airmen," said Henrik. The blame must be his alone: he must try to convince them of that, then only one person would die. "My family doesn't know about them—just me."

Ubi smiled. "Oh yes? Well, of course not. I don't suppose they speak Dutch or German, do they?"

"No," said Henrik.

"Pity," said Ubi, replacing his pistol in its holster. "Because I would like to ask them if I could bring them some food. They must be hungry."

Henrik stared at the soldier. "You'd do that?" he stuttered, his voice breaking with emotion.

"Yes, I would." He shrugged. "How much longer is this war going to go on? One month? Six months? Who can tell, but why should more men die?" He looked down at Henrik with what appeared to be fondness. "We're not going to win, yet if I took these men in we would shoot you and your son, and your daughter-in-law, and who wants that?"

Henrik said nothing. Then he turned to Mike and pointed at Ubi. Then he pointed at his own heart, twice, and placed his finger against his lips. It was the only way he could think of saying what he could not say.

He waited to see if they understood. They

did. Mike reached forward, offering a hand to Ubi, who shook it, smiling as he did so.

Ubi said to Henrik, "Nobody knows about this, Henrik. Understand?"

Henrik nodded. "Except God," he said.

## 15

Val spoke to Willy the day after her visit to the doctor's surgery. It was in the evening, and the two of them were alone in the house, Annie having gone out for a meeting of her wool group. They unravelled old woollen garments, rolling up the wool for re-use, and exchanged news as they did so. It was, Val had suggested, the clearing house for local gossip—and now, she realised, she would be of prime interest in that respect: talked about, disapproved of, the moment her aunt left the circle.

Willy was doing the washing up when she spoke to him. He liked to scrub the pots energetically, priding himself on making them gleam.

"I've something to tell you, Willy," she began.

He continued with his task. "This one's getting old. Metal's thin."

"That's because you scrub it too hard." She paused. "Are you listening to me, Willy? It's something important."

"I can listen and do this at the same time."

She waited a moment. "I'm going to have a baby."

He laid the pot down on the sink and turned to face her. "You? You're going to have a baby?"

"Yes," she said. "Not for some time yet, and the doctor hasn't said definitely. But I think so."

She heard his breath coming in short spurts. "Why?" His voice was strained.

"Well, I just am. I'm going to have a baby."

His eyes were wide. "But you're not married."

"No, but you can still have babies if you're not married."

This took a little while to sink in. "I know about all that," he said. "You been doing all that with him? Even you?"

She lowered her eyes. "Even me, Willy. Yes. Since you ask."

"And now he's dead," muttered Willy. "So what are people going to say?"

She was prepared for this. Willy, for all his innocence, was acutely aware of what people might say. That came, she imagined, from having been laughed at by others; you became sensitive to their sneers. "I don't care what people say." She did, of course.

Willy sat down. "But you can't have people talking about you. You can't have that. Talking. Laughing. Pointing their finger and saying, **She's got no husband, but there's a baby, you know.** You can't have that."

"People always talk, Willy. You have to live with it. Let them talk." She paused, the old rhyme from childhood returning—the playground mantra of the bullied: **Sticks and stones may break my bones but words will never hurt me.** She recited it now to Willy.

"Words can hurt," he said. "They can."

"Well, there's far worse things going on," she said.

He became silent. She watched him, the mental effort of whatever he was thinking about writ large on his face.

"I could marry you," he said at last. "I'll marry you and then it'll be all right."

She held him in her gaze. She realised that he meant it; that this was no idle offer, this was a proposal.

"But Willy . . ."

"Cousins can marry. Lots of cousins marry."

She shook her head. "Not lots, Willy. Sometimes maybe . . . And anyway, we aren't proper cousins. We're what they call **connected . . .**"

"And there ain't nothing wrong with it. You can have a proper church wedding and all."

"Oh, Willy . . ."

"And it would mean that I'd be your baby's dad. A baby needs a dad. He needs somebody to help him."

She knew she had to stop him before he went any further.

She looked for a reason that he would understand. "I can't marry you, Willy. I can't do that because you marry people you love—and we aren't in love, are we? I like you, I like you very much, but you aren't in love with me and I'm not in love with you. That means we can't get married."

He said nothing.

She spoke hurriedly, putting the matter beyond further discussion. "So while I'm really grateful to you for the offer—and it's a kind idea, really it is—we just can't get married." She paused. "So, soon enough I'll make up my mind about what I'm going to do—I'll probably go away somewhere—and then I'll tell you. You can come and visit me."

It worked. He smiled at the invitation to visit. "And bring things for your baby?"

"Of course," she said. "And if it's a boy, he'll want to spend a lot of time with you."

He beamed with pleasure. "I can teach him things," he said. "Since he won't have a dad, I can do that."

"Of course you can, Willy."

She left the room so that he should not see her tears. She went outside, into the darkness. Here and there a chink of light escaped the blackout curtains, but otherwise there was nothing. A dog barked somewhere, and she found herself thinking of Peter Woodhouse and how he had been caught up in the madness of war—a necessary madness, as somebody had put it. She looked up into the sky and wondered how her desperate willing that Mike should be alive could make any difference in a world as large and indifferent as this one was. The answer, of course, was that it could not, and that no amount of hope and prayer had the slightest impact. There was no justice, no fairness; there was nothing that would guarantee that we rather than they won. There was just chance, and death, and the emptiness that death brought.

She went back inside. Willy had finished his work on the pot and was looking about for something else to polish or put away. She crossed the room to him and planted a kiss on his cheek. "I'm so proud of you," she said.

He blushed. "Can't think why," he said.

## 16

News came through Mees, who listened to the BBC and Radio Oranje regularly. He was optimistic, and his optimism buoyed their mood. "It won't be long now. The British are very close to Eindhoven," he said. "That's not far away. We'll be able to hand you over."

"And the Canadians?" asked Mike.

"Not far away either."

"It's hard being cooped up here. I'm sorry, but it's hard."

Mees understood. "There's no point trying to pass you down the line," he pointed out. "You're safe here. Our friend helps."

**Our friend** was his name for Ubi. He liked him less than Henrik did. "Can you trust a German?" he had asked.

"Yes," came Henrik's reply. "The Germans do what they say they're going to do. And besides, he's taking as much risk as we are. He's also looking down the barrel of a gun if he's found out."

In September they heard artillery in the distance, and when Ubi came to see them,

as he did every day, he said there were rumours that Nijmegen had been taken. Mees
said to him, "Do you want to desert? We'll
shelter you, you know."

He thought about it, but at last said that
he would not. The **Oberfeldwebel** would
step up searches if he did, as a traitor was
an irresistible quarry. He would be keener to
find him than he was to ferret out Resistance
people; it would just create trouble.

"When the time comes, I'll give myself
up," he said.

That month, Eindhoven was liberated.
"They're fifteen miles away," said Mees. "We
can start counting the days."

In the garrison, the duties remained much
the same. They did patrols; they logged en-
tries in their book of buildings searched.
They came across a small cache of arms in
a house near the canal. They set fire to the
house, its occupants having fled, and lifted
the two pigs they found in the back yard and
took them back to the garrison in a handcart. One of the men had been a butcher,
and he did the slaughtering, being badly bitten in the leg by one of his victims in the
process. Ubi watched, sickened by the sight.

More blood, he thought. Pig's blood, human blood. Blood.

Some of the men talked openly about the end of the war. One had been listening to a clandestine broadcast that spoke of the Russians' progress. There was talk of the rape that would follow. Ubi thought of his mother and his sister. He wondered whether they could flee west, where the Americans might hold the Red Army in check.

The **Oberfeldwebel** gave the occasional pep-talk. He told the men that every great victory was preceded by set-backs. There was a secret weapon that would make the V2 rockets look tame. It was not long before it would be unveiled, and then Churchill and Stalin would change their tune. In the meantime, they had their work to do and they would do it.

One morning the **Oberfeldwebel** decided that it was time to make a show of force. The entire unit—all twelve men—would accompany him and the **Feldwebel** on a march around the town. This would show any elements of the population who thought they might be giving up that they were still very much in control.

As they made their way down the main
street, they encountered Mees, who was
walking Peter Woodhouse, no longer wearing his compromising collar but being led on
the end of a string with a makeshift noose. The
dog became tense as the sound of marching
approached. When the men drew level with
him, he growled and began to bark. Mees
struck him on the back with the rolled-up
newspaper he was carrying, but this had no
effect. The barking became hysterical. Mees
looked as apologetic as he could, because he
saw the Germans looking in his direction,
and tugged at the string lead. Enraged, Peter
Woodhouse slipped out of his collar.

There was nothing Mees could do other
than shout and run after him. But it was too
late: Peter Woodhouse had reached the first of
the Germans and had lunged at the boots
of one of the men. The soldier kicked out at
him and Peter Woodhouse attacked again.

It was Ubi who managed to get him under
control. Surprised by the familiar smell of
someone whom he had by now got to know,
Peter Woodhouse calmed down and began
to lick his friend's hand. The **Oberfeldwebel** shouted an order and another of the

men stepped forward, loosened his belt, and put it round Peter Woodhouse's neck.

"Dietrich," shouted the **Oberfeldwebel.** "Take that dog round the corner and shoot him."

Ubi frowned. "He's just a dog," he muttered. "Can't we just . . ."

He was not allowed to finish. A small group of children had gathered, and the **Oberfeldwebel** gestured towards them. The locals might need to be taught a lesson from time to time, but shooting a dog in front of children was unnecessary.

Ubi tried to dissuade the **Oberfeldwebel,** but his pleas had no effect. "You've been given an order," came the response. "Carry it out unless you want to face the consequences."

He stood for a few moments while Mees approached the **Oberfeldwebel,** begging him to excuse the dog. "He meant no harm," he said. "He was over-excited, that's all."

The **Oberfeldwebel** signalled him away with a movement of his pistol. "I will not have my men attacked by dogs," he said. "Consider yourself fortunate that you are not being placed under arrest yourself."

Mees knew that he must not be arrested.

He knew far too much about what people in the area were doing to subvert the occupation to allow himself to be handed over to the Gestapo. He could not run the risk of compromising those whose identity he knew. He made a gesture of acceptance and moved off.

Ubi began to lead Peter Woodhouse away. The men were told that they could break for a smoke, and they did so, sitting on the edge of the town fountain, lighting up and talking among themselves. Round the corner, in the small deserted alley that led off the main street, Ubi dragged Peter Woodhouse into the doorway of a now closed tobacconist shop. The dog looked up at him and tried to lick his hand again. Ubi drew his pistol.

He pulled the trigger, the shot reverberating against the walls of the houses in the narrow street. The bullet, aimed up in the air, sped harmlessly away.

Peter Woodhouse cowered. "Go," hissed Ubi, aiming a kick at the dog's rump. "Run."

At first Peter Woodhouse simply continued to cower, but then a second kick, sharper than the first, made him move away. Ubi reached down to pick up a small stone at the edge of the road. He threw this at the dog as hard as he could and it connected with his snout, making him yelp. Slowly he began to move away, and then he broke into a faster run when Ubi sent another stone rattling down the street.

A week later, they heard the sound of tanks, an unmistakable low growl coming from the south. There was some gunfire, but that did not last long, and the sound of the approaching tanks grew much louder. At three o'clock the following afternoon, a tank drew up at the bridge on the edge of the town, allowing a platoon of infantry to run down the road, dropping for cover from time to time as they tested the town's defences. A few shots were fired from the direction of the garrison, and these drew a fusillade of machine gun fire from two separate positions. A white flag cloth quickly appeared at one of the garrison windows—a towel, it seemed—and this was waved energetically until a small line of men came out of the front door, their hands raised high in surrender. Almost immediately the bell in the church began to toll and people appeared in the streets. Dutch flags, hidden in anticipation of this day, were waved by excited children.

Mees ran to the house where Mike and the navigator were hiding. He led them out into the street and urged them on to the main square. They blinked at the light. A woman threw her arms around Mike and kissed him. The navigator looked stunned, and kept glancing up at the sky, as if expecting imminent attack.

They watched as the Germans were given their instructions. Two Allied soldiers kept guard over them, occasionally prodding them with the butts of their rifles and kicking in their direction. An officer appeared and reprimanded the men; then he spoke to the **Oberfeldwebel** in pidgin German. Mees came up and drew the officer aside, telling him that one of the garrison had collaborated with the Resistance.

"Don't point him out to me," said the officer. "They'll kill him."

"I can give you his name," said Mees. "He deserves consideration."

The officer nodded, and wrote it down in his notebook. The **Oberfeldwebel** watched.

Mike and the navigator did not know

what to do. They spoke to the officer after he had finished with the **Oberfeldwebel.** He said, "Don't do anything just now. We'll ask somebody to come and fetch you. It's all a bit mixed up at the moment, but the situation will become clearer in due course." He looked at the two airmen. "Is there anything I can do for you in the meantime? Need anything?"

Mike nodded. "Could you send a message to our unit? They don't know we're alive."

The officer nodded. "Write the details down. I'll try to get it sent from Eindhoven."

One of Mees's friends appeared with Peter Woodhouse. The officer frowned. "What's this?"

Mike smiled as he explained. "Our dog. Our unit's mascot. He was shot down with us."

The officer looked astonished. "He was in the plane?"

"Yes," said Mike. He noticed that the **Oberfeldwebel** was staring at the dog. "Sir, you must take one of those men into protective custody."

The officer looked irritated. "Why?" He

indicated Mees. "This man's already spoken to me about him."

"No, you must." Mike's voice had a note of urgency in it.

The officer bristled. He was a captain, and a senior one at that, but he was not sure if he outranked this scruffy aviator. "I'm not sure you can tell me what to do."

Mike fixed him with a cold stare. "I'm a serving officer. I'll take him as my prisoner."

The officer's lip curled. "He's under my custody."

Mees said, "I'll take him. He can be a prisoner of the Resistance."

The officer shook his head. "Don't be ridiculous. I don't know who you are." He hesitated. He had seen the **Oberfeldwebel** looking at Ubi, and he understood. Stepping forward, he pointed at Ubi. "You—you there. You come with me."

Mees quickly translated the command. His relief was palpable.

Ubi stepped forward. He looked at Mike and smiled. Then he bent down and patted Peter Woodhouse gently on the back. "War's over," he murmured.

The dog looked up at him. He was not sure: this was the man who had kicked him and thrown stones at him. The canine memory for that sort of thing is a long one. But something told him that all that was over. He had no word for it, but dogs can forgive, and he did.

## 17

Val asked Willy to peel the potatoes for their dinner that night. She had three large eggs, given to her by Archie. She had told him that she did not feel entitled to them, as he had already given her two that week, but he insisted. She was going to make egg and potato pie—a dish that she knew both Willy and Annie particularly liked. The white sauce would have to be made without butter, but the richness of the eggs would make up for that.

It had not been a good day. She had felt unwell early in the morning, which might have been morning sickness, she thought, or might have been something unconnected with the pregnancy. She had examined herself in the full-length mirror on the outside of her wardrobe, standing naked, sideways and then full on, to see whether her body was changing shape. She thought it was, although how big would the baby be at this stage? Tiny, she decided. The size of a mouse, perhaps, tucked away in her stomach somewhere vaguely down there: precise female anatomy had never been properly explained at school, although the girls had been taken aside for instruction and a visiting nurse had shown them a coloured diagram that none of them had properly understood. It was all tubes, she thought, and the baby was somewhere at the end of one of them, in the womb, wherever that was. She relaxed her muscles and her belly sagged—more so than normal, she thought. So she was beginning to show, she told herself: people would be able to tell in a month, perhaps a little longer.

She looked at her bust. She had never been proud of it because she thought it was too schoolgirlish, too small. She had seen the women painted on the fronts of the American planes at the base—some of them completely naked, others wearing very little, and they all had much larger busts. They held them out before them like those carvings seamen had on the prows of sailing ships; that's what men liked, it seemed: women with that sort of bust, not one like hers. And yet Mike had said that her body was "just perfect," and she thought he had meant it.

Now he would never see her like this.

He would never see her carrying his child. He would never be able to put his hand on her stomach and feel the baby move within, which is what she had been told fathers-to-be liked to do—to feel the life they had helped to create. That would not happen.

A few days earlier she had been able to tell herself that she might see him again. She had felt that if she gave up all hope for him, she would somehow be bringing about his death. It was a superstitious belief: talk of a man dying and you make it happen. People said something like that; she had heard them. So you didn't speculate as to somebody's chances, or at least not openly.

But then she started to admit to herself that the possibility of his survival was, as they had told her, extremely slender. And what had made it worse was that the day before, when she had delivered eggs to the base, Sergeant Lisowski had asked her whether she wanted any of Mike's things. He had been as tactful as he could, saying that she could just "look after" them and give them back if he ever returned, but she knew that what was happening was a disposal of his effects. There was not much, he said: some personal family photographs that would go back to his family in Muncie, along with his diary and an inscribed wristwatch that had his father's initials on it. But there were some other things—small things—that they would not normally send all the way back to the States and she might like as mementos.

She had said she would like them, and he had gone off to fetch a linen drawstring bag. He had given it to her without opening it to show her the contents, and it was not until she had returned to the house that she went to her room and opened the neck of the bag.

There was a penknife. There was a set of navigator's calipers; there was a bow tie with red and blue stripes. There was the framed picture he had taken of her. She laid these things out on the bed and then knelt at the side and let her head rest on the quilt. She reached for the bow tie, put it to her lips and kissed it. She wiped her eyes with the back of her hand. She muttered "Mike" and then "My love, my love," and she repeated these words over and over again, her tears making the bedcover moist, their salt in her mouth.

Now, as Willy peeled the potatoes for the egg and potato pie, she stood in the door-

way and stared at his back. Should she have
let Willy marry her? There would have been
raised eyebrows, as many people would think
that a woman should not take up with a man
who was not quite all there. It was as if doing
that would be to take advantage of him in
some undefined way—sexual, perhaps. But
he would be loyal, and kind, because both
of these qualities were in his nature, and he
would not make her unhappy.

But then she told herself that what she
had said to him—even if it was intended
to be a simple explanation readily understood by somebody like him—was, in fact,
the right thing to say. She believed that you
married for love—you had to if you wanted
it to work. She knew that there were women
who married for money or for land, but
were they truly married in the real sense of
the word? Or were they just signing up for
a business arrangement in which they gave
what women gave their husbands in return
for a roof over their heads and the necessities
of life? It was possible that Willy would find
somebody who would actually love him, and
he needed to have that chance. There could
well be a girl somewhere, a farmer's daugh-

ter maybe, who would be right for him. She would be plain, perhaps, but strong and resourceful. She would cook and darn clothes and keep the kitchen range well stoked up. And if she were a farmer's daughter and there were no sons, then Willy could succeed to a farm and have his own place. That was possible, just possible.

Willy finished peeling the potatoes. He turned to Val and said, "All done. Good potatoes too. None of those black things in them—what do you call those black things, Val?"

"Eyes," she said.

He smiled. "That's right—eyes. No eyes."

She crossed the room to stand beside him. The eggs were in a brown paper bag, and she reached into this to extract one of them. "Look at this," she said. "I think I know which hen laid this one. She's a Rhode Island Red, and she's bigger than the others."

He took the egg from her gingerly. "Shall I put it in the pan?"

"Yes, and then we'll put the other ones in with it and fill it with water. They need to be hard-boiled for our pie."

He said, "That's six minutes at least."

She nodded, and remembered that Willy had difficulty telling the time. She had tried to teach him when she realised this, but he had struggled to master the concept of minutes to the hour. Why, he asked, if you counted up to thirty up to the figure six, did you then start counting down? Her explanation, she feared, had been less than clear and had merely added to his confusion.

They put the egg pan on the stove and switched it on. It was an unsophisticated electric cooker, and it took a long time to get to temperature. But they were lucky; plenty of people had nothing so advanced, and relied on ranges fuelled by wood or coal.

Willy was looking out of the window. "That sergeant fellow," he said. "Did you invite him?"

She frowned. "No. Is he outside?"

"He's coming by here," said Willy. "Maybe he wants more eggs."

She moved to the window and looked out. Sergeant Lisowski was making his way down the front path—and he had a dog with him.

"He's got hold of another dog," said Willy.

"He must have been missing Peter Woodhouse." He turned to Val. "Ain't that nice, Val? Him getting another dog like that."

She did not answer. Making her way to the front door, she took a deep breath, brushed her hair back from her forehead, and opened to the sergeant's knock.

Peter Woodhouse leapt up at her. It was a headlong dive, and she reeled under the onslaught. She almost fell over, but righted herself as the dog managed to lick her face, covering her with dog spittle. He was whimpering, the sort of excited whimpering that comes when a dog is overcome with emotion.

Sergeant Lisowski stood there beaming. "He remembers you," he said. "He hasn't forgotten."

"I-i-is it really him?" she stuttered.

"Yes," said Sergeant Lisowski. "It's Peter Woodhouse. Look at the collar."

She struggled to get a sight of the collar. There was so much fur, so much wriggling dog muscle, that it was difficult to see the inscription. But it was there.

And then the full significance of this hit her, and she let out a scream.

"He's alive," said Sergeant Lisowski. "He'll be back in two or three days."

She screamed again. Willy was there now, and he was struggling to understand what was happening.

"Mike made it," said Sergeant Lisowski. "They sent the dog first because he didn't need a seat. Mike's waiting for a plane that's going out there soon. It'll bring him back."

Val flung her arms around the sergeant. He smelled of cooking, she thought, because he spent his days in the cookhouse. She kissed him on his neck, his chin, his cheek. He kissed her back and said, "I shouldn't kiss another fellow's girl, but what the heck."

They told Val that she could see him the day after his return. The colonel, who had returned from London, saw Mike while Val waited outside the office. It was the day after VE Day, when the formal capitulation of Germany had occurred, and there were still signs of the previous day's celebrations. Somebody had tied a balloon to a fire bucket, and it was still there, half deflated.

"Well, it's over," said the colonel. "At

least, this bit of it." He paused. "And I think I know what you want to talk to me about."

Mike told him that they wanted to marry as soon as possible and would like his permission. The colonel suppressed a sigh. These wartime marriages were troublesome; he had seen many of them come unstuck once the glamour faded—as it did. He gave his permission. And then he said that Peter Woodhouse, U.S. Air Force, Dog First Class, could be officially reinstated as a mascot, if that was all right with the people who owned him, but was not to fly without permission. Mike thanked the colonel, and said that he felt one forced landing was enough for any dog.

The colonel laughed. "And your own future?" he said. "I've heard that you might want to stay in. Is that correct?"

Mike nodded. "I like flying, sir. It's what I want to do with my life." When he had entered the air force, he had had only a vague interest in flying. Now that had all changed, and he had discovered it was the thing that he wanted to do above all else.

He tried to explain it to the colonel. "When I'm up there, sir, up above the clouds, I just feel . . . well, I feel that I'm in the right

place—for me, that is. That's where I have
to be."

The colonel smiled. There was no need
for that feeling to be explained to him; he
knew. "Uncle Sam will still need pilots. And
I think I can recommend you."

It was a strange moment for Mike. He
had committed himself to a career, and he had
chosen the woman he wanted to marry. It
seemed to him as if the contours of his life,
which had always been uncertain, were now
set out as clearly and firmly as the lines on
any map.

Willy gave Val away, leading her down the
aisle of the small church not far from the post
office. She was visibly pregnant by the time
of the wedding, but people pretended not to
notice. Archie, uncomfortable in an unac-
customed suit, sang the hymns loudly and
out of tune. Afterwards, they went to the
pub, where the landlord had laid out some
of the tinned food that Mike had purloined
from Sergeant Lisowski.

He had told her that their future would
still be uncertain. There was still work for
the air force to do in Europe—they had been

warned that this would not finish any time soon—and he hoped she would not mind if they did not make it to Muncie, Indiana, just yet. She said that she could accept that, as long as they went there sometime.

The honeymoon was the last three days of the leave the colonel had granted Mike. They travelled in a borrowed car, using American fuel, to a small port in Cornwall and climbed on the cliffs. They looked out in the direction of France, far away at that point, and were both for a moment silent with their thoughts.

A breeze came up off the sea. She asked, inconsequentially, "What are you thinking of?"

He turned to look at her. "I guess I was thinking of Peter Woodhouse."

She smiled. She had no idea why she should have been thinking of Peter Woodhouse just then, but she was.

"So was I," she said.

He smiled. "Do you think that it happens?"

"What happens?"

"Synchronicity."

She looked puzzled. He was studying engineering—or had been—and that made him a scientist, she supposed; she knew nothing of science, and the words that went with it.

He explained. "It's what happens when people start doing things—or thinking things—at the same time." He paused. "They say that it happens a lot with married couples." He blushed—neither of them was used to the fact of marriage. In the bed and breakfast in which they were staying, he had spoken the words "my wife" with such hesitation and awkwardness as to attract a look of doubt to the owner's face. Mike had intercepted the glance to the hand, and to the rings—that had allayed suspicion, but the fact still seemed strange to him. How did married people behave? Was he convincing as a married man?

Val liked the idea. "I wouldn't have to ask you to do things," she said. "I'd just have to think them."

"And I'd do what you wanted," said Mike. "Exactly."

They spent a great deal of their time talking about the future. She seemed to have an insatiable appetite for information about Muncie and Indianapolis. What colour would the roof be? It would be red—he had no hesitation in answering that. And the kitchen? It would have everything, he promised, including a refrigerator large enough to walk into—well, almost—and cupboards with sliding doors.

And she asked what they would do.

He frowned. "Do?"

"Yes, what would we do . . . with our time?"

He looked thoughtful. "Go for drives in the car. Have you heard of drive-in movie theatres?"

She had not, and he explained. "They're going to be big. Every town's getting one now. You park your car, you see, and you watch the movie from the car. Twenty-five cents a person, and they sell hot dogs, popcorn . . . everything."

"I'd like that."

"Of course you would. We'd go every week—maybe twice a week."

"America," she sighed. It seemed an impossible dream: safety, refrigerators, drive-in movies. If only the war would end, with them alive when it did. She closed her eyes and thought that if that happened, then she might stop doubting that God existed and say yes, of course he does, because he would have brought them through this. It was almost a challenge to him, if he was there: prove it to me.

Suddenly an idea occurred to her. "Do people believe in God in Muncie?" she asked.

He looked surprised. "But of course they do," he answered.

"All of them?"

"Pretty much." Then he said, "And here? Don't people believe here?"

She thought for a moment. "They say they do, but I'm not so sure that they do—underneath. Maybe they **hope** that he's there."

"It's easier if you believe," he said. "It makes you feel a bit . . ." He trailed off.

**Braver,** she thought. **It makes you feel braver.**

"It makes you feel braver?"

He smiled. "Boy, do we need that."

It was the closest he came to telling her

how frightened he was, but she understood, and she steered the conversation away, onto something less real. She asked about drive-in movie theatres, and about where the sound came from. Did you leave your windows open?

He smiled at her. "You'll see," he said.

TWO

# HE HATED THE WAR

## 18

A small square of roughly cut brown bread, stale and heavy, with a mug of lumpy soup scraped out of an urn. No meat in the soup, but a rancid smell that could have come from meat, an unfortunate horse, perhaps, or an ancient pig; a thin layer of grease, too, across the surface that suggested the same origins.

Ubi took it gratefully, warming his hands on the mug, which was made of tin and conducted heat well. It was early May, and the air was far from warm, even if the hedges were green once more and there were wildflowers everywhere, and early blossom on the fruit trees. The man next to him spilled some of his soup down his chin and onto the jacket of his uniform; his hands were shaking and it was hard for him to bring the mug to his lips. He looked sheepishly at Ubi, who smiled at him encouragingly. There were many who seemed to be fumbling or faltering in unexpected ways—tripping, or stumbling, as if some internal gyroscope had been taken from them. One man, a **Feldwebel** like Ubi, seemed to have lost control of his bladder and sat dejectedly and self-consciously separate from the other men, staring up at the sky as if he were somewhere else, as if this were not him, this reeking, shameful person, a disgrace to the uniform he had so thoroughly ruined. Ubi took him an extra piece of bread that he found near the table where the rations had been handed out, and gave it to him in a gesture of support. The man took it, and looked up at him, briefly, but then looked away again without thanking him.

It was the midday meal. There would be something more at six o'clock, they had been told, although it might not be warm. One of their Canadian captors, a sergeant with a loud voice, had explained—through an interpreter—that they could not expect much more because their own people had robbed the Netherlands of most of its food. "So you see what this brings you," he announced. "What goes round, comes round. Understand?" He looked again at the puzzled faces and repeated his question. "Understand?"

Because of the intervention of Mees and

the captain who had taken their surrender, Ubi had been put into a different prisoner-of-war holding centre from the rest of his unit. The captain had decided that if this were done there would be little risk of retaliation from his former superiors or his colleagues—the chances of their encountering him among the thousands of prisoners of war caught up behind the rapidly advancing Allied lines would be next to non-existent. A note was left with the senior Canadian officer at the makeshift detention camp to the effect that **Feldwebel** Dietrich was alleged to have been helpful to the Resistance and to a group of American airmen. This could be entered on his records, although nobody was sure what records there would be and who would hold them. At the camp itself, there was the barest noting down of name, age, and unit, with nothing said about anything else.

On the third day of his captivity, when they were still bedding down in a field, all two hundred of them, watched over by sentries posted along an ordinary stock fence, the Canadian officer in charge insisted on an examination of every prisoner. In the raw spring air they took off their tunics and their shirts, and lined up in front of a couple of non-commissioned officers. Each man then held out his left arm to be checked for an SS number tattooed on the flesh; this was the mark of Cain that exposed those who had sought cover in the stolen uniforms of less guilty branches of the German forces. One man, exposed in this way, yelled out in protest, turning to the men behind him for support, but was greeted with indifference, even flickers of **Schadenfreude.**

An orderly sprayed them for lice, the fine white powder a cloud of humiliation that hung about them for a few seconds before settling on skin and clothing. Ubi breathed it in, and coughed and spat to rid himself of the chemical taste. He felt like an animal, prodded, probed, and treated for infestation before re-joining the herd of milling figures, clustering together like cattle.

And everywhere he saw the raw hopelessness of defeat, only punctuated now and then by thoughts of how much worse it would have been had it been the Russians who had overrun them. The Russians were bent on revenge, shooting their captives out of hand or waiting for starvation, or death by thirst, to do their work for them; one of the men who had been on the eastern front told them of a unit of Georgian cannibals that had been let loose on German prisoners. They chose the youngest men, the boys of fifteen, even younger, who had been drafted in as the ranks of their elders were steadily diminished. "This happened," he said. "I saw it. They ate the boys."

Ubi did not believe him. Men went mad in war, he thought, but not that mad. Such stories had been put about by the authorities to persuade people to fight when they had lost all enthusiasm for the cause. Ubi had never wanted to fight in the first place. His elder brother had been a communist and had told him that this war was nothing to do with the people of Germany but was fratricidal lunacy inspired by a demented Austrian. His brother had expressed these views once too often, and in the wrong company, and disappeared without a trace one morning. That left Ubi with a mother and a sister, his father having died a few months after the war began.

His mother and his sister were in Berlin, and when news filtered through that the city had fallen to the Russians he sat with his head in his hands, trying as hard as he could not to think about what would happen to them. It was unbearable, and he eventually told himself that they had both been killed, in their sleep, by a direct hit by an American bomb on their flat in Wedding. An American bomb would have been clean and merciful, and they would not have suffered—unlike those who found themselves in the path of Ivan.

They were marched from one place to another, and eventually he found himself being called out at early morning muster and taken to a tent in which a Canadian major, flanked by an interpreter, quizzed him about his service record. There was not much to say, of course; he had had a quiet war, and had not so much as fired a shot in anger. He did not bother to tell his interrogator this, as it sounded such an unlikely story, and anyway would already have been used by those with most to hide.

But that was not what the Canadian wanted to find out.

"We've had information," the major said, referring to a typewritten sheet before him, "that you were of assistance to two American airmen. Can you tell me a bit more about that?"

He hesitated. He did not want to stand out from the crowd in any way. He wanted to be anonymous, just to be one of the hundreds of thousands of defeated soldiers who could not be individually punished for what had happened. He wanted to go home. He wanted to take off this uniform and escape from under the rank cloud that the army carried with it: in good times a miasma of cruelty and noise and raucous singing, and now, in defeat, a dark air of gloom and brokenness. He wanted to sit with a girl in a café and drink coffee and feel the sunlight; he wanted to lie in a bath of soapy water; he wanted to clean and bind the recalcitrant ulcer that had developed on his right foot; he wanted not to smell. Would that ever again be possible? The world was in ruins; there would be no medicines for the dregs of this disgraced army; coffee would be a distant memory; and what would girls want to do

with the men whom they would blame for
bringing this all about?

"Well, tell me," prompted the major.
"What assistance did you provide?"

He saw that the major had cut himself
while shaving and had applied a styptic pencil to the nick.

"I took food," he said.

The major stared at him. "You didn't report them?"

He shook his head. He was tired. What
was the point of going over the things that
had happened in war? The dead stayed dead;
the living preferred to forget. Did anything
else really matter?

"So, you didn't report them and you took
them food? Why did you do this?"

He shrugged. "The war was almost over,"
he said. "And I didn't see any point."

He felt the major's eyes on him. He looked
away. He wanted this interview to come to
an end.

The major turned to the interpreter and
said to him, in English, "Is this man telling
the truth?"

The interpreter answered, "Yes, I think so.
I can't be sure, sir, but liars talk in a different

way—it's just something they do. This man isn't doing that."

The major laughed. "I wish I had your certainty. Mind-reader, are you?"

"It's all there on that piece of paper," pointed out the interpreter. "He seems to be confirming it."

The major turned back to Ubi. "We are sending home a number of prisoners," he said. "They are either very sick or very deserving—mostly sick, although heaven knows what they can do for them back in Germany. A smaller number are men who have done something to help us—men like you. There are very few of those, I might add."

Ubi listened.

"You live in Berlin?"

"Yes."

"Would you like to go back there? The Soviets . . ."

"But you are there, too, I hear."

The major nodded. "The Americans, yes. The British and the French too. You can go if you wish."

He collected his few possessions—a kit bag, a spare shirt that he had tried to launder in cold water.

"Don't tell the other men you're leaving," the major had warned him. "Say that you're being transferred to another prisoner-of-war camp. They might not take it too well."

When he went back to the major's tent, he was told to take off his clothes and change into a new set of clothing they provided for him. The trousers were too large, but he was given an old tie to serve as a belt. They were at least clean, as was the shirt they gave him. There were even fresh underclothes, fastened with drawstrings because elastic was hard to come by. His old clothing was picked up by a Canadian corporal, his face distorted with unconcealed distaste, and thrown on the ground outside.

"Burn all that," snapped the major. "Don't leave it there, for God's sake."

The corporal went outside and gestured to a soldier to fetch a can of petrol. A few drops were sprinkled on the clothing and a match applied. Ubi was surprised at the size of the flames that enveloped his abandoned clothing, and the smoke too. It was his past that was in flames, he thought, and he was grateful. He was cleansed. He had fresh clothing and was being taken back to

Germany, taken home, to find out whether his mother and sister were still alive.

"You're a fortunate man," said the major.

Ubi knew he was right. He wanted to thank the officer for what he had done, but he could not get the words out. Words, it seemed, had deserted him, as if his brain sensed that there was no point in trying to express the immensity of what had happened. Only two reactions to war seemed possible: a silence, as of horror, or a wail of anguish.

"You're fortunate because you're no longer in uniform," the major went on. "These men . . ." He gestured to the corporal and a guard standing at the entrance to the tent. "These men are still in uniform."

Now Ubi found his voice. "You are very kind, sir."

The major sighed. "Doing my job, that's all." He gave Ubi a piece of paper impressed with an official stamp. "You are no longer a prisoner of war," he said. "You are demobilised, as of now. You are a civilian again."

They took him away with two other men. One had a bandaged head and looked dazed and unsure what was happening. The other seemed to be uninjured, but muttered incessantly under his breath in a heavy, unfamiliar dialect. They were driven to another army post, where they waited several hours before being loaded, with other men, into an army truck just as night was descending. The back of the truck was closed, and they saw nothing. One of the men started to sing one of the songs they had been taught, the **Westerwaldlied,** but this was greeted with scowls, and he stopped halfway through a line, awkward and embarrassed.

They were transferred onto a train late at night, into an open wagon into which a few blankets had been tossed. They were not told where the train was going, other than Germany; they would have to make their way home from wherever it was that it stopped. After what seemed like an interminable wait, the engine started its journey; he tried to settle, lying down on one of the blankets, but the train jolted and squeaked and sleep eluded him. Lying awake, he looked sideways through a gap in the slats that made up the side of the wagon, watching such lights as the battered towns possessed. There was an acrid smell; the train had been used for transporting lignite, and his new clothes were soon discoloured with the dust of the cheap coal. He did not care. He was returning to Germany, and whatever had happened to it, it was still Germany; it was still his country.

## 19

With his release document in his hand, Ubi
considered himself lucky: others lingered far
longer than he as prisoners or forced labour-
ers, and many succumbed, particularly those
who fell into the hands of the Russians. Yet
he had a feeling of being cast adrift, at the
beginning of a journey that would be long,
complicated, and beset with bureaucratic obstacles. The original release paper, so potent
in getting him on that train back to Germany, would have a great deal of work to do,
and he feared it would soon lose its power.
There were just too many displaced persons;
there were just too many ration books and
travel passes to be issued for much time to be
spent on the claims of one young man who
had been released early and simply wanted
to get back to a home that probably no longer existed. A whole country had been up-
rooted and turned upside down; everybody
was looking for somebody, and the ether was
full of echoing, plaintive cries: **ich suche
meine Frau; ich suche meinen Sohn**—I

am looking for my wife; I am looking for my son. Scraps of paper were pinned on notice boards, half obscuring one another like the over-abundant leaves of trees in full foliage, each a record of a desperate attempt to find out what had happened to sons, to brothers, to husbands. **Do you know anybody who was at Stalingrad? Did anybody ever mention a Sergeant Kurt Muller from Hamburg, who was posted there?**

Prisoners of war were fed, but those, like Ubi, who were demobilised had to find work if they were to eat. He had no idea whether his mother and sister were still alive; he had not heard from them, and he had found out that the street on which they lived in Berlin had been reduced to rubble. Stories of the atrocities suffered at the hands of the Russians had filtered through: whispered accounts of rape on an unremittingly brutal scale. They said that the bodies of those who were killed had simply disappeared under the broken buildings and would never be recovered. The rats grew fat on this hidden bounty—their tunnels reached places where the efforts of those clearing the ruins would never penetrate.

People said that it was a place of silence, like a city of the dead, shocked by the fate it had brought upon itself.

That first train journey had ended at a station in a small city that had got off fairly lightly in the bombing raids. Almost three-quarters of it was intact, and there was food, too, as it was a market town for the surrounding countryside. Although there was no coal, the woods nearby provided wood for fuel, and people brought this into town each afternoon on hand carts loaded with bark and hand-sawn timber.

The population was less dispersed than in places where the physical destruction had been worse. Yet even so, there were few men, and certainly not enough men of Ubi's age to do the work that needed to be done. He had been intending to join the streams of people he had seen heading to a nearby larger city, but on his first morning he was approached by a woman at the railway station. She asked him whether he could help her: she owned an inn, she said; her husband had been on the eastern front and there was no word of him. "I don't think he will be back," she said. "I like to tell myself other-wise, but I am a realist."

He lowered his eyes. Was she blaming him, in some way, for what had happened? Her tone had been almost accusing, and he thought she might imagine him to be a party member, or an SS man, or something that he had not been.

"In what way do you think I can help?" he asked.

"I need somebody to help me at the inn," she said. "I need somebody to do the man's work. To fix things."

She mentioned that the person who helped her would get a warm room—it was above the kitchen—and his keep. "I have food," she said. "My inn is being used by British officers who are billeted there. Not fighting people—administrators. They're the new government, you see. I prepare their rations." She looked at him meaningfully. "I prepare their rations," she repeated.

Hunger gnawed at his stomach. He had not eaten for eighteen hours, and from somewhere in the station there came the smell of soup. He was dirty.

"I even have hot water," said the woman. "Not much, but enough."

He met her gaze. "I want to get back to Berlin," he said.

She looked at him as if he had said something beyond comprehension. "Berlin is full of Russians," she said. "And it's surrounded."

"I'd like to go eventually."

"But not now?"

"Maybe not now."

She smiled. "So you'll work for me?"

He nodded. He was tired.

They walked back to the inn, which was not far from the station. A British military car was parked outside it, a Union Jack pennant limp in the lifeless air.

"That's the English colonel's car," said the woman. "He has an office next to his room. He prefers to work there."

He nodded. "Do they pay you?"

"Not what I would like, but something. It means I can keep the inn open—most of the others have closed."

She showed him to his room. Her name, she told him, was Ilse Marten. Her father had been a Lutheran pastor, she said, and he had died four years before the war began.

"I am glad he died then," she said. "He was spared the worst of the monster who got us into this."

"This war?"

She looked at him cautiously; she had spoken freely, but now ancient habit reasserted itself. There were still fanatics who had not changed their views, and one had to be circumspect in what one said. He put her mind at rest. "It's a pity they didn't hang him," he muttered. "They got the others—or a lot of them—but he cheated them."

She looked relieved. "Well, that settles that," she said. "If you make a fire under the boiler, you can have some hot water. I have a razor you can use, if you like—it was my husband's."

He mumbled something. What was there to say, beyond the trite expressions of sympathy?

As she had promised, his room was warm, the heat coming from the flue of the kitchen range directly below. This was exposed as it passed up through his room, and there was warmth, too, that came up through the floorboards, along with cooking smells. He later learned that there was coal—it was

not meant for civilians, but the British officers were entitled to it, and they passed it on
to Ilse for kitchen use.

He took off his socks and felt the warmth
underfoot. It took him back to Holland,
where they had enjoyed an ample supply of
wood for heating their barracks. Defeat had
been cold; it had been hunger and cold.

"You may have a bath," said Ilse. "I have
run the water for you. And there is soap."

He had not seen soap for weeks and he
handled it now as if it were something precious. In the bath he noticed that he was
changing colour as the grime came off; it
was as if he were shedding a skin.

She entered the room with a towel, un-
concerned at his nakedness. Nobody seemed
to worry about such things any longer; modesty was unimportant when survival was at
stake.

The towel was clean and smelled of something he could not quite place. And then
he remembered: it was lavender. It was one
of the familiar smells that had simply gone
from his memory, replaced by the overpow-
ering smells of war: smoke, burning rubber,
the stink of putrefaction. There was even a

smell for fear—a sharp, uneasy tang that was something to do with the sweat of frightened men. And now the smell of lavender came back to him, and as he pressed the towel to his face he felt the urge to weep. There was so much to bring tears: the loss of those years of his youth when he should have been happy; his recruitment into a cause of rampage and killing; the pain of others; the humiliation of defeat. He was nothing: the conquerors were here, among them, and he and so many like him counted for nothing.

He went downstairs, where she gave him a bowl of soup. He sat at the kitchen table and tried to control his hunger; it would not do to sink this in a single draught, which is what he wanted to do. He did not want her to think he was that desperate. But he was, and the soup took seconds to disappear.

She was watching, half amused, half pitying. "Let your stomach get used to food," she said. "They say that you can do damage if you eat too much too quickly."

He nodded. "I have been so hungry."

She smiled at him, and poured a small second helping of soup into the bowl. "They expect us to survive on less than half of what they get," she said. "I've seen it in print—in black and white. Our ration is meant to be one thousand calories a day. We don't get even that."

He stared into the soup bowl. Now it was all charity—every scrap came at the will of those put in authority over them. And yet, he thought, this is our payback. This is what we started, if it was indeed true that we started it. He could not remember. There were vague claims: Had Poland provoked Germany? Had it been necessary to attack the Russians because of what they were doing to Germans who had the misfortune to live in the east?

She was saying something to him about work, and he stopped thinking of issues of retribution. He apologised. "I'm sorry—I wasn't listening."

She explained that if he felt strong enough, there was wood to be chopped. She had bought a load of felled oak from a man she knew, but the pieces were too large to fit into the stove. And then there was a window that needed repairing. She had managed to get her hands on a piece of glass that should fit—it was probably stolen from somebody else, but if you started asking questions now-adays you would never get anything done. Everything was stolen, and had he heard: the Russians had removed everything, even things that were bolted down, and sent it back to Russia—whole factories, cranes, even small buildings that could be dismantled and shipped off. And people, too, of course; they were easy to transport: you simply loaded them into the wagons of a train and then unloaded those who were still alive at the other end. Siberia, or somewhere.

"Mind you . . ." she said.

He waited. Mind you, what?

"Mind you, the colonel has shown me photographs that you wouldn't believe. Our people doing the same thing. Packing people off to camps in the east. They died there, you know." She paused. "He had photographs. They're making people—civilians—look at the photographs. Then they say: **See this? See what you people did?**"

He looked away. He would never have al-lowed anything like that. If there was a stain, then it was not on his hands.

He started work after the meal. At four o'clock that afternoon, some of the officers who were billeted at the hotel returned from work. One of them looked at him with distaste, and threw an enquiring look at Ilse. She shook her head.

"He was never in the army or anything," she said in English. She searched for the English word—was there one? "Asthma." She pointed at Ubi's chest.

He did not understand, but the officer merely raised an eyebrow and went off to his room.

Ilse turned to Ubi and told him what she had said. "It's simpler that they don't know," she said. "Especially that one. He likes young men, and it's best for you if he thinks you're . . ." She tapped her chest. "Understand?"

He tried to work out Ilse's age. Ubi was just twenty-three, and he thought that she must be somewhere in her thirties. But two days after he arrived she told him that she was coming up to her twenty-eighth birthday. She had married when she was twenty, and had experienced barely five years of marriage before her husband had been conscripted into the army. She had managed to run the inn by herself, with the help of the staff who had been there since before they bought it; but then those people had retired, or moved for various reasons connected with the war, and she had been obliged to work longer and longer hours. At length it had been only her and two part-time chambermaids, which was why Ubi's arrival was so welcome.

It did not take him long to settle in. The regular meals, the security of being host to the occupying forces, and the warmth and comfort of his room made him happy to stay where he was and not think about going on to Berlin. Winter was approaching, and people said that it would be severe. They said that rations would be reduced and that the slow march of starvation would devour whole swathes of Germany. It was no time to be doing anything adventurous; far better to put up with the tedium of the woodcutting and the other mundane tasks he was expected to perform. It would be madness to go to Berlin at this point, Ilse said; the Russians could seize him on any grounds, or no grounds at all, and spirit him off to a factory or a mine in the Soviet Union. That had happened to hundreds of thousands of Germans, they said; men who were now working in Soviet coal mines or on building sites, repairing the wrecked towns and cities. They would need more as these men, under-nourished and badly housed, died in droves. If you go to Berlin, she said, then that will be you.

He realised that there would be work to do on the inn itself. Little maintenance had been done for years, the neglect going back to a time well before the war. There was a barn at the back, full of old agricultural im-plements, and behind it, half covered by a frayed tarpaulin, some sort of round wooden structure that intrigued him. It was like a vast towering vat, a straight-sided wine bar-rel, perhaps, the height of at least three men, and of vast capacity. There was lettering on the side of it, but it was difficult, with the tarpaulin and the effect of weathering, to make out what this said.

On the second day he asked her. "That thing out there. That big barrel."

They were standing in the kitchen, where he was drying plates before stacking them on the shelves.

She smiled. "Big barrel? I suppose you could call it that."

He waited for the explanation. She had moved over to the window and was looking out towards the barn.

"It's a **Motodrom**," she said. "It's a fairground thing. You ride your motorcycle round and round and then you go up the wall and you carry on going round and round on that. You defy gravity. Fairground stuff."

The shape, the writing: of course.

"I know what a **Motodrom** is," he said. "I've seen one before."

"Well, that's what that is."

He shook his head in disbelief. "You have a **Motodrom . . .**"

"It's pretty decrepit. It hasn't been used for years."

He looked out of the window towards the barn. "Amazing. A **Motodrom.** You know, when I was a boy there were fairground people who came to Berlin. They must have been from somewhere deep in the south, because they spoke with a very broad Bavarian accent. You'd think they were singing half the time. They had a **Motodrom.** I used to spend my pocket money on tickets to watch them. I loved it."

She looked at him indulgently. "I suppose that when you're a boy, something like that is very exciting."

"It was. It was the most exciting thing I'd ever seen."

"I can imagine that," she said. "Noise. Danger. Speed. The things that boys like." And men, she thought; hence this war.

"I thought then," Ubi continued, "when I was a boy, that is, that I'd give anything—anything—to have a **Motodrom.** I thought it would be the finest thing in the world to own a **Motodrom.**"

Ilse laughed. "I'll sell you mine. Not that you—or anybody else—would want to buy it." Then she said, "You know what the English officers call it? It's called a wall of death over there, they told me. One of them was interested in it. The fat one with the moustache. He said he'd seen one in England and that's what they called it."

Ubi asked where it came from.

"It belonged to my husband's uncle. He had no children and he left it to him. My husband said he'd get it going again one day. The uncle always said there was good money in it."

"He'd ride it himself?"

She came back from the window and looked at him in a way that conveyed that she did not wish to talk about her husband.

The knowledge that he had somewhere to stay—and the sense of security this brought—meant that the fractured, fitful sleep patterns that had been with him since his conscription were fading, and his nights becoming restful once again. He began to look forward to the moment when he finished the washing up after the evening meal—a task that Ilse had been eager to off-load—and he could go up to his room, throw off his clothes, and sink into the haven of laundered sheets and a down mattress. It was unfathomable luxury for him after army beds, and then no bed at all. The dreams that came to him were vague and confused: he was in Holland, then he was somewhere else altogether, in a landscape he did not recognise; he was back at school, writing in an exercise book, dimly aware that he was being tested in some way; he was in the company of his brother who had gone missing, who in his dream embraced him and told him that everything was all right, even though he was dead.

In a vivid dream that recurred from time to time he was in the presence of someone powerful. They were walking somewhere and the other person was singing some little song under his breath, chopping at wildflowers with a walking stick. And he knew his name—that was the astonishing thing; he called him Ubi and asked him if he had anything he wanted to say to him. Was this the Führer himself? Surely not, because he knew Ubi's name and he looked different, although he was wearing something that looked like a uniform.

He told Ilse about these dreams one day, and she said that it was very common to dream about their vanished leaders. "So many people have told me this happens to them," she said. "It's because they penetrated our lives so deeply. You dream of things like that, you know."

"And you?" he asked. "Do you dream about them too?"

She shook her head. "Not that I know of. But then they say, don't they, that everyone has his particular nightmares."

"And yours?" he asked.

She hesitated before answering. "The Jews," she said. "I dream about the Jews."

He watched her. He saw her lower her eyes.

"We murdered them," she said. "We took their houses, their businesses, everything. Then we sent them away to be killed."

He did not say anything. People were only just beginning to talk about these things, and many simply refused to believe them. How could so many people be disposed of in that way? Surely it was impossible.

But he knew it was true. "It happened," he said.

She met his eyes. "It's our fault," she said. "We all became murderers. And it was not just the Jews—it was the Gypsies and the insane and all sorts of people. All marched off to be killed."

He wanted to do something for her evident pain. "You didn't do it personally," he said. "You're only accountable for things you do personally."

She wanted to believe him, but it seemed to her that the crime was just too big; it required a whole nation to commit something on that scale. "There were some Jews here, you know," she said. "The party people painted signs on their doors. They broke their windows. I saw some of them doing it; I saw them from my kitchen window. And what did I do? Nothing. I stood and watched."

"You would have got into trouble if you'd tried to do anything," Ubi said. "People were sent to prison for less."

"Oh, I know that," she said, suddenly sounding weary. "But the fact remains that I did nothing. And now we're paying for that. All this hardship is because of what we started."

"We can begin again," said Ubi. "They might make us pay, but they can't make us all pay with our lives."

She was staring at him. "You're ready to start again?" she asked.

"Of course. And Germany will start up again. You watch."

"I'm watching," she said wearily.

. . .

There were ten officers billeted at the inn. Five
of them spoke German—two of them with
a facility approaching the fluency of a native
speaker. One was an intelligence officer; the
others were part of the military government
for that part of the British sector. They were
mostly concerned with mundane matters—
transport and provisions, criminal justice;
two had been lawyers in civilian life and now
found themselves dealing with the crimes
of desperate people—and with the control of
disease. Theft had become an almost natural
response to shortage; if you were hungry, you
stole—there was a simple, inarguable logic
to that response. People who were not prepared to steal died. But they perished, too, of
typhus and dysentery, and of sheer neglect;
they died because nobody cared very much
for them, not even their fellow citizens.

One of the German-speaking officers asked
Ubi whether he would like to learn English.
"I could teach you," he said. "I'm sure you'll
be a quick learner. And, as payment, you can
help me with my German—I still get things
wrong from time to time. And people are

always using colloquial expressions that I've never come across before. It would be helpful to learn a few more of those."

He readily agreed, and the lessons were conducted each day in the twenty minutes before dinner. Ilse liked to work in the kitchen by herself, and did not ask Ubi to help. "You'll have plenty to do once the plates are cleared," she said.

He sat with the officer in the small parlour at the front of the inn. The officer had a book that he lent to Ubi; it had pictures of everyday things in it with the English nouns printed below.

"A hat," said Ubi, pointing to a picture of a man in a bowler hat, under which the word **hat** appeared.

The man was looking towards the camera and smiling broadly. Ubi switched to German: "He doesn't look guilty, does he?"

The officer looked surprised. "Why should he look guilty?" he asked.

Ubi shrugged. "I suppose it's because so many people look guilty. I suppose I've come to expect it." He paused. "But then the man in this picture is English, isn't he?"

"I think so," said the officer. "Look at the

red buses in the background. That's always a giveaway, I find."

"The English have nothing to feel guilty about," said Ubi.

The officer smiled. "Nice of you to say that," he said. "But we also have a history, you know."

Ubi stared at the officer. His face was unremarkable, although there was a certain pleasing regularity to it. His eyes were clear, and he looked straight at you when he spoke. That was an ability that came with never having done anything he was ashamed of, thought Ubi.

There was a picture of a family drinking tea. Each person, and each item, was labelled with the appropriate English word: **father, mother, son, daughter; cup, saucer, teaspoon;** and so on. Through the window could be seen a **tree** and a **hill.** It was a world that seemed to suit the softer nature of the words, even if **Vater** and **Mutter** clearly came from the same place as **father** and **mother.** This was not a language to shout in, thought Ubi; this was not a language with which to articulate threats, or invade, or terrify others.

He was a quick learner, and he was soon able to read the cyclostyled newsletters that the British prepared for their own troops. The officer helped him with this, encouraging and complimenting as he stumbled through the easily smudged text. There was piece about fraternization; a warning not to trust German civilians.

"Do not talk to these people," read Ubi, enunciating each word carefully. These people . . . Who were these people? **Me?**

The officer looked apologetic and switched to German to explain. "They don't really mean ordinary people. They mean people who might have been SS or something like that. People who haven't accepted the outcome. That's what this means."

"But it says ordinary civilians," said Ubi.

"We don't follow rules in quite the same way as you people do," said the officer. And then, as if to himself, "That's the trouble. I mean, the trouble with you people, so to speak."

And then, looking out of the window, and as if talking to himself rather than to Ubi, the officer continued, "I don't want to be here, you know. Like most people, I don't want to be here at all."

"But if you weren't here," said Ubi, "wouldn't it be even more terrible?"

The next two years passed quickly for Ubi. He was kept busy in the inn, and soon became indispensable not only in the kitchen, but in the performance of a range of maintenance tasks. He became skilled in woodwork and in plumbing, and even managed to fathom and sort out the building's antiquated electrical wiring. He generally kept to himself; the war had been a waking nightmare and now he wanted nothing so much as the peace and quiet of a modest, uncomplicated life. In April 1948 he had news of his family, thanks to the help of the officer who had been teaching him English. He used contacts in the British sector in Berlin to make enquiries on Ubi's behalf, and came up with the address of the landlord who had owned the building in which they had lived. This man responded, and told him that unfortunately his mother had been killed when a mortar shell came through the window in

May 1945. His sister had gone to live with one of the other residents—a widow—and had stayed there until quite recently. He was sorry to report that she had become ill—it was typhus, he believed—and she, too, had died. She had a young child, he said, and the widow had looked after the little boy. The widow had moved, but he had her address as she had done some work for him and he was still in touch with her. She had a small job and she was hard up, but the boy was still with her, he thought.

Ilse found him in the kitchen with the letter on the table in front of him. There was a pile of onion skins beside it, and when she saw his tears she smiled. "Don't you know what to do?" she chided. "When you're peeling onions, you should have a tap running nearby. It stops you crying."

She laughed, and scooped the onion skins away to put in the compost. And then she realised her mistake.

He gestured to the letter, inviting her to pick it up. She read the first few sentences and then dropped it back on the table. She put her arms around him. "Ubi, Ubi . . ." Somehow, in that moment, she felt that the sorrows of Germany had crystallised, and she wept too—not just for this woman and her daughter, who were just two amongst millions, but for everything, for all the hatred and injustice and revenge; for all the immeasurable pain.

He told her that he should get back to Berlin, even if only to see what remained of their home, which might be nothing but an empty space; in pictures, Berlin looked a wasteland, a place in which troglodytes eked out an existence in the basements of ruins. Ilse tried to dissuade him, but she knew that he had to go. She had heard that from so many others, who had said that they were drawn back to the place where it happened, to the site of their loss.

"And there's a child," he added. "My sister's child. I must see him." He was virtually alone now; he had lost all his family, and this unknown child was all he had.

"Of course you must."

"I feel responsible, you see."

A few weeks earlier he and Ilse had become lovers, shyly and with very little being said about it. He had worked for her for over two years, and had become indispensable about the inn. He had repaired the roof—a task that took over eight months—and had replaced rotten timbers on the ground floor, scouring bombsites for wood, shaping each by hand. It was comfort and tenderness that lay at the heart of their relationship, rather than passion. It was as if they were children lost in a wood, holding on to one another in the darkness.

"If you go to Berlin," she said, "will you come back here?"

She did not say "come back to me," as she did not want him to feel trapped.

He replied that he would. "Of course I shall." And then he said, "And I'll ask you to marry me then."

She hardly dared speak, but she managed to say, "Can I?"

"Because of . . ." She hardly ever mentioned her husband, but he knew that he was called Erik. "Because of Erik?"

She nodded. "I suppose he's dead, but . . ."

"I think he must be."

It was as if his words were an official confirmation. "Then in that case, I can," she said.

They left the discussion at that. He told

her that he would be no more than a few weeks in Berlin and would be back before she knew it. She smiled, and kissed his forehead gently. She said a prayer, silently, because she believed in God and she thought that he did not.

"You can bring the child back," she whispered. "There's room for a child here."

He stared at her, moved by her generosity. That had been evident from the very first day, when she had accosted him at the station, and it had continued: the soups, the comfortable bed, the laundering of his shirts, the bottles of Burgundy diverted from the supplies of the British officers. "Are you sure?"

"Of course."

"I don't know anything about him," said Ubi. "I don't even know who the father is." An unspoken word hung in the air between them: **Russian.**

On the evening before he was due to leave, one of the British officers, a newly arrived one—they were always changing—removed the tarpaulin from the abandoned **Motodrom.** Several of his fellow officers joined him, some still in uniform, having just come off duty. They shouted to one another, and their laughter drifted back to the inn, where Ubi and Ilse were watching from a window.

Ubi turned to Ilse. "Did they ask you?"

She shrugged. "One said something about taking a look at it. Not that young one. The one with the bad skin—he asked me."

Ubi wondered what they intended to do, and was about to ask her when he heard the motorcycle. One of the younger officers appeared from round the side of the building, riding an army motorbike.

He looked at Ilse. "Do you think . . ."

"They'd be mad," she said. "But then the British are mad—everybody knows that."

The officers had managed to open a door in the side of the **Motodrom.** The motorbike was now driven up to this and the rider dismounted and pushed it inside.

Ilse opened the window at which she and Ubi were standing. She shouted out towards the officers. "Careful. That's very dangerous."

The officers waved back gaily, but paid no attention.

They heard the sound of the motorbike

engine reverberating inside the **Motodrom,** and then a thud, followed by silence.

Laughter broke the silence, followed by raucous shouting, and then more laughter.

"Boys," said Ilse. And then she thought about the war, and she thought **boys** again.

## 20

He had been prepared for the destruction he found in Berlin, although people he met there kept telling him how bad it had been a few years back, in 1945. "You wouldn't believe it," said the only one of his friends from school he managed to locate. Stoffi suffered from asthma, and that had saved his life, as he had been given a wireless operator's job that kept him far from the front line, almost up to the end. "You wouldn't believe the stench, Ubi. Everywhere. Weeks, months of stench, because many of the Russians, the real peasants, came from places where there was no proper sanitation and they didn't know. The other thing they didn't know about was watches. They'd never had watches, and so they stole every watch they could get their hands on. They wore them all the way up their arms—five or six under each sleeve. But you couldn't laugh at them when they rolled their sleeves up and the watches appeared, because they could fly into a rage without any warning. Anywhere.

Everywhere. You wouldn't believe it, Ubi; you wouldn't."

At first, he listened without making any comment of his own. Invasion—defeat—was a brute fact about which one could say very little, even if one was the guiltless victim. But in our case, he thought, we are far from guiltless and so can say even less. We did it to them, and now they're doing it to us. Who could blame the Russians?

"We're surrounded," said Stoffi. "And they'll turn the screws. Of course they will."

"But what can they do? What about the others? The Americans? The British? The French?"

Stoffi shrugged. "They're surrounded too—at least in Berlin. They say the Russians are already making it more difficult for them to reach us here. They say that bridges are being repaired, or railway lines need work—that sort of thing." He paused, to make a strangling motion with his hands. "They could squeeze us just like that, you know."

At least the streets were now clear of rubble. The burnt cars had been removed and rebuilding had long since started. There were people on the streets, and they seemed to have proper shoes—or many of them did—and the trams and trains were running. The furtiveness that he had noticed in the early days of defeat seemed less common here; people walked, rather than scurried; they looked one another in the eye, rather than shiftily, warily; there were political notices and newspapers. There were still echoes of hopelessness—that indefinable air with which he had become so familiar—but there was something else now, something quite different: a sense of a future. People were doing things purposively; they were doing things that seemed to matter to them; Germany was making things again and these things were beginning to appear in shops.

Stoffi allowed him to sleep on the floor of the basement room he occupied. He gave him food and accompanied him when he went to look for the widow whose address he had been given.

"People move a lot these days," Stoffi warned Ubi. "Don't be too disappointed if you find this woman has gone."

But she had not. She answered the door in

a neat apron, her hands covered with flour. She had been kneading dough.

He told her who he was, and for a few moments she stared at him in confusion. Then, as she made sense of what he had said, she raised her hands to her face. When she lowered them, there were traces of flour on her eyebrows and cheekbones. She sat down heavily on a chair in the entrance hall and shook her head.

"I thought you were all gone," she said. "All of you."

He told her that he had been taken prisoner and had been released early. He told her how he had obtained her address.

"I thought I should see my nephew," he explained. "I think my sister would have wanted that."

"Of course, of course. Your nephew . . ."

He waited. Children had died, too, many of them from malnutrition. Was he too late?

She stood up. "Your nephew will be coming back very soon. A friend of mine has taken him to the shops. He won't be long."

She invited them in. The flat was neat, but spartan in its furnishing and decoration. Poverty manifested itself in the absence of anything of any value; people had sold their possessions in difficult times. A family heirloom might have been exchanged for a few loaves of bread; an item of jewellery—a ring, a brooch—could have brought in a few kilos of donkey meat.

As he waited, he tried to make conversation. He asked about what had happened to his mother and his sister, but she was able to tell him very little. She had been somewhere else when his mother's flat had been hit; and his sister, whom she did not know very well, had died rather quickly. She had taken the child in because there did not seem to be anybody else and it was her duty, she said, as a Christian. She did not know where either of them was buried; so many people, she said, had shallow graves that were either unmarked or only temporarily recorded. He asked the widow about the days after the Russians had arrived, but she clearly did not want to talk about that. She shuddered, though, involuntarily, and then started to discuss a Russian film she had seen the previous day. It had been beautifully filmed, she said, and if it had been propaganda, then that side of it had been lost on her, as she had no Russian.

The friend returned with the boy half an hour later. She was carrying a large paper bag into which groceries had been stuffed; at her feet, clinging onto her skirts, was a small boy of about three. He was wearing a tight-fitting cap that failed to cover his ears and a shabby red coat, and he stared at Ubi and Stoffi with the unembarrassed curiosity of the very young.

The child was dark-skinned, his black hair knotted with small curls.

Ubi smiled at the boy, and then looked at the widow. She held his gaze, almost defiantly, as if she were daring him to say something.

"What's his name?" he asked.

"Klaus," she said.

Ubi stepped forward and bent down to address the child at his level. He reached out for the boy's right hand, and held it briefly in his own. "So you're Klaus," he said. "And I'm your uncle."

The boy looked at the widow, as if to ask permission to respond. She smiled encouragingly, but he was too timid to say anything.

Ubi stood up again. The widow stepped back; she had been about to whisper something into his ear. "An American father," she said.

He looked at the child again. "I see."

She nodded. "It was not easy for your sister," she said. "People abused her because of the child's being mixed race. Some people actually spat at her."

His chest felt tight. "This man . . . the father . . . was she . . ."

The widow knew what he was trying to ask. "No, don't think that. She said he was kind to her. And people had to make whatever arrangements they could in those times, you know."

He let out his breath slowly. "Did he know about the child?"

The widow shrugged. "He may have—I don't know. Your sister told me that he had been sent somewhere else. He was a sergeant. She showed me a photograph."

The child was watching him with widened eyes. He reached into his pocket and took out a small bar of chocolate, which he unwrapped. He offered it to the small boy, who hesitated, and then took it from him.

"We need to talk," said Ubi.

The widow nodded. "I would appreciate it if you were able to help in some way."

"I'll take him," said Ubi. "If you don't mind letting him go, I'll take him back with me. I have a place to live, and I'm going to be getting married. We shall look after him well."

The widow hesitated, but not for long. "I would have been happy to continue," she said. "I would never have turned him out, but it's such a struggle to get by . . ." She looked at him hopelessly. It was a miracle, it seemed to him, that people managed to continue. From somewhere within themselves they found the will to persist, to scrape a living, to patch and mend, to find small ways of expressing their sense of beauty—a few flowers plucked and put in a cracked egg cup serving as a vase; a printed picture cut from a magazine and pasted on cardboard; a splash of colour in a threadbare dress.

He reached out and touched her arm. "I understand," he said. "And I'm very grateful to you—I really am."

"You have work back there?" she asked. "Real work?" The labour draft had sucked up able-bodied men for construction, but the pay was minimal.

He told her about the inn. "My fiancée"— it was the first time he had used the word of Ilse—"my fiancée owns it."

"Ah."

He noticed a change in her expression. Was it envy? When most had nothing, the possession of something had to be concealed. So he said, "It's not a big place. It's a very modest concern. Just a few rooms."

He was right; it had been envy, because the look disappeared.

"Klaus will be well fed," he said.

She prickled with resentment. "I've done my best on what I get."

He was quick to reassure her. "I'm sure you have. And he looks very healthy, doesn't he?"

He did not, and they both knew it. But she accepted the compliment, and then turned to Stoffi and asked him where he lived. Ubi bent down again to speak to the child, who continued to look at him with his wide, dark eyes, wondering whether to trust him. The chocolate had gone, leaving a smudge on the boy's upper lip. Ubi reached into his pocket and took out another bar, handing it over with a flourish. This brought a shy grin to the small face as his nephew reached out to take possession of the treasure.

They agreed that Ubi would leave the following week, once the child had had the chance to get used to his company. He would visit each day, and familiarity—and chocolate— would do its work. But as the day of departure approached, so its possibility receded. The boy had no papers, and the widow, at whose address he was registered for ration purposes, lived in the Soviet zone. Just as Stoffi had said, road and rail transport between Berlin and the outside world was now being deliberately cut by the Russians, as were transfers of food from the countryside to the non-Soviet zones of the city.

"Stalin has two big weapons," said Stoffi. "Starvation and isolation. Watch him use them. Just watch him. There is nothing that man would not do."

They attended a meeting—an impromptu gathering of neighbours addressed by a local liaison official. Somebody, a thin man wearing horn-rimmed glasses, brandished a French newspaper, with its headline **Berlin crisis: a challenge for the West.** "They say here that America's going to give up," he said. "That's what the French think. Listen."

He read out a few sentences, which he translated into German.

"The French!" called a woman from the back of the crowd. "What do they know? They're defeated, just like us."

"Not quite," said the liaison man. "But the Americans are not going to abandon us. There's an agreement."

This brought laughter.

"No," shouted the official. "No, you're wrong. General Clay isn't going to let it happen."

"What can he do?" someone shouted.

"They can force their way in."

"With tanks? That'll be a war between America and Russia. And we'll be in the middle."

A voice at the front said, "The way we were not all that long ago."

Other views were expressed. "General Clay won't risk that. He knows what the Russians are like." And "There's not much he can do. Look at the number of Russian

HE HATED THE WAR    251

tanks—they say they're bringing more in every day. Piling them up. America's a long way away. How can they compete?"

The official was becoming irritated. "We shouldn't talk about things that haven't happened yet," he said. "We need to keep calm. The whole situation will probably be sorted out soon enough. The roads will reopen."

"Says who?" a man called out.

"We're finished," said the man with horn-rimmed glasses. "The Russians have got us. We're finished."

The following day, when Stoffi came back to the flat, he had managed to buy half a large cured sausage and a loaf of crusty bread. They shared this, adding to the feast a piece of cheese that Ubi had bought from a woman on a tram—a mobile black marketeer selling her goods between stops.

Stoffi had news. He was an electrician, and his job was at Templehof airport, which meant that his finger was on the pulse. "They're going to do it," he said. "They've already started."

"There are so many rumours," Ubi sighed. "How can one tell?"

Stoffi shook his head. "No, this is true. This is happening. They're going to airlift everything in. The Russians can't close the air corridors."

Ubi looked doubtful. "Everything?"

"Yes," said Stoffi. "Everything the city needs." He told Ubi that his boss at the airport had been briefed. They would be busy, he said, because the planes would be coming in non-stop.

Ubi said that he thought it would be impossible. "There are too many people," he said. "Think of the amount of food you'd have to bring in. Think of it."

"A lot," agreed Stoffi. "But then the Americans have lots of planes. And the British too."

"And coal," said Ubi. "You can't fly electricity in."

"Coal too," said Ubi. "My boss said it would be everything—including fuel."

It seemed impossible, but Stoffi assured Ubi that the planes were already coming in. "Tomorrow," he said. "Come to Templehof tomorrow. Come and see for yourself."

"I need to think about getting back," said Ubi. "I need to go home."

Stoffi laughed. "Too late, Ubi," he said. "The roads, the railway—they're not going to open them. We're surrounded by Russia now. And that means you're in Berlin, I'm afraid, until . . . until all this ends."

Over the next few days, Ubi realised that Stoffi was right, and he was trapped: travel would be impossible, particularly with an undocumented three-year-old boy. He would wait it out; the blockade could not last forever, people said, and the Russians would soon realise how unpopular they were making themselves. Stoffi shook his head. "You don't know these people," he said. "They don't think like us."

Ubi wrote to Ilse; mail was still getting through by air, although it took some days to be dispatched, and was sporadic. He told her that he would stay in Berlin for the time being, but would return when everything died down. Stoffi had said that he could get him a job at Templehof airport unloading planes. Flights were coming in now every few minutes, as the airlift began in earnest. People were needed to unload aircraft after they landed; the work was reasonably well paid, and food was provided at the end of each shift. There were worse ways, he said, of spending what would be, he felt, the short days of a crisis that would surely blow over soon enough.

"I look forward so much to seeing you again," he wrote at the end of the letter. "I miss you more than I can say, my dearest one, my love."

He looked at the sentence he had just written. He had not told her that before; he had not told her that he was in love with her, not in so many words. **I am no Goethe,** he thought. But now he said it, and something deep within him shifted: an emotional barrier that had been in place ever since the day he donned a uniform; a barrier that had stood between him and the outside world, a barrier designed to show others how strong and self-sufficient he was. It was the same, he thought, with so many men, with all the soldiers of the world perhaps, who were made to seem what in reality they just were not.

# THREE
# IN FRIENDSHIP'S
# HANDS

## 21

After their brief honeymoon, Mike returned to duty at the airfield and Val went back to work on the farm. Archie had pretended not to notice her pregnancy, but now, with a certain embarrassment, he asked her about her plans.

"Your baby," he said, looking anywhere but at the obvious bulge. "He'll be an American, I suppose. Now that you . . ."

She smiled. "His dad is, so I suppose he'll be too. I'm not sure how these things work."

Archie nodded. "And you too—you'll be going over there?"

"Eventually."

"With the baby?"

"Well, I'd hardly leave him here, would I?"

He smiled. "Of course. I wasn't thinking." He paused. "Which means you won't be working here much longer."

She told him that she would work for a couple of months longer. She could do most things, but would probably avoid the heavier tasks, if he did not mind. "Then I'll leave and wait for the baby."

"And what if they send your husband away?" asked Archie. "They won't be here forever, what with the war ending, and all that. You don't need all those planes now that them Germans have given up, do you?"

"We'll see," said Val. "Mike says that they have to keep the planes somewhere, and he thinks they'll probably keep his people here for a while. He said they might have to go to Germany itself."

Archie shook his head. "They don't want to go over there," he said. "Bad place, that. And bombed to pieces, judging from the pictures in the paper."

Something was still clearly bothering him, and he looked at her enquiringly. "He's still over at the base," he ventured, "but you're at your aunt's place. Haven't they got housing for married couples?"

She saw him blush.

"No," she said. "They haven't. Not at the base. But we have a room at my aunt's, and he can spend weekends with me there. We get by."

He quickly changed the subject. They would need to attend to the hens, he said. The fox had somehow found his way into the coop the previous night and taken the cockerel and two of his spouses. "More than he could eat," Archie said, shaking his head. "I'm going to get my hands on that fellow one of these days."

She settled back into her routine. Archie was careful about giving her only light work, and he also insisted that she go home early each day. "You have to rest," he said. "In your condition."

She had been concerned about Willy. She had been worried that he would be possessive, and that he would resent Mike's return, but her fears proved unfounded. On the first occasion that Mike stayed overnight, Willy was quiet over dinner and she thought that it was through resentment. But when Mike addressed a few remarks to him—asking him whether he had ever flown—this brought forth a torrent of questions. What happened if one of your engines stopped—did the other keep the plane in the sky? What would happen if a wheel hit a rock on the runway? Could a plane fly upside down?

Mike answered his questions patiently, and with good humour. He had seen enough of Willy in the past to know that even if he found it difficult to deal with things that were a bit complicated he was still kind, and loyal, and could hold down a job as long as it was not too demanding. He understood all that, he assured Val. "We had a guy like that in the store," he told her. "He swept the floor and stacked the shelves, although he sometimes put things in the wrong place. His life's ambition was to be one of the sheriff's deputies—he used to wear a badge he'd picked up for a dime, but of course he could never be the real thing."

Val thought this was sad. "To want to be something that you can never be—that seems sad to me."

"And yet that's what life is like for a lot of folks," said Mike. "Not everybody has our luck."

She had not thought of it as luck, but now that he spoke of it in those terms, she could see that this was what it was. It had been luck that had brought them together, when they had been born into such different worlds. It was as a result of luck that his plane had come down on a field rather than a wood. It was luck that those Dutch people had hidden him, and it was luck that that

German soldier had decided to do what he did. Everything was reducible to luck—right back to being born, and the circumstances in which that took place.

But could you ever do anything about your luck, or was it an immutable hand of cards, dealt out once and to be played throughout life, with no possibility of change? She had sometimes thought about that. People said that you got the luck you deserved; that if you behaved selfishly or cruelly, you would get the luck that came with such behaviour—and that, of course, was bad luck.

Mike's luck had held out, she thought. So many fliers had not come back; he had told her about the melancholy duty of clearing out a friend's locker—as they had done with his, when they thought he had died in the crash. That duty was one that cropped up time and time again, but was every bit as hard the fourth or fifth time as the first.

Although they were married, she felt that she had no more than a tenuous hold on him. He belonged to the air force, it seemed, rather more than he belonged to her. If it was the air force's will that he should be sent somewhere, then what she felt about that counted for nothing. And so when he came to Annie's house one evening and told her that there was something he wanted to discuss with her in the village pub, she knew that this would be the news she was dreading—that of his posting.

Her hands shook as she took the small glass of cider he had bought her. He noticed; he was concerned that she was still working on Archie's farm and would have preferred her to rest. She had said that it was better to remain active; that a baby thrived if its mother still did the things she normally did.

"Are you worried about something?" he asked.

She took a sip of the cider, savouring its sweetness. "About you," she said. "I know what you're going to tell me."

She could tell from his expression it was not going to be good news.

"I'm going to Germany," he said. "I'm going to be flying transport planes. C-47s. They're really just military versions of DC-3s."

She looked at him blankly. She knew nothing of planes, although she could recognise the sort he flew.

"There's a base at Wiesbaden," Mike went

on. "We took it over from the Germans. I'm going to be there."

She stared into her cider. **I'm** going to be there. **I'm . . .**

"And us?" she asked.

He bit his lip. "We'll be fine."

"But you'll . . ."

"I have to be over there, yes, and at the moment they won't let us take wives." He paused, and reached for her hand. "In the future, maybe. In fact, definitely: the air force doesn't like to split families."

"Then why—"

He cut her short. "Some posts are unaccompanied. It's just the way they are. They aren't sending me to Hawaii—it's to a country we've just been at war with. It's different."

"Couldn't you ask to go to Hawaii?"

He laughed. "Everybody wants to go to Hawaii. That's what Hawaii is for—it's a reward."

"Or even California? What about California?"

He shook his head. "I have to go where I'm sent. It won't be forever. Maybe you'll be able to come over next year. Who knows?"

There was something else he wanted to

discuss with her. "You could be sent to the States, you know. They can arrange that. You don't have to stay here."

She had not expected this. "Without you?"

"Yes. You'd get housing on a base, maybe." He was trying to sound optimistic. "Or you can go to my mom and dad. In fact, that would be much easier."

"In Muncie, Indiana?"

He smiled. "Yes, in Muncie, Indiana. You've always wanted to go there. You said . . ."

"But that was with you. I don't want to go there by myself."

He had spilled some of his beer on the table, and now he traced a pattern in it with a finger. "They'd look after you," he said. "And the baby too."

"But I don't know them. I'd be a stranger."

"You wouldn't. You'd be my wife. That's not a stranger."

She shook her head. "And it'd be different, wouldn't it? With the baby and everything. Even some of the words—you call nappies diapers, don't you?"

"That's not a problem, surely."

She was struggling with tears. "It could be for me."

He took her hand again. "All right, all right." He sounded defeated, and she felt a pang of guilt. After what he had gone through, she should not make it harder for him than it was. "You stay here. Have the baby at your aunt's place. We'll be together later, but in the meantime . . ." He tried again to appear positive. "In the meantime, you'll be comfortable here with your aunt and with Willy. And there's Peter Wood-house. He can stay with you, of course."

She hesitated, but finally decided. "He's your dog now. Take him to Germany with you. He's an American dog."

He grinned. "Do dogs think like that? Do they care about these things? British dogs, American dogs . . . it's all the same to them."

She smiled for the first time that evening, and he pressed her hand in his, encouraging her. "Probably is," she said. "But still. He's used to you. You take him."

He looked thoughtful and almost agreed. But then he shook his head and explained that it would be better for him to stay. "This base is all right," he said. "But who knows what it'll be like over there. No, this is his place. This country. This place probably smells right to him—you know how dogs are with their smells."

She did not argue. "He could go back to the farm—to Archie. He'll look after him."

"The best thing for him," said Mike.

She felt the baby kick, and she took his hand and placed it on her stomach. He thought about what she had said about Peter Woodhouse. American babies, British babies . . . even German babies . . . They were all the same. Things went wrong only after they were born.

He wanted to say something, but no words came. **Being close to death can make us look at the world with different eyes . . .** It was what the chaplain at the base had said to him on his return. He was referring to the crash, of course, but it had occurred to Mike that the observation could be interpreted more widely; given that the human lifespan was so short, it might apply throughout life. We were always close to death, young or old: we did not have all that long. He had been about to say something to that effect, but he stopped himself; he had heard that the chaplain liked nothing more than a theological discussion, and had been known to detain a busy man for over an hour in the exploration of some abstruse point. On one famous occasion he had even held up a mission—delaying the departure of avenging angels by almost ten minutes.

## 22

He was already in Wiesbaden when the baby arrived. Annie went to the base to hand over the letter that one of the air force clerks had promised to get delivered within two or three days—unlike the normal post, which could take weeks to reach an overseas address. She wrote: **Your baby son has arrived safely. I am writing to tell you this because Val is still in the hospital and they don't want her to do anything very much just yet. We'll send a photograph as soon as we can arrange one, but Val said: "Tell Mike that he looks just like him." He took a long time to arrive—it wasn't easy for her, labour being that long and all, but he's here now, safe and sound, and as strong and as hungry as can be. One of the nurses says that American babies are all like that—all very strong—and maybe she's right. Val sends you her dearest love. She says to tell you that she thinks of you all the time, and that she knows you will love your new little Thomas Barnes Rogers the moment you see him, which she**

**hopes will be very soon. She sends you all her love and asks you not to worry about anything—she has everything she needs and is very happy.**

It was five days before she was allowed home, and then only on the strength of a promise from Annie that she would enforce bed rest for a further week. She had lost more blood than they would have liked, but gradually her strength returned. Thomas Barnes Rogers—"such an impressive name for a baby" said Annie—or Tommy, as he had already become, was bundled up in ancient lace baby clothes from Annie's attic and wheeled about in a carriage pram that the midwife had summoned up from somewhere. Willy doted on the new arrival, and would talk of nothing else over meals. Was Tommy sleeping enough? Should the district nurse be asked to come to listen to his chest? Was the house warm enough for him? Small babies did not like draughts—they could get croup from them, he had been told. You could never be too careful when they were that small.

"Calm down, Willy," said Annie. "Babies are tough little things—especially large babies like this one. If he gets his milk regularly and the air in his room is kept warm, he'll thrive all right, you mark my words."

"Auntie's right," said Val. "You don't want to wrap babies up too much. Their skin needs air on it. Nurse said that herself. That's exactly what she said."

"I know a thing or two," said Willy resentfully. "I've read them books too."

"Of course you have, Willy," said Annie. "And Tommy will be fine, with you and Val looking after him, and the whole village behind him, egging him on. He's going to grow into a fine little boy before any of us knows it."

There were extra rations for a nursing mother, and Archie made sure that there was no shortage of eggs, butter, and cream. "Cream is what you need," he said to Val, standing awkwardly at the door of her room when he came to visit, fingering the brim of his cap, embarrassed to enter this room of mother and baby equipment, of bottles and towels, and the soft, slightly sour-milk smell of a tiny infant. "I can get you plenty of cream now."

She asked him what he thought of the

baby. He edged into the room and peered into the cradle. "He's a proper healthy nipper," he said. "Got your eyes, I think."

She laughed. "That's what Willy thinks too."

"And when will they let your fellow come back?"

She sighed. "I don't know, Archie. I'll go over there, I think, once everything's sorted out. There's not much housing yet—even for officers."

He raised an eyebrow. "You told me that before. I thought they always looked after officers. There are always houses for officers."

"Not over there there's not."

Archie nodded. "You'll see him soon enough, I expect." He moved away from the cradle. "And young fellow-my-lad over there will keep you busy meanwhile."

She enquired about the farm; was he coping now that she was no longer working? He replied that he was, but that there were things he was having to give up. There would be no turnips next year, he thought, but the field he normally grew them in could do with a rest anyway.

"And Willy?" he said, looking over his

shoulder towards the kitchen, where Willy and Annie could be heard conversing. "Do you think he might want to come and work at my place?"

"You could ask him. I don't see why not."

Archie looked thoughtful. "He's a good boy, that."

Val agreed; and she was not just saying that. Willy was a good boy, even if he was impetuous at times and even if he did go on and on about some subjects—babies currently, but that would change as something else attracted his attention.

Willy's enthusiasm for Tommy proved not to be a passing phase. Not only did he continue to talk incessantly about him—thoughts of the baby occupying his every waking moment—but he proved to be a staunch ally in the watches of the night, when Tommy awoke to be fed and he would make tea for Val, averting his eyes if he brought it to her as she was feeding the baby. Then he would wait outside the door until she called him back in, when he would take Tommy in his arms and rock him, murmuring in the low voice that the baby seemed to find calming. Val watched, and thought of how nobody would ever have dreamed that Willy would show qualities like this, would behave like the most devoted of fathers.

She had spoken to him about Archie, and had been surprised by Willy's easy acceptance of the suggestion that he should leave the farm he was on.

"That would be all right with me," he said. "I like Archie."

"He's a nice man to work for," said Val. "He never asks you to do too much. He's kind."

Willy nodded. "And it'll be easier for me to look after Tommy if I work there," he said. "Closer, you see. I can get back here quicker."

She was silent. The attachment was deeper than she had imagined.

She tried to be gentle. "Of course, Tommy and I are going to have to go one of these days, Willy. Not now, mind, but maybe . . . well, maybe in a few months' time." She paused. "Mike will be counting the days until he sees his boy for the first time."

Willy looked away. "I know that," he said.

The next day an idea occurred to her. The vicar visited and spoke to her about the christening. "Have you discussed baptism with the father?" he asked, searching his memory for the name. He had married them, after all, and he did try to remember all the names, but it was difficult.

"Mike," she said. "No, I haven't spoken to him, but he'll not mind. I can write to him."

The vicar said he thought this was the thing to do. "I'm a great believer in early baptism," he said. "As early as possible, I always say."

She smiled. The vicar always said **I always say**; round and round in a circle, **I always say I always say . . .**

"And godparents?" he asked.

She had given the matter no thought, but that did not stop her replying. "Willy, I think."

The vicar inclined his head. "He'll be very proud of that, I suspect."

"He will be."

"And the others? It's normal for a boy to have two godfathers and one godmother. And the other way round, **mutatis mutandis.**" He smiled apologetically.

"Is that Latin?"

He laughed. "Yes, it is. I know I shouldn't quote Latin—people don't always like it—but somehow . . ."

She said, smiling, "We all do things we shouldn't do. Quoting Latin is not the worst thing you could do."

"The other godparents?"

The answer came just as easily as it had with Willy. "There's Archie Wilkinson up at the farm. You know him?"

"A good man," said the vicar.

She looked at the vicar's shoes. They had been good shoes once, she thought, well made black shoes in a style she had seen described as Oxfords. But now there were cracks in the leather, like lines across a furrowed brow. Of course, shoes had needed coupons for a long time, and now they were reduced to only three a week, to cover everything. It was worse than in wartime, because now they had to clothe all those people in Germany who had nothing but the rags they stood up in. They started it, and it was their fault, she thought, but they were still people, and a lot of them were women and children who presumably had not wanted war in the first place; not really, even if there were those photographs showing them waving flags and saluting Hitler just like the men.

"And my aunt," she said. "She'd love to be godmother."

"I'm sure she would," said the vicar. "But will you be discussing it with . . . with . . ."

"Mike."

"Yes, Mike. Ask the father, I always say, even if he's not there. He should be asked."

She said she would do that, and she wrote about it in her next letter. He wrote back, **Whatever you want, my darling. Everything for you. You're the one! Everything.**

Now she could ask Willy, and the others too. But speaking to Willy, she felt, was the most important.

He listened attentively, nodding his head as she spoke. Then, when she had finished, he said, "Godfather?"

"Yes. The vicar holds a service. We all go— even Tommy. And the vicar splashes him with water . . . well, not actually splashes, just pours a little over his head." She paused; sometimes it was difficult to work out just what Willy knew. "You must have seen it, Willy."

"Of course I've seen it," he said. "Lots of times, down at the church."

"Well, there you are. You know all about it."

He looked thoughtful. "Godfather? That's like . . . like being a father, sort of, when the father isn't there? Like that?"

She hesitated. "Well, it's not quite that. It's not quite like being the father. That's different, you see. A father's—"

He cut her short. "I know that." He gave her a reproachful look. He was sensitive to being thought not to know things; if people thought that he knew nothing, they were wrong. Often, they were the ones who failed to grasp something that he knew perfectly well. How animals felt, for instance, or what the clouds meant for the weather ahead, or the various types of bird nest, or what was wrong with the country. And here was Val implying that he did not know what godfathers were for. "Of course, I know that. But when the father's away somewhere, or dead, or something, then you still have the godfather, don't you?"

"You could put it like that. But the main thing is that the godfather's kind to the baby. He remembers birthdays—that sort of thing."

Willy grinned. "I can do that," he said.

"Of course you can, Willy."

The vicar's cracked shoes projected from under his white cassock, the hem of which was frayed, as everything was after five years of war and the shortages that war brought. There was even a smell to parsimony, some said: a thin, musty smell of things used beyond their natural life, of materials patched up, cobbled together, persuaded to do whatever it was they did well after they should have been retired. And it was true of people too—with both young men and young women in uniform, those left behind to do the day-to-day jobs seemed tired, overworked, made to carry on with their duties well after they should have been pensioned off. And now the vicar looked up at his small congregation and took a deep breath, as if summoning up for the task ahead what little energy he had left.

Val sat in the front pew, flanked by Annie and Willy, with Archie, stiff in his ancient suit, on the other side of Willy. The vicar closed his eyes as he spoke, only opening them occasionally to look out on the heads of those in the pews: the familiar words required no reading; he had uttered them countless times before. At first Val only half listened, being preoccupied with Tommy, who was awake but silent in her arms, all but completely covered in the christening robe Annie had made for him from scraps of white cotton and lace. But then she found herself following the vicar's words, drawn in by the poetry of the liturgy.

"Beloved," he said, and Val thought, **That's us;** and he continued, "you hear in this Gospel the words of our Saviour Christ, that he commanded the children to be brought unto him . . . You perceive how by his outward gesture and deed he declared his goodwill toward them; for he embraced them in his arms, he laid his hands upon them, and blessed them. Doubt not therefore, but earnestly believe, that he will likewise favourably receive this present infant; that he will embrace him with the arms of his mercy . . ."

Val did not think that God existed, but

she liked the idea that he was there, even if it was no more than a fond hope—that thing that people called faith. Even the vicar, she thought, must have his doubts, because if God did exist, then why had he let all those people die in the war; all those innocent people herded into those camps and murdered; all those besieged Russians starving to death, eating rats to keep alive; all those children who died under the rain of bombs? Why did he allow all that when by one movement of his finger he could have obliterated the Nazis and their works, stopped the slaughter and the suffering?

But now the vicar held the little bundle in his arms and reached for a tarnished silver spoon on the edge of the font. He had said that the water would be warm—as warm as the River Jordan, he smilingly assured her; and he sprinkled a few drops on Tommy's forehead. The child's eyes opened, surprised, unfocused, but he did not cry, and he was handed back to her as she struggled to keep from crying herself. She was thinking of Mike, who would have been so proud at this moment, and would have put his arm around her, she thought. She missed him so painfully. It was an insistent, raw ache of longing, assuaged from time to time by the joy of having Tommy. But as the weeks of separation drew into months, she found it increasingly hard to remember what the man she had married had been like. Even his face was becoming blurred in her memory now; their times together re-membered, but in such a way as to make her ask herself whether she was recalling them correctly. What did his voice sound like? What did he say to her when he spoke about Indiana and the life he had led there? What did he whisper to her in their moments of intimacy?

Her dreams began to disturb her. He ap-peared in some of them, but it was only to tell her that he had found somebody else, or to reveal that he was actually dead and they had not got round to telling her yet, and he was sorry that she was the last to hear. In her dreams she always said that it did not matter, that she still loved him, but for some reason when she tried to address him he was not there, but was in an unfamiliar place somewhere else, a place that was something like the air force base but with no planes, just tractors. As places do in dreams, it had a fluid identity; it was a farm, and then it was not a farm but the village, and then part of a landscape that she did not recognise but that must have been Muncie, Indiana.

He came back on leave when Tommy was four months old, and again five months later. They went to Cornwall, where they had spent their honeymoon, and stayed for a week in a boarding house where the food was cold and generally unpalatable. The woman who ran it offered to babysit, and they went to the local cinema, the Electric Palace. After the film, they called in at a pub where a pianist played "The White Cliffs of Dover" and everybody started to sing. Looks were exchanged—looks of relief, coupled with nostalgia. A man, a perfect stranger, bought Mike a drink, saying, "In case people haven't said thank you." Mike said, "We did it together," and the man nodded, but said nothing further.

Eventually, on another long leave, he told her that he was likely to be in Germany for some time yet. "You'll have to come," he said. "There's somebody on the base who can arrange a place for us now. Nothing special, but it'll be a roof over our heads."

"When?" she asked.

"Next week," he said. Then he added, "You'll have to tell Willy as tactfully as you can—you can see how attached he's become to Tommy."

She sighed. "He lives for him." It was true, she thought. And then there was the unspoken fear that, for Tommy, Willy was his father. Mike was a stranger to the boy, who was now almost two.

Mike shrugged. "I guess he'll get used to it."

"He will. He'll be sad, though."

He said that he thought that sadness, mostly, never lasted very long. "It's not the way people are made," he said. "We're made to get moving, to get on with the next thing. To look to the future."

He was right, she thought, but it would still be hard for Willy, who had no next thing, at least as far as she could see.

. . .

She broke the news of her departure to Willy as gently as she could. For a few moments he was silent; then he looked away, avoiding her eyes.

"I'm sure I'll be back," she said. "From time to time. Quite often, in fact."

He glanced at her quickly, and then his gaze slid away once more.

"You won't," he muttered.

"Willy!" she exclaimed. "Don't be like that. I wouldn't tell you I'd be coming back if I wasn't going to. Of course I'll come back to see you and Annie—and Peter Woodhouse. To see everybody, in fact."

His face was full of reproach. "No, you won't. You may think you will, but you'll be far away, won't you? Over in Germany, and then what? That place in America? That Indiana? You won't come back from there—it's too far."

He was right, of course, and she realised it. Yet she had no stomach for a real leave-taking—there had been so many of those in the war years, when goodbye had meant goodbye as never before.

"I'll do my best," she said. "And I'll write to you."

She suddenly became aware that Willy
was crying. She put her arms about him, but
he tried to push her away, as a child avoiding an embrace might do. She wanted to cry
too; for everything, for the war, for Willy's
loneliness, for the ache that separation or the
prospect of separation brought with it. She
wanted to cry for the world that seemed to
have come to such an abrupt end: the world
of England before the war, when everything
had seemed so secure. Now England itself
seemed to be built on shaky foundations. England was changing into something else—a
country where everything had been shaken
up and spilled out in a quite other pattern
from that which she had been used to. They
had known what they were fighting for, but
now that they had it, it seemed to be something quite different.

"I wish you wouldn't cry, Willy," she said.
"You're going to be fine."

He wiped at his eyes clumsily. "What
about Tommy?" he asked.

"Tommy will write too. And I'll send you
photographs."

It occurred to her that Willy was hoping

for a different response—that Tommy could somehow be left behind.

"He has to be with his father," she added quickly. "You do see that, don't you?"

With a supreme effort, Willy nodded. "I hope he'll be all right," he said. "Over there in Germany . . ."

He left the sentence unfinished.

"He'll be well looked after. The U.S. Air Force has schools. Swimming pools, playgrounds—everything."

He wiped his eyes again. "When he's bigger he could come and visit the farm," he said. "He could help me and Archie."

She seized at this. "Of course he could. That's a lovely idea, Willy."

"He could pick plums," Willy went on. "Small fellow like that can climb up on the branches without breaking them. He could reach the plums."

"Yes," said Val. "He could do that all right, Willy—when he's bigger."

One of the other wives in Wiesbaden, the wife of a major, took her out for coffee shortly after she arrived and asked her about her life before she was married. "I'm just curious, you see. A lot of the men married, didn't they? I often wonder what it's been like for their wives—coming from somewhere different and then being taken back to the States where they have no family, you know. It can't be easy."

Val told her about being a land girl. She told her about meeting Mike and the dances at the base.

The major's wife smiled. "I always knew I was going to marry Bill. From about sixteen, I think." She paused. "I don't think he knew, though."

They both laughed.

"And now?" said the major's wife. "What about now?"

"I'm happy. We're together. And that's the important thing."

"Of course it is."

"So I feel that my life—our life, I suppose—is just starting."

This brought a nod of the head. "And there's your little boy—a cute little guy. You're lucky."

"Yes. I know that."

"But," said the major's wife. "But . . ."

"But what?"

"The Russians. Berlin. These extra duties. Bill says . . ."

Val waited.

"Bill says we're in for a long haul. They're going to have to fly everything in—food, coal, the whole lot. The British, ourselves—everyone's going to have to keep them alive. He says he can't see how we can do it." She sighed. "Was life meant to be like this, do you think? I mean, when you think about what we really want—to find somebody, fall in love, get married, and so on. Have kids. Enjoy ourselves. And what do we get instead? World War Two. The Russians. Berlin."

"Oh well . . ."

The major's wife smiled. "You English people," she said. "I don't get you. You say things like **oh well** and then you carry on as if nothing ever happened."

"Do we have any choice?"

"Maybe not."

"So we may as well say **oh well.**"

"Maybe."

Later, when Mike came off duty, he told her that he was going to have to go to a different base for emergency duties. She and Tommy were to stay where they were.

"Berlin?" she asked. The papers had been full of the news of the blockade.

He nodded. "I'm going to be flying non-stop, more or less. Every pilot we have."

He moved forward to embrace her, and she felt that familiar feeling of longing that had never once gone away when she was in his presence. She wanted the moment to be frozen; she wanted to be with him, exclusively and alone, with nothing else around them. She wanted to hold him to her and not to let him go from her. Ever. Ever.

He drew back, and looked at her fondly. "Sometimes," he said, "the world has other plans for people, doesn't it? But the people themselves . . . the people . . ."

"Yes?"

"The people themselves have to hold on to their own plans . . . and hope that they get the chance to carry them out."

They were standing in the kitchen. She took his hand. She held it gently: a hand that guided planes; a human hand. "Please be careful."

He smiled at her. "I'll take care. I always do."

"But especially careful. More careful than ever before."

He put a finger against her lips, as much to silence as to reassure her. "Yes," he said. "Don't worry."

## 23

Returned to Archie's farm, Peter Woodhouse became once more a farm dog, housed in an old crate. Archie had been pleased by his return, as was Willy, who now worked six days a week on the tasks that the older farmer was beginning to find more difficult, with his troublesome hip and his increasing breathlessness. The doctor had said that Archie should retire altogether; his remaining years, he urged, would be better spent—and more numerous—were he to hang up his boots and sit in the warmth of the farmhouse kitchen.

"You've got that young fellow helping you," the doctor said. "There's plenty of hard work in him and you've done your bit." He spoke with conviction, but without much hope that his advice would be heeded; in his experience, farmers rarely retired, tending to die on the job. It was what they wanted, he supposed, although he could still spell it out to them.

"You won't last all that long," he said, "if

you don't take things easily. That chest of
yours . . ."

"Lasted me until now," said Archie. "Still
got the puff to keep me going."

"Yes, but . . ." The doctor sighed.

"When I go, I go," said Archie. "Same
as with animals. They know when it's time.
They just keep going until the time comes,
and then they go."

Peter Woodhouse, of course, was no longer a young dog. Like his owner, he appeared to have something wrong with a hip,
and walked with a marked limp. This did
not stop him trying to keep up with Willy
when he drove the tractor, but he could not
carry on for long, and soon fell panting by
the wayside, watching Willy disappear down
the farm lane. For the most part, he lay in his
kennel, or immediately in front of it, where
there was a large paving stone that warmed
with the sun. On the rare occasions when
visitors arrived in the farmyard, he would
give a few desultory barks, and then sidle up
to them in a show of unqualified affection.
"He's no guard dog, that one," said Archie.

Willy defended Peter. "Doesn't mean he
isn't brave," he said. "He went up with them

in those planes of theirs. He's seen action—
which is more than most dogs can claim."

Archie smiled. "Yes. Good pilot, they say."

He had a new collar, given him by the airmen at the base when he left. Inscribed on
it, burned into the leather with the tip of a
soldering iron, was **The Good Pilot Peter
Woodhouse.** A visitor noticed this—a reporter from the local weekly who was doing
an article on rights-of-way through farms.
He asked about its meaning, and Archie explained about the dog's time as a U.S. Air
Force mascot.

"You serious?" asked the reporter.

"Yes, of course. They took him up with
them."

The reporter's incredulity grew. "In their
planes? Over to Germany?"

"So I've been told," said Archie. "Apparently, he liked flying."

The reporter whistled. "What a story," he
muttered.

A photographer came to take a picture
of Peter Woodhouse in front of his kennel.
Then he took a shot of the collar and its inscription. In due course an article appeared
on the front page of the weekly newspaper

published in the nearby market town. **The Good Pilot Peter Woodhouse,** it was headed, with the sub-heading **Brave dog helps fliers on wartime missions.** There was a picture of Sergeant Lisowski, whom the paper had approached for comment. "He was given an honourable discharge," the sergeant said. "He did his bit."

Willy beamed with pleasure when he saw the paper. He bought every copy for sale in the post office, cut out the article, and sent one off to Val in Germany. She sent a postcard back on which she had written: **Our Peter Woodhouse! The hero!**

Annie was more reserved. "I'm not sure that Peter Woodhouse needs to be in the papers," she said. "What if that Ted Butters sees it? He can read, you know, same as anyone else."

Willy shook his head. "Ted Butters wouldn't dare do anything."

Annie looked dubious. "I'd put nothing past him," she said.

They were looking at the tractor, which was misfiring and emitting white smoke.

"The injectors," said Archie. "Do you know about those, Willy?"

Willy nodded, but looked blank at the same time.

Archie showed him. There were so many things that Willy knew nothing about, but the farmer had found him to be a quick learner, in spite of everything. If you engaged his attention, he could pick things up, and you would not know, then, that he was slow. Now Archie showed him how to remove the exhaust manifold so that they could work out which cylinder was pumping out white smoke from unburnt fuel.

"There," said Archie. "You see over there? That's the culprit."

"Can we fix it?" asked Willy.

Archie did not reply. A small brown van was making its way up the lane towards the farmyard, and Archie was gazing at it. "That's Ted Butters," he muttered.

They watched as Ted Butters drew to a halt at the farmyard gate. He got out of the van, opened the gate, and then drove through, omitting to close it again behind him.

"Hey!" shouted Archie. "The gate. You didn't close the gate. We've got livestock . . ."

Ted Butters ignored him.

"You!" he said, pointing at Willy. "Where's my dog?"

Archie felt Willy stiffen and bristle. He put a restraining hand on the young man's arm. "Listen to me, Butters," he began. "You come on my land, you talk to me—understand?"

Ted Butters turned to face Archie. "Very well," he said. "I've got the same question for you—where's my dog?"

"He ain't your dog any more, Butters," said Archie firmly. "You mistreated him. You know you did. He left you."

Ted Butters snorted with anger. "You stole him, more likely. That dog cost six quid, and you stole him."

Willy now joined in. "He left you," he said. "He ran away."

Ted Butters looked at him contemptuously. "Liar," he said. "Not that you'll know the meaning of the word."

Willy flushed. "I know what it means."

Ted Butters rolled his eyes. "That's a good one," he said. He took a few steps forward to get a better view of the farmyard. He noticed Peter Woodhouse's kennel, and the dog lying down, half inside, half outside.

"So what's that over there?" he sneered.

He walked purposively over towards the kennel. Archie hobbled after him.

"You leave that dog alone, Butters," Archie shouted.

Ted Butters did not turn round, but began to walk more quickly towards the kennel. As he approached it, Peter Woodhouse stirred, and then sat up. He sniffed at the air, and fixed his gaze on the angry farmer.

Ted Butters was now a few paces away. He called out to the dog, who rose to his feet, and began to growl. Butters looked about and spotted a stone on the ground. He bent down to pick this up, and made a gesture as if throwing it at the dog. "Don't you growl at me, my lad," he muttered.

The action of picking up the stone was enough. Deep in his memory, Peter Woodhouse recognised the smell of the man who had tormented and beaten him. Now, with almost no hesitation, he lurched forward, baring his teeth. Ted Butters stopped in his tracks, and then threw the stone, the missile hitting the dog on the top of his head with a dull thud. For a moment, Peter Woodhouse seemed to topple, but he soon righted himself and his eyes flashed with hatred. Hurling himself forward with something midway between a yelp and a growl, he charged at Ted Butters, sinking his teeth into the man's leg and then momentarily disengaging before latching onto his flailing arm.

Willy rushed forward and seized Peter Woodhouse by the collar, wrenching him bodily off his victim. Ted Butters, freed of the dog, aimed a kick at Peter's flank but missed, losing his balance as a result, and falling heavily to the ground. Archie, now at the fallen farmer's side, bent down to help him to his feet.

Once upright, Ted Butters brushed away Archie's hand. "That dog's dead," he spat out. "He'll be shot. I'm going straight to Bill Edwards."

"You asked for it," said Willy, his voice high with indignation. "You threw a stone at him. What do you expect a dog to do?"

"He'll be shot," replied Ted Butters, wincing with pain. "The police shoot dogs that attack people. You know that as well as I do."

"Not if they're just defending themselves," countered Archie. "There's a difference."

"I'll shoot him myself," said Ted.

Archie stepped forward. "If you come on my land with a shotgun you'll get more than you bargained for."

Ted Butters gave him a murderous look. "The police will be here," he said. "You'll see." He stormed off towards his van, and they noticed, as he went, that there was blood on his trouser leg where Peter Woodhouse had bitten him. Archie looked anxious; Ted Butters was right about dogs being shot if they attacked people. There had been a case the previous year where that was exactly what had happened; a dog had savaged a ten-year-old girl and had been shot the same afternoon by Bill Edwards. Bill had disliked doing it, but had been given instructions by the station sergeant in the nearby town, who had not been prepared to listen to any of the owners' pleas for mercy.

Willy suddenly started to run towards the retreating farmer. Archie moved to intercept him, but was too slow. Willy grabbed at Ted and jerked him back off his feet. Then he appeared to shake him, as a dog might shake a rabbit, before dropping him on the ground.

"Willy!" Archie shouted. "Let him be."

Willy stood over Ted, his face flushed with rage. "You beat that dog," he yelled. "You deserve everything you get."

Reaching Willy's side, Archie pushed him roughly away and bent down to help Ted to his feet.

"You've added assault to the charges," Ted spluttered. "Grievous bodily harm, I shouldn't wonder."

Archie glanced at Willy over his shoulder, warning him off. A small trickle of blood was emerging from Ted's right nostril, his nose having felt some of the impact of his fall.

"You brought all this on yourself, Ted," Archie muttered. "You always were like that, you know. Caused trouble wherever you went."

"You stole my dog," said Ted.

Archie shook his head. "We've been through that, Ted." He paused. A solution was dawning on him. "How much to settle?" he asked.

Ted Butters rubbed at his nose, his hand

coming away bloodied. He was a farmer after all, and his farmer's instinct was coming into play. Money could sort out most issues, judiciously applied, and this might be one of them. "Fifteen quid," he said, glaring over Archie's shoulder at Willy in the background.

"Twelve pounds ten shillings," countered Archie. "He's getting on a bit now, that dog."

"Fourteen," replied Ted Butters. "And half a dozen hens—good layers."

Archie looked at Willy, who had started to walk over towards Peter Woodhouse's kennel. "All right," he said. "Fourteen quid and four hens."

## 24

The job that Ubi took on at Templehof involved six ten-hour shifts a week. It was unremittingly hard work, every bit as physically demanding, he thought, as working in a mine, but there were the meals, which were rich and sustaining, and there was the pride of competition, too, which made a difference. Each crew kept a note of the times it took to open the hatches of the incoming aircraft and unload the cargo onto the waiting trucks. With the planes coming down every couple of minutes, the ground operation was as slick and precise as the airlift itself. There was a room in which they could spend a few minutes recovering after each unloading, but the drone of the departing aircraft would soon merge into that of the next descending, a ceaseless background sound, like that of the waves on a shore.

Everything that the city needed was brought in this way—across the invisible air bridge that linked Berlin with the West. The Russians had closed every ground route into the city, ruthlessly strangling the three non-

Soviet sectors. It would not be long, they calculated, before the task of keeping hundreds of thousands of people alive would prove just too much, even with the might of the Americans behind it. How could you bring in enough food to feed that many people day after day? You could not. How could you bring in sufficient coal to generate a whole city's power? You could not.

Many of those who did the unloading were volunteers, working for the free meals alone; some, like Ubi, who was given charge of a crew, were paid. Some of the money he earned went to Stoffi as rent for the floor that was his bed; some of it went to the widow, for Klaus. His own needs were small enough, and he was used now to poverty and paucity.

He wrote every other day to Ilse, even when he was tired at the end of a gruelling shift, his ears ringing with the sound of the aircraft engines. In her replies, she sent him long accounts of the doings of the British officers. There was the story of the junior maid in the hotel, who had taken up with one of the officers, and now had confessed to being pregnant. There was the story of the officer who had taken an interest in the **Motodrom.** He had managed to get hold of some paint from somewhere and had offered to paint it for her. She had accepted, but was worried that they would take it away from her. **They can requisition things they need,** she wrote. **What if they decide the occupying forces need a** Motodrom? She was fond of it, in a curious way, and was even wondering whether it might be rescued as a paying attraction. A local mechanic had been to see her about it. He and a friend were keen to disassemble it and move it to a field on the edge of town. People would pay to come and watch it being ridden. They would charge admission and then would split the proceeds with her. What should she do about that? Should she accept?

He wrote back and told her about his airlift duties. **I am black from unloading coal,** he said. **Then the next plane comes in and it's carrying sacks of flour. So I become white. Now, your** Motodrom: **yes, you should let other people use it, but you mustn't give it away. A** Motodrom **is an unusual thing, and you're lucky to have it. I can help you**

**when I come back. I can help you run it, and perhaps we can let the mechanic be the rider, if that's what he wants.**

She responded that the officer had finished the painting. She had offered to pay him something, but this had just caused surprise, and even offence. He had looked at her sideways; did she not understand who they were? She was a German civilian, one of the vanquished, and he was one of the conquerors. The offence might have been less had he been one of the men, but he was an officer. She said that he had bitten his lip and declined her offer in a voice that sounded as if he were being strangled. **They are very proud men,** she wrote. And then she added, **Not that we should accuse others of being proud.** He reread that sentence, and knew that she was right. There was something very deep in the soul of his country that made it want to dominate; that thing, that lurking quality, was wounded now, but it would find a new way to express itself one day. He did not want that to happen; he had hated the strutting and the arrogance, but he knew that it was still there, even if bullied into submission. He had seen it in people's eyes: the glint that told him those fires were not entirely or everywhere extinguished.

Her letters were the high point of his day. When one failed to arrive, as sometimes happened during the blockade, he went back to the last one he had received, and often found that it contained new things to think about. His time now was largely filled with work, punctuated by visits to the widow and Klaus. The boy was getting used to him, and looked forward to the chocolate passed on from the American fliers. On one occasion Ubi received half a carton of cigarettes from an airman who had just been told that he was to be posted home at last, and was feeling generous. He was able to exchange that for a new pair of boy's shoes and a barely worn child's overcoat. The widow said, "I'm rationing his chocolate," but he suspected that she ate much of it herself, and had once seen traces of it about her lips. But everyone had become like that, he realised; these were still times of bare survival. The coat went missing after a few weeks and he did not believe her protestations that

it had been left on a tram. He did not accuse her of trading it on the black market,
but he was certain that this was what had
happened.

They were unloading medical supplies. The
cartons were light—bandages and pills did
not weigh a great deal—and they completed
their task in not much more than ten minutes. There was mail to be loaded for the
return journey, but, unusually, there was
no urgency. The plane required a repair, and
that would take over twelve hours. The crew
would be stood down for at least eight of
those and could go off into the city if they
wished. They went ahead with the loading,
though, so that the plane would be ready for
take-off the moment the repairs were finished. Every lost hour meant less cargo, and
that could be translated into hunger or cold
for somebody in the beleaguered city. It was
while Ubi was bringing in the last of the mail
sacks that the pilot emerged from the flight
deck. Ubi moved to the side to let him pass,
and for a moment the two men were side
by side. The pilot glanced at him briefly

and then stopped. He reached out to put a hand on Ubi's shoulder, and the two men looked into each other's faces.

There was no doubt in the mind of either, but for a few moments nothing was said. There had been so many painful moments of recognition that people were wary. Recognition could mean denunciation and arrest; there were full dress trials that had resulted from a passing glance in the street.

"It is you, isn't it?" Mike said. "Holland?"

Ubi was silent.

"It is, isn't it?"

Mike's smile gave him the reassurance he needed. "Yes, it's me."

Mike moved forward and flung his arms round Ubi. "You protected us."

Ubi made a gesture of helplessness. "The war was over."

"It wasn't. You took a big risk. And our dog too. You saved his life." Mike released him from the hug. "And here you are," he said.

"You're speaking German," said Ubi.

Mike laughed. "I've learned. Classes at the base. I have an ear, I'm told. I picked up a bit of Dutch too . . . back then."

"So did I."

Mike gestured to the loaded mail bags. "And this is what you're doing?"

"For the time being. I want to get back to the West. I have a fiancée back there, but there's a small boy here—my sister's son. She died."

Mike lowered his eyes. "I'm sorry."

"It's difficult," said Ubi. "Papers and so on. And now the blockade."

"Ah, papers. Papers control our lives, don't they?" Mike hesitated. "I reckon I owe you."

Ubi said nothing.

Mike looked at his watch. Night and day made little difference to the working of the air bridge, but he could see that it was coming up for dinner time. "When do you finish your shift?" he asked.

"Now," said Ubi. "You were the last plane—for us, at least."

"I don't really know Berlin," said Mike. "Are there any restaurants left standing?"

Ubi nodded. "There's Der Kleine Friedrich not far from here. They say it's good. I've never been."

"And they have food?"

"Some."

Mike smiled as he placed a friendly hand on Ubi's shoulder. "Will you let me buy you dinner? As a thank-you."

Ubi protested that Mike did not need to thank him for anything.

"I know that," said Mike. "But I want to."

"In that case, yes."

Der Kleine Friedrich was in the basement of a building that had miraculously survived the destruction round about it. The blockade had dimmed the electric light bulbs that festooned the entrance to the bar, but inside, strategically placed candles gave a nightclub air of complicity and decadence. A small band, consisting of a pianist, a violinist, and a clarinettist—all emaciated and well into their sixties—made a brave attempt at cheerfulness, mixing Dixie and Weimar in a curious mish-mash of time and place.

They sat by the bar while a table was prepared for them. Ubi, who had been unable to change out of his working clothes, seemed ill at ease; Mike, in his flying jacket and boots, was insouciant, and largely indifferent to the thinly disguised condescension of the barman.

Mike asked Ubi about his experiences as a prisoner of war. He heard about Ilse and the billeted British officers. He heard about the search for his sister and for Klaus.

"It hasn't been as bad for me as it has for so many," said Ubi. "I haven't really suffered."

Mike shrugged. "Luck, I guess. We were lucky that you found us back there. It might have been very different. Some of your people . . ." He stopped.

Ubi looked down at the floor. "You can say it. I know it happened."

Mike looked at him. "They shot their prisoners."

Ubi looked up at him and met his gaze. "I know."

Mike reached for his drink. He was not given to anger, but there were moments when he felt it welling up within him. These people—the Germans—needed to have it brought home to them just what they had done. The country was full of people who said it was nothing to do with them—not a swastika in sight, not a party badge; a whole ghost country that had somehow disappeared when the Allies had arrived.

"I didn't want any of that to happen," said Ubi. "I don't expect you'll believe me, but I didn't."

Mike put down his drink. He felt immediately guilty. This was the man who had possibly saved his life. He reached out and placed a hand on Ubi's arm. "Of course I believe you. And I'm sorry—I'm tired. I've been flying too much, and it's tricky stuff. Coming in over the rooftops, missing the chimneys by inches. It takes it out of you."

Ubi nodded. "The people are very grateful," he said. "They can't quite believe that you're doing what you're doing, all for us. We were your enemies, and now you're doing this for us."

"War isn't the only thing," said Mike. "You get over it."

They raised their glasses to one another, repeating their first, tentative toast.

"So what now?" asked Mike.

Ubi explained about getting back to Ilse. "I'll wait. When it's possible again, I'll take my nephew back there."

Mike hesitated. "It might be possible," he said.

"What do you mean?"

"Did you hear about that man who did an involuntary trip? One of the loaders was shut in by mistake and had to take a cold ride back to Cologne."

Ubi said they had been warned to be careful. That man could have frozen to death.

"So if you and the boy," Mike continued, "were to stow away, we might not notice you until we had taken off and were well on our way. Do you see what I mean?"

Ubi looked about him. The habit of the last few years had become ingrained: circumspection, caution, silence.

Mike noticed, and smiled. "Look," he said. "You're free now. Nobody can harm you. That's all over."

Ubi looked at him with gratitude. It was so different for these Americans; they'd never had a government founded on hate. "When?" he asked.

Mike scratched his head. "Those repairs will be done by morning. We'll probably be off duty tomorrow, but we'll be flying in the next morning. Could you and your nephew be there?"

Ubi thought. Security at the gates was tight, but mostly for those going out. Theft had been a problem, and the authorities were getting tougher.

"I could try," he said. "It could be hard to get Klaus in, but I'm friendly with one of the security men. He's German—we were at school together. He might be persuaded."

Mike reached into the bag he had with him—halfway between a briefcase and a rucksack. He took out a carton of cigarettes. "Would this help to smooth the way?"

"I think my friend smokes," said Ubi, smiling.

Klaus was wrapped in as many layers of clothing as they could manage, which made him look like the cocoon of some flying insect. The widow smothered him with kisses and urged Ubi to be careful. He thanked her and promised that he would send her money when he was able to do so. "I'm very grateful to you," he said. "I shan't forget."

He had reported in sick for the day. Arriving at the airport an hour or so before the time that Mike had given him, he saw that his friend was on duty, as they had planned it. Ubi had the papers to get in, and the friend explained to his superior that the child had an appointment to be seen by a doctor who was coming in on one of the flights. "I've seen the documents," he said. "And everything's in order."

The superior was busy with something else, and nodded his approval. They were in.

They waited in the unloading area. Ubi entertained the little boy with a toy he had brought with him—a small tin monkey on a string. He fed him pieces of chocolate and pointed out the stream of planes as they came in. The child watched wide-eyed, confused by the din of activity; at one point he wailed in fear, but was pacified by a particularly large piece of chocolate. Ubi watched the sky. It was a fine winter afternoon, with the sun painting the trees and buildings with gold. The aeroplanes appeared as specks of reflected light in the sky, grew larger and darker, and dropped down onto their perilous approach route through the buildings.

He knew the identifying number of Mike's aircraft, but he almost missed it as it did a balletic turn on the apron in preparation for unloading. But he saw it in time to follow the truck onto which his team would unload the cargo. He had already seen them and spoken to one or two of them.

"Why are you here?" his deputy asked. "You were meant to be sick."

"I have to look after this boy today," said Ubi. "I've brought him in to see the planes."

"You shouldn't."

"Well, I have."

He stood aside as the cargo of rice was unloaded. When the last sack had been dragged and manhandled into the truck, he approached the loading bay door and began to clamber into the plane. Hands reached out to help him; others took the child from him and spirited him into the storage area of the fuselage.

Mike said to him, "Everybody on board knows. They're okay. I told them what you did."

He was aware that he was being looked at with interest by two other men in flying gear. One of them made a thumbs-up sign; the other smiled.

"Sit down over there," said Mike. "Hold on to the boy."

They were not refuelling, and they had to

take their place in the line of aircraft readied for departure. The pitch of the engines rose, and in his terror Klaus clung more tightly to Ubi, who hugged him and tried to reassure him with half-remembered nursery rhymes, the words of which were lost in the roar of the engines and the rattling of the aircraft's fuselage. **Hänschen klein / ging allein / in die weite Welt hinein . . . Sieben Jahr / trüb und klar / Hänschen in der Fremde war . . .**

Eventually the terrified child fell asleep, and was still sleeping when the plane dropped down one hundred and twenty miles later to make a bumpy landing on American asphalt in the western zone.

"Guess what?" said Mike to the control tower wireless operator. "I believe we have stowaways."

# FOUR
# MOTODROM

## 25

Ilse had prepared an attic bedroom for Klaus immediately above the room she occupied with Ubi. She had brightened up a counterpane by sewing onto it animal shapes cut from a bolt of red felt. She had been given the felt, a precious commodity, as a present and had been keeping it for some special purpose; this, she decided, was the moment to use it. There was an elephant with trunk raised, a line of camels, and a bloated hippopotamus. She had not anticipated the small boy's reaction to the sight of the quilt, which had been one of fear, and a terrified seeking of refuge behind Ubi's legs.

Ubi sought to reassure her. "He'll get used to it," he said. "Remember what children in Berlin have seen."

She understood. She had been surprised by the resilience of children, when she knew what they had witnessed. There were gangs of them everywhere, it seemed, groups of semi-feral youngsters who survived among the city ruins, living from hand to mouth, emerging to steal whatever they could lay their hands on before slipping back into the shadows. Theft was their lifeline, although some of them, boys as well as girls, knew that more money could be made in prostitution and took advantage of the fact, beyond the reach of the authorities, their tired, world-weary faces reflecting their loss of childhood and the daily pain of their furtive, degraded lives.

At least Klaus had had a home and an adult to look after him. But now, having lost the security of the widow's flat in Berlin and the familiar routine of his life there, he was uncertain and confused. Ilse's advances to him were culinary, but the dishes she concocted herself, which included treats she was sure he would never have seen in Berlin, were often rebuffed without any explanation; questions addressed to him were rarely acknowledged, and he withdrew into a sullen and resentful private world.

"Grief," said a friend, a nurse, who had tried—and failed—to get through to him.

"And there's no cure for that," said Ilse.

The nurse shook her head. "Love," she

said. "And patience." She added, as an afterthought, "Time."

Ilse knew her friend was right: she would give this child those three things and he would get better, just as Germany itself would recover from its nightmare. She could already see it happening around her; a factory had opened in their town and it was turning out furniture—functional items at first: beds and chests of drawers that were even being exported to France, people said—but that was just the beginning; there would soon be more expensive things. The inn itself was doing well; the British officers had moved on—they had their own buildings now—but Germans themselves were beginning to travel and look for places to stay. There was money again; not much, and there was a limit to what it could acquire, but the grinding poverty of those first few years was slowly being relieved. It showed in people's demeanour: the broken, almost dazed look of defeat was no longer universal. People were smiling again; wearily, cautiously perhaps, but smiling nonetheless.

Ilse and Ubi married. Their wedding was

a quiet affair: there was no family to invite on Ubi's side, apart from two cousins in Hamburg, who for various reasons were unable to make the journey; Ilse's parents had recently divorced and were uncomfortable about attending together. It was simpler, she thought, for them to marry with the minimum of fuss, which is what they eventually did.

Ubi had acquired a motorcycle—a battered machine that he spent long evenings restoring. They used this for their honeymoon trip, three days of meandering through countryside so untouched by the war that it might never have happened. Klaus was looked after by one of the maids in the hotel who had become fond of him, and spoiled him with treats of marzipan animals she made from sugar and almonds acquired from her black-marketeer lover.

Klaus started to call Ilse **Mutti.** She cried the first time he did this, struggling to contain her sobs. Ubi asked her what was wrong, and she whispered her reply to him. He stroked her hand. They had been trying for a child of their own, with no success, and he feared it would never happen. She said to him, "I think that he loves me now," and he replied, "He does; of course he does."

Two years passed. Klaus began school, and showed an aptitude for anything requiring manual skills. His teacher praised him for his politeness, and rewarded him with gold stars on his exercise books. He was happy enough at school, although from time to time he was bullied because he looked different from the other children. He said one day, "Why is my hair like this? Will it change?"

Ilse said, "It's lovely hair, Klaus."

"They laugh at me."

"Who? Who laughs at you?"

"Some boys."

She wanted to find the perpetrators and shake them, but Ubi persuaded her that Klaus would have to fight his own battles. "Things will change," he said. "Germany is going to be different. Nobody is going to torment anybody again."

Ubi finished the restoration of the **Motodrom.** He had as yet no plans for it, although he had taken to practising riding it—tentatively at first, making quick forays from the angled lower section to the vertical wall, before dropping back to the safety of the lower level. Then, emboldened, he completed his first full ride, soaring higher until he sped around just below the level of the raised viewing platform. Ilse and Klaus came to witness this, and shrieked with admiration as Ubi waved to them with one hand while steering with the other.

"One day," said Ubi, "we'll start this thing properly. We'll open it to the public."

Ilse smiled. "Perhaps."

"But we must," insisted Ubi. "What's the point of having a **Motodrom** if you don't use it?"

"Perhaps," she repeated.

Early in 1950, Ubi decided to write to Mike. They had not met again since Mike had flown him from Berlin; Ubi, though, had thought of his friend from time to time and had wondered whether he was still stationed in Germany. There was a certain embarrassment for him in contacting Mike—he felt that it could be seen as an attempt to ingratiate himself, which he was reluctant to do. People like Mike had every reason to dislike Germans, and he felt that he did not wish to press himself upon him. Yet he wanted him to know about Klaus, and how he had settled, and how their lives were getting better. He wanted to express gratitude for what Mike and his fellow Americans had done. The Russians had wanted to punish Germany, and had done so; their plan was to transform the country into one giant potato farm, people said, a feudal empire given over to the growing of food for Russia. America had been different; it was helping them back on their feet, and he wanted to say thank you, again, for that.

He addressed his letter to Mike at his base in Wiesbaden. In it, he told him what had happened since his return. He put in a picture of Klaus, standing beside Ilse, holding the small wooden figure of Pinocchio Mike had found abandoned in a Berlin ruin— a dead child's toy, he thought. Pinocchio's nose had been broken, and was half its original size, but the paint on his cheeks was still bright and rosy. He told Mike about the improving fortunes of the inn, and about the restoration of the **Motodrom.** He invited him to visit them if he ever had the chance to travel their way. He signed the letter, **Your grateful friend, Ubi.**

He received no reply. After a few weeks he wrote again, a shorter note this time, in which he asked whether his original letter had been delivered. This time there came a response—a brown envelope, on which his name and address were typed. Ilse handed it to him in the office at the inn.

"He's answered you now," she said. "Your first letter must have been lost."

Ubi opened the envelope. The letter within was typed, on paper that had a printed military heading. Glancing at the signature before he read it, he saw that it was not signed by Mike.

**Dear Herr Dietrich,** the letter began, **I am writing in reply to your recent letter addressed to Lieutenant Michael Rogers. I regret to inform you that Lieutenant Rogers lost his life in an aircraft accident in May 1949. This incident occurred in Berlin, during the airlift. I have forwarded your letter to his widow, who is now living in England.**

Ubi read the letter several times before

passing it on to Ilse. He was mute. She read it and shook her head. "One more," she said.

He nodded, and reached out to take the paper back from her. "I feel very sad," he said.

"Of course you must," she said. "Perhaps you can write to his wife. This major . . ." She gestured to the letter. "You can write to this major and ask him to forward a letter to his wife."

"Yes," said Ubi. "I shall." He paused. "It would have been a landing accident, you know. It was so dangerous—all those planes circling above Berlin, round and round, and then having to drop down over the buildings. No wonder they crashed."

She was watching him. "Do you think there will come a time when we stop hurting one another?"

He was surprised by her question. "Hurting one another?"

"Yes. The Berlin blockade: what was that but an attempt by the Russians to hurt Berlin—to hurt all of us."

He sighed. "The Russians are full of anger. But then . . ." He sighed again.

She waited for him to continue.

"But then there is such a thing as righteous anger, don't you think?"

He was right, she thought.

He turned away. "But I wonder how long we are going to be punished? How long will we have to hang our heads in shame for what we did? All our lives, do you think? All our children's lives too?"

She shrugged. "Perhaps for all of our lives." The thought seemed impossibly bleak—a life sentence. "I don't know. Unless they forgive us."

"They won't," he said. "The British will. The Americans and the French too. But not the Russians. I don't see them doing that, do you?"

He composed the letter to Val that evening. He had never met her, but Mike had told him a little bit about her during the conversation in the bar in Berlin. He had never written a letter of this nature before, and he decided to write it first in German and then ask Ilse to translate it into English for him. **I have been told the sad news of your husband's accident,** he began. **This causes me sorrow. Your husband was most kind to**

**me. I shall remember him with great af-
fection.** He showed it to Ilse, who said that
it was perfect. "The English do not like to
make a big fuss," she said. "They are very reserved. Such a letter will be a great comfort
to an English person."

## 26

The air force was generous. As the widow of an officer killed in action, Val was entitled to a pension. She could go to the United States if she wished and would be assisted in finding accommodation and employment. She could go wherever she wanted to go, and efforts would be made to help her find her feet wherever she chose to settle.

Mike's family said that she was welcome to come to Indiana, where his grandparents would take her in and provide a home for Tommy. It would be on their farm, they said, but there was an elementary school quite close and Tommy could go there. Muncie was ten miles away, and she might get a job in the town if she wanted one. They knew somebody in a local bank who could get her a job as a trainee book-keeper. You would never want for work if you were a book-keeper, they said.

It was not an easy decision. She was missing Mike with an intensity that she had never thought possible. It was a feeling of emptiness, a dull ache, constantly present, impossible to subdue by any of the nostrums that people suggested—busying yourself, consciously thinking of other things, counting your blessings, and so on. None of this worked. In her view, their short marriage had been perfect; not once had she felt any irritation or anger; not once had the thought crossed her mind that this partnership between two people of such different backgrounds could turn out to be ill-starred. She had begun to be American, talking of Indiana as home, conversing with the other air force wives on their terms, wearing what they liked to wear, laughing at the same things, becoming a member of what seemed to be a large club of infinite possibilities. But now all that had turned to dust because her rationale for being like this had disappeared. The new person she had become was all to do with Mike, and now that he had gone, the new identity had gone too.

She wrote to Mike's family to thank them for their kindness, but explained that she would return to her aunt's house. It would be easier to care for Tommy there, she said, although she did not say why this should be so. Their reply was one of disbelief. How could it be easier to care for a child in England, where there were still shortages and money was tight? Did she not think that she owed it to her son to bring him up in a place where there were opportunities? She could have written back to ask **What do you know of England?** But she did not do so; she realised that Mike's grandparents simply wanted to have their grandson's little boy, and that was something that he would have understood. She wrote back a conciliatory letter. Yes, she understood all the points they raised; yes, Tommy would have many opportunities in America, but she still felt on balance it would be better for him if she were happy, too, and she had never been to America and could not be sure that she would be happy there. What if she did not like it? What if she felt lonely and cut off from her family back in England?

She went home earlier than she had planned. The air force had been prepared for her to stay in the officers' accommodation on the base, but she thanked them and said that this would not be necessary. She left everything behind—virtually all the possessions they had accumulated together, taking only photographs and clothing; she was ending a chapter and she did not wish to be cluttered with things of the past.

After a day or two at home it was as if she had never been away. Annie was still running the post office, her room was as she had left it, and there were even clothes in her wardrobe that still fitted her. Annie had installed a cot at the end of Val's bed; this was for Tommy, although he was now of an age to sleep in something larger. She had also bought him several new sets of clothes, although these were already too small for him; Mike had been tall, and Tommy was taking after him.

One thing was different: Willy had moved into Archie's farmhouse, where he occupied the spare room at the back of the house. Archie's arthritis had become worse, and he now spent most of the day immobile in the kitchen, following what was happening on the farm with an old pair of army field binoculars. He did not need to watch too closely; Willy had taken the farm in hand, had clipped the hedgerows and cropped the patches of rank grazing land. New fruit trees had been planted, and new silos built. He had even managed to find the wire for new fences and had put these up himself, while repairing some of the older sections of fencing that went back fifty or sixty years.

At first, Willy was shy. Tommy had forgotten him, of course, and Willy, puzzled by his reticence, kept his distance. But that soon changed, and it was not long before he was showing the boy around the farm and teaching him to look for eggs in the hen coop.

"He loves being with you, Willy," said Val. "He talks about you non-stop, you know."

Willy beamed with pleasure. "He has the makings of a farmer," he said. "It shows."

Val smiled, but she had her reservations. When would Tommy realise that Willy had his limitations? And might not somebody like Willy hold back a child? She reflected, with regret, on the sort of father Mike had been, and on the fact that Tommy would probably have no recollection of him in later life. She would try, of course, to keep his memory alive, but it would mean little to a child of Tommy's age.

Tommy started at the village school. Now that he was out of the house for the entire morning, Val looked for a job. A new medical practice had opened up in the town a few miles away and they needed a receptionist. Val applied and was appointed. She enjoyed the responsibility and the variety that the work provided, and it meant, too, that she met people.

Annie asked her if she would remarry, and she shook her head. "Not for a long time," she said.

"I can understand that," said Annie. "But the heart gets better, you know. Give it the chance, and it'll get better."

Val laughed. "Who'll want me? A man doesn't like to take on a woman with another man's child. Men steer clear of that sort of thing."

Annie disagreed. "Any man who gets you will be very fortunate," she said.

Then Willy proposed. Archie had unwittingly put the idea in his head. He had disclosed that he would be moving to a stockman's cottage that had been lying empty on the farm, and Willy could have the main farmhouse, if he wished; he was used to it now, and it was easy to run the farm from there.

Willy said to Val, "Archie's given me the house. He says I can live there by myself."

"That's kind of him, Willy," said Val. "And you're good to him—anybody can see that."

Willy brushed the compliment aside. "It's a big place," he said. "Too big for one person."

"Then get somebody to share it with you," said Val. "There's that tractor man down at Dunbar's place who's looking for somewhere. He might—"

Willy did not let her finish. "Or you," he said.

Val stared at him. "Me? But I live with Auntie—here—at the post office."

Willy reached out to take her hand. His skin felt rough. Val laughed nervously. "I could come to visit you," she said.

"That's not what I meant," said Willy. "You and I . . . well, we could get fixed up together."

She caught her breath. "I don't think

so, Willy. It's very kind of you, of course, but . . ."

"Because I love you," said Willy. "I've always loved you—right from the beginning."

He spoke with such disarming frankness that her heart gave a leap. "That's kind. Thank you, Willy."

"No, I mean it." He paused, looking askance at her. "You don't think I'm stupid, do you?"

She assured him that she did not.

"Because all I want to do is to look after you," he said. "And Tommy."

She knew that what he said was true: that was what he wanted. And then she thought about her own feelings, and how she was sure that she would never stop loving Mike, and that if she were to accept Willy's proposal she could still do that; she had always thought it possible to love more than one person at the same time, and there were, after all, different types of love, as people learned in wartime, when, in the knowledge of the fragility of any human plans, they made do, took what they could get, learned to patch things together. She was tired. If she married

Willy she would have a place to live and there would be somebody who loved Tommy to look after both of them. The world was an uncertain place, full of disappointment. She wanted to protect Tommy from that, whatever should happen to her. "If I marry you," she said to Willy, "will you let me . . ." She hesitated, searching for the right way of expressing what she had in mind. "Will you let me decide what to do?" No, that was not quite right. "You see," she went on, "I want to play my full part . . ."

He smiled. "But of course you can do that. I don't mind."

Annie received the news in silence. Then, trying hard to conceal her surprise, she said, "It'll be good for Tommy."

"Yes," said Val. "It will."

Annie gave her a searching look. "Is that why you're doing it?"

Val bit her lip. "He's a good man."

"I know that," said Annie. "But . . ."

"There are different ways of being happy," said Val.

Annie nodded. "You're a good girl, Val Eliot," she said.

Val was embarrassed by the compliment. But there was something else. "And Archie has told him that he can take over the farm," she said. "He'll let to him for a very small rent, and then he says he'll come into it eventually— when Archie goes."

Annie raised an eyebrow. "That's a generous gift."

"Archie has no family."

"No," said Annie. "Nor does he. But now he does, you see."

## 27

In 1951, Ilse received an invitation to a wedding in a village in Oxfordshire. One of the British majors, the one who had taught Ubi English, had left the army and taken a job as a teacher in a boys' boarding school. He was marrying the daughter of the local doctor and had sent an invitation to Ilse, with whom he had maintained a correspondence since leaving Germany. Ubi had also been invited, but was unable to make the journey as somebody had to stay behind to look after the hotel. He was uncomfortable, too, about going to England. "They might not want to see us . . . just yet," he said.

Ilse laughed at him. "But they've invited us," she pointed out.

"I don't mean them—the major. I don't mean him. I mean people in general. What if we turned a corner, and there was Winston Churchill?"

This brought more laughter. "Mr. Churchill would be very polite. I'm sure he would say **guten Tag.**"

It was not a journey undertaken lightly.

In Germany things were returning to normal, step by cautious step; in England the Festival of Britain, an ambitious official effort to persuade people to address the future with optimism, was under way, but people still felt bruised by years of privation. Travel was still a luxury for both nations.

Ilse bought a new dress for the wedding and made the journey by train to Calais, where she boarded the ferry to Dover. The following day she arrived at her small hotel in the village where the wedding was due to take place. At the wedding, although the major and his bride were polite and welcoming, the other guests seemed stand-offish. She sensed that she was being pointed out as the German guest—the subject of whispers and sideways glances.

She had a day in hand after the wedding before she had to get back to Dover for her return ferry. She had with her the diary in which she had written Val's address, and she asked the woman who kept the hotel whether it would be possible to get there and back in a day. She and Val had exchanged letters since that first letter of sympathy, writing to one another every two or three months, as pen friends. Val had said that if Ilse ever came to England she should come to see her, and Ilse had reciprocated. Neither had imagined that either would ever take up the invitation, but now Ilse found herself feeling a certain curiosity about her unmet friend.

The hotel-keeper told her that it would not be a complicated trip. There was a bus that stopped at the edge of the village; this would take her all the way to a town near Val's village. She could go from there by taxi.

She sent a telegram to warn Val of her arrival, not knowing whether it would reach her in time. She arrived at the post office, to which she had addressed her letters to Val. Annie greeted her warmly; the telegram had been received a few hours earlier. "I know all about you," she said. "I'll telephone Val and tell her you're here."

Val collected her in the farm van and took her back to meet Willy and Tommy. The two women's conversation was stilted at first, but after a while it became more relaxed.

"Our husbands had a very good friendship," said Ilse.

Val sighed. "War is unnatural—friendship isn't."

"Yes," said Ilse. "We women know that."

Val thought: **We had to fight, though, and it was because of you.** But she stopped herself, because she knew that forgiveness demanded that such thoughts be put to one side.

Ilse caught her bus back to her hotel late that afternoon. She felt herself becoming emotional when she said goodbye to Val and to Tommy.

"You will continue to write, won't you?" she asked Val as they stood at the bus stop.

"Of course," promised Val. "It will be much easier now that you have seen the farm and we've met. Much easier."

The bus took Ilse off, its tired engine spluttering as it drew away from the stop. She waved to Val and Tommy through the window beside her seat. The window was dirty, and somebody had traced a message on its surface: **Harry loves Geraldine: true.** She raised a finger and wrote underneath it, **I have a true friend.** It was an odd, childish thing to do. Harry, who had written the other message, was probably sixteen or seventeen—unless, of course, it was Geraldine who had written those words, in the hope that what she said was true was really the truth.

Everything changed. A great wave of prosperity washed over Germany as the pinched, hungry years of the fifties gave way to a decade of plenty. In Britain, crisis followed crisis, as the world folded in over a country that was exhausted to its very bones. The youthful vanquished rebuilt and prospered; the aged victors looked on in puzzlement as their lucrative empire crumbled. Ilse sold the inn to a wealthy businessman who wanted it for a brother-in-law who had managed to escape from the East. Ubi moved the **Motodrom** to a site in the countryside. There was a house attached to the field in which the **Motodrom** now stood, and that became their home. A young mechanic, an enthusiastic motorcyclist, was taken on as the principal rider, and he brought with him a friend who joined him on the wall. A new road had been built nearby, an arterial highway that brought a stream of visitors to the attraction.

Ubi said to Ilse, "Did you ever imagine this? Ever?"

They were sitting outside the **Motodrom;**

inside, the roar of motorcycles and the rattle of the wooden planks that made up the wall reached a climax. The cheers of the crowd became raucous applause.

"They're enjoying it," said Ilse. And then, "I would never have believed we would be doing this. Running a **Motodrom**?"

"Yes. And everything else. The war. Klaus. Us." He smiled at her and touched her hand gently. "Very few people imagine their own future accurately. And then they're often pleasantly surprised."

Ubi occasionally rode the **Motodrom** himself, but he knew that Ilse did not like it, and he was careful in the routines he performed. The two young men had no such scruples and shot up and down, their paths intersecting with a bravado that made the spectators gasp with pleasure.

"If you kill yourselves," Ilse warned them, "you'll have only yourselves to blame."

"No we won't," said the younger of the two. "We won't be around to blame anybody."

"Don't tempt providence," Ilse retorted.

Ubi taught Ilse how to ride a motorcycle— not on the **Motodrom,** but sedately on the roads. She enjoyed this, and he bought her a modest machine of her own. He acquired for himself a large Ducati, painted red, and with gleaming chrome. They rode away together at weekends, leaving Klaus with Ilse's aunt and putting the young men in charge of the **Motodrom.** They rode down to Munich and to Regensburg. They joined a motorcycle club; Ubi became president while Ilse was elected treasurer. Klaus watched. He said, "I'm going to get a motorcycle, too, one day."

"One day," said Ubi, non-committally.

A month later, Ilse wrote to Val: **How do you stop a boy doing dangerous things? One of the young men who works on our** Motodrom **has somehow got hold of a miniature motorcycle and I caught him putting Klaus on it.**

**You can't stop them,** came the reply. **Boys do foolish things. It's what they do.**

Things went well for Val and Willy too. They had moved from the post office to live on the farm, and Willy had helped Archie get the stockman's cottage into order. They had installed a bath and a new range in the farmhouse kitchen, and she had sewn new curtains from material that Annie had obtained from somewhere. Annie was always getting hold of material, somehow or other—it had become a bit of a family joke. On good days, Archie would come up from his cottage and sit with her in the kitchen—where it was warmest—to look out on the fields that he could no longer work in, because of his arthritis. He knew every inch of the land, she thought, every inch. He would have cared for it, year after year, and his father would have done exactly the same, without complaint, without questioning their destiny to nurture this little bit of England for their lifetime, and then hand it over to the next generation to do the same.

Tommy would not do that, though, and they would have to find somebody else to run the farm in due course. Val knew, even when he was still a small boy, that he would do something different; that he would be an engineer. He was fascinated by machinery and how things worked. When he was seven, she bought him a book called **The Boy's Book of How Everything Works,** which contained cutaway illustrations of the insides of ships and locomotives and even planes. It was all laid out there, in coloured diagrams, and he had pored over these, often with Willy, discussing the mechanisms that made these things work. Willy was learning every bit as much as Tommy was, she felt; she overheard a conversation about jet propulsion.

"Where does the air go, Tommy?"

Tommy had taken Willy's finger and moved it to a place on the drawing. "It goes in there. You see? There. And then it gets heated up and it comes out there with a whoosh."

"Which makes the plane go forward?"

"Yes, Willy. Forward, you see."

She smiled at the memory. It did not matter to Tommy that Willy was slow to take new things in; the boy seemed to take that in his stride, and even took pleasure in explaining something that Willy was not immediately grasping. And later, when Tommy was old enough to understand, she explained to him about how Willy had agreed to look after them and how he worked hard to make up for the fact that they had lost his real father.

"He flew an aeroplane," she said. "Your first dad. He was a pilot."

"In the war?"

"Yes, in the war, as I've told you, lots of times—remember?"

"He was American?"

She nodded. "Yes, he was American, Tommy. He came from a place called Muncie, Indiana. He used to tell me about it."

"But you never went there?"

She took a moment to answer. That was an unfulfilled promise in a way—to Mike. Perhaps she would honour it some day, and she would take Tommy and show him the place where his father came from. "No, I didn't go there myself. But maybe one day you and I . . ."

"Yes. Yes. Please."

"We'll try."

She took a deep breath. She could so easily cry, but children became very anxious if an adult cried without reason—or without a reason they could comprehend. "There's another thing about your first dad—he was a very brave man. Some day you'll understand just how brave he was, but for now just believe me—he was a brave man."

He was watching her.

"And here's yet another thing," she said.

"We had a dog, you know. We had a dog with a funny name."

"How funny?"

"He was called Peter Woodhouse. And you know what? He sometimes went off with your dad in his plane. He was what they call a mascot."

"What's that?"

"It's an animal that people sometimes have to keep them company—they sometimes think that a mascot brings good luck." She paused. "Which I think might just be true."

He looked unconvinced. "How can an animal bring you good luck?"

She shrugged. "I don't quite know. But they do, I think. They can help when you're in danger. That's what those pilots thought."

"My dad thought that?"

"I think he probably did."

The boy looked thoughtful. "Do animals go to heaven when they die? Like people?"

One could answer from one's head, she thought, or from one's heart.

"I don't know," she replied. She touched him lightly on his head; on the sandy-coloured hair that came from his father. "But perhaps . . . just perhaps, they do. Perhaps dogs, for instance, go to a special heaven for dogs."

"With lots of bones for them to chew?"

She laughed. "Yes, with lots of bones, and plenty of smells. Dogs would love that, don't you think? Plenty of smells for them to sniff at."

"And rabbits to chase?"

"Yes, lots of rabbits. The rabbits that had been bad on earth, maybe—they'd be sent to dog heaven, which wouldn't be so much fun for them. The good rabbits would go to a place where **they** chased the dogs."

"Was Peter Woodhouse a good dog?"

"A very good dog."

"So he'll be in dog heaven?"

She smiled. "Yes, I expect he will be. Doing his job—which is to watch over us, I think. You and me. He'll be watching."

# FIVE
# AFTERWARDS

## 28

In June 1981, in the southern German city
of Regensburg, a meeting took place in the
office of a quietly spoken lawyer. The lawyer,
Franz Huber, was careful, almost fussy, in his
manner; this suited his practice, which was
mostly concerned with domestic affairs—
family property, wills, and the like—and with
the day-to-day issues of small businesses. He
had a talent for persuading clients to adopt
what he described as the "wise and cautious
solution" to the complexities of their affairs.
He was fond of saying, "Nobody has ever
regretted erring on the side of caution"—an
observation that, under any scrutiny, would
soon be shown to be false, but Herr Huber
had little interest in missed opportunities.

"Frau Dietrich," he said, tapping his pencil discreetly on the edge of his desk. "This
English lady? May I ask: Have you known
her for a long time?"

On the other side of his desk, Ilse tried to
conceal her irritation. She had never liked
Herr Huber, even if Ubi had thought highly

of him. They had had few professional dealings—there was not much call for that—but Ubi knew him from the swimming club they had both been members of, and had mentioned him from time to time. She knew that Ubi had placed his affairs in Herr Huber's hands, and she knew that this would mean she would have to deal with him in due course.

"Many years," she replied.

"And your husband knew her too?"

She nodded. "It was through him that we met, you see—a long time ago. My husband knew her husband, and that was how I knew about her. It was one of those strange things that happened in those days. People were brought together in odd ways."

He raised an eyebrow. "I don't wish to pry," he said. "But here you are, proposing to give your two employees a half share in the business, while you and this English lady go off on this trip you've been talking about . . ."

She kept her temper. There was no point in antagonising the man. "She has a name, Herr Huber. Mrs. Rogers. I call her Val. The

English are less formal than we are, as I'm sure you're aware."

"Yes, of course. Mrs. Rogers. Forgive me. Well, I really want to make sure that this Mrs. Rogers isn't persuading you to take this step. The late Herr Dietrich—your husband, of course—would not have wished you to divest yourself at this stage of the business he had built up. She is a newcomer, so to speak . . ."

She shook her head. "She is not a newcomer, Herr Huber. She has been coming to see me for years now. And we're only going away for a couple of months." And there was more. "These two employees have been with me for six years now. They have been very loyal."

The pace of the pencil-tapping increased—until he noticed that her eyes were fixed on it, and he rapidly put it away.

"You're going off on your motorcycles," he muttered.

"On one motorcycle," she corrected him. "I have a great deal of experience with motorcycles, as you can imagine. Herr Dietrich and I used to go on our holidays that way.

We rode all the way down to Italy. A large motorcycle is very comfortable for the pillion passenger—just as it is for the driver."

She saw a thin smile play about his lips. She did not have to justify herself to him, she thought. "The important thing is to be happy." Who had said that? Oh, hundreds of people, she thought; hundreds and hundreds of people through the ages, and all of them right. Because it was the important thing— the most important thing of all, when you came to think about it.

She glanced out of the window. There was a large tree directly outside, and its branches were moving in the breeze. In the distance, a hillside rose up to meet the pale summer sky. Perhaps it would be best to explain to him what had happened; this dry, essentially humourless lawyer might just understand— if she explained the history.

"My husband served in the war," she said.

She held his gaze. There was a flicker; just a flicker.

"And in the course of his service, he met an American airman."

His face was immobile. **He doesn't wish to be reminded.**

He spoke. "I see. An American airman."

"Yes. And then they met later on—during the Berlin Airlift."

Herr Huber relaxed. That was a different narrative, with a different set of victims.

"The American was married to an English-woman. He met her when he was stationed in England during the war. She came with him when he was based here in Germany—they were down in Wiesbaden, although he had to fly all over. He was one of the pilots who went into Berlin."

He was comfortable now. "That was so very important," he said. "If they hadn't done that ..." He shrugged. "The Soviets would have taken everything eventually. I doubt if we would be here today, having this conversation. We have a lot to thank the Americans for."

Ilse said, "You are right. It was very important. And they were brave men."

"Of course they were."

"He was one of the ones who was killed," she continued. "It was towards the end of the blockade—just days before, I think. They had to fly in all sorts of conditions. I don't think it was anybody's fault. Something went wrong, and his plane went down. We were in touch with his widow afterwards."

"Wartime friendships," said Herr Huber. "They can be very strong, I think."

"His widow went back to England—to her people."

Herr Huber nodded. "It's always best," he said. "If you can go home, that's the best thing to do. Always." He paused. "And then?"

"I wrote to her—my husband, you see, was not a very good correspondent. Men aren't, you see, and wives have to . . ." She trailed away. He was looking reproachful.

"**Some** men, Frau Dietrich. **Some** men— not all of them."

She inclined her head. "Yes, you're right— not all men. But, as I was saying, we wrote to one another over the years. Every year there was a Christmas card—that sort of thing— and a letter as well. She married again. She lived on a farm, over there; I went to see her, and then she came over to Germany every other year to stay with us."

The lawyer inclined his head. "I under- stand, Frau Dietrich—and it is not for me to interfere in your plans."

"No," she said. "It is not."

. . .

Dust, white dust of the sort that for its fineness took time to settle, was thrown up in a small cloud behind them as Ilse applied the brakes of the motorbike. It was hot, and when she switched off the engine the air was filled with the screech of cicadas. Someone in the distance was cutting wood with a buzz-saw, the old branches of a vine perhaps, because there were vineyards stretched out across the slopes of the hillsides here.

She silently coasted the heavy bike into the shade thrown by a sculpted birch tree. These trees formed a regimented line along the edge of the village; below them the land fell away sharply to the plains below. On the other side of the road was the village, a cluster of buildings ascending to a tangle of woods above which the sky, pale in this heat, was dizzying in its emptiness.

The village had no proper piazza, the public space being the area in front of the shops and houses that made up the main street. At the end of this one-sided street was a church, its open door looking to all intents and purposes like the mouth of a cave. At least it would be cool in there, with the rock as its floor and the shelter it provided from the relentless sun.

They stretched when they dismounted, taking off their helmets and putting them on the seats of the motorcycle before they stretched their legs. They had been riding non-stop since Florence that morning; the day before they had ridden all the way from Milan, and both had felt the aches that came with such a long spell on the road.

Now, though, there was lunch to look forward to, and the village at least boasted a proper restaurant with umbrellas outside and a table of old men sitting smoking and nursing glasses of the local red wine.

They sat at one of the other tables outside. There was a greeting from the table of locals, who had smiled at the sight of two women on a motorbike, and smiled even more when they saw their age. This would be talked about for days, analysed and speculated upon in a village where nothing ever happened other than the arrival of passers-by.

The proprietor brought them a large bottle of carbonated water. They sipped on this while they scrutinised the menu, which offered what it described as the "particular delights of the region."

Ilse said, "Well, I feel we're really on our way now. Home seems a long way away."

"It does," said Val. "And it is."

"With all its cares."

"Yes, with all its cares. Your wall of death . . . It's in good hands, isn't it?"

"Those two young men are completely reliable," said Ilse. "They're never happier than when they're going round and round, making the girls scream with delight. All our young men have been the same."

Val laughed. "What girl wouldn't like to see a young man going round and round a wall of death?" She paused. "Did you ever go on it yourself?"

Ilse nodded. "I used to—now and then. I rode one of the smaller bikes. I sometimes went on when Ubi was riding. He enjoyed it. He was never really happy running the inn, but when we gave that up to concentrate on the **Motodrom** he was very happy."

Val lifted her glass of water to her mouth. The bubbles were sharp on the tongue; tiny needles of sensation. "You must miss him," she said.

Ilse looked back at her. "Yes, just as you must miss Mike."

"When you marry again," said Val, "you don't talk about that too much. You're meant to be over it, but you aren't, you know. Not really."

"We have our boys, of course."

"Yes," said Val. "And Tommy's a good son. Now that he's working in London I don't see so much of him—and he's got his own young family now. Your Klaus—do you see a lot of him?"

"It's not too far to Stuttgart," said Ilse. "Three hours or so. He's doing well. He's never liked motorbikes since he fell off one when he was just a boy. He loves cars— which is why he's working for those people in Stuttgart—but motorbikes, no. He disapproves of my riding, you realise?"

Val smiled. "I think it shows we brought them up right if they disapprove of our behaviour."

"Perhaps. No, you're right. You're right."

The proprietor came to take their order.

"You've ridden down here all the way from Germany?" he asked.

"We have," answered Ilse. "And we're going on to Naples. Then Sicily. Palermo."

The proprietor suppressed a smile.

"You could join us if you like," said Val. "Do you have a motorbike?"

The proprietor laughed. "I have a wife," he said.

Ilse made a gesture of disappointment. "Oh well."

They were brought their food.

Afterwards, with coffee on the table, they sat under the shade of the umbrella and looked down onto the plains.

"You know," said Val, "there was something I was told that I don't think I ever passed on to you."

"Oh?"

"Yes. Mike told me. He said that when they were in Holland—when they were hiding from . . ." She stopped herself.

"From the Germans," Ilse supplied.

"Yes. But it was a long time ago. Let's say, different Germans."

"Something happened?"

"Yes. They had a dog with them."

"I heard about that," said Ilse.

"And your husband, your Ubi, was ordered to shoot the dog."

Ilse winced.

"But he did not," continued Val. "He saved the dog's life by firing a shot in the air."

Ilse was silent. "He did that?" she asked at last.

"Yes," said Val.

Ilse looked down at the tablecloth. "I'm glad you told me that," she said. "I'm very glad."

"You never knew it?"

"No. But I'm grateful you told me, because it makes me proud of him."

They were both silent. Then Ilse said, "Do you think it's possible to love somebody who isn't there any longer? To carry on loving him?"

Val looked up at the sky. A hint of a cooling breeze had sprung up and it touched her now. Swallows dipped and swooped in pursuit of prey in the higher layers of air; tiny dots of pirouetting black. The question was not a casual one, she thought; this was as important as anything they had said to one another. "Of course it is," she said. "Of course."

"Are you sure?"

"Yes, I'm quite sure." And then she added, "Look up there; look at the birds."

"What about them?"

"Nothing."

She thought: **You can go on loving people a long time after they have left you; you can love them every bit as much as you loved them when they were still here. Love lasts. Love grows stronger. Love lasts a lifetime, and beyond.**

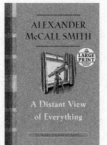

# The Gospel of Mary
## of Magdala

### JESUS AND THE FIRST
### WOMAN APOSTLE

# KAREN L. KING

*The Gospel of Mary of Magdala: Jesus and the First Woman Apostle*

Published in 2003 by Polebridge Press, P.O. Box 6144, Santa Rosa, California 95406.

Cover image: "Mary Magdalene" courtesy of and © Robert Lentz. Color reproductions available from Bridge Building Images, www.BridgeBuilding.com.

Photographs of PRylands 463 courtesy of the John Rylands University Library of Manchester.

Photograph of POxy 3525 compliments of the Ashmolean Museum, University of Oxford.

ISBN 0-944344-58-5

### Library of Congress Cataloging-in-Publication Data

King, Karen L.
  The Gospel of Mary of Magdala : Jesus and the first woman apostle /
Karen L. King.
      p. cm.
  Includes bibliographical references.
  ISBN 0-944344-58-5
  1. Gospel of Mary--Criticism, interpretation, etc. I. Title.

BT1392.G652K56 2003
229'.8--dc22                                         2003062350

# Table of Contents

## Part III
## The Gospel of Mary
## in Early Christianity

# Preface

Several foundations provided grant support to allow for work on this manuscript, and I would like to acknowledge my appreciation to them: the George A. and Eliza Gardner Howard Foundation, the Women's Studies in Religion Program of the Harvard Divinity School, and the Graves Foundation. In addition, my thanks to the National Endowment for the Humanities for a Travel to Collections Award (1996), which allowed me to make my own transcription of the fragments in Berlin, Oxford, and Manchester. For their hospitality and help, I would like to thank Dr. William Brashear, Dr. Günther Poetke, and Dr. Ingeborg Müller from the Ägyptisches Museum und Papyrussammlung, Berlin; Dr. Revel A. Coles, Papyrology Rooms, Ashmolean Museum, Oxford; and Dr. Peter McNiven of the Rylands Museum, Manchester.

The study of the *Gospel of Mary* which follows has benefited from many voices. Over the course of preparing this manuscript, I made presentations to numerous academic conferences, university courses, church groups from a wide range of Christian denominations, and feminist spirituality workshops. The critical and constructive responses of these groups has had a substantial impact on my own thinking about the meaning and significance of the *Gospel of Mary*. I would like to thank all those whose questions, comments, and objections led to beneficial rethinking and reworking of this manuscript. For the time and effort they gave in reading various portions of the manuscript and supplying vital critique and support, I would like to offer my sincere thanks to Francois Bovon, Ann Brock, Constance Buchanan, Robert Funk, Anne McGuire, Elaine Pagels, Hans-Martin Schenke, and Elisabeth Schüssler Fiorenza. I offer yet again my gratitude to Tom Hall, whose generous labor saved me from numerous grammatical infelicities and taught me salutory lessons along the way. My warm thanks, too, to Daryl Schmidt and Hershey Julien for their careful corrections of the final manuscript, and to Char Matejovsky for her professionalism and consistently good advice. My most profound thanks belong to Hal Taussig who read the manuscript in multiple versions, providing both critical response and encouragement when I needed them most. I would like to dedicate this book to him as an indication of my heart-felt gratitude for his friendship.

# Abbreviations & Sigla

## Abbreviations

| | |
|---|---|
| *ABD* | *The Anchor Bible Dictionary.* Ed. David Noel Freedman. 6 vols. New York: Doubleday, 1992. |
| *Acts* | *Acts of the Apostles* |
| *AgHer* | Irenaeus, *Against Heresies* |
| *ANF* | *The Ante-Nicene Fathers.* 10 vols. Ed. A. Cleveland Coxe. Grand Rapids, MI: Wm B. Eerdman's Publishing Company, reprint 1979. |
| *ApJas* | *Apocryphon of James* |
| *ApJohn* | *Apocryphon of John* |
| *1ApocJas* | *First Apocalypse of James* |
| *2ApocJas* | *Second Apocalypse of James* |
| *ApocPaul* | *Apocalypse of Paul* |
| *ApocPet* | *Apocalypse of Peter* |
| BCE | Before the Common Era |
| BG | Berlin Codex (Berolinensis Gnosticus) |
| *BkThom* | *Book of Thomas the Contender* |
| CE | Common Era |
| *Col* | *Colossians* |
| *1 Cor* | *First Corinthians* |
| *2 Cor* | *Second Corinthians* |
| *Deut* | *Deuteronomy* |
| *Did* | *Teaching of the Twelve Apostles (Didache)* |
| *DSav* | *Dialogue of the Savior* |
| *Eph* | *Ephesians* |
| *Gal* | *Galatians* |
| *GMary* | *Gospel of Mary* |
| *GNaz* | *Gospel of the Nazarenes* |
| *GPet* | *Gospel of Peter* |
| *GPhil* | *Gospel of Philip* |

| GSav | Gospel of the Savior |
|------|---------------------|
| GThom | Gospel of Thomas |
| GTruth | Gospel of Truth |
| HistEccl | History of the Church |
| Jas | James |
| JECS | Journal of Early Christian Studies |
| John | Gospel of John |
| Luke | Gospel of Luke |
| Mark | Gospel of Mark |
| Matt | Gospel of Matthew |
| NHC | Nag Hammadi Codex |
| NHLE | The Nag Hammadi Library in English, 3rd ed. Ed. James M. Robinson and Richard Smith. San Francisco: Harper and Row, 1988. |
| NRSV | New Revised Standard Version |
| Od | Odyssey |
| OrigWorld | On the Origin of the World |
| PetPhil | The Letter of Peter to Philip |
| 1 Pet | First Peter |
| 2 Pet | Second Peter |
| POxy | Papyrus Oxyrhynchus 3525 |
| Prov | Proverbs |
| PRyl | Papyrus Rylands 463 |
| PiSo | Pistis Sophia |
| Q | Synoptic Sayings Source (Quelle) |
| Rev | Revelation |
| Rom | Romans |
| SoJsChr | Sophia of Jesus Christ |
| TestTruth | Testimony of Truth |
| 1 Tim | First Timothy |
| 2 Tim | Second Timothy |
| Wis | Wisdom of Solomon |

## Sigla

[ ] Square brackets in the translation indicate that a lacuna exists in the manuscript where writing once existed; the enclosed text has been restored by scholars.

( ) Parentheses in the translation indicate material supplied by the translator for the sake of clarity.

< > Pointed brackets indicate a correction of a scribal omission or error.

# Part I

## The Gospel of Mary

Papyrus Rylands 463, recto

*Chapter 1*

# Introduction

## Early Christianity & the Gospel of Mary

Few people today are acquainted with the *Gospel of Mary*. Written early in the second century CE, it disappeared for over fifteen hundred years until a single, fragmentary copy in Coptic translation came to light in the late nineteenth century. Although details of the discovery itself are obscure, we do know that the fifth-century manuscript in which it was inscribed was purchased in Cairo by Carl Reinhardt and brought to Berlin in 1896. [1] Two additional fragments in Greek have come to light in the twentieth century. Yet still no complete copy of the *Gospel of Mary* is known. Fewer than eight pages of the ancient papyrus text survive, which means that about half of the *Gospel of Mary* is lost to us, perhaps forever.

Yet these scant pages provide an intriguing glimpse into a kind of Christianity lost for almost fifteen hundred years. This astonishingly brief narrative presents a radical interpretation of Jesus' teachings as a path to inner spiritual knowledge; it rejects his suffering and death as the path to eternal life; it exposes the erroneous view that Mary of Magdala was a prostitute for what it is—a piece of theological fiction; it presents the most straightforward and convincing argument in any early Christian writing for the legitimacy of women's leadership; it offers a sharp critique of illegitimate power and a utopian vision of

3

spiritual perfection; it challenges our rather romantic views about the harmony and unanimity of the first Christians; and it asks us to rethink the basis for church authority. All written in the name of a woman.

The story of the *Gospel of Mary* is a simple one. Since the first six pages are lost, the gospel opens in the middle of a scene portraying a discussion between the Savior and his disciples set after the resurrection. The Savior is answering their questions about the end of the material world and the nature of sin. He teaches them that at present all things, whether material or spiritual, are interwoven with each other. In the end, that will not be so. Each nature will return to its own root, its own original state and destiny. But meanwhile, the nature of sin is tied to the nature of life in this mixed world. People sin because they do not recognize their own spiritual nature and, instead, love the lower nature that deceives them and leads to disease and death. Salvation is achieved by discovering within oneself the true spiritual nature of humanity and overcoming the deceptive entrapments of the bodily passions and the world. The Savior concludes this teaching with a warning against those who would delude the disciples into following some heroic leader or a set of rules and laws. Instead they are to seek the child of true Humanity within themselves and gain inward peace. After commissioning them to go forth and preach the gospel, the Savior departs.

But the disciples do not go out joyfully to preach the gospel; instead controversy erupts. All the disciples except Mary have failed to comprehend the Savior's teaching. Rather than seek peace within, they are distraught, frightened that if they follow his commission to preach the gospel, they might share his agonizing fate. Mary steps in and comforts them and, at Peter's request, relates teaching unknown to them that she had received from the Savior in a vision. The Savior had explained to her the nature of prophecy and the rise of the soul to its final rest, describing how to win the battle against the wicked, illegitimate Powers that seek to keep the soul entrapped in the world and ignorant of its true spiritual nature.

But as she finishes her account, two of the disciples quite unexpectedly challenge her. Andrew objects that her teaching is strange and he refuses to believe that it came from the Savior. Peter goes further, denying that Jesus would ever have given this kind of advanced teaching to a woman, or that Jesus could possibly have preferred her to them. Apparently when he asked her to speak, Peter had not expected such elevated teaching, and now he questions her character, implying that she has lied about having received special teaching in order to increase her stature among the disciples. Severely taken aback, Mary begins to cry at Peter's accusation. Levi comes quickly to her defense, pointing out to Peter that he is a notorious hothead and now he is treating Mary as though she were the enemy. We should be ashamed of ourselves, he admonishes them all; instead of arguing among ourselves, we should go out and preach the gospel as the Savior commanded us.

The story ends here, but the controversy is far from resolved. Andrew and Peter at least, and likely the other fearful disciples as well, have not understood the Savior's teaching and are offended by Jesus' apparent preference of a woman over them. Their limited understanding and false pride make it impossible for them to comprehend the truth of the Savior's teaching. The reader must both wonder and worry what kind of gospel such proud and ignorant disciples will preach.

How are we to understand this story? It is at once reminiscent of the New Testament gospels and yet clearly different from them. The gospel's characters—the Savior, Mary, Peter, Andrew, and Levi—are familiar to those acquainted with the gospels of *Matthew, Mark, Luke,* and *John.* So, too, is the theological language of gospel and kingdom, as well as such sayings of Jesus as "Those who seek will find" or "Anyone with two ears should listen." And the New Testament gospels and *Acts* repeatedly mention the appearance of Jesus to his disciples after the resurrection. Yet it is also clear that the story of the *Gospel of Mary* differs in significant respects. For example, after Jesus commissions the disciples they do not go out joyfully to preach the gospel, as they do in *Matthew;* instead they weep, fearing for their lives. Some of the teachings also seem shocking coming from Jesus, especially his assertion that there is no such thing as sin. Modern readers may well find themselves sympathizing with Andrew's assessment that "these teachings are strange ideas."

The *Gospel of Mary* was written when Christianity, still in its nascent stages, was made up of communities widely dispersed around the Eastern Mediterranean, communities which were often relatively isolated from one other and probably each small enough to meet in someone's home without attracting too much notice. Although writings appeared early—especially letters addressing the concerns of local churches, collections containing Jesus' sayings, and narratives interpreting his death and resurrection—oral practices dominated the lives of early Christians. Preaching, teaching, and rituals of table fellowship and baptism were the core of the Christian experience.[2] What written documents they had served at most as supplemental guides to preaching and practice. Nor can we assume that the various churches all possessed the same documents; after all, these are the people who wrote the first Christian literature. Christoph Markschies suggests that we have lost 85% of Christian literature from the first two centuries–and that includes only the literature we know about.[3] Surely there must be even more, for the discovery of texts like the *Gospel of Mary* came as a complete surprise. We have to be careful that we don't suppose it is possible to reconstruct the whole of early Christian history and practice out of the few surviving texts that remain. Our picture will always be partial—not only because so much is lost, but because early Christian practices were so little tied to durable writing.

Partly as a consequence of their independent development and differing situations, these churches sometimes diverged widely in their perspectives on essential elements of Christian belief and practice. Such basic issues as the content and meaning of Jesus' teachings, the nature of salvation, the value of prophetic authority, and the roles of women and slaves came under intense debate. Early Christians proposed and experimented with competing visions of ideal community.

It is important to remember, too, that these first Christians had no New Testament, no Nicene Creed or Apostles Creed, no commonly established church order or chain of authority, no church buildings, and indeed no single understanding of Jesus. All of the elements we might consider to be essential to define Christianity did not yet exist. Far from being starting points, the Nicene creed and the New Testament were the end products of these debates and disputes; they represent the distillation of experience and experimentation—and not a small amount of strife and struggle.

All early Christian literature bears traces of these controversies. The earliest surviving documents of Christianity, the letters of Paul,[4] show that considerable difference of opinion existed about such issues as circumcision and the Jewish food laws[5] or the relative value of spiritual gifts.[6] These and other such contentious issues as whether the resurrection was physical or spiritual were stimulating theological conversations and causing rifts within and among Christian groups. By the time of the *Gospel of Mary*, these discussions were becoming increasingly nuanced and more polarized.

History, as we know, is written by the winners. In the case of early

Christianity, this has meant that many voices in these debates were silenced through repression or neglect. The *Gospel of Mary*, along with other newly discovered works from the earliest Christian period, increases our knowledge of the enormous diversity and dynamic character of the processes by which Christianity was shaped. The goal of this volume is to let twenty-first-century readers hear one of those voices—not in order to drown out the voices of canon and tradition, but in order that they might be heard with the greater clarity that comes with a broadened historical perspective. Whether or not the message of the *Gospel of Mary* should be embraced is a matter readers will decide for themselves.

## Discovery and Publication

Where did the *Gospel of Mary* come from?

Over a hundred years ago, in January of 1896, a seemingly insignificant event took place on the antiquities market in Cairo. A manuscript dealer, whose name history has forgotten, offered a papyrus book for sale to a German scholar named Dr. Carl Reinhardt.[7] It eventually became clear that the book was a fifth-century CE papyrus codex, written in the Coptic language (see Box 1). Unbeknownst to either of them, it contained the *Gospel of Mary* along with three other previously unknown works, the *Apocryphon of John*, the *Sophia of Jesus Christ*, and the *Act of Peter*.[8] This seemingly small event turned out to be of enormous significance.

Dr. Reinhardt could tell that the book was ancient, but he knew nothing more about the find than that the dealer was from Achmim in central Egypt (see map of Egypt, p. 12). The dealer told him that a peasant had found the book in a niche of a wall,[9] but that is impossible. The book's excellent condition, except for several pages missing from the *Gospel of Mary*, makes it entirely unlikely that it had spent the last fifteen hundred years unnoticed in a wall niche. No book could have survived so long in the open air. It may be that the peasant or the dealer had come by it illegally and, hence, was evasive about the actual location of the find. Or it may have been only recently placed in the wall and accidentally found there. In any case, we still don't know anything specific about where it lay hidden all those centuries, although the first editor, Carl Schmidt, assumed that it had to have been found in the graveyards of Achmim or in the area surrounding the city.[10]

---

Box 1    **COPTIC LANGUAGE**

Although the *Gospel of Mary* was originally composed in Greek, most of it survives only in Coptic translation. Coptic is the last stage of the Egyptian language and is still in liturgical use by Egyptian Christians, called Copts. The oldest known Egyptian language was written in hieroglyphs, always on stone or some other durable material. In addition, Egyptians also wrote on papyrus, and for this they used a different script called hieratic, employed almost solely for writing sacred literature. A third script, called demotic, was developed for everyday transactions like letter-writing and book-keeping. Each of these scripts is very cumbersome, utilizing different characters or signs to represent whole syllables, not just individual sounds as in English. Sometime during the late Roman period, probably around the second century CE, scribes started writing the Egyptian language in primarily Greek letters, but adding a few from demotic Egyptian. This process made writing Egyptian much simpler and more efficient. Since Coptic script was used almost exclusively by Christians in Egypt, we can assume that Egyptian Christians were the ones who translated and preserved the *Gospel of Mary*.

---

Dr. Reinhardt purchased the book and took it to Berlin, where it was placed in the Egyptian Museum with the official title and catalogue number of Codex Berolinensis 8502. There it came into the hands of the Egyptologist Carl Schmidt, who set about producing a critical edition and German translation of what is now generally referred to as the Berlin Codex (see Box 2).

From the beginning, the publication was plagued by difficulties. First of all, there is the problem of the missing pages. The first six pages,[11] plus four additional pages from the middle of the work, are missing. This means that over half of the *Gospel of Mary* is completely lost. What happened to these pages? Carl Schmidt thought they must have been stolen or destroyed by whoever found the book. The manuscript itself was found protected inside its original leather and papyrus cover (see photo, p. ii),[12] but by the time it reached Carl Schmidt in Berlin, the order of the pages had been considerably jumbled.[13] It took

---

$\text{Box } 2$     **THE BERLIN CODEX**

The book Reinhardt bought in Cairo in 1896 turned out to be a fifth-century papyrus codex. Papyrus was the most common writing material of the day, but codices, the precursor of our book form, had come into use only a couple of centuries earlier, primarily among Christians. The codex was made by cutting papyrus rolls into sheets, which then were stacked in a single pile, usually made up of at least 38 sheets. Folding the pile in half and sewing the sheets together produced a book of about 152 pages, which was finally placed inside a leather cover. The *Gospel of Mary* is a short work, taking up only the first 18¼ pages of a codex that itself is relatively small in size, having leaves that measure on average only about 12.7 cm long and 10.5 cm wide. (See photos, pp. 19–27.)

---

Schmidt some time to realize that the book was nearly intact and must therefore have been found uninjured. In an uncharitable and perhaps even rancorous comment, Schmidt attributed the disorder of the pages to "greedy Arabs" who must also have either stolen or destroyed the missing pages,[14] but to this day nothing is known about their fate. We can only hope that they lie protected somewhere and will one day resurface.

By 1912 Schmidt's edition was ready for publication and was sent to the Prießchen Press in Leipzig. But alas! The printer was nearing completion of the final sheets when a burst water pipe destroyed the entire edition.[15] Soon thereafter Europe plunged into World War I. During the war and its aftermath, Schmidt was unable to go to Leipzig and salvage anything from the mess himself, but he did manage to resurrect the project. This time, however, his work was thwarted by his own mortality. His death on April 17, 1938, caused further delay while the edition was retrieved from his estate and sent to press.[16] At this point, another scholar was needed to see its publication through, a task that ultimately fell to Walter Till in 1941.[17]

In the meantime, in 1917 a small third-century Greek fragment of the *Gospel of Mary* had been found in Egypt (Papyrus Rylands 463) (see Box 3). Being parallel to part of the Coptic text, it added no new passages to the *Gospel of Mary*, but it did provide a few variants and

---

**Box 3    PAPYRUS RYLANDS 463 (PRyl)**

This Greek fragment of the *Gospel of Mary* was acquired by the Rylands Library in Manchester, England, in 1917, and published in 1938 by C. H. Roberts.[18] Like POxy 3525, it was found at Oxyrhynchus in northern Egypt, and dates to the early third century CE. It is a fragment from a codex—it has writing on both sides of the papyrus leaf—and exhibits a very clear literary script. It measures 8.7 cm wide by 10 cm long, although most fibers measure only 8.5. cm. The front of the fragment contains the conclusion of Mary's revelation and the beginning of the disciples' dispute over her teaching. After a short gap, the dispute continues on the other side of the fragment and ends with Levi leaving to announce the good news (*GMary* 9:29-10:4; 10:6-14). (See photos, pp. 1 and 35.)

---

additional evidence about the work's early date and its composition in Greek. Till incorporated this new evidence into his edition,[19] and by 1943, the edition was again ready to go to press. But now World War II made publication impossible.

By the time the war was over, news had reached Berlin of a major manuscript discovery in Egypt near the village of Nag Hammadi. As chance would have it, copies of two of the other texts found within the Berlin Codex along with the *Gospel of Mary* (*Apocryphon of John* and *Sophia of Jesus Christ*) appeared among the new manuscripts. No new copies of *Gospel of Mary* were found at Nag Hammadi, but publication was delayed yet again as Till waited for information about the new manuscripts so that he could incorporate this new evidence into his edition of the Berlin Codex. But the wheels of scholarship grind slowly, and finally in exasperation, Till gave up. He confides to his readers:

> In the course of the twelve years during which I have labored over the texts, I often made repeated changes here and there, and that will probably continue to be the case. But at some point a man must find the courage to let the manuscript leave one's hand, even if one is convinced that there is much that is still imperfect. That is unavoidable with all human endeavors.[20]

At last in 1955, the first printed edition of the text of the *Gospel of Mary* finally appeared with a German translation.

Till was right, of course; scholars continue to make changes and add to the record.[21] Of foremost importance was the discovery of yet another early third-century Greek fragment of the *Gospel of Mary* (Papyrus Oxyrhynchus 3525), which was published in 1983 (see Box 4).[22] With the addition of this fragment, we now have portions of three copies of the *Gospel of Mary* dating from antiquity: two Greek manuscripts from the early third century (P. Rylands 463 and P. Oxyrhynchus 3525) and one in Coptic from the fifth century (Codex Berolinensis 8525).

---

## Box 4  PAPYRUS OXYRHYNCHUS 3525 (POxy)

This tiny and severely damaged papyrus fragment of the *Gospel of Mary* in Greek was found during excavations of the town of Oxyrhynchus, along the Nile in lower (northern) Egypt. Published in 1983 by P. J. Parsons, it is now housed in the Ashmolean Library at Oxford.[23] It dates to the early third century CE. The fragment has writing on only one side, indicating that it came from a roll, not a codex (book). Because it was written in a cursive Greek script usually reserved for such documentary papyri as business documents and letters rather than literary texts, Parsons suggested that it was the work of an amateur. What remains is a very fragmentary fragment indeed. It contains approximately twenty lines of writing, none of them complete. The papyrus measures 11.7 cm long and is 11.4 cm at its widest point, but the top half is only about 4 cm wide. The restoration is based largely on the parallel Coptic text. It contains the Savior's farewell, Mary's comforting of the other disciples, Peter's request to Mary to teach, and the beginning of her vision (*GMary* 4:11-7:3). (See photo, pp. 91.)

---

Because it is unusual for several copies from such early dates to have survived, the attestation of the *Gospel of Mary* as an early Christian work is unusually strong. Most early Christian literature that we know about has survived because the texts were copied and then recopied as the materials on which they were written wore out. In antiquity it was not necessary to burn books one wanted to suppress (although this was occasionally done); if they weren't recopied, they disappeared through neglect. As far as we know, the *Gospel of Mary* was never recopied after the fifth century; it may have been that the *Gospel of Mary* was actively suppressed, but it is also possible that it simply dropped out of circulation. Either way, whether its loss resulted from animosity or neglect, the recovery of the *Gospel of Mary*, in however fragmentary condition, is due in equal measure to phenomenal serendipity and extraordinary good fortune.

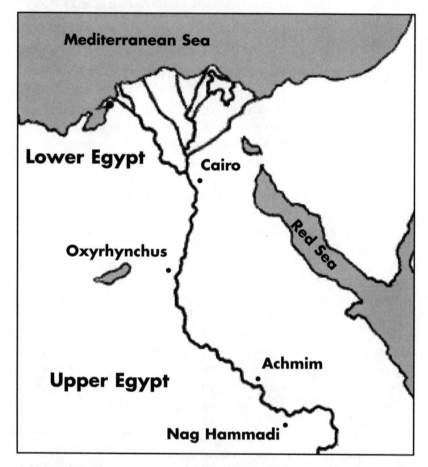

Achmim is located in central Egypt along the Nile, less than a hundred miles from the site of another important manuscript find near Nag Hammadi. Oxyrhynchus, the site of the discovery of the Greek fragments of the *Gospel of Mary*, lies far to the north.

# Chapter 2

# Translation

## Papyrus Berolinensis 8502,1

**1**  (*Pages 1-6 are missing.*)

**2**  *The nature of matter*
"… Will m[a]tter then be utterly [destr]oyed or not?"
²The Savior replied, "Every nature, every modeled form, every creature, exists in and with each other. ³They will dissolve again into their own proper root. ⁴For the nature of matter is dissolved into what belongs to its nature. ⁵Anyone with two ears able to hear should listen!"

**3**  *The nature of sin and the Good*
¹Then Peter said to him, "You have been explaining every topic to us; tell us one other thing. ²What is the sin of the world?"
³The Savior replied, "There is no such thing as sin; ⁴rather you yourselves are what produces sin when you act in accordance with the nature of adultery, which is called 'sin.' ⁵For this reason, the Good came among you, pursuing (the good) which belongs to every nature. ⁶It will set it within its root."

[7]Then he continued. He said, "This is why you get si[c]k and die: [8]because [you love] what de[c]ei[ve]s [you]. [9][Anyone who] thinks should consider (these matters)!

[10]"[Ma]tter gav[e bi]rth to a passion which has no Image because it derives from what is contrary to nature. [11]A disturbing confusion then occurred in the whole body. [12]That is why I told you, 'Become content at heart, [13]while also remaining discontent and disobedient; indeed become contented and agreeable (only) in the presence of that other Image of nature.' [14]Anyone with two ears capable of hearing should listen!"

## 4   The Savior's farewell

[1]When the Blessed One had said these things, he greeted them all. "Peace be with you!" he said. [2]"Acquire my peace within yourselves!

[3]"Be on your guard [4]so that no one deceives you by saying, 'Look over here!' or 'Look over there!' [5]For the child of true Humanity exists within you. [6]Follow it! [7]Those who search for it will find it.

[8]"Go then, preac[h] the good news about the Realm. [9][Do] not lay down any rule beyond what I determined for you, [10]nor promulgate law like the lawgiver, or else you might be dominated by it."

[11]After he had said these things, he departed from them.

### Papyrus Oxyrhynchus 3525

[11] ... having said [th]ese things, he de[parted.]

## 5   Mary comforts the other disciples

[1]But they were distressed and wept greatly. [2]"How are we going to go out to the rest of the world to announce the good news about the Realm of the child of true Humanity?" they said. [3]"If they did not spare him, how will they spare us?"

[4]Then Mary stood up. She greeted them all, addressing her brothers and sisters, [5]"Do not weep and be distressed nor let

## 5   Mary comforts the other disciples

[1][But they were distressed, weeping greatly.] [2]"How [are we to] g[o to the rest of the world preaching the good] news of the Rea[lm of the child of true Humanity?" they said. [3]"For if] they [did not spare him,] how will they keep [away from] us?"

[4][Then Mary stood up and greeted] them; she tenderly kissed [them all and said, "Brothers and sisters, [5]do not

## BG 8502

your hearts be irresolute. ⁶For his grace will be with you all and will shelter you. ⁷Rather we should praise his greatness, ⁸for he has prepared us and made us true Human beings."

⁹When Mary had said these things, she turned their heart [to]ward the Good, ¹⁰and they began to deba[t]e about the wor[d]s of [the Savior].

6 **Peter asks Mary to teach.** ¹Peter said to Mary, "Sister, we know that the Savior loved you more than all other women. ²Tell us the words of the Savior that you remember, the things which you know that we don't because we haven't heard them."

³Mary responded, "I will teach you about what is hidden from you." ⁴And she began to speak these words to them.

7 **Vision and mind** ¹She said, "I saw the Lord in a vision ²and I said to him, 'Lord, I saw you today in a vision.'

³He answered me, 'How wonderful you are for not wavering at seeing me! ⁴For where the mind is, there is the treasure.'

⁵I said to him, 'So now, Lord, does a person who sees a vision see it <with> the soul <or> with the spirit?'

## POxy 3525

weep, do not be dis]tressed nor be in doubt. ⁶[For his grace will be w]ith you sheltering you. ⁷Rather [we should] praise his [great]ness, ⁸for he has united us and [made (us)] true Human beings."

⁹[When Ma]ry [said these things] she turned their mind to[ward the Good ¹⁰and they began to debat]e about the sayings of the Savio[r.

6 **Peter asks Mary to teach** ¹Peter said to] Mary, "Sister, we know that you were greatly [loved by the Sav]ior, as no other woman. ²Therefore tell us t[hose wor]ds of the Savior which [you know] but which we haven't heard."

³[Mary] re[plied, "I will] rep[ort to you as much as] I remember that is unknown to you." ⁴[And she began (to speak) the]se words [to them].

7 **Vision and mind** ¹"When [the Lord] ap[peared] to m[e] in a vision, ²[I said], 'Lord, today [I saw y]ou.'

³"He replied, ['How wonderful you are … ' "]

## BG 8502

[6]The Savior answered, 'A person does not see with the soul or with the spirit. [7]'Rather the mind, which exists between these two, sees the vision an[d] that is w[hat … ]'

**8** (Pages 11-14 are missing.)

**9** *The ascent of the soul*
[1]" '… it.'

[2]"And Desire said, 'I did not see you go down, yet now I see you go up. [3]So why do you lie since you belong to me?'

[4]"The soul answered, 'I saw *you*. You did not see me nor did you know me. [5]You (mis)took the garment (I wore) for my (true) self. [6]And you did not recognize me.'

[7]"After it had said these things, it left rejoicing greatly.

[8]"Again, it came to the third Power, which is called 'Ignorance.' [9][It] examined the soul closely, saying, 'Where are you going? [10]You are bound by wickedness. [11]Indeed you are bound! [12]Do not judge!'

[13]"And the soul said, 'Why do you judge me, since I have not passed judgement? [14]I have been bound, but I have not bound (anything). [15]They did not recognize me, but I have recognized that the universe is to be dissolved, both the things of earth and those of heaven.'

[16]"When the soul had brought the third Power to naught, it went upward and saw the fourth Power. [17]It had seven forms. [18]The first form is darkness; [19]the second is desire; [20]the third is ignorance; [21]the fourth is zeal for death; [22]the fifth is the realm of the flesh; [23]the sixth is the foolish wisdom of the flesh; [24]the seventh is the wisdom of the wrathful person. [25]These are the seven Powers of Wrath.

[26]"They interrogated the soul, 'Where are you coming from, human-killer, and where are you going, space-conqueror?'

[27]"The soul replied, saying, 'What binds me has been slain, and what surrounds me has been destroyed, and my desire has been brought to an end, and ignorance has died. [28]In a [wor]ld, I was set loose from a world [an]d in a type, from a type which is above, and (from) the chain of forgetfulness which exists in time. [29]From this hour on, for the time of the due season of the aeon, I will receive rest i[n] silence.' "

### Papyrus Rylands 463 (PRyl)

[29]" '… for the rest of the course of the [due] measure of the time of the aeon, I will rest i[n] silence.' "

## BG 8502

[30]After Mary had said these things, she was silent, [31]since it was up to this point that the Savior had spoken to her.

## 10 The disciples' dispute over Mary's teaching

[1]Andrew responded, addressing the brothers and sisters, "Say what you will about the things she has said, [2]but I do not believe that the S[a]vior said these things, f[or] indeed these teachings are strange ideas."

[3]Peter responded, bringing up similar concerns. He questioned them about the Savior: "Did he, then, speak with a woman in private without our knowing about it? [4]Are we to turn around and listen to her? Did he choose her over us?"

[5]Then [M]ary wept and said to Peter, "My brother Peter, what are you imagining? [6]Do you think that I have thought up these things by myself in my heart or that I am telling lies about the Savior?"

[7]Levi answered, speaking to Peter, "Peter, you have always been a wrathful person. [8]Now I see you contending against the woman like the Adversaries. [9]For if the Savior made her worthy, who are you then for your part to reject her? [10]Assuredly the Savior's knowledge of her is completely reliable. That is why he loved her more than us.

[11]"Rather we should be

## PRyl 463

[30]After she had said these [words], Mary was sile[n]t, [31]for the Savior had spoken up to this point.

## 10 The disciples' dispute over Mary's teaching

[1]Andrew sai[d, "B]rothers, what is your opinion of what was just said? [2]Indeed I do not believe that the S[a]vior said these things, for what she said appears to give views that are [dif]ferent from h[is th]ought."

[3]After examining these ma[tt]ers, <Peter said>, "Has the Sa[vior] spoken secretly to a wo[m]an and <not> openly so that [we] would all hear? [4][Surely] he did[not want to show] that [she] is more worthy than we are?" ...

[6]"... about the Savior."

[7]Levi said to Peter, "Peter, you are al[ways] rea[dy] to give way to you[r] perpetual inclination to anger. [8]And even now you are doing exactly that by questioning the woman as though you're her adversary. [9]If the Savio[r] considered her to be worthy, who are you to disregard her? [10]For he knew her completely (and) loved her stea[df]ast[ly].

[11]"Rath[e]r [we] should be ashamed and, once we have clothed [ou]rselves with the

## BG 8502

ashamed. We should clothe ourselves with the perfect Human,
acquire it for ourselves as he commanded us, [12]and announce the
good news, [13]not laying down any
other rule or law that differs from
what the Savior said."

[14]After [he had said these]
things, they started going out [to]
teach and to preach.

[15][The Gos]pel according to
Mary

## PRyl 463

p[erfec]t Human, we should do
what [w]e were commanded.
[12][We] should announce [the]
good n[e]ws as [the] Savior
sai[d], [13]and not be la[y]ing
down any rules or maki[n]g
laws."

[14]After he had said [the]se
things, Le[vi] le[ft] (and)
began to anno[unce the good
ne]ws.

[15][The Gospel according to
Mary]

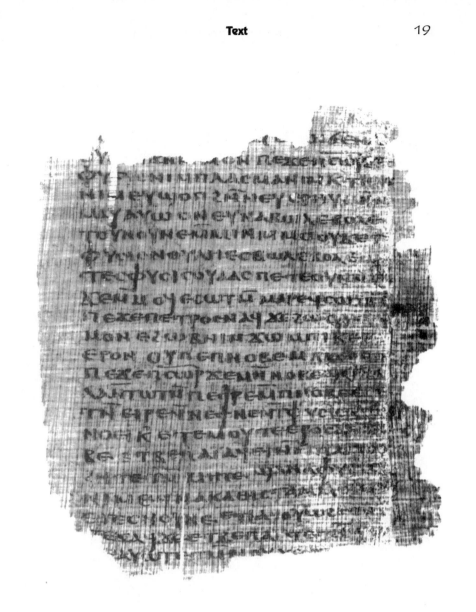

Page 7 of the *Gospel of Mary* from the Berlin Codex. Ägyptisches Museum u. Papyrussammlung SMB Inv.-Nr. P8502. Foto: Margarete Büsing. Used by permission.

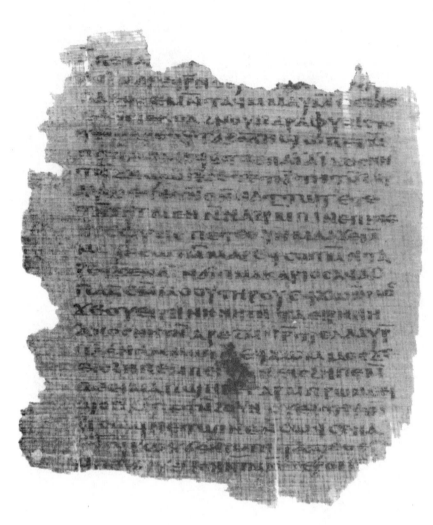

Page 8 of the *Gospel of Mary* from the Berlin Codex. Ägyptisches Museum u. Papyrussammlung SMB Inv.-Nr. P8502. Foto: Margarete Büsing. Used by permission.

Page 9 of the *Gospel of Mary* from the Berlin Codex P8502.
Staatliche Museen zu Berlin - Preußischer Kulturbesitz
Musterabzug für die Fotoabteilung. Foto: Karin Marz. Used by
permission.

Page 10 of the *Gospel of Mary* from the Berlin Codex P8502.
Staatliche Museen zu Berlin - Preußischer Kulturbesitz
Musterabzug für die Fotoabteilung. Foto: Karin Marz. Used by
permission.

Page 15 of the *Gospel of Mary* from the Berlin Codex. Ägyptisches Museum u. Papyrussammlung SMB Inv.-Nr. P8502. Foto: Margarete Büsing. Used by permission.

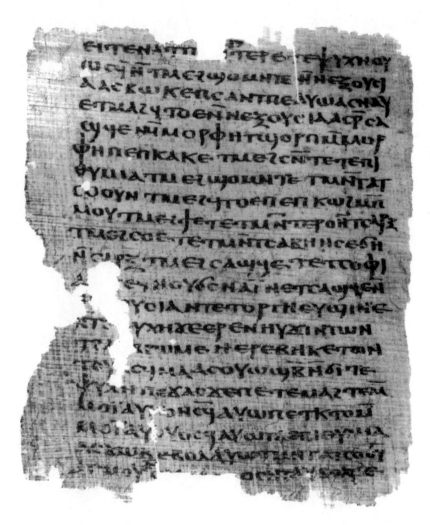

Page 16 of the *Gospel of Mary* from the Berlin Codex. Ägyptisches
Museum u. Papyrussammlung SMB Inv.-Nr. P8502. Foto:
Margarete Büsing. Used by permission.

Page 17 of the *Gospel of Mary* from the Berlin Codex. Ägyptisches Museum u. Papyrussammlung SMB Inv.-Nr. P8502. Foto: Margarete Büsing. Used by permission.

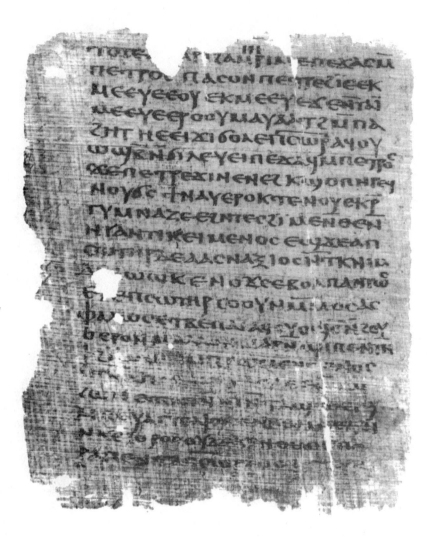

Page 18 of the *Gospel of Mary* from the Berlin Codex. Ägyptisches Museum u. Papyrussammlung SMB Inv.-Nr. P8502. Foto: Margarete Büsing. Used by permission.

Page 19 of the *Gospel of Mary* from the Berlin Codex. Ägyptisches
Museum u. Papyrussammlung SMB Inv.-Nr. P8502. Foto:
Margarete Büsing. Used by permission.

*Chapter 3*

# Gospel, Revelation, Dialogue

Since the first six manuscript pages of the Berlin Codex, constituting approximately one third of the text, are missing, and no Greek fragments of this portion of the text exist, we are left ignorant of how the work actually begins. The first surviving page opens in the middle of a discussion between the Savior and his disciples. However, both the commissioning scene (4:8–10) and the reference to the death of the Savior (5:3) which appear later in the text indicate that the setting is a post-resurrection appearance of the Savior to his disciples.[1] Indeed, all the commissioning scenes from the New Testament gospel literature occur after the resurrection.[2] The disciples in the *Gospel of Mary* must already know about the Savior's death, since they fear that they might suffer the same fate.

Post-resurrection appearances are found in all four of the New Testament gospels and *Acts*, as well as many other early Christian writings such as *First Apocalypse of James* and *Dialogue of the Savior*.[3] While they function to substantiate the reality of Jesus' resurrection, these appearances portray the post-resurrection period primarily as a time when Jesus gave special teaching[4] and commissioned disciples to go forth and preach the gospel.[5] Post-resurrection scenes typically include at least some of the following elements: the appearance of the risen

Lord, rebuke of fearful or grieving disciples, the association of special teaching with the risen Lord, the disciples as the recipients of the teaching, the mention of opponents, persecution for holding secret teaching, and a commissioning scene.[6] All of these elements are found in the *Gospel of Mary*, although it is focused heavily upon presenting the Savior's teaching, whether in his own words or through Mary's account of the revelation to her.

The title appended to the text identifies this book as a "gospel," a term commonly associated with a story of Jesus' life and teaching. But for the earliest Christians it meant not so much a biographical account as the "good news" of the kingdom[7]; it indicated the message and promise of the Savior, not the genre of the work. Indeed, the *Gospel of Mary* better fits the formal conventions of a post-resurrection dialogue.[8] It is structured as a series of dialogues and departures: 1) the dialogue between the Savior and the disciples, followed by the Savior's departure; 2) the dialogue among the disciples, followed by their departure (or at least Levi's departure) to preach the gospel; 3) the dialogue between the Savior and Mary, ending in her silence; and 4) the dialogues between the soul and the Powers, culminating in the soul's departure from the world to its final resting place.

These dialogues not only communicate the content of the *Gospel of Mary*, but they also emphasize the dialogical character of its teaching and their messages are amplified by the work's structure. For example, the structural similarity between the two main dialogues (1 and 2) authorizes Mary's teaching and her leadership role by placing her in a position parallel to that of the Savior: it is she who steps into the Savior's place by turning the other disciples toward the Good and providing them with advanced spiritual instruction. Moreover, while the first dialogue stands alone, the other three dialogues are embedded within one another, creating an ordered layering of teaching that draws the reader deeper and deeper inward. In the outer layer of the dialogue, the disciples are fearful and contentious, mistakenly concerned with the survival of their physical shells and jealous of their standing in the group. The next layer models the true disciple: Mary's complete comprehension of the Savior's teaching is signaled by her stability, her capacity to comfort and teach the Savior's words, and ultimately by her restful silence. The final and innermost layer of the dialogues takes place between the soul and the Powers, circling inward and upward toward the triumphal journey of the soul out of darkness and ignorance to exuberant joy and eternal rest. Both the content and the configuration lead the reader *inward* toward the stability, power, and freedom of the true self, the soul set free from the false powers of ignorance, passion, and death. In this way, the structure of the *Gospel of Mary* reproduces the same message as the Savior's teaching: "Acquire my peace *within yourselves*!... For the child of true Humanity exists *within you*. Follow it! Those who seek for it will find it."[9]

The repeated motif of departure also binds together content and structure, conveying the message that understanding requires a change of situation and action. The Savior's departure signals the eventual departure of the disciples, such that going out to preach the gospel becomes a step on the soul's journey to the Divine. The hearers are not to remain in this world, but are to follow the path of the Savior in preaching the gospel even as they are to follow the child of true Humanity within, the path forged by the soul in overcoming the Powers in the ascent to the Good. The repetition of the commission to preach, once at the end of the first dialogue and again at the conclusion of the gospel, functions formally to tie the Savior's departure to the disciples' mission to preach. Preaching the gospel is the direct consequence of understanding the Savior's message.

Throughout the journey of the soul toward comprehension, dialogue is key. The model for this dialogue is the ancient ideal of a pedagogical relationship in which the teacher's words and acts comprise a model to which the disciple ought to conform. Ancient culture was deeply suspicious of writing if it became detached from this intimate model, and Christians very early transformed this widespread ideal by understanding Jesus—not Scripture—as the truest revelation of God. As the second century theologian Irenaeus of Lyon argued, the incarnation of Jesus made God visible, so that by "becoming what we are, He might bring us to be even what He is Himself."[10] Irenaeus insisted: "We could have learned in no other way than by seeing our Teacher, and hearing His voice with our own ears, that, having become imitators of His works as well as doers of His words we may have communion with Him, receiving increase from the perfect One, and from Him who is prior to all creation."[11] For Irenaeus, both what one saw of the Lord and what one heard from him were equally to be enacted. While in many respects Irenaeus' theology differs significantly from that of the *Gospel of Mary*,[12] they agree that following the Savior requires both comprehension of his teaching and imitation of his actions. For the *Gospel of Mary*, communion with God was formed in dialogue with the Savior; the relationship between teacher and student cultivated an accurate understanding of divine reality and a pattern for ethical behavior. The message of the dialogue form is that relationship is fundamental to salvation, both that between teacher and student and that formed among the disciples in the community of faith and in their mission.

In the *Gospel of Mary*, first the Savior and then Mary take up the role of the teacher—the Savior by answering the questions of his followers, Mary by recounting her dialogue with him. Dialogue is the primary form of instruction because it insists upon the active participation of the student. The Savior attempts to inculcate proper attitudes in his disciples—for example by warning them not to fear the dangers that lay ahead, or by praising Mary's behavior when she had a vision of him: "Blessed are you for not wavering at the sight of me!" Her stability showed that she had overcome the fear that usually accompanies the appearance of a divine being. The interaction aims not at domination by the teacher, but at bringing the student to the level of the teacher; the Savior seeks to meet the needs of the disciples and raise their level of understanding as much as possible, even to the point where they are able to succeed him. The Savior has clearly been successful in this aim with Mary, since she is able to take his place after his departure. When the disciples are distressed at the Savior's departure, Mary comforts them precisely by turning their hearts and minds toward a discussion of the Savior's words. She responds to their request for teaching not in order to put herself above them, but in order to meet their need to understand more fully.

While dialogical pedagogy does presume that the teacher's status is higher than that of the student, this difference is neither permanent nor absolute; it should wane and at last disappear as the student progresses. The disciples are to find and appropriate the truth of the Savior's teaching for themselves, at which point they will no longer need a teacher. Indeed the Savior warns them against looking for some hero to save them; they are to look within: "Be on your guard so that no one deceives you by saying, 'Look over here!' or 'Look over there!' For the child of true Humanity exists within you."[13] Rather than accept an external authority, they themselves are to discover the truth in order to achieve the freedom and efficacy of the undominated soul.

The Savior's teaching against illegitimate domination pervades the *Gospel of Mary*. He explicitly instructs them not to "lay down any rule beyond what I determined for you, nor promulgate law like the lawgiver, lest you be dominated by it."[14] Elaine Pagels has pointed out that Peter's attempt to denounce Mary as a liar recalls such other attempts to silence women as that of *1 Cor* 14:34: "the women should keep silence in the churches; for they are not permitted to speak, but should be subordinate, *even as the law says*."[15] So too the Powers attempt to maintain their domination over the soul by judging and condemning it, much as in a law court. But the knowing soul resists and undermines their domination by refusing to play their game and by offering truth in the place of deception. It is true that both where Peter and Andrew challenge Mary, and where the Powers challenge the soul, the *Gospel of Mary* exposes how dialogue can foster harmful relationships as well as salutary ones. But it also offers a strategy for overcoming that harm: Speak the truth to power, call enslaving law and condemnation by their true names—deception and domination. True teaching does not deceive and dominate, it frees. Thus while dialogue by itself is not always good, it is crucial to creating proper relationships.

In the *Gospel of Mary* I tend to translate "kingdom" as "realm" precisely because the text's language itself is straining to articulate a sense of reality in which power is exerted for spiritual freedom not royal domination. So, too, the language of the "Son of Man" strains against the *Gospel of Mary*'s ideal of a nongendered space in which men and women exercise leadership based on their spiritual development and the resulting capacity to meet the needs of others. Here the phrase "Son of Man" is translated "child of true Humanity".

The dialogical form and content of the *Gospel of Mary* work together to communicate true teaching about the gospel of the Divine Realm. The soul's journey past the wicked Powers provides a narrative portrait of perfect humanity moving inward to discover the divine Good within. Here the soul, the true self, is purged of all its ignorance and attachment to the body. It is powerful and joyous. This vision of the perfected self forms the core of the text's deepest teaching. Both the content and the structure prompt the reader to look inward, toward the true self.

The form of post-resurrection dialogue also functions to authorize the *Gospel of Mary*'s teaching—even in the face of opposition—by attributing it to revelation. Here again form, function, and content work together. Many early Christian writings indicate that teachings received through appearances or visions of the risen Savior were considered to have a special validity. Already in *Galatians*, for example, it is clear that Paul considers the teaching that he received in a revelation of Jesus Christ to be more trustworthy than that which is passed on by mere humans.[16] Similarly, the authority of *Revelation* derives from its claim to record "the revelation of Jesus Christ" given to John.[17] The post-resurrection setting of the *Gospel of Mary* similarly functions to authorize its teaching.

By showing that Mary takes over important functions of the Savior, especially in comforting the disciples and providing them with special teaching, the *Gospel of Mary* associates opposition to Mary with opposition to the Savior. Those who oppose her oppose the Savior, and are on the side of the Powers who fight against the soul's escape. And having grounded its teaching on the authority of the Savior, the *Gospel of Mary* situates that teaching within the context of inter-Christian debate about salvation, the nature of sin and the world, the fate of the soul, the reliability of apostolic authority, and the question of women's leadership roles.

# Part II

## The Savior's Teaching in the Gospel of Mary

Papyrus Rylands 463, verso

## Chapter 4

# The Body & the World

The Savior's teaching makes up the substantial core of the *Gospel of Mary*, and Jesus is the central figure in salvation. He is called the Lord and Savior, and his teaching holds the key to eternal life with God. But the interpretation of that teaching in the *Gospel of Mary* differs radically from other common understandings. While it affirms the death and resurrection of Jesus, these events are not the core of Christian belief but rather the occasion for the disciples' mission to preach the gospel. The *Gospel of Mary* focuses instead on Jesus as a teacher and mediator of divine revelation. The Savior teaches that at death, the human body dissolves into the elements out of which it came; only the spiritual soul is immortal and lives forever. This knowledge leads people to discover the truth about themselves—that they are spiritual beings made in the Image of God—and it allows them to overcome the worldly attachments and bodily passions that lead to suffering and death. Therefore the final goal of salvation is not the resurrection of the body at the end of the age, but the ascent of the soul to God—both in this life by following the Savior's teaching, and at death when the bonds between the body and the soul are loosened beyond time and eternity. There is no hell and no eternal punishment in the *Gospel of Mary*'s teachings, for God is not conceived as a wrathful ruler or judge, but is called simply the Good. Nor is God called Father, for gender, sexuality, and the social roles ascribed to them are part of the lower material realm. Even the true spiritual nature of human beings is non-gendered, so that people are truly neither male nor female, but simply Human in accordance with the divine Image of the transcendent Good. Moral effort is centered on inner spiritual transformation, not on sin and judgment. Service to others is primarily understood as teaching people to follow the words of the Savior and preaching the gospel of the Divine Realm. The establishment of excessive laws and rules within the Christian community is understood as a tool for domination and is unnecessary for proper order.

These teachings were no doubt shaped not only in conversation and controversy with other Christians, but also, as we will see, in the crucibles of ancient intellectual and social life among the diverse societies under Roman imperial rule. While Jesus and most of his earliest followers were Jews, Christianity quickly spread around the edges of the Eastern Mediterranean, from Rome to Egypt, garnering Gentile followers as well as Jews living outside of Judaea/Palestine. The earliest extant Christian literature, the letters of Paul, documents the spread of Christianity through Asia Minor to the imperial capital of Rome itself during the first decades after the death of Jesus in Jerusalem. When Gentiles encountered the teachings of Jesus, many of the earlier connections to Jewish faith and practice receded, while the belief systems and world views of the new Gentile Christians brought other issues to the fore. Tensions over whether Gentiles who accepted Jesus needed to be circumcised or follow dietary laws gave way to other concerns. Some elements already in the Jesus tradition became more prominent, especially when they intersected with philosophical speculation and popular pieties. The *Gospel of Mary* provides one example of these kinds of Christianity.

The *Gospel of Mary* presents many familiar sayings of Jesus, but they are interpreted in a framework that may seem foreign to modern readers used to reading the literature of the New Testament as part two of the Bible, following the Hebrew Scriptures of the Old Testament. Interpreting the life and deeds of Jesus and his followers as the fulfillment of Hebrew Scriptures was crucial to early Christian claims that faith in Christ had superseded Judaism and indeed that Christians were the true Israel. By the fourth and fifth centuries this perspective was able to claim the name of orthodoxy for itself and condemn other views as heretical. In contrast, the theology of the *Gospel of Mary* shows almost no ties to Judaism since it developed out of the thought world of Gentile philosophy.

Yet the fact is that determining the proper relationship to Judaism became the single most important factor in distinguishing orthodoxy from heresy in the early period. Scholars themselves have been so influenced by the dominant orthodoxy that they have divided early Christianity into three basic types following this same factor. I call this the Three Bears story of Christian origins; that is perhaps somewhat flippant, but the illustration works too well not to use it. Jewish Christianity is *too much* Judaism and takes too positive an attitude toward Jewish practices like Sabbath observance and synagogue attendance. Gnosticism is *too little* Judaism or takes too negative an attitude toward Jewish scriptures and traditions. While orthodoxy is *just right*, drawing a firm line between Christians and Jews while simultaneously appropriating Jewish scripture and tradition for its own by claiming that they can be properly interpreted only in the context of their fulfillment by Christ.[1]

While this modern division of Christianity accurately reproduces the politics of normative Christian identity formation, it does not accurately describe how Christianity developed. Jewish Christianity and Gnosticism are modern inventions that have allowed scholars to categorize the diversity of early Christianities into a simple and indeed simplistic scheme, dividing the tremendous diversity of early Christianity into two basic types: orthodox and heretical. This scheme emphasizes the differences between orthodox and heretical theologies, overlooking the many similarities that existed. The real situation was much more convoluted and complex than this binary division suggests. Moreover, this scheme has allowed scholars almost effortlessly to classify the *Gospel of Mary* as a work of Gnostic heresy without looking carefully at what it is saying or striving to understand what it tells us about the development of early Christianity. One scholar even questioned whether the *Gospel of Mary* was Christian at all![2]

The old master story of the history of early Christianity is now being challenged and rewritten, primarily on the basis of newly discovered early Christian works. Not only the works from Nag Hammadi[3] and the Berlin Codex, but the *Gospel of the Savior* (recently discovered in the Berlin Egyptian Museum[4]), a new version of the *Gospel of Matthew* from the Schøyen Codex,[5] and other works not yet published are providing new grounds and resources for rethinking the history of Christian beginnings. The *Gospel of Mary* will play an important part in forging a new story.

Historians and theologians will need to take great care in how this story is written. Because orthodoxy has made the relationship to Judaism a central focus for defining Christian identity, the impact on Jewish-Christian relations must be a vital consideration. Some would argue that a work like the *Gospel of Mary*, which presents a type of Christianity largely unaffected by ancient Judaism, could further an anti-Jewish stance within Christianity. There is, however, no evidence of anti-Judaism within the *Gospel of Mary* itself, whereas the orthodoxy that developed in the fourth and fifth centuries was supersessionist by definition, and provided a basis for the gravely problematic dogma that God had rejected the particularism and literalism of Judaism in favor of Christianity's universal salvation and allegorical interpretation of Scripture. The depictions of both Judaism and Christianity presupposed by this dogma are inaccurate stereotypes. As we know too well in the twenty-first century, this kind of Christian anti-Judaism has led to horrific anti-Jewish and anti-Semitic acts since the ascendancy of Christian hegemony under the late Roman empire. Yet as Christian theologians continue to struggle against this heritage, my hope is that a more complex and more accurate history of early Christian development will strengthen their efforts while at the same time engaging the fact that Christianity in all its early forms was shaped within the pluralistic context of Greco-Roman society. This realization is especially important since Christianity is now a world religion. Most Christians today live outside of Europe and North America, so that the teachings of Jesus continue to be read and interpreted in a wide variety of cultural contexts. A complex history will take into account the situation of ancient pluralism in which ancient Christianity arose and, in so doing, may afford some insights into what it means to be a Christian in our own pluralistic world. My immediate point here, however, is a much smaller issue: that the prevailing orthodox view about the relationship of Christianity to Judaism, which we blithely characterize as the Judaeo-Christian tradition, was far from obvious to those by and for whom the *Gospel of Mary* was written. Because Christian identity had not yet been fixed in an orthodox form, alternative interpretations of Jesus' teachings were simply a part of the dynamic processes by which Christianity was being shaped. It is one of these alternatives that we will be exploring here.

One way to imagine the *Gospel of Mary* is to ask how someone with little or no real knowledge of Judaism, but steeped in the world view of ancient philosophical piety, would hear the teaching of Jesus. So powerful and pervasive is the prevailing perspective of orthodoxy that modern readers may well agree with Andrew that "indeed these teachings are strange ideas."[6] Strange to us perhaps, but not to the early Christians. They drew heavily upon popular Greek and Roman philosophy and piety, a fact obvious even in the canonical literature of the New Testament. Although written in the second century, the *Gospel of Mary* reflects a stream of interpretation reaching far back into the early decades of first century Christianity.

In order to imagine how the teachings of Jesus were heard among those for whom Platonism and Stoicism were common ways of thinking, it is important to give a brief overview of some of the ideas from those traditions that most strongly intersected with the *Gospel of Mary*'s teaching. Centuries before the *Gospel of Mary* was written, Plato had argued that a true lover of wisdom cultivates the soul and is not concerned with the pleasures of the body.[7] Since death is nothing more than the release of the soul from the prison[8] of the body,[9] he argued, the wise take care for the eternal well-being of the soul, not the crude and immediate demands of the body. Only through disciplining the body and avoiding as much as possible physical contacts and associations could the soul come to understand the truth of its own nature and the truth of Reality.[10]

Plato based these views on a distinction between what is eternal, immutable, uncreated, and known only through the mind (the Ideas or Images) and what is finite, mutable, created, and subject to sense-perception (the material world). The first is the Divine Realm of Reality, the latter the mortal realm.[11] The Divine Realm is completely free from evil of any kind, but evil cannot be done away with in the material world because evils are a part of mortal nature.[12] The created world was formed by imposing the pattern of the Divine Realm upon the material universe. Everything that is good and beautiful in the material world was made in the Image of the truly Good and Beautiful. That which is mortal and evil, however, has no Image in the Divine Realm because mortality and evil have no place in it.

There are, Plato says, "two patterns in the unchangeable nature of things, one of divine happiness, the other of godless misery." The character of each human soul is shaped by the pattern it follows. Fools led by their own ignorance and self-deception are, he says, unaware that "in doing injustice they are growing less like one of these patterns and more like the other."13 The wise, on the other hand, seek to conform as much as possible to the Image of the Divine. The goal of life, then, is to flee the mortal world with all its evils by becoming as much like the Divine as possible. Plato's character Socrates advises: "we should make all speed to take flight from this world to the other, and that means becoming like the Divine so far as we can, and that again is to become righteous with the help of wisdom. . . . In the Divine there is no shadow of unrighteousness, only the perfection of righteousness, and nothing is more like the Divine than any one of us who becomes as righteous as possible."14

"Fleeing the mortal world" could be accomplished both in this life through the cultivation of the soul by living a wise, free, and just life in this world, and in the next through the ascent of the soul to the Divine Realm at death. In this system, justice is meted out not by judges and courts of law, but by the workings of the universe. In this life, Plato wrote, the penalty of people's conduct "is the life they lead answering to the pattern they resemble."15 The good life is its own reward in this world. But the life one leads also determines one's fate at death. Unless fools change their unjust and immoral behavior, at death the Divine Realm will refuse to accept them and they will be forced to dwell on earth "for all time in some form of life resembling their own and in the society of things as evil as themselves."16 The wicked, Plato said, will be reincarnated into a form appropriate to their character: cowardly and unrighteous men become women; light-minded men become birds; and so on down to the most senseless and ignorant of all who become sea slugs.17 But those who attain a likeness to God through righteousness and wisdom are able to ascend forever out of the mortal sphere.18 Thus the only real punishment for wickedness is, so to speak, self-inflicted. Justice is built into the order of Reality itself.

For many people, however, the cosmos assumed a very different aspect. The early Stoic philosophers, for example, were largely materialists who rejected the existence of an immortal, immaterial soul. They argued that the universe and everything that exists is material by nature; even the soul is material, although it is made of particularly fine "stuff." The ethical teaching of the Stoics was very influential in antiquity, largely because much of it was very practical and focused on concerns of daily life. They taught that most external conditions are beyond a person's control, and that people achieve peace of mind only by focusing moral development on the interior attitudes that are under one's control. You can't help being short or having a beautiful nose, being born into poverty or slavery, but shaping an appropriate attitude toward those conditions is within your power. The Stoics argued that virtue is achieved not by fighting against the way things are, but by living one's life in accord with nature and reason.

For Stoics, the ideal state of the wise and virtuous person was *apatheia*. *Apatheia* literally means "without passion"; our word "apathy" derives from it. But while "apathy" in English implies passivity and disinterest, the Stoic teaching is much more active, insisting that the passions should be rooted out and destroyed, since evil is caused by the four cardinal passions: pleasure, desire, distress, and fear. There is a tendency in modern thinking to regard feelings as irrational or at least as non-rational. But the Stoics treated the emotions primarily in terms of their cognitive character.[19] They thought that the passions arise not out of feeling, but through ignorance and false belief. The four primary passions derive from the cognitive capacity to distinguish between good and bad, between present and future. In this scheme, pleasure is defined as "judgment that what is presently at hand is good"; desire as "judgment that something still in the future is good or valuable"; distress as "judgment that what is presently at hand is bad"; and fear as "judgment that what is still in the future is bad."[20] The diseases of the soul are caused by accepting value judgments that are *false*. Only sound teaching and accurate knowledge of the truth about Reality can heal people of the diseases that wrack the whole self, body and soul. Hence the cardinal virtues of the wise person are moral insight, courage, self-control, and justice, all of which help a person make correct judgments and instill the character necessary to render those judgments into right behavior and attitudes. Moreover, many Stoics held that because the passions arise out of *false* ideas that have hardened into fixed dispositions of the soul, they need to be completely wiped out rather than merely moderated. Only complete extirpation of the passions could lead the soul to internal stability and tranquility.

By the time the *Gospel of Mary* was written, ideas from Platonists and Stoics had permeated popular culture in the eastern Mediterranean in much the same way that we modern Americans are all armchair psychologists, talking about childhood traumas, neuroses, and complexes whether or not we've ever actually read Freud. To greater or lesser degrees the ideas of these thinkers had become removed from their earlier literary and intellectual contexts. They had poured out of the relatively close parameters of the Greek city-state and spilled over the broad geographical area and the diverse cultures encompassed by the Roman empire. Shifts in time and place meant that the social, political, and intellectual contexts within which people reflected upon such topics as human nature, justice, and ethics had shifted as well. The variety of the languages and cultures encompassed by the Roman empire ensured that Greek ideas were woven into new fabrics and turned to new constructions. In the pluralistic mix of ancient urban life, ideas that had been separate and indeed logically incompatible began to cohabit. The Stoic ideal of *apatheia*, for example, could be neatly grafted onto a Platonizing, dualistic conception of ethics as conflict between the body and the immaterial soul.

Historians have some idea of how the elite philosophers of the early Roman empire developed Platonic and Stoic ideas. But we know less about the form in which such ideas reached the general population, and how they were actually interpreted and employed by the vast semi-literate or illiterate majority of the population.[21] If the *Gospel of Mary* is any indication of popular thinking,[22] then it is clear that Plato's teaching had moved in directions that would no doubt have astonished him. A resurrected Jesus instructing his followers to tend their immortal souls and extirpate their passions in good Stoic fashion, so that at death they could outwit and defeat the wicked Powers who would try to stop them on their heavenly journey—such a portrait tells us that we have come a long way from the dinner party conversations of Athens' elite male citizens. Comparisons of the *Gospel of Mary*'s thinking with the ideas of Plato and the Stoics will allow us in some measure to chart the distance. There are four points of significant confluence: the association of evil with material nature, the need for correct knowledge of Reality to free the soul from the influence of the passions, an ethical orientation toward conformity with the pattern of the Good, and the ascent of the soul to the Divine Realm at death. But in each of these areas, the *Gospel of Mary* develops its thinking out of the Jesus tradition, and that made an enormous difference in both its theological content and social dynamics. In order to grasp further the significance of these ideas, they will be discussed below in greater detail under four rubrics: 1) the body and the world, 2) sin, judgment and law, 3) the Son of Man, and 4) the rise of the soul.

## The Body and the World

The extant portion of the *Gospel of Mary* opens in the middle of a dialogue between the Savior and his disciples constructed in a question-and-answer format. The topics are framed around questions from the disciples, followed by extended answers from the Savior. Each answer concludes with the formula, "Whoever has two ears to hear should listen," a saying well-attested in the Jesus tradition.[23]

The first topic of the existing dialogue concerns the nature of the material universe. One of the disciples asks: "Will matter then be utterly destroyed or not?" The Savior responds that although all material things form an interconnected unity,[24] they have no ultimate spiritual value and in the end will dissolve back into their original condition, which he calls their "root."[25]

The language in which the question and its answer are framed shows the influence of contemporary philosophical debates over whether matter is preexistent or created. If matter is preexistent, then it is eternal; if it is created, then it is subject to destruction. Only a few early philosophers, such as Eudorus of Alexandria (first century BCE),[26] held that matter was created out of nothing, although this position later became widely accepted. A more common position for the early period is reported by Cicero when he discusses the Platonists:

> But they hold that underlying all things is a substance called 'matter,' entirely formless and devoid of all 'quality,'. . . and that out of it all things have been formed and produced, so that this matter can in its totality receive all things and undergo every sort of transformation throughout every part of it, and in fact even suffers dissolution, not into nothingness but into its own parts.[27]

This concept presumes that matter has no form or qualities of its own; it is simply the substratum that is subject to being formed or produced.

The Savior agrees: everything will dissolve back into its own proper root. It does not matter whether things occur by nature, whether they have been molded out of formlessness, or whether they have been created from nothing, all will return to their original condition. He doesn't take a clear position on whether that natural state is formlessness or nothingness, but either way his point is clear: "anyone with two ears" should realize that because the material realm is entirely destined for dissolution, it is temporary, and therefore the world and the body have no ultimate spiritual value.

For both Plato and the *Gospel of Mary*, there are two natures, one belonging to the material world and one to the Divine Realm. Evil belongs only in the material world and is associated with the finite and changing character of material reality. The nature of the Divine Realm is perfect Goodness, unchanging and eternal. The material world is the place of suffering and death; the Divine Realm offers immortality in peace. The dualism between the material and the Divine is definitely sharper in the *Gospel of Mary* than in Plato, but we would do well not to exaggerate it. The Savior argues that the material world is destined to dissolve back into its original root-nature; he does not say that it is evil and will be destroyed.

The position that the world is fleeting is hardly new to Christian thought. Paul had written that "the form of this world is passing away,"[28] and the *Gospel of Mark* says that "heaven and earth will pass away."[29] The difference is that they expected this dissolution to be the prelude to a new creation. For the *Gospel of Mary*, there will be no new creation. Dissolution is the final state, when everything that is now mixed up together will be separated and return to its proper "root"—the material to its formless nature or nothingness, and the spiritual to its root in the Good.

What difference does it make, we might wonder, whether one conceives of final salvation to be a future life with God in a new and righteous world, or spiritual life with God beyond time and matter? Clearly for all parties concerned, the question about the ultimate fate of the world was bound up with ethics. This linkage can be seen explicitly in *2 Peter*:

> But the day of the Lord will come like a thief, and then the heavens will pass away with a loud noise, and the elements will be dissolved with fire, and the earth and the works that are upon it will be burned up. Since all these things are thus to be dissolved, what sort of person ought you to be in lives of holiness and godliness, waiting for and hastening the coming of the day of God, because of which the heavens will be kindled and dissolved, and the elements will melt with fire! But according to his promise we wait for new heavens and a new earth in which righteousness dwells (2 *Pet* 3:10–13).

Knowing that this world will end calls people to give priority to what will not end. The author of *2 Peter* claims that the divine power of "our God and Savior Jesus Christ" has granted "great promises" through which "you may escape from the corruption that is in the world because of passion, and become partakers of the divine nature" (*2 Pet* 1:1, 4). Believers are admonished to supplement their faith with virtue, their virtue with knowledge, their knowledge with self-control, and their self-control with steadfastness, godliness, brotherly affection and love.[30] They can do this because they have been cleansed from their old sins.[31] But if they turn away from this path, they will be subject to God's judgment, condemnation, and punishment.[32] The *Gospel of Mary* agrees with the teachings of *2 Peter* on many issues: that the ultimate dissolution of this world should call people to turn to God; that passion is at the root of the world's corruption; that believers are called to the divine nature, to faith, virtue, and knowledge. Where they part company concerns how they understand sin and judgment.

## Chapter 5

# Sin, Judgment, & Law

After hearing that matter will be dissolved, Peter asks, "What is the sin of the world?" The Savior responds, "There is no such thing as sin." For modern readers who perhaps too narrowly associate Christianity with the doctrine of the fundamental sinfulness of humanity, this statement could be shocking. But the Savior's surprising response needs to be read in the context of the discussions about matter which both precede and follow it. While the *Gospel of Mary* clearly defines sin differently from its common interpretation as wrong action or as the transgression of moral or religious laws, Christian theology generally understands sin as the condition of human estrangement from God. And this meaning is closer to the sense of the *Gospel of Mary*, in which the Savior is primarily concerned to orient the soul toward God.

The substantive difference is not the nature of sin, but the nature of the human body. Contrary to the view that later became basic to Christian orthodoxy, the *Gospel of Mary* does not regard the body as one's self. Only the soul infused with the spirit carries the truth of what it really means to be a human being. Since matter will eventually dissolve back into its constituent nature, the material world cannot be the basis for determining good and evil, right and wrong. Compare the *Gospel of Philip*:

... neither are the good good, nor the evil evil, nor is life life, nor death death. This is why each one will dissolve into its original source. But those who are exalted above the world will not be dissolved, for they are eternal (*GPhil* 53:17–23).

From this perspective, sin does not really exist insofar as it is conceived as action in the material world, which will be dissolved. At death the soul is released from the body and ascends to rest with God beyond time and eternity. The corpse returns to the inanimate material substance or nothingness out of which it arose. As a result, ethical concern is focused upon strengthening the spiritual self since it is the true, immortal, real self.

For the *Gospel of Mary*, the sinfulness of the human condition, the estrangement from God, is caused by mixing together the spiritual and material natures. While insisting that no sin exists *as such,* the Savior goes on to clarify that people do produce sin when they wrongly follow the desires of their material nature instead of nurturing their spiritual selves. He describes this sin as "adultery," an illegitimate mixing of one's true spiritual nature with the lower passions of the material body.[1] To sin means that people turn away from God toward concern for the material world and the body because they have been led astray by the passions. The disciples themselves produce sin by acting "according to the nature of adultery" (3:4). The metaphor fits the Savior's point quite well. Like adultery, sin joins together what should not be mixed: in this case, material and spiritual natures. Attachment to the material world constitutes adulterous consorting against one's own spiritual nature.

This attachment, the Savior says, is what leads people to sicken and die: "for you love what deceives you" (3:8). People's own material bodies deceive them and lead them to a fatal love of perishable material nature, which is the source of the disturbing passions, as well as physical suffering and death. This suffering, however, is deceptive because true knowledge can never be based upon unreliable bodily senses. When the soul "tries to investigate anything with the help of the body," Plato writes, "it is obviously led astray."[2] True Reality can be apprehended only when thought is free of all physical contact and associations.[3] This is basically what the Savior means when he tells Mary of Magdala: "Where the mind is, there is the treasure" (*GMary* 7:4). Turning the soul toward God would therefore not only lead people away from sin, it would overcome suffering and death. But people cannot accomplish this without true knowledge, since they are driven by the passions.

Yet there is hope: "For this reason, the Good came among you, pursuing (the good) which belongs to every nature. It will set it within its root" (*GMary* 3:5–6). God came to humanity in order to establish people in their true nature and set them up firmly within their proper "root," the natural good within themselves. The word "root" is used twice in the text (*GMary* 2:3; 3:6). Like English, the Coptic and Greek terms have a wide range of metaphorical implications: cause, origin, source, foundation, proper place, and so on. Here the "root" of perishable matter is contrasted with the proper "root" of a person's true spiritual nature which the Good will establish.

In 3:10-14, the Savior goes on to develop this distinction between matter and true nature, relying again upon the Platonic distinction between the changeable material world and the immutable world of Ideas (or Forms).[4] He says that "matter gave birth to a passion which has no Image because it derives from what is contrary to nature" (*GMary* 3:10). To say that passion "has no Image" means that it is not a true reflection of anything in the immutable Divine Realm. Because the passions are tied to suffering and deception and because no evil or falsehood belong to the Good, no divine Image of passion can really exist because true Reality belongs only to the Divine Realm. One might even say that "matter has no Image" because it lacks a heavenly origin and is contrary to the true nature of spiritual Reality; everything which is true and good is an Image of the divine Reality above.[5]

But that does not mean that the suffering caused by the passions is not real; passions lead to a disturbing confusion that wracks the entire body. The *Gospel of Mary* says that people suffer because they are led by the unnatural and deceptive passions of the body. The material nature of the body is the source of the disturbing passions, as well as of suffering and death. Peace of heart can be found only by turning away from conformity to this false nature, and forming one's true self to "that other Image of nature"[6] which the Good came to "set within its root." The teaching of the *Gospel of Mary* agrees very strongly with the Stoics that proper judgment based on a sure knowledge of Reality is necessary to overcome the devastating influence of the passions. It turns in a more Platonizing direction, however, in thinking that the diseases of the soul are caused in large part by people's failure to understand that their true nature is not material, but spiritual. It also agrees with Plato's basic principle that although the immutable, spiritual Realm does not appear in this material world as it is in and of itself, it can be known through Images. The *Gospel of Philip* puts it this way:

> Truth did not come into the world naked, but it came in types and images. The world will not receive truth in any other way (*GPhil* 69:7–11).[7]

When the Savior admonishes his disciples to "become contented and agreeable in the presence of that other Image of nature" (*GMary* 3:13), he is admonishing them to conform to the pattern of the Divine Realm. "That other Image of nature" is the reflection of the heavenly Realm that allows Divine Reality to be comprehended in the material world. It is this Image which the Savior will later admonish his disciples to seek within themselves. By turning toward the Good, the soul comes to follow its true spiritual nature and is no longer disturbed by the confusion of the body. The implication may be that if people were to conform to the spiritual nature of the Good, as the Savior teaches them, all the troubling confusion of the body would cease, and they would find both physical health and inner peace in this life, as well as attain salvation at death.

As was discussed above, the distinction between "the nature of matter which has no Image" and "that other Image of nature" is based on a philosophical distinction between the material world of sense perception and the Divine Realm. Although Plato considered the lower material world to be only an inferior copy of the higher Divine Realm of true Being, he still thought it was as good as it could possibly be, and beliefs about it were still useful, if not absolutely reliable. But in the *Gospel of Mary*, these views take on a more strictly dualistic cast in the light of human suffering. Confidence in material things is now equated with the deception that leads to death. "Anyone with two ears should listen," the Savior concludes (3:14).

Where the *Gospel of Mary* departs radically from the elite teachings of Plato and the Stoics is its insistence that sure knowledge comes only through the revelation of the Savior. Through Jesus' teachings, believers have access to a true understanding of the spiritual realities and therefore the possibility of salvation. The *Gospel of Mary* is less confident than the ancient Greeks that humans can discern the truth of things through the exercise of reason. Yet while less optimistic about the condition of life in the material world than is Plato, it is also more utopian in regarding the soul's spiritual orientation to God as the source of healing and salvation. In taking this position, the *Gospel of Mary* marks out one of its decidedly Christian features.

Intimately tied to these ideas about the nature of the world and sin are the Savior's teachings about law and judgment. When he commissions the disciples to go out to preach the gospel, he charges them: "Do not lay down any rule beyond what I determined for you, nor promulgate law like the lawgiver, or else you might be dominated by it" (*GMary* 4:9–10). Levi repeats this injunction at the end of the work before going forth to preach (10:13). How are we to understand this command? The "lawgiver" is surely a reference to Moses and hence to Jewish law. We know from other early Christian literature that in the first century considerable controversy among both Jews and Christians arose over how to interpret Jewish law. The *Gospel of Matthew*, for example portrays Jesus in conflict with other Jews over whether it is lawful to heal or to pluck grain on the Sabbath. When Jesus is charged with lawlessness, he responds that "The Sabbath was made for humans, not humans for the Sabbath" (*Mark* 2:27) and again "It is not what goes into a person, but what comes out that determines whether a person is clean or not"(*Matt* 15:11).[8] Yet he also says:

> Think not that I have come to abolish the law and the prophets; I have come not to abolish them but to fulfill them. For truly, I say to you, till heaven and earth pass away, not an iota, not a dot, will pass from the law until all is accomplished. Whoever then relaxes one of the least of these commandments and teaches people to do so, shall be called least in the kingdom of heaven; but whoever does them and teaches them shall be called great in the kingdom of heaven (*Matt* 5:17–19).

For the *Gospel of Matthew*, the issue is not whether to obey the law or not, but how to understand properly what the law demands. In his letter to the Galatians, Paul strongly opposed other apostles by insisting that Gentiles who believe in Jesus Christ need not be circumcised or follow the purity laws regulating food preparation and consumption. He concludes, "We ourselves, who are Jews by birth and not Gentile sinners, yet who know that a person is not justified by works of the law but through faith in Jesus Christ, even we have believed in Christ Jesus, in order to be justified by faith in Christ, and not by works of the law, because by works of the law shall no one be justified" (*Gal* 2:15–16). For Paul, the law is from God, but it is not adequate to bring about salvation. "So the law is holy, the commandment is holy and just and good," Paul writes in *Rom* 7:12. And again, "Do we then overthrow the law by this faith? By no means! On the contrary, we uphold the law!" (*Rom* 3:31). In the end, however, "There is now no condemnation for those who are in Christ Jesus. For the law of the Spirit of life in Christ Jesus has set me free from the law of sin and death" (*Rom* 8:1–2).

But these questions about the Jewish law, so crucial to early Christian self-definition, are not at issue in the *Gospel of Mary*. Rather the Savior is cautioning his disciples against *laws they themselves set*; it is these that will come to rule and restrict them. The Savior's command in the *Gospel of Mary* belongs to intra-Christian debate about the source of authority for Christian life and salvation, not the relationship to Jewish law. The reference to the "lawgiver" appears to be merely a remnant carried over from another setting where the relationship to Jewish law was an issue. But now in a Gentile context, the rejection of law has come to have a very different meaning. The Savior's point in the *Gospel of Mary* is that spiritual advancement cannot be achieved through external regulation; it has to be sought by transformation within a person. Not Mosaic law, but *Christian* regulations are seen to be the problem. This point is strengthened by noting that when Levi repeats the Savior's injunction, he leaves out any reference to "the lawgiver," saying only that they should "not lay down any other rule or law that differs from what the Savior said" (10:13).

Why emphasize this point by repeating it? Two scenes in the *Gospel of Mary* allow us to grasp more fully what was at stake. The first appears in the dialogue between the soul and the Powers who judge and condemn the soul, seeking to keep it bound under their domination. The second Power, Ignorance, in particular provides an explicit example of false judgment (9:8–15). It commands the soul "Do not judge!"—but it is the one who has judged and condemned the soul, declaring that it is bound by wickedness! The soul responds by declaring that it has not judged; it has not bound anything, even though it has been bound—not of course by wickedness, but by its attachment to the body and the world. Now that it has left these behind, the soul is no longer subject to the condemnation of Ignorance nor of any other Power. Judgment and condemnation for sin belong to the lower world; once the soul has been set free, the Powers no longer have any power over it. This scene evinces a deep distrust of moral systems of law, styling them as a tool of illegitimate power based on the desire to dominate, ignorance of divine Reality, and vengeful wrath. The rules and laws set by the Savior are understood to lead one to spiritual freedom; they are free of the kind of ignorant and vicious judgments fed by the passions of the lower world. We can easily grasp the logic behind this stance by thinking about situations in our own world where legal systems and law enforcement are dominated by practices and policies that are fundamentally unjust or that serve only to bolster or ensure the status and safety of some groups, but not others. South Africa under apartheid is a notable example, but even in the United States unequal practices are all too often concomitant with differences in race or economic status.

Another scene exemplifying the text's attitude toward law and judgment appears in the dialogue between Mary and Peter. He does not understand the teachings of the Savior, and yet he judges Mary by calling her a liar. His words incite conflict among the disciples, leading Levi to point out that he is acting like a hot-head and treating Mary as though she were his adversary, not his sister. Levi recalls the words of the Savior in an attempt to dispel the conflict and bring the disciples back to their mission to preach the gospel. In this scene, Peter vociferously rejects Mary's words and denounces her because he is jealous that the Savior seemed to prefer her, a woman, to himself—and he tries to bring the other male disciples over to his point of view by including them in his charge. According to the Coptic version, he asks: "Did the Savior, then, speak with a woman in private without our knowing about it? Are *we* to turn around and listen to her? Did he choose her over *us*?" (BG 10:3b–4). The Greek version reads: "Surely he didn't want to show that she is more worthy than *we* are?" (PRyl 10.4). But that appears to be exactly the case. Levi rejoins: "If the Savior considered her to be worthy, who are you to disregard her? For he knew her completely and loved her steadfastly" (PRyl 10:9–10). The Coptic pushes the point even more strongly: "Assuredly the Savior's knowledge of her is completely reliable. That is why he loved her more than us" (BG 10:10).

By supporting Mary, the *Gospel of Mary* makes it clear that leadership is to be based upon spiritual achievement rather than on having a male body. Clearly Mary is spiritually more advanced than the male disciples; because she did not fear for her life at the departure of the Savior and did not waver at the sight of him in her vision, she is able to step into the Savior's role and teach the others. She thereby models true discipleship: the appropriation and preaching of the Savior's teaching.

Elaine Pagels has suggested that the Savior's injunction was written specifically against Paul's attempt to silence women by appeal to the law.[9] His first letter to the Corinthians says:

> As in all the churches of the saints, the women should keep silence in the churches. For they are not permitted to speak, but should be subordinate, as even the law says. If there is anything they desire to know, let them ask their husbands at home. For it is shameful for a woman to speak in the church (*1 Cor* 14:33b–35).[10]

There is no such law in the Hebrew Scriptures, although *1 Timothy* appeals to *Genesis* to make a similar point:

> Let a woman learn in silence with all submissiveness. I permit no woman to teach or to have authority over men; she is to keep silent. For Adam was formed first, then Eve; and Adam was not deceived, but the woman was deceived and became a transgressor (*1 Tim* 2:11–14).

*1 Timothy* is attributed to Paul, although it is pseudonymous, having been written in the early second century, and merely asserts Paul's apostolic authority to authorize its message. Could the *Gospel of Mary* have known these passages? I find no obvious evidence that it knew them directly, but the issue of women's leadership roles in the churches was wide-spread and appeal was made to law, whether natural or written, to support various positions.[11] The portrayal of the conflict between Mary and Peter, followed as it is by a repetition of the Savior's injunction not to lay down any laws beyond what he commanded, clearly suggests that any regulation forbidding women's teaching was one of those laws set by the disciples which would have the effect of injecting illegitimate domination into the life of the Christian community. Any such regulation must necessarily be the product of jealousy and a deep misunderstanding of the Savior's teaching.

Because the *Gospel of Mary* was in circulation for over three hundred years, we have to assume that the Savior's command against oppressive laws was interpreted in a variety of contexts by various groups of readers. It could have been read as resistance to the establishment of various kinds of external restraints—not only certain aspects of Jewish law, but also the formation of an exclusive Christian canon,[12] restrictions on prophecy and visionary revelation, the exclusion of women from official positions of leadership, or even against colonial Roman law. If we are to imagine a second or third century setting in Egypt, for example, it is quite possible that many people would associate a "lawgiver" as readily with the Romans as with Moses. In the end, however, it is the law *that they themselves set* that would come to rule and restrict them. Spiritual advancement is to be sought within, not through external regulation. The context for this kind of command in the *Gospel of Mary* applies most clearly to intra-Christian controversies, not to relations with Jews or Romans.

*Chapter 6*

# The Son of Man

The Coptic phrase ⲡϣⲏⲣⲉ ⲛ̄ⲡⲣⲱⲙⲉ (Greek υἱὸς τοῦ ἀνθρώπου) is usually translated "Son of Man." In the *Gospel of Mary* the "Son of Man" is the child of true Humanity, the Image of the Divine Realm that exists within every person. It is identified as the true Image of nature to which the disciples are supposed to conform, the image of humanity's true spiritual nature.[1] In his farewell to the disciples, the Savior tells them: "The child of true Humanity exists within you" (4:5). The Savior commands them: "Follow it! Those who search for it will find it" (4:6). The verb "to follow," says Pasquier, "in the *Gospel of Mary*, as with certain Stoics and Pythagoreans, appears to have the meaning of 'grasping something as a model'. . . in order to become in turn a model oneself; in short, in this context, it requires the idea of an identification."[2] To find and follow the child of true Humanity within requires identifying with the archetypal Image of Humanity as one's most essential nature and conforming to it as a model. Those who search for it will find it, the Savior assures his disciples.

Note how one is *not* to find it: by looking outside of oneself. The *Gospel of Mark*, for example, understands the Son of Man to be a messianic figure who will come in clouds with power and glory in the end times (13:26). In contrast, the *Gospel of Mary* admonishes: "Be on your guard so that no one deceives you by saying, 'Look over here!' or 'Look over there!'" This warning shows a knowledge of apocalyptic eschatology, such as we see in the *Gospel of Mark* and many other sources, but it rejects it entirely. The *Gospel of Mary* does not understand "Son of Man" as a messianic title and never uses it to refer to Jesus. For the *Gospel of Mary*, the Son of Man is not the Savior Jesus, but the true self within. Nor does the phrase mean simply "human being," as it does for example in Jesus' saying that the son of man has nowhere to lay his head (*Matt* 8:20). For the *Gospel of Mary*, it refers to the ideal, the truly Human. Plato had posited the existence of a Form of Man (Greek *anthropos*)[3] existing in the Divine Realm apart from all the particular humans that share in that Form.[4] The *Gospel of Mary* has interpreted Jesus' traditional teaching about the child of true Humanity to refer to this archetypal Form of Man, possibly in conjunction with the statement in *Genesis* 1:26–27 that humanity was created in the image of God, male and female.

But there are significant differences. For Plato, the Form of Man was clearly imagined as a male image; indeed Plato had suggested in the *Timaeus* that women were deviations from the ideal male norm, divergences which had resulted from cowardice. That cannot be the case in the *Gospel of Mary*, for when Mary comforts the disciples, she admonishes them: "We should praise his greatness, for he has prepared us and made *us* true Human Beings" (5:7–8). The Coptic term underlying the translation "true Human Beings" is ⲚⲢⲰⲘⲈ; Greek ἀνθρώπους. Both terms can refer either to humanity in general or to male persons, much as the English word "man." The use of the plural here, however, includes both Mary and the male disciples, so the meaning must be generic. Furthermore, they were already human beings in the strict sense; the Savior after all did not turn them from asses into humans, as happened to an unfortunate character in Apuleius' story, *The Golden Ass*; there a man had unwittingly been magically transformed into an ass and was made human again only by the intervention of the Goddess Isis. In the *Gospel of Mary*, being made human means that the Savior's teaching has led the disciples to find the Image of the child of true Humanity within. They have grasped the archetypal Image and become truly Human.

Levi's reiteration of the Savior's teaching at the end of the work reinforces this interpretation: "We should clothe ourselves with the perfect Human, acquiring it for ourselves as the Savior commanded us" (10:11). Here, too, the notion of the perfect Human (Coptic:

ⲡⲣⲱⲙⲉ ⲛⲧⲉⲗⲓⲟⲥ; Greek: τέλειον ἄνθρωπον) refers to the Savior's earlier admonition to find the child of true Humanity within.[5] To find the child of true Humanity within or to put on the perfect Human means to come to know that one's true self is a spiritual being whose roots are nourished by the transcendent Good. Salvation means appropriating this spiritual Image as one's truest identity.[6]

Scholars have sometimes inaccurately equated Mary's statement that the Savior made the disciples truly Human with Jesus' statement in the *Gospel of Thomas* that he will make Mary male. The passage in the *Gospel of Thomas* reads,

> Simon Peter said to them, "Let Mary leave us, for women are not worthy of life."
> Jesus said, "I myself shall lead her in order to make her male, so that she too may become a living spirit resembling you males. For every woman who will make herself male will enter the kingdom of heaven" (*GThom* 114).

Much as the scene later in the *Gospel of Mary*, this passage also pits Peter against Mary but the import of the Savior's teaching is quite different. In the *Gospel of Mary*, the Savior uses the generic term, "human being" (Coptic: ⲣⲱⲙⲉ), and he makes both Mary and the male disciples into Human Beings. In the *Gospel of Thomas*, Jesus uses the non-generic term "male" (Coptic: ϩⲟⲟⲩⲧ) and he specifically says that he will make Mary male, and other women "will make themselves male resembling you males." The difference in gender imagery is striking. However we interpret Jesus' saying in the *Gospel of Thomas*—and numerous suggestions have been made such as conforming to the male ideal or taking up asceticism—it clearly understands the male condition to be superior to that of women. Not so for the *Gospel of Mary*. It is straining to articulate a vision that the natural state of humanity is ungendered, while constrained by language that was suffused with the androcentric values of its day.[7] But the vision is clear: for the *Gospel of Mary*, the divine, transcendent Image to which the soul is to conform is non-gendered; sex and gender belong only to the lower sphere of temporary bodily existence. The theological basis for this position lies in the understanding that the body is not the true self; the true self is spiritual and nongendered, even as the divine is nonmaterial and nongendered. Remember that God is not called Father in this work, but only the Good, a term that in Greek can easily be grammatically neuter. In order to conform as far as possible to the divine Image, one must abandon the distinctions of the flesh, including sex and gender.

## Chapter 7

# Vision & Mind

After the Savior departs, Peter asks Mary to disclose any words of the Savior which she knew, but which were unknown to the other disciples (6:1–2). Mary reports a dialogue she had with the Savior. It began with her telling the Savior that she had seen a vision of him.[1] She did not waver at the sight, but immediately acknowledged the Lord's presence. He, in turn, praised her for her steadfastness, saying: "Blessed are you for not wavering at seeing me. For where the mind is, there is the treasure" (7:3–4). The term "wavering" carries important connotations in ancient thought, where it implies instability of character.[2] Mary's stability illustrates her conformity to the unchanging and eternal spiritual Realm, and provides one more indication of her advanced spiritual status. The saying about treasure reinforces the Savior's praise. The term "mind" points the reader back to Mary's earlier ministry to the other disciples in which "she turned their mind toward the Good" (POxy 5:9). It is because Mary has placed her mind with God that she can direct others to the spiritual treasure of the Good.

The saying about treasure is often quoted in early Christian literature.[3] For example in *Q*, an early collection of Jesus' words used by the writers of *Matthew* and *Luke*, the saying is used to warn people against greed and attachment to ephemeral wealth.[4] In the *Gospel of Mary*, however, the saying introduces Mary's next question and points ahead to the Savior's response. She asks whether one receives a vision by the soul or the spirit. The Savior responds that "a person does not see with the soul or with the spirit. Rather the mind, which exists between these two, sees the vision and that is what . . ." Unfortunately, the text breaks off here and we are left without the rest of the Savior's answer, but it is clear that he is describing the tripartite composition of the true inner self: it is made up of soul, mind, and spirit. Enough remains of the Savior's response to glimpse an intriguing answer into a very difficult issue: how does a prophet see a vision?[5] The mind conveys the vision, functioning as a mediator between the spirit and the soul.

Early Christians were fully part of ancient Mediterranean society and shared the concepts common to that culture. It was widely believed that gods and spirits communicated with people through trances, possessions, and dreams. Opinions differed about how that occurred, and the issue was widely discussed among ancient scientists, philosophers, and physicians. Christians also had differing opinions on the matter, depending upon which intellectual tradition they drew upon. In the *Gospel of Mary*, the Savior is taking a very specific position on the issue. The significance of his answer to Mary can be better appreciated by comparing it with the views of the church father Tertullian, who wrote *A Treatise on the Soul* (*De anima*) at the turn of the third century. He discussed this same issue, but took a different position than the *Gospel of Mary*.

Both Tertullian and the *Gospel of Mary* valued prophetic experiences highly and considered them to be authoritative for Christian teaching and practice. They believed that only the pure could see God in visions, because sin and attachment to the things of the flesh dim the spiritual comprehension of the soul. There the similarity ends. They disagreed on almost every other important issue.

The most fundamental basis of their disagreement rests on conflicting views about what it is to be a human being. Tertullian understood a person to be made up of a body and soul, joined in a completely unified relationship.[6] The mind is the ruling function of the soul, not something separate from it. He maintained that the soul, as well as the body, is material. It is shaped in the form of the human body and even "has its own eyes and ears owing to which people[7] see and hear the Lord; it also has other limbs through which it experiences thoughts and engages in dreams" (*De anima* 9:8). Souls are even sexed: "The soul, being sown in the womb simultaneously with the flesh, is allotted its sex simultaneously with the flesh such that neither substance controls the cause of sex" (*De anima* 36:2). He regarded male souls to be superior to female souls by nature.[8] Thus sexual differentiation and gender hierarchy are natural to the soul's very existence.

For the *Gospel of Mary*, a human being is composed of body, soul, and mind.[9] The mind is the most divine part of the self, that which links it with God. The mind rules and leads the soul, so that when the mind is directed toward God, it purifies and directs the soul toward spiritual attainment. As the Savior said, "Where the mind is, there is the treasure" *(GMary* 7:4). In contrast to Tertullian's view, the body is seen as merely a temporary shell to which the soul has become attached. It is this attachment of the soul to the body that causes sickness and death. At death the soul leaves the body and ascends to its immortal rest, while the material body returns to its originally inanimate, soulless nature. The *Gospel of Mary* also denies that souls are sexed; sexuality and the gender differences inscribed on the body belong to the material nature that the soul must transcend. Differences between men and women are therefore ultimately illusory since they don't belong to the true self, but only to bodies that will cease to exist at death. They belong to the world of matter and the passions, not the spiritual Realm.

Because their views about human nature diverged, Tertullian and the author of the *Gospel of Mary* also disagreed about the nature of sin and salvation. Tertullian believed that the soul was polluted from the moment that pagan birth rituals were performed under the influence of the devil.[10] Because of the pollution of the soul, the body was actively sinful. Only the regeneration of the soul through faith in Christ, sealed in baptism and confirmed through proper instruction in the rule of faith, could purify the soul and lead a person out of sin. The final hope of the believer was for the physical resurrection of the body, including the material soul.[11]

As we have seen, the *Gospel of Mary* defines sin as the adulterous relationship of the soul to the body. When the soul becomes attached to the body, it is overcome by the frailties and passions of the material nature, leading to sickness and death. By turning away from the body and recognizing one's true self as a spiritual being, the self can find the child of true Humanity within and conform to that Image. This knowledge will allow the soul to escape the illegitimate domination of the flesh and ascend to rest with God. The teaching of the Savior brings the salvation of the soul, not the resuscitation of a corpse.

Their views about how prophecy occurs are directly tied to these views. Tertullian held that all souls have some measure of original goodness on the basis of which they can prophesy.[12] Hence after a soul has been purified by embracing the Christian faith and accepting baptism, it is capable of prophesying.[13] Prophetic experience occurs when the soul steps from the body in ecstasy:

> Accordingly, when sleep comes upon bodies (for sleep is the comfort that is peculiar to it), the soul, being free, does not sleep (because sleep is alien to it), and since it lacks the assistance of the limbs of the physical body, it uses its own.... This power we call ecstasy, the departure of the senses and the appearance of madness (*De anima* 45:2, 3).[14]

Ecstasy ("the departure of the senses and the appearance of madness") is common in sleep, and Tertullian associates this state with dreaming. Not all dreams, however, are prophetic. Dreams can come from three sources: demons, God, or the soul itself.[15] In true prophecy, the soul is moved by the divine Spirit and experiences ecstasy.[16] Only this madness signals the divine presence:

> ... ecstasy, that is being out of one's senses, accompanies the divine gift. For since human beings have been formed in the Spirit, they must be deprived of sense perception particularly when they behold the glory of God, or when God speaks through them, since they have been manifestly overshadowed by the divine power (*Against Marcion* 4:22).[17]

According to the *Gospel of Mary*, however, it is not the soul that sees the vision, but the mind acting as a mediator between the sensory perceptions of the soul and the divine spirit. This view was widely held among Christian theologians.[18] For example, the second-century theologian and martyr, Justin,[19] argued that God is invisible, and thus "the vision of God does not occur with the eyes, as with other living beings, but He can be grasped only by the mind, as Plato says; and I believe him" (*Dialogue with Trypho* 3). The famous third-century Egyptian theologian, Origen agrees:

God, moreover, is in our judgment invisible, because He is not a body, while He can be seen by those who see with the heart, that is the mind, not indeed with any kind of heart, but with one which is pure (*Against Celsus* 6:69).[20]

The *Gospel of Mary* clearly agrees that only spiritually advanced souls have visionary experiences. Mary, for example, is praised by the Savior because she has not wavered at the sight of him.[21] The Savior ascribes Mary's stability to the fact that her mind is concentrated on spiritual matters. Mary has clearly achieved the purity of mind necessary to see the Savior and converse with him. The vision is a mark of that purity and her closeness to God.[22] Note, too, that her stability is in marked contrast with the contentious fearfulness of the other disciples. Because the mind is not associated with the senses, it is not dimmed in the presence of the Spirit. Madness and ecstasy are not necessary characteristics of true prophecy from the *Gospel of Mary*'s point of view; rather the purified mind is clear and potent.

In short, Tertullian and the *Gospel of Mary* differ in their conceptions of the fundamental nature of the person (whether human nature is fundamentally material or spiritual), the character of sexual differentiation and gender roles (whether natural or illusory), and the role of the human mind in relationship to God (whether dimmed or potent). It is clear, even from this brief overview, that the discussion of how prophecy occurred was intertwined with such central issues of early Christian theology as attitudes toward the body, the understanding of human nature, sexuality and gender roles, and views about the nature of sin and salvation. All these issues are at stake in answering the question: "Lord, how does a person see a vision?"

## Chapter 8

# The Rise
# of the Soul

When the story resumes after the four-page hiatus, we are in the middle of an account of the rise of the soul to God. Mary is recounting the Savior's revelation about the soul's encounters with four Powers who seek to keep it bound to the world below. The missing beginning of the account must have included the soul's encounter with the first of the four Powers, probably named Darkness.[1] When the extant portion of the text resumes, the second Power, Desire, is addressing the soul, which replies and then ascends to the next level:

> And Desire said, "I did not see you go down, yet now I see you go up. So why do you lie since you belong to me?" The soul answered, "I saw you. You did not see me nor did you know me. You (mis)took the garment (I wore) for my (true) self. And you did not recognize me." After it had said these things it left rejoicing greatly (*GMary* 9:2–7).

Desire here attempts to keep the soul from ascending by claiming that it belongs to the world below and the Powers that rule it. The Power assumes that by attempting to escape, the soul is claiming that it does not belong to the material world. From Desire's point of view

that is a lie; since it did not see the soul come down from the world
above, it thinks the soul must indeed belong to the material world.
But the soul knows better and exposes the Power's ignorance. It is
true, the wise soul responds, you did not recognize me when I
descended because you mistook the bodily garment of flesh for my
true spiritual self. Now the soul has left the body behind along with
the material world to which it belongs. The Power never knew the
soul's true self—as the Power has itself unwittingly admitted by saying
it didn't see the soul descend. The response of the soul has unmasked
the blindness of Desire: the Power had not been able to see past the
soul's material husk to its true spiritual nature. But the soul did see
the Power, thereby proving that its capacity to discern the true nature
of things is superior to Desire's clouded vision. Having thus exposed
Desire's impotence and lack of spiritual insight, the soul gleefully
ascends to the third Power.

> Again, it came to the third Power, which is called Ignorance.
> [It] examined the soul closely, saying, "Where are you going?
> You are bound by wickedness. Indeed you are bound! Do not
> judge!" And the soul said, "Why do you judge me, since I
> have not passed judgment? I have been bound, but I have not
> bound (anything). They did not recognize me, but I have rec-
> ognized that the universe is to be dissolved, both the things
> of earth and those of heaven" (*GMary* 9:8–15).

Again the Power attempts to stop the soul's ascent by challenging
its nature. Ignorance judges the soul to be material, and therefore
bound by the wickedness of the passions and lacking in discernment:
"Do not judge!" it commands. But the soul turns the tables: it is the
Power of Ignorance who is judging; a soul is bound to the lower
world, not by its material nature but by the wicked domination of the
Powers. This soul is innocent precisely because it acts according to the
nature of the spirit: it does not judge others nor does it attempt to
dominate anything or anyone. It has knowledge of which Ignorance is
ignorant; it knows that because everything in the lower world is passing away, the Powers of that transitory world have no real power over
the eternal soul.[2] The soul's rejoinder to the Power here is a kind of
applied restatement of the Savior's teaching about sin and nature given
earlier in the text: "There is no such thing as sin" (*GMary* 3:3). Only
because of the domination of the flesh does sin even appear to exist.

Without the flesh—which is to be dissolved—there is no sin, judgment, or condemnation.[3] The soul for its part rejects any kind of judgment and domination, associating them with the Power of Ignorance. The soul's insight into its own true spiritual identity enables it to overcome the illegitimate domination of the Power. Again, the wit in the passage lies in the fact that it is the Power itself which has acknowledged that the soul's knowledge is true: wickedness is due only to the domination of the flesh. This insight frees the soul and it moves upward to the Fourth Power.

> When the soul had brought the third Power to naught, it went upward and saw the fourth Power which had seven forms. The first is darkness; the second is desire; the third is ignorance; the fourth is zeal for death; the fifth is the realm of the flesh; the sixth is the foolish wisdom of the flesh; the seventh is the wisdom of the wrathful person. These are the seven Powers of Wrath. They interrogated the soul, "Where are you coming from, human-killer, and where are you going, space-conqueror?" The soul replied, saying "What binds me has been slain, and what surrounds me has been destroyed, and my desire has been brought to an end, and ignorance has died. In a [wor]ld, I was set loose from a world [an]d in a type, from a type which is above, and (from) the chain of forgetfulness which exists in time. From this hour on, for the time of the due season of the aeon, I will receive rest i[n] silence" (*GMary* 9:16–29).

The names of the seven Powers of Wrath may correspond to the astrological spheres that control fate,[4] but above all they show the character of the Powers that attempt to dominate the soul: desire, ignorance, death, flesh, foolishness, and wrath. Their collective character and name is Wrath.

Like the other Powers, Wrath seems disturbed at the soul's passage and questions both its origin and its right to pass by. But again the Power ignorantly plays into the hands of the wise and playful soul who knows that it derives from above and is returning to its true place of origin. Wrath charges the soul with violence, stating that it is a murderer (because it has cast off the material body) and a conqueror (because it has traversed the spheres of the Powers and overcome them). These terms of approbation are greeted happily by the soul who reinterprets them, affirming that indeed the material elements and the body that bound it in lust and ignorance have been overcome and it is free from bondage. The soul dramatically contrasts the subjection to material bonds, desire, and ignorance it has escaped, with the freedom of the timeless realm of silence and rest to which it ascends; it distinguishes the deceitful image below from the true Image above, and mortality from immortality. Even as the soul finally finds perfect rest in silence,[5] so, too, does Mary become silent, modeling in her behavior the perfect rest of the soul set free.[6]

At the temple of Apollo in Claros, Greece, archaeologists found a stone bearing a late second-century CE inscription that reads:

> When someone asked Apollo whether the soul remained after death or was dissolved, he answered, "The soul, so long as it is subject to its bonds with the destructible body, while being immune to feelings, resembles the pains of that (body); but when it finds freedom after the mortal body dies, it is borne entire to the aether, being then forever ageless, and abides entirely untroubled; and this the First-born Divine Providence enjoined."[7]

The belief that the soul could leave the body at death and ascend to an eternal life of peace beyond the heavenly spheres, while not the only view of death or the afterlife in antiquity, was widely held in the late Roman period.[8] But the confidence of Apollo's oracle that the journey would be an easy one was not widely felt. A successful conclusion was far from assured. More often the soul's passage was thought to be fraught with numerous perils that few could overcome.

A glimpse into the soul's trials after death is given in the *Apocalypse of Paul*, one of the works discovered near Nag Hammadi, Egypt, in 1945. This work is an elaboration of the visionary journey that Paul described in *2 Corinthians*:

> I must boast; there is nothing to be gained by it, but I will go on to visions and revelations of the Lord. I know a man in Christ who fourteen years ago was caught up to the third heaven—whether in the body or out of the body I do not know, God knows. And I know that this man was caught up into Paradise—whether in the body or out of the body I do not know, God knows—and he heard things that cannot be told, which man may not utter (*2 Cor* 12:1–4).

Of course, this unnamed man was most likely Paul himself. The author of the *Apocalypse of Paul* draws upon Paul's own account, but does not share his reticence about revealing what he saw and heard. This author is happy to imagine everything and tell all. In the *Apocalypse of Paul*, the third heaven is only the beginning of Paul's journey. At the fourth heaven, he sees angels whipping a soul who had been brought out of the land of the dead. When the soul asks what sin it has committed to deserve such punishment, the toll-collector brings out three witnesses who accuse it of various misdeeds. Obliged to face the truth, the sorrowful soul is cast down again into a body that had been prepared for it. In the fifth heaven, Paul sees an angel with an iron rod and others with whips, all goading souls on to judgment. He manages to get past them and on to the sixth heaven only because his guide is the Holy Spirit. In the seventh heaven, an old man seated on a luminous throne and dressed in white interrupts Paul's ascent, demanding to know where he is going, where he has come from, and how Paul thinks he will be able to get away from him. Paul replies with the correct answers and, at a prompt from his guide, gives the old man a sign that allows him to proceed. He then joins the twelve apostles and ascends with them to the ninth heaven, and finally goes up to the tenth heaven where he greets his fellow spirits.

This account contains many of the elements common to ancient stories of the souls' rise. Antiquity was home to a wide variety of post-mortem scenarios that involved rewarding the righteous and punishing the wicked. Such views were sometimes elaborated with stories about the righteous ascending directly to God.[9] Views about the judgment of the dead could be combined with the idea that angelic (or demonic) gate-keepers or toll-collectors attempt to stop souls and send them back into bodies. These notions were based on current astrological beliefs that the planets were powers who governed the fate of all beings in the world. The soul's ascent was seen as an attempt to escape from their arbitrary and unforgiving rule by successfully passing through each of the planetary spheres. Sin was considered to be a determinative impediment to escape because sinful souls, unable to pay the price, were returned to the flesh—presumably to try to do better. Moral purity was absolutely essential since ultimately only the souls of the good would ascend.

Yet because of the journey's extreme dangers, it was sometimes held that moral purity and righteousness alone might not be enough. Preparation was necessary to ensure safe passage. Special guidance, revealed knowledge, and ritual signs contributed to the success of the journey.[10] Instruction about the obstacles that would confront the soul and how to overcome them was required. This instruction often included learning the questions the gate-keepers would pose and the traps they would set. Having the right answers and the capacity to see through their devious machinations could protect the soul. Given that after-death experience undoubtedly presupposed esoteric knowledge, the necessary instruction obviously had to be based on revelation. This information could come through reports of a visionary journey through the heavens such as Paul took, or it could be given by a divine messenger-instructor such as the Savior in the *Gospel of Mary*. Additionally, ritual purification and empowerment were often considered essential to aid the soul in its journey. Such purification most often included baptism[11] and ritual enactment of the ascent itself,[12] but it could include other rites and magical practices as well, some of them quite elaborate.[13]

Popular views of this sort were often combined in various ways with philosophical speculations which envisioned the soul as an immortal being that would return to its divine origins when released from the bonds of the mortal body; it had come down from the stars or from some luminous realm beyond the material world and would return there at death. In the process of descent, the soul or its vehicle had acquired accretions that needed to be removed in order for the soul to ascend back to its divine sphere. As one account from the Hermetic corpus describes it,

And then (the soul) rises upward through the structure of the heavens. And to the first zone of heaven he gives up the force which works increase and decrease; to the second zone, the machinations of evil cunning; to the third zone, the lust which deceives people; to the fourth zone, domineering arrogance; to the fifth zone, unholy daring and rash audacity; to the sixth zone, evil strivings after wealth; and to the seventh zone, the falsehood which lies in wait to work harm. And then, having been stripped of all that was worked upon him by the structure of the heavens, he ascends to the substance of the eighth sphere, being now possessed of his own proper power; and he sings, together with those who dwell there, hymning the Father; and they that are there rejoice with him at his coming. And being made like to those with whom he dwells, he hears the Powers, who are above the substance of the eighth sphere, singing praise to God with a voice that is theirs alone. And thereafter, each in his turn, they mount upward to the Father; they give themselves up to the Powers, and becoming Powers themselves, they enter into God. This is the Good; this is the consummation for those who have got knowledge (*Poimandres* 1:25–26a).[14]

Many accounts in late antique literature describe the soul's journey past the guardians.[15] Often angelic guards are represented as the instruments of justice. The gate-keeper in the *Apocalypse of Paul*, for example, rightly judged a soul's wickedness and sent it back into the body until like Paul it should be purified through faith. But in other accounts the gate-keepers are presented as wicked and ignorant beings who are wrongly trying to keep pure souls trapped below. In the *First Apocalypse of James*, for example, the Lord warns his brother James about the difficulties he will face:

"A multitude will arm themselves against you in order to seize you. And in particular three of them will seize you—the ones who sit as toll collectors. Not only do they demand toll, but they also take away souls by theft. When you come into their power, one of them who is their guard will say to you, 'Who are you or where are you from?' You are to say to him, 'I am a son, and I am from the Father.' He will say to you, 'What sort of son are you, and to what father do you belong?' You are to say to him, 'I am from the Pre-existent Father, and a son in the Pre-existent One.'... When he also says to you, 'Where will you go?' you are to say to him, 'To the place from which I have come, there shall I return.' And if you say these things, you will escape their attacks" (*1ApocJas* 33:4–24; 34:15–30).

Here the toll-collectors are clearly malevolent thieves who steal souls. But the questions they ask only demand that James know his true identity and place of origin. Knowledge is sufficient to escape their attacks. His moral condition is not an issue, and there is no hint of judgment for sins.

In the *Gospel of Mary*, however, we find both themes: the malevolent character of the gate-keepers and the moral judgment of the soul. When combined they produce an astonishingly sharp image of the gate-keepers as tools of false justice and offer a satirical critique of the unjust nature of power in the world below. The dialogues between the soul and the Powers show that their domination is based on lies, blind ignorance, and false justice; their condemnation of the enlightened soul for wickedness and violence is rooted in their own blindness, lust for power, and ignorance of the Good. The soul opposes their lies with truth, their adultery with purity, their ignorance with knowledge, their judgment with refusal to judge, their blindness with true vision, their domination with freedom, their desire with peace, and their mortal death with life eternal. The soul's entire battle with the Powers focuses on overcoming their illegitimate domination.

Although it is quite possible that this section on the rise of the soul was originally a separate literary source only later incorporated into the dialogue framework, it amplifies important themes in the Savior's teaching raised during the initial dialogue with his disciples. In the account of the soul's rise, salvation is conceived as overcoming the passions, suffering, and death that are associated with the physical body and the lower world. The Savior's admonition not to lay down any law is elaborated as we see the Powers, sitting like corrupt judges in a law court, working to condemn the soul in its struggle to escape their domination. Law, it would seem, is set up to work on the side of those who wish to enslave the soul. The soul's refusal to judge is also a refusal to be bound by their unjust and ignorant laws. Those who judge, the Savior teaches, are ruled by laws that can then be used to judge them. Such laws are really domination; such knowledge as the Powers offer is really ignorance.

The whole dialogue between the soul and the Powers is characterized by a sharp contrast between the world above and the world below. The Divine Realm above is light, peace, knowledge, love, and life; the lower world is darkness, desire, arrogance, ignorance, jealousy, and the zeal for death. More is going on in this contrast than merely a simple belief in the immortality of righteous souls, or even the struggle against the arbitrary powers of fate. The dialogues instruct the reader in the truth about the very nature of Reality by contrasting it with the deception that characterizes life in the world. The dialogue of the soul with the Powers stresses as does no other ancient ascent account the unjust nature of the Powers' illegitimate domination. In so doing the *Gospel of Mary* presents a biting critique of how power is exercised in the lower world under the guise of law and judgment.

How are we to understand this critique? The *Gospel of Mary* is clearly a religious work aimed at freeing the soul from the bonds of suffering and death; there is no outright call for political rebellion or explicit criticism of either local or imperial Roman domination. But cannot a religious work incorporate a political message? Indeed if we overlook the subversive implications of the *Gospel of Mary*, I think we miss one of its most important elements.

It has been a commonplace to exclude covert forms of resistance from consideration as real political activity. In fact, religious teaching like that of the *Gospel of Mary*, which points the soul toward peace in the afterlife, is often seen not only as apolitical, but as anti-political—an escapist ideology that serves only to distract people from effective political engagement by focusing on interior spiritual development and flight from the material world with all its troubles and demands. Research among social scientists has changed this view dramatically. Let me cite at length the conclusion of the most influential researcher in this area, James Scott. He writes:

> Until quite recently, much of the active political life of subordinate groups has been ignored because it takes place at a level we rarely recognize as political. To emphasize the enormity of what has been, by and large, disregarded, I want to distinguish between the open, declared forms of resistance, which attract most attention, and the disguised, low-profile, undeclared resistance that constitutes the domain in infrapolitics. ... For contemporary liberal democracies in the West, an exclusive concern for open political action will capture much that is significant in political life. The historic achievement of political liberties of speech and association has appreciably lowered the risks and difficulty of open political expression. Not so long ago in the West, however, and, even today, for many of the least privileged minorities and marginalized poor, open political action will hardly capture the bulk of political action. Nor will an exclusive attention to declared resistance help us understand the process by which new political forces and demands germinate before they burst on the scene. How, for example, could we understand the open break represented by the civil rights movement or the black power movement in the 1960s without understanding the offstage discourse among black students, clergy, and their parishioners?

Taking a long historical view, one sees that the luxury of

relatively safe, open political opposition is both rare and recent. The vast majority of people have been and continue to be not citizens, but subjects. So long as we confine our conception of the political to activity that is openly declared, we are driven to conclude that subordinate groups essentially lack a political life or that what political life they do have is restricted to those exceptional moments of popular explosion. To do so is to miss the immense political terrain that lies between quiescence and revolt, and that, for better or worse, is the political environment of subject classes. It is to focus on the visible coastline of politics and miss the continent that lies beyond.

. . . Finally, millennial imagery and the symbolic reversals of folk religion are the infrapolitical equivalents of public, radical, counterideologies: both are aimed at negating the public symbolism of ideological domination.[16]

It is just such opposition and reversal that characterizes the soul's dialogues with the Powers.

As Scott points out, groups labeled heterodox or heretical have always been significant sites for ideological resistance. We might do well to remember here that the Romans persecuted Christians under the charge of atheism and undermining the public good. Such groups stand at a critical distance from the dominant society, a distance that enables them to articulate "an original attitude toward the meaning of the cosmos."[17] Their politics are often cultivated among what the famous sociologist Max Weber marvelously called "pariah-intelligentsia."[18] His point is that this kind of resistance does not necessarily arise among those who *reject* the values of the dominant society, so much as among those who were very deeply committed to them and feel *betrayed* by the failures of leaders to live up to the values they espouse.[19] The fact that the *Gospel of Mary*'s critique is couched in the fantastic terms of the religious imagination should not lead us to ignore its political import. Its critique of the body and the world with its suffering and its wrathful rulers draws its power precisely from an uncompromising commitment to the values of justice, peace, and stability pervasive throughout the Roman world. It is these elements of Roman ideology that provoke the feeling of betrayal. From this perspective, the *Gospel of Mary* is not aimed at nihilism, but at cultivating an uncompromising, utopian vision of spiritual perfection and peace rooted in the divine Good, beyond the constraints of time and matter and false morality. Social criticism and spiritual development were irrevocably linked together in this vision.

The criticism offered by the *Gospel of Mary* is very general; it does not seem aimed at anything or anyone in particular. Such generality is part of the strategic method of covert resistance, for it affords both discretion (one can easily deny that any criticism was intended) and potential long-term effectiveness (since it allows for adaptation to diverse and changing circumstances). Like other Christian works such as the New Testament *Book of Revelation*, the *Gospel of Mary* holds that the world is under the control of malevolent beings. This doctrine not only explains the existence of evil and injustice, but also locates an object at which resistance can be aimed. The *Gospel of Mary* makes it possible for people to see the struggle against violence in their own situations as part of a necessary and justified resistance against Powers that seek to keep people enslaved to their passions: anger, desire, lust, envy, greed. The mythic framework of the *Gospel of Mary* allows the spiritual, the psychological, the social, the political, and the cosmic to be integrated under one guiding principle: resistance to the unjust and illegitimate domination of ignorant and malevolent Powers.[20] It also offers a strategy for that resistance: preaching the gospel and appropriating the teachings of the Savior in one's own life.

At one level, the *Gospel of Mary* invites the reader to discern the true character of power as it is exercised in the world. It insists that ignorance, deceit, false judgment, and the desire to dominate must be opposed by accepting the Savior's teaching and refusing to be complicit in violence and domination. People need to accept the spiritual freedom, life, and peace that they *already possess* because their true nature is rooted in the Good; the Savior admonishes his disciples to seek and find the child of true Humanity within. Knowing the truth about oneself and opposing the false powers that rule the world are foundational to achieving spiritual maturity and salvation.

At another level, the ascent of the soul can also be read as a guide for following a spiritual path that leads from fear and instability of heart, such as that which the disciples evince after the Savior's departure, to the unwavering faith and peace exemplified by Mary. In this scenario, the Powers represent the forces within the soul that it must overcome. Unfortunately we do not know what it took to overcome the first Power, since its encounter with the soul is lost in a lacuna.

The second Power is overcome by the soul's knowledge of its own spiritual nature. By rejecting the body as the self, it can overcome the false power of desire. The third Power, Ignorance, is overcome by knowledge of the transitory nature of the world. In order for the soul to overcome this power, it must root itself in the Good by abandoning the moral economy of sin and judgment which is tied to the world of the flesh. By turning to the Good, the soul establishes a foundation for the self's identity in what is enduring and true. The final Power is the strongest, a combination of all those the soul had already faced, but now appearing united in the single countenance of Wrath. Its seven names truly reveal the nature of rage: darkness, lust, ignorance, zeal for death; it is the power of the kingdom of the flesh; its "wisdom" is folly; its tools are violence: killing and conquering. But what the soul has come to realize is that violence is impotent. Whereas the Power of Wrath claims that the soul belongs under its domination because the soul itself employs violence by rejecting the body and conquering the Powers, the soul describes these acts as release from death, desire, and ignorance. The soul learns to reject violence by recognizing that it is contrary to the spirit of the Good. The overt violence of wrath cannot harm the soul because the soul does not belong to the kingdom of the flesh but to the Realm of the Good.

As we have seen, the spiritual condition toward which the soul "ascends" is characterized by light, stability of mind, knowledge, and life; the condition it must overcome is described as darkness, desire, ignorance, and death. The true wisdom of the Savior opposes the foolish "wisdom" of the flesh, which thrives on false powers of wrathful judgment and violence. We see these contrasted in the *Gospel of Mary*'s portraits of Peter and Mary. Peter judges and condemns Mary out of his jealousy and inclination to be hot-tempered; because his spiritual sight is clouded, he is unable to see past the transitory distinctions of the flesh to recognize the truth of Mary's teaching. Mary, on the other hand, shows stability of mind and teaches the words of the Savior, bringing comfort and knowledge to the other disciples. The contrast of these two characters illustrates the nature of the soul's inner ascent to spiritual perfection.

The ascent of the soul is an act of transcendence. It is figured as the soul's escape from the suffering of the mortal body and the Powers that seek to bind it. Viewed as a purely external event, ascent could be mere escapism. But before the soul can ascend it must be prepared to face the Powers of Darkness, Desire, Ignorance, and Wrath. This preparation involves recognizing one's own true spiritual nature, accepting the truth revealed in the teachings of the Savior, rejecting the false ideology of sin and judgment which is tied to domination by the flesh and the passions, and eschewing violence in any form. The capacity to overcome evil requires that one has perceived the Good-beyond-evil and molded oneself to its Image and nature. One has to acquire peace and find the child of true Humanity within, making no laws beyond those laid down by the Savior—lest the laws that are made come to dominate those who made them. Viewed as a purely internal event, ascent could be apolitical and individualistic. Yet the account of the rise of the soul unites internal spiritual development with resistance to external forces of evil in the practice of preaching the gospel to others. In so doing, the *Gospel of Mary* promulgates an alternative vision of the world, one that has the potential to overcome the passions and the violence that separate the soul from God.

## Chapter 9

# Controversy over Mary's Teaching

Although the *Gospel of Mary* is largely preoccupied with presenting the Savior's teaching, a substantial portion is also taken up with conflict among the disciples. Just before the Savior departed, he had commanded the disciples to go preach the good news. But rather than immediately setting out, they were overcome with distress and weeping, filled with doubt. "How are we going to go out to the rest of the world to preach the good news about the Realm of the child of true Humanity" they worried; "If they didn't spare him, how will they spare us?" (*GMary* 5:2-3). Mary at once stepped in to comfort them, turning their heart-mind[1] toward the Good so that they began to discuss the Savior's words. The Greek version says that she "tenderly kissed them all" (5.4).[2] Her words seem to have restored harmony among the apostles.[3] This concord is strengthened when Peter addresses Mary as their "sister" and acknowledges that the Savior had a special affection for her; he asks her to tell them anything the Savior may have told her which the other disciples have not heard. She agrees and gives them an extensive account of a vision and dialogue she had with the Lord. At this point, however, the disciples' concord is shattered by Andrew who breaks in with an accusatory challenge, denying that she could have gotten these teachings from the Savior because they seem strange to him. Peter is even more contentious, question-ing whether the Savior would have spoken to her in private without their knowledge. He apparently cannot accept that the Savior would have withheld such advanced teaching from the male disciples and given it to a woman, expecting them to "turn around and listen to her" (*GMary* 10:4).

Some modern commentators are startled by this sudden antago-nism to Mary.[4] Up to this point, the relations among the disciples have seemed quite congenial, even affectionate. Peter himself had readily acknowledged that Mary was Jesus' favorite among women and that there were occasions when Jesus had spoken with her when the other disciples weren't present, yet it would seem that the other disciples—or at least Andrew and Peter—are simply not prepared for Mary's response to Peter's request. It apparently went far beyond Peter's expectations. He had asked Mary only to tell them what the Savior had said to her that the other disciples hadn't heard, but the distinctive teaching she recounted didn't come simply from conversa-tion with Jesus during his life; she had had a vision of the Lord and received advanced teaching from him. In the Coptic version, Mary really rubs it in: she says that she has teaching that has been *hidden* from them. It is not a matter of chance that she knows things they do not; it is because the Savior singled her out. The fact that she has received a vision further emphasizes her purity of heart and mind, since according to ancient thought, spiritual experience of this kind would not have been possible without unwavering mental strength and moral purity. The Savior himself acknowledged these qualities in her when he said, "How wonderful you are for not wavering at seeing me" (*GMary* 7:3).

Now Mary weeps, no doubt disturbed not only because Peter is suggesting that she has made everything up and is deliberately lying to her fellow disciples—whom she had just kissed so tenderly—but Mary is also distressed at the rivalry and animosity his words suggest. At this point Levi steps in, and we may assume that his words express the author's perspective on the situation. Levi's rebuke of Peter is blunt, especially in the Coptic version: He tells Peter not only that he is being hot-headed as usual, but that if he persists he will find himself on the side of their adversaries, the Powers, rather than on the side of the Savior. Although in the Greek version Levi says only that Peter was "questioning the woman as though you're her adversary," it seems to me that the Coptic version has rightly brought out the implication of Levi's rebuke: divisive rivalry, judgment, and anger are characteristics of the Powers, not of the Savior's true disciples. As Levi insists, the Savior considered Mary worthy, and if he loved her more than the other disciples, it was because he knew her completely. Who did Peter think he was to disregard or reject her? But just as one begins to think that he himself is being belligerent by provoking Peter, Levi shifts to a conciliatory "we": "We should be ashamed," he says, no longer blaming Peter alone but encompassing all the disciples including himself. At stake is not merely the behavior of an individual or two, but the harmony of the whole group and their mission to preach the gospel. Remember that in the Greek version Mary had said that the Savior "has united us and made us Human Beings" (*GMary* 5:8). Repeating the Savior's injunctions, Levi reminds them, "We should clothe ourselves with the perfect Human . . . and go forth to preach the gospel, not laying down any rules or laws." And with the departure of Levi (or all the disciples), the gospel comes to an end.

But this abrupt ending is fraught with ambiguity. Did the disciples accept Levi's rebuke? Did they understand Mary's teaching? Were they able to return to harmonious unity and work together, supporting and comforting one another, or did they each go off alone, harboring resentment and misunderstanding? We are not even sure who left to go preach. The Greek version tells us that only Levi left and began to announce the good news. What about the others? Did they just stand there? The Coptic version says "they" started going out to preach. But who was included in this "they"? Mary and Levi? Andrew and Peter? All the disciples? Can we really trust that all these apostles fully understood the Savior's teaching and preached the gospel of the Human One in truth? None of this is answered. We know only the content of the gospel that the author thinks the apostles *should* have preached.

How are we to understand this scene? *The Gospel of Mary* clearly sides with Mary and Levi against Andrew and Peter, but why question Mary's integrity at all if the work wishes to affirm her teaching? And why give the work such an ambiguous ending? Modern commentators have suggested that this scene reflects real conflicts, in which Peter and Mary (or Peter/Andrew and Mary/Levi) represent different positions under debate or different groups in conflict with each other within second century Christianity.[5] They suggest that Mary's teaching and leadership are challenged in the work because they were challenged in reality. But rather than resolve the problem, this solution raises a host of new questions. Does the final scene in the *Gospel of Mary* reflect actual conflict between the historical figures of Peter and Mary? If so, what were the tensions about? Or were Peter and Mary (Andrew and Levi) only narrative representatives for opposing Christian groups or differing theological positions? If so, who were those groups? What positions did these figures represent? And with each of these questions, we have to ask what was at stake in the conflict. Whose perspective does the *Gospel of Mary* represent? What does the *Gospel of Mary* tell us about Christianity in the second century? We must also recognize that the characters and conflicts represented in this work would no doubt be read differently in later centuries, including our own. How? We'll take up these questions in chapter 14, but before we can answer them, we need to look more closely at how the *Gospel of Mary* describes the issues that are under contention.

The dialogue among the disciples is framed by the Savior's admonition to preach the gospel, beginning with the disciples' fear of the consequences and ending in Levi's exhortation to do as the Savior had commanded. This structural design signals that the main issue concerns preaching the gospel. By portraying most of the disciples as fearful and uncomprehending, even antagonistic, the *Gospel of Mary* clearly raises doubts about whether these disciples are ready to take up the apostolic mission. Their reluctance to preach the gospel indicates that some of the disciples have not understood the Savior's teaching. They are still caught up in the attachment to their bodies and appear to be still under the domination of the Powers who rule the world. They have not found the child of true Humanity within or conformed to the Image of the perfect Human. The attacks of Peter and Andrew on Mary demonstrate even more convincingly that they are still under the sway of passions and false opinions; they have failed to acquire inward peace, and out of jealousy and ignorance are sowing discord among the disciples. How can they preach the gospel of the Realm of the Human One if they do not themselves understand its message? In the absence of an established leadership, a fixed rule of faith, or a canon of scripture, determining the meaning of Jesus' teaching rests almost entirely upon judgments about the reliability of the witnesses who preach it. If the closest disciples of the Savior have not understood his message, how will people ever know what he truly taught? The *Gospel of Mary* has put in question the practice of basing authority solely on claims of having been the Savior's disciple and having received from him a commission to preach the gospel. Even being a witness to the resurrection does not appear to have been sufficient.

The *Gospel of Mary* does, however, portray two disciples as reliable: Mary and Levi. Both work to bring unity and harmony to the group by calling the other disciples back to consideration of the words of the Savior. Mary in particular is portrayed as a model disciple, comforting the other disciples and offering advanced teaching from the Savior. Both her steadfastness and her vision of the Savior demonstrate the strength of her spiritual character. It is no accident that the Savior loved her more than the others; that love and esteem is based on his sure knowledge of her. More than any other disciple, she has comprehended the Savior's teaching and is capable of teaching and preaching the gospel to others. She shows no fear at the prospect of going forth to preach because she understands how the soul overcomes the passions and advances past the Powers that attempt to dominate it. The *Gospel of Mary*'s portrayal of Mary and Levi makes it evident that demonstrable spiritual maturity is the crucial criterion for legitimate authority. The spiritual character of the persons who preach is the ultimate and most reliable basis for judging the truth of the gospel that is preached.

This criterion fits well with ancient expectations. As we said above, teachers were supposed to manifest their teaching in their actions, providing instruction not only by what they said but by how they lived. The personal character of the teacher was considered to be fundamental to his or her capacity to instruct. (And yes, albeit few in numbers, women teachers of philosophy were known in antiquity.[6]) We have to remember too that when the *Gospel of Mary* was written, no rule of faith or fixed canon had yet become commonly accepted. In the early centuries, Christians often based claims for the truth of their gospel on demonstrations of the power of the Spirit in prophecy and healing or in high standards of moral living. Thus representing the steadfast and irenic character of Mary and Levi would go a long way toward establishing the *Gospel of Mary*'s authority.

The *Gospel of Mary* seems most concerned with challenges to the truth of its teaching by other apostles within the Christian community. If Andrew and Peter are examples, those challenges were basically of two kinds: 1) the rejection of new teachings based on prophecy or private revelation, and 2) gender. We know from other Christian writings of the first and second centuries that these were very real issues in this period. Irenaeus, for example, denied that the apostles possessed hidden mysteries that had been delivered to them in private,[7] and he charged the heretics with inventing and preaching their own fictions.[8] So, too, Mary understood Peter's accusation to imply that she had made up everything she was reporting. The *Gospel of Mary* defends her against these charges through Levi's defense and the portrait of her character. Levi's two-pronged defense of Mary begins by attacking Peter's character: Peter, well-known as a hot-head, is sowing division among the apostles themselves. He then affirms that the Savior knew Mary completely and loved her best. And just as Levi considers the Savior's judgment of Mary to be decisive in ending the dispute, so the *Gospel of Mary* affirms her teaching by emphasizing the strength of her relationship to the Savior. That the Savior judged her rightly is illustrated by the work's portrait of her as an unflinching and steadfast disciple, worthy of receiving visions and advanced teaching. Levi's defense is at once remarkable and unremarkable. Unremarkable because the standards for legitimacy are those found widely in the earliest literature: apostolic witness to the resurrection and the demonstration of spiritual gifts, in Mary's case prophetic visions and inspired teaching. Yet because all the apostles in the text can claim to be witnesses to the teaching ministry of Jesus, both before and after his resurrection, and all received his commission to go forth and preach the gospel, her qualifications are not sufficient to defend her from attacks by fellow apostles. The crux of the defense, then, rests on the remarkable intimacy of Mary's relationship to the Savior: as Levi states, he did love her more than the other disciples. The fact that Andrew's objection to the "strangeness" of Mary's teaching is never explicitly answered leaves the issue he raises in the hands of the reader. As I have suggested above, there are multiple points of contact between the content of the revelation to Mary and the Savior's teaching earlier in the work; but ultimately the reader will have to decide whether they are sufficient to exonerate her or not.

The second challenge to Mary's authority as a teacher and apostle concerns gender, an issue that is explicitly raised in the text three times. In the first instance, Peter says to Mary: "We know that the Savior loved you *more than the rest of women*" (*GMary* 6:1). The second time, Peter protests, "Did (the Savior) speak with a *woman* in private without our knowing about it? Are we to turn around and listen to *her*? Did he choose *her over us*?" (10:3–4). Finally, Levi responds: "Peter . . . I see you now contending against the *woman* like the Adversaries" (10:8). The repeated references to Mary's womanhood makes it clear that at least one aspect of Peter's problem was that she was a woman. He apparently had no difficulty with the fact that Jesus preferred her to other women, but he couldn't accept the fact that Jesus preferred her to the male disciples—or even worse that they would have to "turn around" and accept instruction from a woman. Levi's response shows that he recognized that Peter's problem had to do at least in part with Mary being a woman, and he makes it clear that the Savior did indeed love her more and gave her special teaching because she, a woman, was worthy. He thereby implies, of course, that she was indeed more worthy than they were.

The issue of gender is raised not merely to score a point in the interminable battle of the sexes. Mary's gender is also crucial to the *Gospel of Mary*'s theology, especially the teaching about the body and salvation. As we said above, for the *Gospel of Mary* bodily distinctions are irrelevant to spiritual character since the body is not the true self. Even as God is non-gendered, immaterial, and transcendent, so too is the true Human self.[9] The Savior tells his disciples that they get sick and die "because you love what deceives you" (*GMary* 3:7–8). Peter's fault lies in his inability to see past the distinctions of the flesh to the spiritual qualities necessary for leadership. He apparently "loves" the status his male sex-gender gives him, and that leads to pride and jealousy. The scene where Levi corrects Peter's ignorance helps the reader to see one of the primary ways in which people are deceived by the body. Authority should not be based on whether one is a man or a woman, let alone on roles of socially assigned gender and sexual reproduction, but on spiritual achievement. Those who have progressed further than others have the responsibility to care and instruct them. The claim to have known Jesus and heard his words was not enough. One had to have appropriated them in one's life. Leadership is for those who have sought and found the child of true Humanity; they are to point the way for others, even as the Savior did. And such persons can be women as well as men. According to the *Gospel of Mary*, those who fail to understand this fact are, like Peter, mired in the materiality and passions of their lower natures. Worse yet, they risk finding themselves on the side of the Adversaries, for those who oppose women's spiritual leadership do so out of false pride, jealousy, lack of understanding, spiritual immaturity, and contentiousness. Rejecting the body as the self opened up the possibility of an ungendered space within the Christian community in which leadership functions were based on spiritual maturity.[10]

The *Gospel of Mary* takes two very strong positions concerning the basis of authority: that spiritual maturity, demonstrated by prophetic experience and steadfastness of mind, is more reliable than mere apostolic lineage in interpreting apostolic tradition, and that the basis for leadership should be spiritual maturity not a person's sex. On those foundations rest not only its claims to possess the true understanding of Jesus' teachings, but also to have a vision of Christian community and mission that reflected the Savior's own model as a teacher and mediator of salvation.

Further, its portrait of Mary offers an alternative to sole reliance on apostolic witness as the source of authority. Although she, too, knew the historical Jesus, was a witness to the resurrection, and received instruction from the Savior, these experiences are not what set her apart from the others. Throughout the *Gospel*, Mary is clearly portrayed as an exemplary disciple. She doesn't falter when the Savior departs. She steps into his place after his departure, comforting, strengthening, and instructing the others. Her spiritual comprehension and maturity are demonstrated in her calm behavior and especially in her visionary experience. These at once provide evidence of her spiritual maturity and form the basis for her legitimate exercise of authority in instructing the other disciples. She does not teach in her own name, but passes on the words of the Savior, calming the disciples and turning their hearts toward the Good. Her character proves the truth of her revelation and by extension authorizes the teaching of the *Gospel of Mary*—and it does so by opposing those apostles who reject women's authority and preach another gospel, laying down laws beyond those which the Savior determined.

# Part III

## The Gospel of Mary in Early Christianity

Papyrus Oxyrhynchus 3525

## Chapter 10

# The Jesus Tradition

Readers acquainted with the New Testament will find much that seems familiar in the *Gospel of Mary*: the characters of the Savior, Peter, and Mary; the vocabulary of gospel, kingdom, and law; and the post-resurrection scenario[1] in which the Savior meets with his disciples, commissions them to preach and teach, and then departs. Yet they will also encounter striking differences: unfamiliar terms and ideas appear and the Savior's words are sometimes puzzling. Usually scholars explain the similarities by assuming that the *Gospel of Mary* borrowed from or was influenced by the New Testament gospels and at least some of the letters; they characterize the differences in terms of deviance from the canonical norm. But this picture is not accurate, for it misrepresents the dynamics of early Christian life and practice.

As I noted earlier, the *Gospel of Mary* was written before the canon had been established. At that time there was keen debate over the meaning of Jesus' teachings and his importance for salvation. And because Jesus himself did not write, all our portraits of him reflect the perspectives of early Christians. Since the end of the eighteenth-century, historians have been asking how those portraits developed.[2] After long and painstaking investigation, they have constructed the following picture[3]: Jesus said and did some things that were remembered and passed down orally. People did not repeat everything he said and did, but only what was particularly memorable or distinctive, especially what was of use in the early churches for preaching, teaching, ritual practices, and other aspects of community life. His parables and his sayings (called aphorisms) were often so striking, so pithy and memorable, that they were repeated again and again. A saying like "Blessed are the poor," for example, would surely have struck people as remarkable—for who thinks poverty is a blessing! In the process of being passed down, his words and deeds were interpreted and elaborated. The *Gospel of Matthew*, for example, interpreted the saying about poverty allegorically: "Blessed are the poor *in spirit*" (*Matt* 5:3); while the *Gospel of Luke* read it as a pronouncement against injustices tied to wealth and greed: "But *woe to you who are rich*, for you have received your consolation" (*Luke* 6:24). Some materials were adapted to fit the needs of developing communities for worship or mission; others were elaborated to address new situations that arose. Some sayings attributed to Jesus in the gospels came from early Christian prophets who claimed to have received revealed teaching from the Lord in the Spirit—for the early churches did not necessarily distinguish between the words of the historical Jesus and the revelation of the risen Christ to inspired prophets. Traditions about Jesus were used and passed down primarily in oral form as part of the living practice of early Christians. As Helmut Koester writes, "Sayings of Jesus were known because they had been established as parts of a Christian catechism; the passion narrative was known because it was embedded into the Christian liturgy."[4] Gradually various elements of oral tradition were frozen in writing, sometimes as a collection of Jesus' words like the *Gospel of Thomas* or *Q*, sometimes in a narrative like the *Gospel of Mark*.

These writings give us glimpses of how the Jesus tradition was being used and interpreted by the earliest Christians, but it would be historically incorrect to think they reflect the full breadth of early Christian interpretation of that tradition. While recent discoveries like the *Gospel of Mary* and the *Gospel of Thomas* have started to fill in some gaps, they also prove that theological reflections in the first centuries of Christian beginnings were much more diverse and varied than we had ever realized. Moreover, only a few of the many writings by early Christians have survived. And even if all the early Christian literature *had* been preserved, those written sources would represent only a fraction of the full story, because the gospel was spread primarily by mouth and ear: it was preached and heard. Most people in the ancient world could neither read nor write. Christian ideas and practices developed in the primarily oral contexts of evangelizing, prayer and worship, preaching and prophesying. The sounds of those voices are lost to us forever.

Nor did the written gospels play the same role in early Christian life that they have in our own literate, print societies. Again and again in antiquity we hear that people were suspicious of books. Indeed, when Irenaeus argued for the authority of the four gospels in the late second century, he had to counter the views of Christians who claimed that "truth was not transmitted by means of written documents, but in living speech; and that for this reason Paul declares, 'We speak wisdom among the perfect but not the wisdom of this cosmos'."[5] True teaching was communicated directly through speech, and the most powerful and authoritative kind of speech was prophetic revelation—the divine voice, with the power to create the universe, reaching into people's lives through inspired teachers and prophets.

Moreover, as the literary sources that have survived were copied and passed on, they were sometimes altered to suit new situations and theological demands. A striking example of this can be seen in the literary relationships among the gospels of *Matthew*, *Mark*, and *Luke*. The overwhelming majority of historical-critical scholars maintains that the authors of *Luke* and *Matthew* knew the *Gospel of Mark* and adapted it to fit their own interpretations of Jesus' teaching and ministry.[6] Not only that, but materials could easily be added on to the end of works, like the final saying in the *Gospel of Thomas* (114) or the longer ending to the *Gospel of Mark* (16:9–20), to say nothing of both intentional and accidental changes that undoubtedly occurred in the process of manually copying the manuscripts.[7] By the beginning of the second century, these processes had resulted in a highly diverse body of gospel material all claiming to present the words and deeds of Jesus.

For over a century, scholars have sought to reach behind these diverse portraits to discern what the historical Jesus really said and did, as well as how early Christians elaborated and interpreted that heritage. One tool they have developed to further this task is source criticism, which seeks to determine which texts were known and used in writing later works. The operative assumption is that the earliest sources would be closest to first-hand accounts and therefore historically and theologically the most reliable, while the later a gospel was written the less reliable it would be. The *Gospel of Mark*, for example, is considered to be the first written gospel and therefore scholars have relied upon it heavily in their attempts to paint historical portraits of Jesus. Later gospels are seen to be valuable for research on the historical Jesus only when they offer new, independent information that goes back to the earliest period. Enormous labors have gone into this enterprise because so much is at stake for theological politics. To claim that one's beliefs rest on the sure foundation of Jesus' teachings and deeds is a powerful assertion of theological legitimacy. To claim that a gospel's teaching deviates from that foundation is an implicit assertion that it is heretical. At stake is the whole basis of Christian orthodoxy and normative Christian identity.

The attempt to determine whether or not the author of the *Gospel of Mary* knew the New Testament texts is therefore not a neutral exercise, but one fraught with theological consequences. From the beginning, assertions that the *Gospel of Mary* is heretical rested upon assertions that it was a late composition both dependent upon and deviant from the New Testament. By measuring its theology against the later established norms of canon and creed, scholars impugned its theological value. Robert McL. Wilson, for example, in a brief study on "The New Testament in the Gnostic *Gospel of Mary*" concluded that "The *Gospel of Mary* presents clear allusions to all four Gospels, in addition to some that are more doubtful. There are two possible references to the First Epistle of John, and Levi's reference to 'putting on the perfect man' seems to recall Ephesians and Colossians."[8] This dependence upon later sources indicated to him that the *Gospel of Mary* was not a reliable witness to the earliest Jesus tradition and, moreover, in his judgment its novel ideas established its deviant character. Thus the *Gospel of Mary* was deemed to be historically unreliable and theologically heretical.

We have to ask two questions: First, is it true that the *Gospel of Mary* is dependent upon New Testament sources? Second, is it legitimate to judge its teaching to be heretical based on comparison with later norms of orthodoxy? The second question will be considered in chapter 14; this chapter and those that follow will inquire more carefully into its possible relationships to other early Christian traditions, especially those represented in the New Testament gospels and Paul.

## The Jesus Tradition in the Gospel of Mary

The initial problem with Wilson's conclusion is that in the absence of direct citations it is not at all clear where the author of the *Gospel of*

*Mary* derived its material about the Savior's teachings. Even Wilson concluded that "the writer's practice is to make use of echoes rather than quotations. . . . There are few full citations, and no real attempt at exegesis; rather are the allusions worked into the text, and it is sometimes difficult to identify the source."[9] Many of the "echoes" in the *Gospel of Mary* can be traced to the earliest layers of the Jesus tradition and were widely dispersed throughout early Christian literature. Sayings like "Anyone with two ears to hear should listen" or "seek and you will find" could have come from any number of literary sources or oral traditions. In addition, since none of the supposed citations shows evidence of the distinctive language of any particular gospel author, it is impossible to be sure which if any gospels may have been known to the writer of the *Gospel of Mary*. By the early second century, the terminology, themes, characters, and narrative structure of the Jesus story were part of the shared thought-world of early Christians, and the *Gospel of Mary*'s use of language was typical of this idiom of Christian theological reflection.[10]

Moreover it is impossible to imagine that the interpretation of the Jesus tradition in the *Gospel of Mary* arose as a "deviation" from the New Testament. The *Gospel of Mary* itself claims to rely directly upon apostolic witnesses to the Savior's teaching after the resurrection. Its authority is based on direct revelation of the Savior, and it appeals to the apostolic witness of Mary Magdalene. We cannot, however, take this claim at face value since it was standard procedure for Christians to ascribe their beliefs to apostles; the New Testament gospels and several of the epistles are well-known examples of this practice.[11] As we will see below, the evidence instead suggests that the *Gospel of Mary* developed an early, independent interpretation of the Jesus tradition within a Gentile Christian context. It knows of other interpretations, but it does not draw upon them as sources for its own teaching; rather when it alludes to other early Christian traditions, it does so primarily to oppose them. Therefore, we should not imagine that the author of the *Gospel of Mary* sat down and read the New Testament gospels and letters, and from those sources generated its interpretation of the Jesus tradition. It is much more conceivable that the author was drawing upon other oral or literary sources, now lost to us, in which the sayings of Jesus were already being understood in terms of popular Platonizing cosmology and Stoic ethics. At the same time, the *Gospel of Mary* evinces a knowledge of alternative traditions, some of which it agrees with and some of which it opposes.

In order to account for both the similarities of the *Gospel of Mary* to other early Christian writings and its distinctive theological development, it is necessary to move away from source criticism. The reason is that this method tends to conceive of literary relationships in static and passive terms, as imitation, borrowing, influence, or some such reiteration of the past. New approaches, collectively called intertextuality, focus instead upon the ways in which authors absorb, transform, or transgress the traditions they appropriate. They tend to stress the ways that authors allude to prior written and oral materials in contexts of struggle. Each work labors to displace other interpretations in order to supersede them. This kind of practice is not so much a question of influence or borrowing as it is a matter of confrontation; authors shape meaning by resituating known materials in ways that can at once present their own views and displace prior readings. The *Gospel of Mary* is replete with evidence of this kind of struggle. The most apparent example is the conflict among the disciples over Mary's revelation, but intertextual analysis shows that even the words of the Savior are shaped by constantly referring the reader beyond the text to alternative interpretations it is seeking to displace. It is as though the Savior is making asides designed specifically to counter other, erroneous interpretations of his sayings. We can never be sure precisely what the author knew or intended, or what associations early readers might have, for we could well be making links that they did not[12]; nevertheless, we can spell out the intertextual allusions we hear that may have been options for ancient readers as well. This procedure is at least an advance over the methods that privilege the New Testament canon in a way early Christians did not, since no fixed canon existed in the first and second centuries.

Let's take as an example *GMary* 4, which Wilson characterizes as "a 'farewell discourse' woven from New Testament texts."[13] Just before the Savior departed, he delivered a short speech, consisting of three parts: peace, warning and admonition, and commission to preach. All three allude to material familiar from other Christian literature, but in the *Gospel of Mary* the order, sequence, and meaning of the sayings are distinctively different. Compare, for example, his greeting of peace with that in other texts:

- *GMary* 4:1: "When the Blessed One had said this, he greeted them all. 'Peace be with you!' he said. 'Acquire my peace within yourselves!'"

- *John* 14:27: "'Peace I leave with you; my peace I give to you; not as the world gives do I give to you. Let not your hearts be troubled, neither let them be afraid.'"
- *John* 20:19: "Jesus came and stood among them and said 'Peace be with you.'"
- *John* 20:21: "Jesus said to them again, 'Peace be with you. As the Father has sent me, even so I send you.'"
- *John* 20:26: "The doors were shut, but Jesus came and stood among them, and said, 'Peace be with you.'"
- *Luke* 24:36: "And as they were saying this, Jesus stood among them and said to them, 'Peace to you!'"[14]
- *Sophia of Jesus Christ* (NHC III) 90:14–91:2, 10–12, 20–23: "After he rose from the dead, his twelve disciples and seven women continued to be his followers and went to Galilee onto the mountain called 'Divination and Joy.'... The Savior appeared, not in his previous form, but in the invisible spirit. ... And he said, 'Peace be to you! My peace I give to you!'" (After a long dialogue, the Savior commissions the disciples to preach.)
- *Letter of Peter to Philip* 140:15-23: "Then Jesus appeared saying to them, 'Peace to you [all] and everyone who believes in my name. And when you depart, joy be to you and grace and power. And be not afraid; behold, I am with you forever.'" (Then the apostles go out to preach, in peace.)

The greeting of peace is common in much ancient literature, and ancient readers may immediately have connected it with a variety of genres and milieus (epistolary greetings, farewells, and so on).[15] In the Christian gospels and dialogue literature, however, the greeting of peace consistently introduces an appearance of Jesus to the disciples. It appears to have become a kind of signal for special instruction or a commissioning, almost always in the context of a post-resurrection appearance.[16] The author may reasonably have expected readers to interpret the Savior's greeting in the *Gospel of Mary* as such a signal.[17] But if they did, their expectation receives a startling twist because the Savior tells them to "acquire my peace *within yourselves*." That they were not prepared for. The *Gospel of Mary* emphasizes the interiority of the peace in a way that is missing in the other accounts. Elsewhere, the peace is meant to allay their fears, whether because they are startled by the epiphany of the risen Savior in their midst or because they need comfort in the face of his impending death (*John* 14:27). But here the command of the Savior relates directly to finding the child of true Humanity within.

That difference leads to the warning that follows: "Be on your guard so that no one lead you astray, saying 'Look over here! or Look over there!' For the child of true Humanity exists within you" (*GMary* 4:3-5). Here, too, the author may reasonably have expected readers to make connections with similarly phrased warnings in other texts:

- *Mark* 13:5-6, 9 (cf. *Matt* 24:4-5; *Luke* 21:8): And Jesus began to say to them, "Take heed that no one leads you astray. Many will come in my name, saying, 'I am he!' and they will lead many astray.... But take heed to yourselves."
- *Mark* 13:21–26 (cf. *Matt* 24:15–24, 29–30; *Luke* 21:25–27): "And then if anyone says to you, 'Look, here is the Christ!' or 'Look, there he is!' do not believe it. False Christs and false prophets will arise and show signs and wonders, to lead astray, if possible, the elect. But take heed; I have told you all things beforehand. But in those days, after that tribulation, the sun will be darkened, and the moon will not give its light, and the stars will be falling from heaven, and the powers in the heavens will be shaken. And then they will see the Son of Man coming in clouds with great power and glory."
- *Q* 17:22–24 (cf. *Luke* 17:22–24; *Matt* 24:26–27): And he said to the disciples, "The days are coming when you will desire to see one of the days of the Son of Man, and you will not see it. And they will say to you, 'Lo, here,' or 'Lo, there.' Do not go out, do not follow. For as the lightning flashes and lights up the sky from one side to the other, so will the Son of Man be in his day."
- *Luke* 17:20–21: Being asked by the Pharisees when the kingdom of God was coming, he answered them, "The kingdom of God is not coming with signs to be observed; nor will they say, 'Lo, here it is!' or 'There!' for behold, the kingdom of God is in you."
- *GThom* 3: "If your leaders say to you, 'Look, the kingdom is in the sky,' then the birds of the sky will precede you. If they say to you, 'It is in the sea,' then the fish will precede you. Rather, the kingdom is within you and it is outside of you. When you know yourselves, then you will be known, and you will under-

stand that you are children of the living Father. But if you do not know yourselves, then you live in poverty, and you are the poverty."
- *GThom* 113b: "(The kingdom) will not come by watching for it. It will not be said, 'Look, here!' or 'Look, there.' Rather, the kingdom of the Father is spread out upon the earth, and people do not see it."

The structural similarities are key. Except for *Mark* 13:5–6, each saying is composed of three parts:

1. some formulation that places the readers in opposition to others, either as an explicit warning (against false leaders, prophets, or messiahs) or in an implicit controversy setting (as when the Pharisees ask Jesus a question in *Luke* 17:20–21).
2. the formula: 'lo, here' 'lo, there.'
3. a statement about the true location or arrival of the Son of Man or the kingdom.

The first part is always composed to fit the saying into the work's narrative context, and identifies those of whom the readers should be wary. Note that most opponents are identified only in very general terms: "no one," "anyone," "they." The aim is to counter any opposition, wherever it comes from. This generality allows readers to determine for themselves who the opponents are, supplying more definite connections with opponents from their own local contexts, even though it would appear from what follows that the *Gospel of Mary* has apocalyptic prophets especially in mind. And here the phrasing makes it appear that the Savior does not foment controversy, but only guards the truth. The second part of the saying is almost identical in all the sources, and hence is the core of the allusion. It is the third part that is always the clincher, for here one finds out the truth:

- *GMary*: The child of true Humanity is within you.
- *Mark*: They will see the Son of Man coming in clouds with great power and glory.
- *Q*: For as the lightning flashes and lights up the sky from one side to the other, so will the Son of Man be in his day.
- *Luke*: The kingdom of God is in the midst of you.
- *GThom* 3: The kingdom is within you and it is outside of you.

- *GThom* 113: The kingdom of the Father is spread out upon the earth, and people do not see it.

The sayings in *Mark* and *Q* appear in apocalyptic contexts where Jesus is describing the travail of the last days and the future coming of the Son of Man. He is warning his disciples against false messiahs and prophets who will lead believers astray. But according to the Savior in the *Gospel of Mary*, those who say that the Son of Man is coming to save you are leading you astray! The warning is directed against any-one who claims that an external power will deliver them. Rather they are to look within themselves for the "Son of Man" because the key to salvation lies in understanding the Savior's teaching about the true nature of Humanity and the self. Here "Son of Man" does not refer to an apocalyptic Savior coming at some future time to usher in the eschatological kingdom; it refers to the Image of humanity's essential spiritual nature located within the self. In any case, "Son of Man" is never used in the *Gospel of Mary* to refer to the Savior. It is not diffi-cult to conclude that the author of the *Gospel of Mary* has formulated this saying specifically against the kind of apocalyptic expectations that appear in *Mark* and *Q*, but the modality is at most by implication, not direct attack. Regardless of whatever the author's intention may have been, any reader familiar with apocalyptic Son of Man theology would have made the connection and seen the critique.

But perhaps the reader would instead have been reminded of say-ings like those in *Luke* 17:20–21 or *GThom* 3 and 113. They are closer in meaning to the *Gospel of Mary*, and provide evidence of a relatively widespread alternative tradition within early Christianity. The author of *Luke* declares that the kingdom is already present. Believers do not need to wait for its coming because it is present in the mission of Jesus and the establishment of the Spirit-filled church. The *Gospel of Thomas* agrees that Jesus' teaching exposes the presence of the kingdom, but it locates the kingdom in creation. It does not look forward to the end of the world, but backward to *Genesis* to imagine the perfection of God's kingdom.[18] Both the world and humanity—made in the image and likeness of God—reveal the Divine Realm. *GThom* 113 says that the kingdom is already spread out upon the earth, if people only have the spiritual capacity to see it. *GThom* 3 further suggests that people have been looking in the wrong places, even as the author of *Deut* 30:10–14 had admonished his readers:

... turn to the Lord your God with all your heart and with all your soul. For this commandment which I command you this day is not too hard for you, neither is it far off. It is not in heaven, that you should say, 'Who will go up for us to heaven, and bring it down?' Neither is it beyond the sea, that you should say, 'Who will go over the sea for us and bring it to us, that we may hear it and do it?' But the word is very near you; it is in your mouth and in your heart, so that you can do it.

The kingdom is not in sky or the sea; rather God's Realm is already present within oneself and in creation. Yet while these sayings appear somewhat similar to the teaching of the *Gospel of Mary*, both *Luke* and *Thomas'* gospels speak of the presence of God's Realm rather than the Son of Man or the child of true Humanity. The *Gospel of Mary* at once nods toward other traditions while displacing them and decentering their teaching about the Realm of God.

After telling the disciples that the child of true Humanity is within, the Savior commands them, "Follow it!" (*GMary* 4:6). Here again the reader may think of other instances in which the command to follow was given, such as:

- *Mark* 8:34b (cf. *Matt* 16:24; *Luke* 9:23): And he called to him the multitude with his disciples, and said to them, "If anyone would come after me, let him deny himself and take up his cross and follow me."
- *Q* 14:27 (*Luke* 14:27; *Matt* 10:38): "Those who do not carry their own cross and come after me, cannot be my disciples."

In both these cases, the command to follow is directly connected with the cross. In the *Gospel of Mark*, the injunction to follow Jesus occurs immediately after he predicts his death and resurrection, and is explicitly interpreted in terms of the discipleship of the cross: those who follow Jesus can expect to suffer trials and persecution, even death. In *Q*, the saying links discipleship with the dangerous mission of preaching the gospel; the missionary will need to abandon family and accept the possibility of persecution. The message of the *Gospel of Mary* is quite different. Although the disciples seem fully aware of

Jesus' death and the possibility of their own martyrdom (*GMary* 5:1–3), the command to follow is not connected with the cross and suffering discipleship or even with preaching the gospel. Instead they are exhorted to locate the child of true Humanity within and follow it.[19] If Mary is any example, following the Human One will lead them to fearlessness, stability of character, and eventually to rest.

Similarly the command to seek and find has a substantially different meaning in the *Gospel of Mary* because it is associated with finding the child of true Humanity within.

- *GMary* 4:7: "Those who search for it will find it!"
- *Q* 11:9–10 (cf. *Luke* 11:9-10; *Matt* 7:7–8): "Ask, and it will be given you; seek, and you will find; knock, and it will be opened to you. For everyone who asks receives, and he who seeks finds, and to him who knocks it will be opened."
- *GThom* 2 (cf. POxy 654.2): "Let whoever seeks continue seeking until he finds. When he finds, he will become troubled. When he becomes troubled, he will be astonished, and he will rule over the All."
- *GThom* 94: "Whoever seeks will find, and [whoever knocks] will be let in."
- *John* 7:34, 36: "You will seek me and you will not find me; where I am you cannot come."
- *John* 13:33: "Yet a little while I am with you. You will seek me, and as I said to the Jews so I am saying now to you, 'Where I am going, you cannot come.'"
- *GThom* 38: "There will be days when you look for me and will not find me."
- *GThom* 92: "Seek and you will find. Yet, what you asked me about in former times and which I did not tell you then, now I do desire to tell, but you do not inquire after it."
- *DSav* 126:6–11 "His [disciples said, Lord], who is it who seeks, and [...] reveals? [The lord said to them,] 'He who seeks [...] reveal ...[...].'"
- *DSav* 129:15 "And [let] whoever [...] seek and find and [rejoice]."

The saying "seek and you will find" is at once simple and enigmatic. What is it that one is supposed to seek and find? Early Christians answered this question in a variety of ways. *Q*, *Luke*, and *Matthew* understood it to be an assurance of the efficacy of prayer. *GThom* 2 understood seeking and finding to be the first two stages in the process of salvation (followed by being troubled, being amazed, and finally ruling over the entire creation). In the *Gospel of Mary*, the assurance that "They who seek (the child of true Humanity within) will find it" is part of its distinctive theology that locates the child of true Humanity within.

In addition to the parallels listed above, the *Dialogue of the Savior* offers important thematic similarities to the *Gospel of Mary*. Indeed Helmut Koester has suggested that the dialogue in *Dialogue of the Savior* is

> a commentary on the eschatological time table which is implied in Gos. Thom. 2. The disciples have sought and have found; but their rule and their rest will only appear in the future. At the present time, the 'rulers' of the cosmos still exercise their authority, and the time at which the disciples will rule over them has not yet come (Dial. Sav. ##47–50). The rest can only be obtained when they can rid themselves of the burden of their bodies (Dial. Sav. #28). Mary, who recognizes this, is praised as a disciple who has understood the all (Dial. Sav. #53).[20]

If Koester is correct, we may be able to see here thematic connections among the *Gospel of Thomas, Dialogue of the Savior,* and the *Gospel of Mary*. All three works understand the process of salvation as seeking and finding, overcoming the rule of the Powers (or 'rulers'), leaving the body, and obtaining rest, and all give Mary Magdalene a prominent role. The only significant difference lies in the *Gospel of Mary's* rejection of ruling as an eschatological goal. These works show that the kind of theology encountered in the *Gospel of Mary* was not entirely distinctive, and some readers may have been acquainted with this kind of theological reflection already.

Moreover Koester has pointed out that the theme of seeking and finding is crucial to the *Gospel of John* as well.[21] There, he argues, it serves a polemic against the kind of Christology that portrayed Jesus primarily as a teacher.[22] Koester concludes:

> It is evident that, for the *Gospel of John*, seeking Jesus—not seeking for the meaning of his words—is the central theme. For both the crowds and for the disciples, the mystery of the

seeking after Jesus is captured in the statement of John 7:34 and 36: "You will seek me and not find me, and where I am you cannot come." In John 13:33, the disciples are confronted with the same mystery: "Yet a little while I am with you. You will seek me, and as I said to the Jews so I am saying now to you, 'Where I am going, you cannot come.'" As far as the hostile crowds are concerned, their inability to find Jesus could simply be explained as the result of their unbelief. However, for the disciples too, the question of being with Jesus after his departure, and reaching the place to which he is going, is central for continuing belief in him. The farewell discourses of the Gospel of John are concerned with this question, because a Gnostic answer was already at hand: those who are prepared spiritually can follow the redeemer to the heavenly realms.[23]

Koester's argument can be easily extended to include the *Gospel of Mary*. It, too, contains the kind of theological reflection that the author of *John* would surely have opposed had he known it. The Savior's revelation teaches the disciples how to prepare themselves to ascend to the heavenly Realm by seeking and finding the child of true Humanity within. Readers who made these intertextual associations would not have understood them in terms of borrowing or influence, but as differing, even conflicting meanings of Jesus' command to seek and find.

The Savior wishes the disciples to find the child of true Humanity within so as to prepare themselves to go forth and preach the gospel. He commissions them to go out, cautioning them against setting excessive rules and laws.

- *GMary* 4:8–10: (The Savior commissions his disciples): "Go then and preach the gospel of the kingdom. Do not lay down any rules beyond what I ordained for you, nor promulgate law like the lawgiver, or else it will dominate you."
- *GMary* 5:1–3: (After the Savior's departure, the disciples) were distressed and wept greatly. "How are we going to go out to the rest of the world to preach the good news of the Realm of the child of Humanity" (the gospel of the kingdom of the Son of Man)?" they said. "If they didn't spare him, how will they spare us?"

- *GMary* 10:11–13 (BG): (Levi admonishes the other disciples): "Rather let us be ashamed and put on the perfect Human and acquire him for ourselves as he commanded us, and preach the gospel, not setting down any other rule or law that differs from what the Savior said."
- *GMary* 10:11–13 (PRyl 463): "Rather let us be ashamed and, clothing ourselves with the [perfect] Human, let us do what we were commanded. Let us proclaim the gospel as the Savior said, not laying down any rules or making laws."
- *Matt* 24:14 (cf. *Mark* 13:10; *Luke* 21:13): (Jesus tells his disciples): "And this gospel of the kingdom will be preached throughout the whole world, as a testimony to all nations; and then the end will come."
- *Mark* 16:15: And (Jesus) said to (the disciples), "Go into all the world and preach the gospel to the whole creation."
- *Matt* 28:18–20: And Jesus came and said to (the eleven disciples), "All authority in heaven and on earth has been given to me. Go therefore and make disciples of all nations, baptizing them in the name of the Father and of the Son and of the Holy Spirit, teaching them to observe all that I have commanded you; and lo, I am with you always, to the close of the age."
- *Luke* 24:45–48: Then (Jesus) opened their minds to understand the scriptures, and said to them, "Thus it is written, that the Christ should suffer and on the third day rise from the dead, and that repentance and forgiveness of sins should be preached in his name to all nations, beginning from Jerusalem. You are witnesses of these things."
- *John* 15:16: (In his farewell discourse, Jesus says): "You did not choose me, but I chose you and appointed you that you should go and bear fruit and that your fruit should abide; so that whatever you ask the Father in my name, he may give it to you."
- *John* 17:18: (Jesus prays to the Father): "As thou did send me into the world, so I have sent them into the world."

Except in the *Gospel of John*, all examples of the commissioning are part of the farewell message of Jesus to his disciples after the resurrection but before his final departure. In *Matthew*, the preaching of the gospel is meant to fill the time before the end; in *Luke* it signals the beginning of the age of the Spirit-filled church. In *John*, no specific commissioning is reported, although references to bearing fruit and being sent into the world are mentioned in Jesus' farewell discourse. The *Gospel of Mary* also sets the commissioning in the Savior's final words, but the gospel does not end with his departure; instead the Savior's admonition to preach the gospel becomes the central topic of discussion among the disciples. As we explored in more detail in chapter 9 above, the entire second half of the *Gospel of Mary* is taken up with exploring the question of who is able to meet the demands of apostleship and preach the gospel in truth.

As Ann Pasquier has pointed out, the order of the Savior's farewell speech in the *Gospel of Mary* indicates a distinctive theological perspective.[24] First the Savior cautions the disciples to guard themselves against error; then he affirms the presence of the child of true Humanity within them; and only then does he commission them to go preach the gospel. This order, Pasquier notes, is the reverse of the *Gospel of Matthew*, where the Savior first says that the gospel of the kingdom will be preached to all the nations (24:14); then he warns the disciples to guard against error (24:23–26); and finally he assures them of the coming of the Son of Man (24:27). The effect in *Matthew* is to see the preaching of the gospel as a precondition for the coming of the Son of Man and the last judgment. In the *Gospel of Mary*, however, the presence of the Son of Man within is the basis for preaching the kingdom. The *Gospel of Mary*'s sequence completely undercuts the apocalyptic message of *Matthew* and replaces it with a call to discover and preach the gospel of the Realm of the child of true Humanity. Readers who compare the two works will perceive conflicting pictures of the Savior's teaching.

The *Gospel of Mary* also provides an answer to the question of who can preach the gospel that differs from the other gospel accounts. The response of the disciples to the departure of the risen Savior contrasts sharply with that represented in parallel scenes in *John*, *Luke*, or *Mark*. In *John*, Mary speaks first, the male disciples are afraid, and then Jesus comes (20:18–19). The reverse order found in the *Gospel of Mary* highlights the way in which Mary assumes the Savior's role in bringing comfort and instruction after his departure. In *Luke*, the disciples are filled with joy after Jesus departs (24:52–53); in *Mark*, they immediately go forth and preach the gospel (16:20); in *John*, it is Jesus who comforts the disciples before his death. In the *Gospel of Mary*, however, after the Savior's departure all the disciples except Mary Magdalene are distressed and weeping—behavior more like the reaction of the disciples at Jesus' arrest (*Mark* 14:50) or during the trial

(*Mark* 14:66–72). In particular, they fear for their lives; "If they did not spare him, how will they spare us?" (*GMary* 5:3). Of course the disciples' fear for their lives was a real and immediate issue widely addressed in early Christian literature, usually within the context of persecution.[25] But in other narratives Jesus has already offered encouragement and comfort before his departure, and the disciples go forth with joy and confidence. In *Acts*, for example, the disciples are portrayed as fearless in their preaching. Or again, the other gospels place Peter's hot-headed behavior and triple denial before the resurrection, while in the *Gospel of Mary* he continues to behave this way even after the Savior departs.

The reader of the *Gospel of Mary* has to wonder what kind of gospel such disciples will preach. Their doubt and fear show they have failed to acquire inward peace. How can they preach the gospel if they do not understand it? They think that following the Savior will lead them to suffering—as *Mark* 13:9–13 insists that it will—but in the *Gospel of Mary* their fear only demonstrates that they have not fully comprehended the Savior's teaching. Since attachment to the body is the source of suffering and death (*GMary* 3:7–11), separation from that attachment frees them: there is no promise of, or desire for a physical resurrection.[26] The conclusion of the *Gospel of Mary* leaves the reader with little confidence that these disciples, especially Peter and Andrew, will be able to preach the gospel of the Realm. And since, as we have noted, the *Gospel of Mary* questions the validity of apostolic succession and authority, it is little wonder that later orthodox theologians, who founded their own authority upon apostolic reliability, would decry the *Gospel of Mary* as heresy. Irenaeus, for example, excoriated those who criticized the apostles: "For it is unlawful to assert that they preached before they possessed perfect knowledge, as some do even venture to say, boasting themselves as improvers of the apostles."[27] But Irenaeus was only one man. Other Christians may have thought differently, dismayed by the ever increasing division expressed in theological polemics and distressed by new laws that functioned only to condemn the views of other Christians.

In every case we have examined, the meaning and function of the Savior's farewell speech is enriched by examining the possible intertextual relations to other early Christian literature and theology. To the degree that readers were conscious of these allusions, they would have understood them in terms of intra-Christian controversy rather than literary dependence, borrowing, or influence. To understand early Christianity, it is crucial to recall that no account of Jesus' words and deeds has come down to us uninterpreted: since he did not himself write anything, there is no direct path back to the historical Jesus. All gospel literature attests first and foremost to the theology and practice of early Christians, all our portraits of Jesus come filtered through the lenses of early Christians' beliefs and practices, and all were forged in dialogue with other views.

## Appendix: Criteria for Determining Literary Dependence

In order to appreciate the intertextual approach used above—and illustrate my intertextual dialogue with source critical approaches—let me elaborate on my own conclusions resulting from the use of the source method. Very little source-critical research has been done on the *Gospel of Mary,* in part because scholars have generally assumed that the author knew and used all four canonical gospels and at least some Pauline literature.[28] Initially, I too held this position, and indeed my own published work to date reflects that assumption.[29] But the more I tried to interpret the *Gospel of Mary* from this perspective, the more problems I saw. I now argue that the application of this method to the *Gospel of Mary* shows that it presents an interpretation of the early Jesus tradition that is independent of any known literary work. While it offers no new information about the historical Jesus, it does provide evidence of a type of early Christian theological reflection previously known only from such detractors as Irenaeus.

Scholars employing historical-critical methods have developed several criteria for determining whether or not a work knew and used another literary work. Internal literary factors are the most important criteria. The usual indicators of literary dependence include the following:

- extensive word-for-word similarity (citation)
- similar arrangement or ordering of materials
- similar narrative context or setting
- the use of a citation formula (e.g., "As it is written . . ." or "This was to fulfill what was spoken by the prophet Isaiah . . .")
- use of language specific to the source work[30]

The more fully a work demonstrates these literary indicators, the more likely it is dependent.[31]

It is also important to consider external factors, such as the rate of literacy in antiquity and the nature of literary composition in a chirographic culture, that is, one in which writing exists but is largely restricted to a professional class of scribes. In a time and place where only a minority of the population could read or write, it is necessary to ask whether similarities among literary works are more likely due to literary or oral processes. This consideration is particularly pertinent in the early stages of Christianity when the accessibility of written works was limited. Much depends upon how we understand the way in which tradition was passed on. If, as Helmut Koester has argued, the most probable scenario is that people knew Jesus' sayings and other materials orally in the context of ritual, instruction, and missionary activity, then the burden of proof falls on those who want to argue that written works are the direct sources of the tradition.[32] As Koester himself notes, however, this conclusion is complicated by the possibility that material from written sources has entered into the mix, interacting with other oral and literary traditions. In that case, the distinction between written and oral sources is not cut and dried. An author may not be quoting from a written source, and yet materials from various written sources may have been inserted into the oral tradition upon which the author is dependent. This appears to be the case with the *Gospel of Mary*. It does not show a direct knowledge of any known written sources, yet neither is it completely independent of the Christian traditions that came to be formulated in the written gospels and the letters of Paul.

Finally, what level of proof is necessary, given that historical investigation never produces absolute certainty? Should one have to prove that the *Gospel of Mary* did not know these other works? Or that it did? Is it enough for scholars to show that it is *possible* for the *Gospel of Mary* to have known a specific work, or do they need to meet the heavier burden of showing that it is *probable*? These considerations are significant in a case like the present one because the conclusion will depend largely on the standards employed. While the lower standards clearly indicate the *possibility* that the *Gospel of Mary* knew the canonical gospels, such a conclusion cannot carry much weight. Since higher standards produce results that rest on a much firmer foundation, they will be used here. To conclude that the *Gospel of Mary* is independent of other known literary works would require proving that the cumulative weight of the evidence shows that it probably did not cite from these works.

A well-known example should help illustrate the significance of these considerations. Both the *Gospel of Matthew* and the *Gospel of Luke* contain a set of sayings usually called the beatitudes:

| *Matt* 5:3–12 | *Luke* 6:20–26 |
|---|---|
| Congratulations to the poor in spirit! | Congratulations, you poor! |
| Heaven's domain belongs to them. | God's domain belongs to you. |
| Congratulations to those who grieve: | Congratulations, you hungry! |
| They will be consoled. | You will have a feast. |
| Congratulations to the gentle! | Congratulations, you who weep now! |
| They will inherit the earth. | You will laugh. |
| Congratulations to those who hunger | Congratulations to you when people |
| and thirst for justice! | hate you, and when they ostracize you |
| They will have a feast. | and denounce you and scorn your |
| Congratulations to the merciful! | name as evil, because of the son of |
| They will receive mercy. | Adam! Rejoice on that day, and jump |
| Congratulations to those with undefiled | for joy! Just remember, your compen- |
| hearts! | sation is great in heaven. Recall that |
| They will see God. | their ancestors treated the prophets the |
| Congratulations to those who work for | same way. |
| peace! | Damn you rich! |
| They will be known as God's children. | You already have your consolation. |
| Congratulations to those who have suf- | Damn you who are well-fed now! |
| fered persecution for the sake of justice! | You will know hunger. |
| Heaven's domain belongs to them. | Damn you who laugh now! You will |
| Congratulations to you when they | learn to weep and grieve. |
| denounce you and persecute you and | Damn you when everybody speaks well |
| spread malicious gossip about you | of you! Recall that their ancestors |
| because of me! Rejoice and be glad! | treated the phony prophets the same |
| Your compensation is great in heaven. | way. |
| Recall that this is how they persecuted | |
| the prophets who preceded you. | |

The word-for-word similarities in these two versions of the beatitudes is striking and seems to indicate a common source, whether written or oral. In some cases, minor differences in language, such as "the poor" versus "you poor," do not cause significant differences in meaning; "the poor" and "you poor" differ only in the rhetorical directness with which the audience is addressed, a feature called "performancial variation."[33] The same is not true of *Matthew*'s addition of "in spirit." To be poor "in spirit" is different from being poor, and very different from *Luke*'s condemnation, "Damn you rich!" For source critics, the common elements of this saying are due to use of a common source; the differences are due to the work of the editors of the two gospels. The editor of *Matthew* has added "in spirit"; the editor of *Luke*, the condemnation of the rich.

By itself, this one beatitude is not sufficient to determine whether or not the gospels of *Matthew* and *Luke* got this saying from the same literary source. It might just as easily have been filtered through different literary or oral sources. The weight of the evidence shifts when we look at the full sequence. Not only do the two gospels contain a number of very similar sayings, but the *order* in which the parallel materials appear is also similar.

| *Matthew* | *Luke* |
|-----------|--------|
| poor | poor |
| grieving | hungry |
| gentle | |
| hungry | weeping |
| merciful | |
| peacemakers | |
| persecuted | persecuted |

It appears that the common source, *Q*, had only four beatitudes: poor, hungry, grieving, persecuted. The *Gospel of Matthew* appears to have added several additional beatitudes, and the order of grieving/hungry is reversed in the two works. Yet the similarity in order of their common material is striking enough to increase the *probability* that the two were based on a common literary source. This supposition is strengthened by consideration of the *Gospel of Thomas*. It, too, contains several beatitudes, but each appears alone, suggesting that the beatitudes circulated singly in the oral tradition. At some point they were strung together in a collection which was known to the gospels of *Matthew* and *Luke*, but not to *Thomas*.

In addition, both *Matthew* and *Luke* place the beatitudes in a longer sermon context: *Matthew* in the sermon on the mount (5-7), *Luke* in the sermon on the plain (6:17–49). That they would both keep the beatitudes as a collection within a sermon may be significant, even though each takes place in a different geographical location.

One hindrance for modern readers might be the lack of a citation formula. If both gospels took the beatitudes from *Q*, why didn't they say so? That fact is not particularly disturbing, however, since the use of citation formulas in antiquity was quite rare. Unlike the modern world where references are required to avoid charges of plagiarism, the Roman world lacked a copyright office, and indeed most early Christian writing was anonymous or pseudonymous. Readers were likely to be offended only if language inappropriate to a person's known character was put on his or her lips.

All these factors indicate a strong possibility that the gospels of *Matthew* and *Luke* used a common source for the beatitudes, and that they each adapted that source for their own purposes. The clinching argument, however, is that this pattern holds true not just for the beatitudes, but for the entirety of the two gospels. Again and again comparison shows patterns of similar language and order. As a result, scholars have come to the conclusion that the cumulative weight of the total evidence falls on the side of literary dependence: the similarities between the gospels of *Matthew* and *Luke* are due to use of common sources, the *Gospel of Mark* and *Q*.

Comparison between the two gospels also demonstrates that differences can easily be accounted for as changes and additions made to reflect the editors' differing theological perspectives and interpretations of common material. This point is important for us because if a later author was quoting, say, *Matthew* and not *Luke*, the later work would be expected to show the secondary editorial features of *Matthew* not present in *Luke*. That is, a later work that reads "Congratulations to the poor!" could have a number of possible sources: oral tradition, *Q*, *Matthew*, or *Luke*. But if it reads "Blessed are the poor *in spirit*," the source is probably the *Gospel of Matthew*. It is not just *possible* that it is the *Gospel of Matthew*, it is *probable*.

If we now apply this method systematically to the *Gospel of Mary*, the results point decidedly toward its literary independence. It does not show a consistent pattern of similarity to any one source or set of sources known to us, whether in word for word citation, ordering of materials, context, or theological emphasis. I have arrived at this judgment for several reasons:

> The closest (often word-for-word) similarities appear only in material that either was very common in the first and second centuries (such as the greeting of peace, the command to follow, or the commission to preach the gospel), or that goes back to the earliest layers of the Jesus tradition (such as the saying about having ears to hear, the command to seek and

find, the characters, and the visionary appearances of Jesus to Mary of Magdala). This material could therefore have derived from any number of sources, oral or written, and no material clearly has to have been derived from any particular known work.

The order and arrangement of the individual pieces of tradition in the *Gospel of Mary* are significantly different from those of any known source.

The post-resurrection setting doesn't require an explanation of literary dependence; it could just as well be due to oral story-telling. The tradition that Jesus appeared to his disciples and gave them teaching after his resurrection is wide spread and, again, points to no specific source known to us.

While this point is rather moot, for the sake of completeness I should note that no citation formula appear in the *Gospel of Mary*.

Finally and most crucially, no specific evidence of secondary editorial labor from known sources appears in the sayings or narrative material.

Moreover the significant differences in the interpretation of common elements of the Jesus tradition do not suggest dependence, but rather point toward a context of independent theological development. I simply can't imagine that our author read the four canonical gospels and then sat down and wrote the *Gospel of Mary*. At the same time, it is clear that this stream of theological reflection was in conversation with other Christian views. Both the formulation of the Savior's teaching and the disputes among the disciples show a clear awareness of interpretations other than its own. The very literary setting of the work, as a revelation from the Savior to known apostles, seems fashioned to claim that its teaching comes directly from God and was conveyed with apostolic authority. These claims indicate a need to gain legitimacy for its views in a situation of competition with other Christians.

Let me summarize my conclusions.

1. Several sayings in the *Gospel of Mary* go back to the earliest layers of the Jesus tradition, and could have come from any number of sources, including oral tradition. These sayings are too

common to attribute to any particular source and show no specific redactional elements from any known literature.

- *ears to hear* (*GMary* 2:5, 3:14; *Mark* 4:9 and many other examples)
- *seek and find* (*GMary* 4:7; *Q* 11:9–10; *GThom* 38, 92, 94; *John* 7:34, 36; 13:33; *DSav* 126:6–11; 129:15).
- *mind (heart) and treasure* (*GMary* 7:4; *Q* 12:34; Clement of Alexandria, *Stromateis* 7.12,77; and many others)
- *look here, look there* (*GMary* 4:3–4; *Mark* 13:5–6 and par.; *Mark* 13:21–26 and par.; *GThom* 3; 113; *Luke* 17:20–21, 23–24)
- *kingdom/Son of Man is within* (*GMary* 4:5; *GThom* 3; 113; *Luke* 17:21)

2. Other sayings in the *Gospel of Mary* were crafted by the early churches, but were wide spread. No specific redactional elements from any known literature are apparent in the *Gospel of Mary*.
   - *peace* (*GMary* 4:1-2; *John* 14:27; 20:19, 21, 26; *Luke* 24:36[34]; *SoJsChr* NHC III 91:21–23; *PetPhil* 140:15–23)
   - *follow* (*GosMary* 4:6; *Mark* 8:34b and par.; *Q* 14:27)
   - *commission to preach* (*GMary* 4:8; 5:2; 10:12; *Matt* 24:14, *Mark* 13:10; *Luke* 21:13; *Mark* 16:15; *John* 20:21).

3. Narrative material that belongs to the life of the historical Jesus was widespread in the oral tradition:
   - Jesus teaching disciples
   - names of disciples and characterizations
   - death of Jesus (only mentioned but not narrated in *GMary* 5:3)

4. Narrative material that belongs to the later church that was also widespread in the early tradition:
   - post-resurrection visions and revelation, especially the report of an individual vision to Mary Magdalene
   - the disciples' reactions to Jesus' departure
   - the mission to preach the gospel

Those materials that belong to the early Jesus tradition and/or the life of the historical Jesus cannot be attributed to a known source without explicit reference to specific editorial materials (categories 1 and 3). Neither can those materials in the *Gospel of Mary* which show knowledge of traditions that were in all likelihood generated after the death of Jesus be attributed to a specific source; rather they belonged to early tradition. Although word-for-word similarities between the *Gospel of Mary* and other early Christian writings are evident, these are best accounted for by source criticism in terms of independent transmission through unknown oral or literary works for three reasons. First, the order and arrangement of materials corresponds to no other known source. Second, the contexts for the sayings differ radically from known works in that they appear in the *Gospel of Mary* in a post-resurrection setting, not during the life of the historical Jesus. Third and most important, no specifically redactional material from any known work is evinced in the *Gospel of Mary*.

Furthermore, if we were to posit that *GMary* 4, for example, is composed of citations from known gospels, we would have to presume that the author of the *Gospel of Mary*

- took phrases or allusions from various written works, a bit here, a bit there (the peace saying from *John* or *Luke*; "lo, here; lo, there" from *Luke, Matthew, Q* or *Mark* (6:2–4); the [kingdom] is within you from *Luke* or *Thomas*; and the proclamation to preach the gospel from *Matthew* or *Mark*);
- ignored the narrative settings of all of the source texts;
- recombined the order in which the sayings are presented;
- added a new setting;
- substituted "son of man" for "kingdom";
- and gave the borrowed pieces a new meaning (the theology of the Human One within).

This process is far too cumbersome to be plausible as a description of how the *Gospel of Mary* was composed.

On the other hand, it is unlikely that the *Gospel of Mary* was among the earliest Christian works. Although its theology attests to the development of a distinctive interpretation of the Jesus tradition among some Gentile Christians, its formulation of the Savior's words and the controversy among the disciples after the Savior's departure offer substantial evidence that the author was aware of other early Christian interpretations of the Jesus tradition. The Savior warns against those who would expect a savior to rescue them—a common theme in apocalyptic works—and he exhorts the apostles not to lay down rules and laws beyond what he prescribed—such as excluding women from leadership in ministry. And it clearly defends Mary's teaching and leadership against attacks by other prominent disciples, attacks that also resonate with intra-Christian controversy. To be sure, source criticism is useful in producing a negative answer; but in view of all these factors, an intertextual approach provides a far more satisfactory explanation of the *Gospel of Mary*.

## Chapter 11

# Paul

The *Gospel of Mary* shows notable similarities in terminology and conceptuality with the letters of Paul. Ann Pasquier, for example, has argued that there are close connections between *Romans 7* and the *Gospel of Mary* 3-4.[1]

- *GMary* 3:3–8, 10–13: The Savior replied, "There is no such thing as sin; rather you yourselves are what produces sin when you act in accordance with the nature of adultery, which is called 'sin.' For this reason, the Good came among you, pursuing (the good) which belongs to every nature. It will set it within its root." Then he continued. He said, "This is why you get sick and die: because you love what deceives you. . . . Matter gave birth to a passion which has no Image because it derives from what is contrary to nature. A disturbing confusion then occurred in the whole body. That is why I told you, 'Become content at heart, while also remaining discontent and disobedient; indeed become contented and agreeably (only) in the presence of that other Image of nature.'"
- *GMary* 4:9–10: "Do not lay down any rule beyond what I determined for you, nor promulgate law like the lawgiver, or else you might be dominated by it."

- *Rom* 7:1-8; 22–23: "Do you not know, brethren—for I am
speaking to those who know the law—that the law is binding
on a person only during one's life? Thus a married woman is
bound by law to her husband as long as he lives; but if her husband dies she is discharged from the law concerning the husband. Accordingly, she will be called an adulteress if she lives
with another man when her husband is alive. But if her husband dies she is free from that law, and if she marries another
man she is not an adulteress. Likewise, my brethren, you have
died to the law through the body of Christ, so that you may
belong to another, to him who has been raised from the dead
in order that we may bear fruit for God. While we were living
in the flesh, our sinful passions, aroused by the law, were at
work in our members to bear fruit for death. But now we are
discharged from the law, dead to that which held us captive, so
that we serve not under the old written code but in the new
life of the Spirit. What then shall we say? That the law is sin?
By no means! Yet if it had not been for the law, I should not
have known sin. I should not have known what it is to covet if
the law had not said, 'You shall not covet.' But sin, finding
opportunity in the commandment, wrought in me all kinds of
covetousness. Apart from the law sin lies dead. ... For I delight
in the law of God in my inmost self, but I see in my members
another law at war with the law of my mind and making me
captive to the law of sin which dwells in my members."

Pasquier lists the following points of agreement between these passages:

- Domination under the law is compared to adultery.
- Adultery is compared with enslavement to passion and it leads
  to death.
- Freedom from the law means overcoming the domination of
  death.
- Sin does not really exist.
- Law, sin, and death are interconnected.
- An opposition is made between the divine law/nature which
  gives life and that fleshly law/nature which imprisons or domi-
  nates one.

According to Pasquier, the *Gospel of Mary* has transformed Paul's attempt to understand the value of Jewish law in the face of the saving event of Christ's death and resurrection by placing his discussion of law within a cosmological setting. This displacement significantly changes the meaning of Paul's message. Whereas Paul contends that Christ came to free humanity from sin, the teaching of the Savior in the *Gospel of Mary* warns against adulterous attachment to the material world and the body. In contrast to Paul, it sees law not as divine and purposeful (*Rom* 7:7, 12–14), but as a tool of domination.

Yet it is not at all clear that the author of the *Gospel of Mary* was purposefully and consciously taking this passage from Paul in order to transform its message. There is no direct citation, and the language and themes of passion, sin, adultery, law, and death can be found in a wide variety of literature—though to be sure not always grouped together in such close conjunction. Since Paul's letters were being circulated fairly widely by the second century, it is possible that the similarities may have led some readers (in antiquity as well as in the twentieth century) to connect the two literary works. But if so, the important issue is not whether *Gospel of Mary* was influenced by Paul, but how reading the two works together would mutually affect their meanings and theological impact.

In *Rom* 7–8, Paul is writing to fellow Christians in Rome about how Gentiles can receive salvation from God through faith in Christ. His argument centers around the question of how Gentiles can overcome the carnal desires and passions to which they are enslaved in the face of their refusal to acknowledge the true God.[2] Paul argues that they cannot overcome these sinful passions through the law, for only through faith in Christ's death and resurrection (or through Christ's faithfulness[3]) will they be able to serve God in the new life of the Spirit.[4] The reference to adultery serves to illustrate the legal status of Gentiles before God. Paul likens the situation of Gentiles who are dominated by sinful passions to that of an adulterous woman: just as freedom from the law of sin is made possible by the death of Christ, so the death of a woman's husband frees her to become a "good wife." During life, faith frees the body from the wicked passions which dominate it, so that at death the gross physical body can be transformed into an immortal spiritual body (*1 Cor* 15:35–57).

In *GMary* 3, the themes of sin, adultery, and death are raised by Jesus in response to Peter's question "What is the sin of the world?"

Paul's concern for the admission of the Gentiles into the community of Israel is not at issue. Instead, the problem is how to understand and overcome human enslavement to passion in view of the material nature of the body and the world, for since the material world is finite and temporary, it cannot be the basis for an ethics that has ultimate and enduring spiritual value. For the *Gospel of Mary*, therefore, sin is not a matter of right and wrong acts; rather it has to do with the improper mixing (adultery) of material and spiritual natures, which in turn leads to the improper domination of the spiritual nature by the material. Salvation is achieved by overcoming attachment to the body and the material world, for it is this attachment which keeps people enslaved to suffering and death. Ultimately, it is attachment to the body that produces sin. From this perspective, sin doesn't really exist, because the material world and the body associated with it are merely temporary phenomena, soon to pass away. The Goodness of God is what will endure, and it transcends mortal distinctions between good and evil.

Both Paul and the *Gospel of Mary* have been misunderstood. Already in the period of the early church, the author of the *Letter of James* strove to ensure that Paul's insistence on faith as the sole route to salvation[5] not be taken to mean that the ethical life is not important: "What does it profit, my brethren, if a person says he has faith but has not works? Can his faith save him? . . . Faith by itself, if it has no works, is dead" (*Jas* 2:14, 17). So, too, the Savior's statement in the *Gospel of Mary* that there is no such thing as sin could easily be read to mean that moral behavior is not important for salvation[6], that people need only look to their own salvation and can ignore their responsibilities toward others. But this reading is as incorrect as the view that Paul did not believe the moral life was important.

Both Paul and the *Gospel of Mary* insist that the proper relationship to God requires strong ethical sensibilities and practice.[7] In the *Gospel of Mary*, these are particularly modeled by Mary of Magdala. Having attained inward peace and stability, she does not fear the possibility of persecution. Nor is she merely concerned with her own salvation, for in comforting and instructing the other disciples she supports them with her words and behavior. Far from even hinting that she is given to licentiousness, arrogance, or self-indulgence, the gospel exhibits the contrary. Peter, on the other hand, models what the spiritually undeveloped person is like: fearful, arrogant, jealous, ignorant. Moreover, the Savior's injunction against establishing any law is obviously intended not to invite licentiousness, but to ensure that moral behavior and ethical judgments derive from spiritual goodness rather than conformity to external constraints. Paul and the *Gospel of Mary* both assume that cultivating the spiritual life will enhance the moral life, and vice versa.

The views of Paul and the *Gospel of Mary* quite naturally appear to be similar: they are dealing with a similar problem (how to overcome sin and death); they have a similar diagnosis of the problem (that desires and passions, signaled by enslavement to the body, lead to death); and they have a similar solution to the problem (the life of the spirit). But in the end they differ irreconcilably because their views of sin and salvation are focused on different concerns and belong to different contexts. For Paul, the main issue is the relation of Gentiles to the Jewish law in the face of Christ's saving death and resurrection; for the *Gospel of Mary*, the problem is understanding the Savior's teaching about the nature of sin itself and the means of overcoming suffering and death. Paul's framing of the issue places him firmly within the thought-world of Judaism, while the *Gospel of Mary* reflects concerns that make sense in a Gentile context in which the intellectual arena is dominated by philosophical debates about the relation of material nature to ethics.

It is highly likely that the *actual behaviors* of those who followed these two views appeared very similar, but the two groups would have understood the *meaning* of their behaviors quite differently. Insofar as people accept the teaching of works like the *Gospel of Mary* or the letters of Paul, their moral reflection is directed by the vision of life and value referents conveyed in the work.[8] Those visions structure particular frameworks within which questions about human relationships, moral choices, loyalties, and religious ideas have meaning and can be answered. Such works offer not only portraits of how things really are, but also views of what ought to be. They don't necessarily answer all the questions, but they provide contexts of meaning within which ethical reflection occurs, within which beliefs, values, and behaviors can be assessed and integrated, and toward which behaviors can be aligned. "The basic vision of reality within which one thinks and experiences is crucial for how ethical issues arise and are dealt with."[9] Therefore the stories we tell, the literature we hold dear, even the films and TV we watch are all crucial to the education of our moral imagination and moral feeling. If they are shallow and authoritarian, so will be our capacity for moral behavior. It matters greatly what kind of stories we live with.

The work of Paul and the *Gospel of Mary* provide very different orientations for thinking about what it means to be a human being. For Paul, the self is a physical, psychic, and spiritual whole. The body is thus fully self, even as the soul is. Paul believed that people without faith perish at death—soul and body. There is no hint of the idea of an immortal life of punishment for unbelievers. When they die, they stay dead. Believers, on the other hand, rise to immortal life with God. The gross physical body is transformed into a spiritual body, immortal and freed from all its mortal passions and suffering. For Paul moral behavior is essential in purifying the body in order for it to be the spiritual dwelling place of God, not in overcoming the attachment of the soul to the body as in the *Gospel of Mary*. As was said above, for the *Gospel of Mary*, the body is not one's real self. Only the soul infused with the spirit carries the truth of what it really means to be a human being. As a result, ethical concern is focused not on catering to the desires of the body, but upon strengthening the spiritual self, for at death the liberated soul is released from the body and ascends to rest with God beyond time and eternity, while the corpse returns to the inanimate material nature out of which it came.

Such views about death and immortality had an impact on how early Christians interpreted persecution and suffering. The case of martyrdom offers an instructive example. In her path-breaking work, *The Gnostic Gospels*, Elaine Pagels pointed out that whether one thinks the body will be saved or not has consequences for attitudes toward martyrdom.[10] The *Gospel of Mary* confronts the issue directly. When the Savior departs, all the disciples except Mary are frightened about what might happen if they go out to preach the gospel. They fear that if the Romans did not spare Jesus, they wouldn't spare them either. They have clearly not understood Jesus' teaching that salvation comes by turning away from the world to God, so that at death the soul is prepared to ascend to its eternal rest. It is, however, not as easy to dismiss the disciples' fear as it is to disregard their lack of understanding. The possibility of persecution must have been very real for the Christians who wrote and read the *Gospel of Mary*. The missionary fervor of the early movement could put men and women in real danger.[11] It is no coincidence that the disciples' fear follows immediately upon the Savior's commission to go forth and preach the gospel. This activity would have exposed them to real risk.

Yet fear of death was universally regarded among early Christians as a failing. The martyr stories invariably portray the hero or heroine as fearless and full of faith. The reality was more ambiguous. Personal accounts written by Christian martyrs before their deaths show that dealing with fear was a substantial preoccupation. Two such accounts have survived. One is the witness of Ignatius, the bishop of Antioch in Asia Minor, who was arrested and taken to Rome for execution sometime during the reign of the Emperor Trajan (98–117 CE). On the way, he wrote letters to several churches and these epistles have been preserved. The other is that of Perpetua, a young mother with a nursing infant, who was put to death in North Africa at the beginning of the third century. She kept a diary during her time in prison, and portions of it were later incorporated into an account of her death called *The Martyrdom of Perpetua*. Knowing they were to be executed, both wrote of the need to overcome their fears in order to be true witnesses of the gospel. They feared not only for themselves but for the fate of those around them. Ignatius was disturbed at the rift within his church in Antioch; Perpetua feared for her infant and for the fate of her younger brother who had died of what appears to be some sort of facial cancer. In the last of his letters, Ignatius gives thanks that unity and peace are restored to his church; Perpetua is able to hand her child over to the care of her parents, and she receives a divine vision confirming that her brother is happy. Only with these situations resolved were Ignatius and Perpetua able to prepare to face the realities of their own deaths. In their accounts, they imagine what it will be like to be torn apart by beasts or face the gladiator's sword. Each manages to find courage in the hope of eternal life, and both believed that martyrdom was the surest way to gain that priceless reward. Ignatius expected that his suffering and imminent death would make him "like Christ," while Perpetua had a vision in which she received the victor's crown of immortality.

Whatever we might think of their willingness to die—whether it was fanaticism or heroism—it is clear that their belief in the reality of eternal life provided courage and a basis for hope. We can surmise that the same could be true for those who followed the teachings of the Savior in the *Gospel of Mary*. Knowing that the mortal body is not the true self should have provided the strength to face persecution; after all, the body would die and dissolve back to its elemental nature no matter what they did, and the Romans could not damage their true spiritual selves or hinder their eternal salvation.

Some Christians claimed that heretics who disbelieved in the physical resurrection also avoided martyrdom. New discoveries have provided examples, however, of theologies that could deny the physical resurrection and still insist that martyrdom was necessary. The *Letter of Peter to Philip* provides one example. In this work, the Lord Jesus Christ takes on a body of flesh and is crucified, but Peter tells the other disciples, "Jesus is a stranger to this suffering" (*PetPhil* 139:21–22). How can this be true? In an appearance to his disciples after the resurrection, the Lord tells them that they have not truly understood his teaching unless they accept the fact that they, too, must suffer even as he had suffered. Suffering is inevitable because preaching the gospel will expose them to the retribution of the powers that rule the world. He tells them:

> "When you strip off from yourselves what is corrupted, then you will become illuminators in the midst of mortal men. You will fight against the powers, because they do not have rest like you, since they do not wish that you be saved. . . . Now you will fight against them in this way, for the rulers are fighting against the inner Human. And you are to fight against them in this way: Come together and teach in the world the salvation with a promise. And you, gird yourselves with the power of my Father, and let your prayer be known. And the Father will help you as he has helped you by sending me. Be not afraid, I am with you forever as I previously said to you when I was in the body." Then there came lightning and thunder from heaven, and what appeared to them in that place was taken up to heaven (*PetPhil* 137:6–13; 137:20–138:4).[12]

Jesus is exempt from suffering—and so are the apostles—not because they will not endure persecution but because pain and death concern only the mortal body, not the true inner self. "Be not afraid," he tells them.

Even after the persecutions ended with the conversion of Constantine early in the fourth century, Christian doctrine would teach that suffering is valuable in itself to overcome human pride and to shape the sinner into an obedient servant of God. In sharp contrast, the *Gospel of Mary* and the *Letter of Peter to Philip* do not ascribe any redemptive value to suffering. It is preaching the gospel that gives life; persecution is only an unfortunate, if inevitable, result of that activity because there are powers that oppose the gospel in the world. Believing the truth of the gospel leads people away from suffering by teaching them to overcome the passions and defeat the powers by putting on the perfect Human.

In this context we might also briefly consider Peter's question, "What is the sin of the world?" Here readers might well think not of Paul, but of the *Gospel of John* where John the Baptist sees Jesus coming toward him and exclaims: "Behold the Lamb of God, who takes away the sin of the world!". (*John* 1:29). If the author of the *Gospel of Mary* intends this intertextual reference, it must be yet another attempt to counter a Christology that was deemed unacceptable. The Savior did not teach that his death, like a lamb led to sacrificial slaughter, atoned for the sins of others; since sin does not exist, atonement is unnecessary. Or rather because sin is attachment to the world, turning from the love of the world to the love of God removes humanity from the power of sin.

The end result is that the *Gospel of Mary* does not teach that people need to suffer in order to gain salvation, nor do people deserve to suffer because they sin. This theology rejects any view of God as a wrathful judge who punishes the wicked for their sins with eternal suffering or who demands that his child atone for the sins of humanity through a horrible death. The *Gospel of Mary* explicitly avoids all description of God except as Good. The Savior's teachings are aimed at freeing people from suffering and death, not punishing them for their sins. The *Gospel of Mary* has no notion of hell. There is no intrinsic value in the atoning death of Christ or the martyrdom of believers or the punishment of souls because there is no such thing as sin. This theology stands in clear contrast to that of other Christians, however much their language and themes resonate with each other.

## Chapter 12

# The Gospel of John

Some possible intertextual relations between the *Gospel of Mary* and the *Gospel of John* deserve our special attention because of the role that each gives to Mary of Magdala. In his farewell discourse in the *Gospel of John*, Jesus comforts the disciples: "Let not your hearts be troubled, neither let them be afraid" (*John* 14:27; cf. *John* 14:1). He tells them that they are to bear witness to the truth, even though they will be persecuted for doing so (*John* 15:18–21; 16:1–3). He prays to the Father that "they may all be one" and asks that they be kept safe from the "evil one." He prays, too, for his own glorification. In the *Gospel of Mary*, after the Savior commissions the disciples to preach the gospel, the disciples are afraid but Mary steps in to comfort them: "Do not weep and be distressed nor let your hearts be irresolute. For his grace will be with you all and will shelter you. Rather we should praise his greatness, for he has prepared/united us and made us Human beings" (*GMary* 5:5–8). In both these scenes, the disciples are comforted with similar words and for a similar reason: the Savior is departing and his followers will face persecution. Both works affirm that the Savior has prepared them and unified them so that they are ready to face what he commanded them to do. And even as the Father glorifies the Son, so Mary calls upon the disciples to praise the Savior's greatness. For readers who connect these two passages, the striking point is that here Mary plays the role of comforter which in the *Gospel of John* is ascribed to Jesus. She has stepped in and taken over the task of comforting the disciples and reminding them that the Savior has prepared them and will shelter them.

In a later scene, the *Gospel of John* shows Mary weeping after the crucifixion, distressed at the Savior's death because she does not know where he is. He appears to her and sends her to tell the good news to the other disciples: "'I have seen the Lord'; and she told them that he had said these things to her" (*John* 20:18). The disciples then receive appearances of the Lord that confirm Mary's message. In the *Gospel of Mary*, Mary also weeps—but at Peter's accusation and at the threat that rivalry may disrupt the unity of the apostolic group, not at the Savior's departure. She had just told them "I saw the Lord in a vision" (*GMary* 7:1) and recounted the words that the Savior had spoken to her. Again the most striking similarity is the narrative context: Both gospels affirm that Mary saw the Lord and gave special revelation to the other disciples, but in the *Gospel of Mary*, Mary's teaching sparks controversy rather than faith. Although Peter had asked her to tell them the Savior's words, he now challenges her veracity and she weeps in response. The *Gospel of John* does not record the response of the disciples to Mary's message, but readers may recall the *Gospel of Luke* at this point: "Now it was Mary Magdalene and Joanna and Mary the mother of James and the other women with them who told this to the apostles; but these words seemed to them an idle tale, and they did not believe them" (*Luke* 24:10–11). *Luke* does not tell us how the women reacted to the disbelief of their fellow disciples, but we may well imagine that they wept. In *Luke*, too, the women's message provokes only doubt and perhaps grief.

The sequence of events in the *Gospel of John* also differs from the *Gospel of Mary* in when the commission to preach occurs. In the *Gospel of John*, Jesus comforts the disciples before the crucifixion; he appears to Mary after the resurrection and she brings the good news to the disciples. Yet in the next scene, we are told that the disciples had locked themselves in a room "for fear of the Jews," implying that they feared that they might be accused even as Jesus had been (*John* 20:19). Now Jesus appears in their midst, saying "Peace be with you. As the Father has sent me, so I send you" (*John* 20:21). In this portrayal, the disciples remain frightened even after Mary had brought them the good news; nor are we told how they reacted to Jesus' commission.

In the *Gospel of Mary*, no specious blame is attached to the Jews. The disciples' fear follows the Savior's commissioning to go out and preach, but it precedes Mary's message about her vision of the Savior. The effect, as I noted before, is to make it clear that not all the disciples have understood the Savior's teaching and not all are prepared to preach the gospel. Mary alone is presented as ready and able to step into the Savior's role.

It would seem that the *Gospel of John* affirms Mary's role as teacher to the other disciples, much as the *Gospel of Mary* does. But their portrayals exhibit significant differences. The *Gospel of John* states that the first appearance of the resurrected Lord was to Mary, and that she was the first to use the confessional title "Lord" to refer to him (*John* 20:18), even as in the *Gospel of Mary*, Mary calls the Savior "Lord." On the other hand, Mary's status is diminished in the *Gospel of John* in that she at first mistakes him for the gardener, and then when she does recognize his voice, she addresses him as "Teacher" (Rabboni), indicating a relatively low standing on the hierarchical scale of Johannine Christological titles. The exegetical sore point, however, is in Jesus' command that she not hold him because he has not yet ascended. Usually scholars interpret this command as indicating that Mary tried to cling to him, not recognizing that his ascent was necessary for sending the Spirit and salvation. The whole scene in the *Gospel of John* works to subordinate Mary's authority as a resurrection witness to that of the male disciples, especially by limiting her commission to bear witness only to the other disciples.

In the *Gospel of Mary*, on the other hand, Mary immediately recognizes the Lord when he appeared and he praises her for her steadfastness of mind. As we've already noted, she takes over many of his roles after his departure and is consistently portrayed as a model disciple and apostle. Still, Mary's weeping is not the strong response to Peter's accusations we might wish for, and it is Levi not Mary who gets the last word in the gospel. Jane Schaberg suggests that by ending with Levi's speech, the author allows male voices to overshadow Mary; silenced, she disappears from the story.[1] But surely her response to Peter does not seriously weaken the overwhelmingly positive portrait of her. Sheila McKeithen contends that Mary's weeping demonstrates her distress at both the disciples' lack of comprehension and their fomenting of discord among the apostles.[2] Her weeping is not a sign of weakness, but compassion. And in the end Levi's speech offers a decisive defense of Mary. She may not get the last word, but she is

entirely vindicated. Even Schaberg notes that of all the gospel literature about Mary of Magdala, the *Gospel of Mary* is the only text where
Mary actually gets to speak in her own defense.

Nonetheless it seems odd that the author of the *Gospel of Mary*
would put Mary's teaching in doubt at all, given that she provides the
primary apostolic authority for the gospel. But then it is also odd that
the *Gospel of John* diminishes Mary's role as a witness to the resurrection by saying that she initially mistook him for the gardener and was
then forbidden to touch him. If the resurrection appearances in *John*
are supposed to affirm the physical character of the resurrection, this
statement is alarming, for it can all too easily be read as a sign that
Mary was confused or that the risen Lord was not palpable.[3] These
surprising oddities should lead us to suspect that something else must
be going on.

In her study of the *Gospel of John*, April De Conick has pointed to
an intertext from Homer's *Odyssey*, the scene in which Odysseus' nurse
recognizes him, even though he is disguised, because of a distinctive
scar on his foot (*Od.* 19.357–60). Similarly, when the murdered
Clytemnestra appears in a play by Euripedes, she expects to be recognized by the wounds that killed her; and Aeneas, the hero of Vergil's
*Aeneid*, recognized several of the dead by their death wounds.[4] So,
too, De Conick argues, the post-resurrection scenes in *John* 20 involv-
ing Mary and Thomas were intended not to prove the physical resurrection of Jesus but to establish his identity. Although Mary
recognized him by his voice, not by his wounds as Thomas did, the
analogy stands.

We may not recognize these intertexts as quickly as did ancient
readers who were raised on the Homeric stories, but the recognition
scene is a widespread topos in ancient literature.[5] In the *Gospel of John*,
the clinching point is made by the risen Lord himself, who says to
Thomas, "Blessed are those who have not seen and yet believe" (*John*
20:29). As the German theologian Rudolph Bultmann noted, the real
Easter faith "is not faith in a palpable demonstration of the Risen Lord
within the mundane sphere"; the authority to preach the gospel had
already been given to the whole community by the bestowal of the
Spirit.[6] Thus, just as the Johannine recognition scenes with Mary and
Thomas obviate the necessity of touching and seeing as a basis for
faith, so the *Gospel of Mary* can be seen to use the attacks of Andrew
and Peter to forestall objections by other Christians against its teaching. Its point is not to argue for a spiritual resurrection, but to insist

that eternal life requires the transformation of the inner Human. Those who expect a savior to come on the clouds of heaven to save them have simply missed the point of the Savior's teaching. Like the *Gospel of John*, it affirms that the apostles saw and heard the risen Savior, but those experiences are not in themselves necessary for salvation.

It is not clear whether the author of the *Gospel of Mary* would have expected readers to connect the appearance accounts in the *Gospel of John* and the *Gospel of Mary*, but for any who did (and later readers surely would have) the association would at once affirm the tradition that the Lord appeared to Mary of Magdala after his resurrection and imparted special revelation to her that allowed her to instruct the other apostles; and it would also work to "correct" any imputation in the *Gospel of John* that Mary was less than entirely worthy of her commission as "apostle to the apostles."

## Chapter 13

# The Apostles

Four apostles appear by name in the *Gospel of Mary*: Levi, Andrew, Peter, and Mary. The very mention of their names conjures up kaleidoscopic images from two thousand years of gospels, acts, sermons, and saints lives, as well as images from painting, sculpture, novels, and cinema. The apostles are the foremost heroes of Christianity, and stories about them have proliferated for centuries, overwhelming their historical deeds with legend, myth, and ritual. Their relics adorn major sites of Christian pilgrimage; their names identify countless churches and cathedrals. Patriarchs and emperors have fought to associate apostolic authority with their own spiritual and temporal power.

Their prestige and popularity, however, obscure the fact that we actually have very little reliable historical information about these first followers of Jesus. Part of the reason for that lies with the nature of the ancient evidence. The modern concept of the person did not exist in antiquity; the apostles are represented in ancient literature not as unique individuals with distinctive psychological profiles and particular biographies, but as types. So, too, in the *Gospel of Mary*: Mary is the ideal of the beloved disciple and the model apostle; Peter is the hot-head and Andrew his side-kick; Levi is a mediator and peace-maker. In the hands of the gospel authors, the disciples were malleable characters who served the writers' own goals and reflected their perspectives. In the *Gospel of Mark*, for example, the disciples are commonly portrayed as misunderstanding Jesus; their incomprehension frequently serves the narrative purpose of giving Jesus the opportunity to clarify his points, correct their mistaken views, or provide secret teaching. In other works, like the *Gospel of Luke*, the apostles figure as faithful witnesses who can attest to Jesus' teachings and deeds. And upon reading that Paul accused Peter of being a hypocrite for ceasing to eat with Gentiles when members of the "circumcision party" arrived in Antioch (*Gal* 2:11–13), we have to ask ourselves whose perspective is being represented. Did it happen the way Paul says? What might Peter have said in response to Paul's accusation? So also in the *Gospel of Mary*, the apostles serve the writer's goals as well. In order to understand those goals, we need to know more about how these literary characters were represented.

Still, we shouldn't lose sight of the fact that these four apostles were historical people as well as literary figures. They were early followers of Jesus who accompanied him on his travels through Galilee and up to Jerusalem. All were Jews, even if little trace of that identity remains in the *Gospel of Mary*. Certain specific historical information attaches to each of them. Levi had been a tax collector. Andrew and Peter were brothers, whose trade was fishing. Mary came from Magdala and was the first to have a vision of the Lord. Peter, too, saw the risen Christ and was a leader in the early mission. These were ordinary people who made extraordinary choices to leave their mundane lives and embark on a dangerous mission to spread the gospel. This much at least is known to us in the twentieth century. What might second-century readers of the *Gospel of Mary* have known about these figures or associated with their names?

## Levi

Both the gospels of *Mark* and *Luke* describe Levi as a tax collector who became a disciple of Jesus (*Mark* 2:14; *Luke* 5:27–29), but neither include him in their list of the twelve. The *Gospel of Matthew* also tells a story about a tax collector (*Matt* 9:9), but his name is Matthew; this Matthew, however, is included in the list of "the twelve" (*Matt* 10:3). This confusion led later tradition sometimes to identify the two, but it is not clear that Levi was widely regarded as one of "the twelve" in the early tradition. He is not mentioned in the *Gospel of John* at all. A certain Levi appears in the second-century *Gospel of Philip*, but he is identified only as the owner of a dye works and probably has no connection with our Levi the tax collector (*GPhil* 63:26). Levi also appears in the *First Apocalypse of James* 37:7, but the text is so fragmentary that it is impossible to say much about the role he plays there.

His striking appearance as Mary's defender in the *Gospel of Mary* is therefore a bit of a surprise. Was he chosen for this role because, like Mary, he did not belong to "the twelve," even though he was an early disciple of Jesus? It is hard to say. But he does appear second only to Mary as one who understood the teaching of the Savior. He takes Peter to task and defends Mary's character, calling the apostles to return to the commands of the Savior and go forth to preach. In the Greek fragment, he alone leaves to spread the gospel. Given his relative obscurity in other literature, this highly prominent role is remarkable, if enigmatic. Perhaps other stories associated with Levi are lost to us. We can only wonder.

## Andrew

Andrew's primary claim to fame is that he was the brother of Peter, and in the earliest literature he appears almost solely in that connection. In the *Gospel of Mark*, he and Peter are portrayed as fishers from Capernaum, the first of the disciples called by the Lord (*Mark* 1:16–18), and Andrew appears regularly in the gospel lists of disciples (e.g., *Mark* 3:18; *Matt* 10:2; *Luke* 6:14; *Acts* 1:13). In the *Gospel of John*, he appears initially as a follower of John the Baptist, but becomes the first disciple called by Jesus and leads his brother Peter to the Lord as well (*John* 1:35–42). He is the only apostle mentioned by name in the extant portion of the newly discovered *Gospel of the Savior*, but unfortunately his words are lost in a lacuna (*GSav* 97:31–32).[1] His only other appearance in the early literature is in the *Gospel of Mary*, where again he appears in close conjunction with Peter and is quickly overshadowed by his brother's presence. Andrew's complaint against Mary receives no direct response either from her or from Levi, both of whom address only Peter. Andrew does not appear again in Christian literature until the end of the second century, when he becomes the hero of the *Acts of Andrew*, a mammoth work that portrays him as a miracle-working missionary sent to Achaea, northern Anatolia, Thrace, and Macedonia. There he is active in breaking up marriages by preaching celibacy and is crucified by an angry husband on the shore of the sea. Eventually Andrew takes a firm place in Christian legend as the apostolic guarantor of the bishop's see of Byzantium, where his role of bringing Peter to the faith becomes a most useful tool in the polemics between Byzantium and Rome over ecclesiastical supremacy.[2] All of this, however, occurs long after the *Gospel of Mary* was written and there is no hint that the author would expect readers to associate anything with Andrew except his filial tie to Peter.

## Peter

Historically Peter,[3] also called Simon and Cephas (*Mark* 3:16; *Matt* 10:2; 16:17–19),[4] was a fisherman from Capernaum on the Sea of Galilee (*Mark* 1:16–18). He accompanied Jesus throughout his ministry and was a prominent member of the inner circle of his followers. He was married, and apparently his wife traveled with him on missionary journeys throughout Asia Minor (*Mark* 1:29–31; *1 Cor* 15:5). Later tradition reports that he was martyred and buried in Rome, but this has been disputed—usually along Catholic-Protestant lines.

Peter plays a prominent role in early Christian literature, and Levi's remark implying that Peter's temper and impetuosity are well-known indicates quite clearly that readers would be expected to know something of the tradition about him. Peter's role in the *Gospel of Mary* has struck some scholars as revisionary,[5] for here Peter does not appear as the illustrious rock upon which Jesus founded the church, but as an ignorant hothead who sowed discord among the disciples. This portrait, however, has a strong basis in early Christian tradition, a tradition which painted Peter as a complex and rather ambiguous character. The *Gospel of Mark*, for example, recounts a scene where Jesus himself called Peter "Satan" (*Mark* 8:31–33): Jesus had just predicted his death and suffering, and Peter had the temerity to tell Jesus he was wrong! Once Jesus had to save Peter from drowning because his faith was too weak to walk on water (*Matt* 14:29–31). At the transfiguration, his fear leads him to offer to build three booths, one each for Moses, Elijah, and Jesus (*Mark* 9:5–6). Still later, Peter insisted that even if everyone else abandoned Jesus, he never would—and this just before he denies him not once, but three times (*Mark* 14:29–31; 66–72), a story recounted not only in *Mark*, but repeated in the other canonical gospels as well. In another scene in the *Gospel of John*, Peter at first refuses to have Jesus wash his feet; but when Jesus says that otherwise Peter will have no part in him, Peter goes overboard in the other direction and demands Jesus wash his hands and head as well (*John* 13:6-11). In Gethsemane, when the disciples fall asleep while Jesus prays, Jesus' disappointment is directed primarily at Peter: "Simon are you asleep? Could you not watch one hour? Watch and pray that you may not enter into temptation; the spirit indeed is willing, but the flesh is weak" (*Mark* 14:37–38). At the arrest, Peter pulls out a sword and cuts off the ear of the high priest's slave Malchus, earning another rebuke from Jesus (*John* 18:10–11). As noted earlier, even Paul had troubles with Peter, and accused him of acting like a hypocrite by changing his behavior to suit his audience (*Gal* 2:11–13).[6] These repeated examples in the early literature consistently portray Peter as a bold fellow, but also as someone who doesn't quite understand what is going on. The *Gospel of the Nazarenes* took a very harsh position on Peter's character and pronounced the final judgment that Peter "denied and swore and damned himself" (*GNaz* 19).

While wide-spread, this characterization of Peter is not the only one. Paul places Peter first in his list of those who saw the risen Christ (*1 Cor* 15:5) and the *Gospel of Luke* attests that he had an individual resurrection appearance (*Luke* 24:34).[7] Paul accepts Peter as a leader in the Jerusalem church and a reliable source of tradition about Jesus (*Gal* 1:18; 2:1–10). He also accedes to Peter the role of "apostle to the circumcised" (*Gal* 2:8), despite the fact that Peter appears hypocritical in his behavior toward Gentiles. The *Acts of the Apostles* broadens Peter's role, making him also the first to receive a vision attesting to the mission to the Gentiles (*Acts* 10). The *Gospel of Mark* paints a rather ambivalent picture of Peter, depicting him both as an intimate member of Jesus' inner circle and as an unreliable blusterer. *Matthew*'s portrait is even more ambiguous, continuing the tradition of Peter as the one who denied Jesus but also offering a unique scene in which Jesus designates Peter as the rock upon which he will found the church, and hands him the keys of the kingdom and the power to bind and loose (*Matt* 16:18–19). The most positive portrait by far, however, is that found in the *Gospel of Luke* and the *Acts of the Apostles*. In his gospel, the author goes to considerable lengths to undermine the tradition of Peter as a continual failure, bolstering his image in preparation for his role as the leading spokesman of the apostles, a powerful miracle-worker, and bold evangelist in the book of *Acts* (1–5,

8–11).[8] The *Gospel of John*, in contrast, minimizes Peter's role in the first twenty chapters, but this changes rather dramatically in chapter 21, where Jesus asks Peter three times if he loves him; Peter answers yes, and Jesus tells him to "Feed my sheep" (*John* 21:15–17). The triple repetition in this dialogue is often understood as a parallel to Peter's triple denial, intended to rehabilitate his status with the Lord and prepare him for his martyrdom (*John* 21:18–19). But there are also telling details that invite comparison of *Luke*'s treatment of Peter with the treatment of Mary in the *Gospel of Mary*. Once Jesus asks Peter if he loves him "more than these," meaning the other disciples, and in the end Peter responds, "Lord, you know everything. You know that I love you" (*John* 21:15, 17). Here Peter's special love is confirmed by the Savior's knowledge of him, even as in *GMary* 10:10 Jesus' love of Mary is confirmed by his knowledge of her. Would readers of the *Gospel of Mary* have seen the similarities here, or was the trope linking love and knowledge too widespread for a specific association of the two passages? Is the *Gospel of John* trying to replace Mary with Peter? or is the *Gospel of Mary* undermining Peter's role? Readers who knew both texts would have to wonder.

Numerous early Christian works are ascribed to Peter, including the canonical letters of *1* and *2 Peter*, the *Gospel of Peter*,[9] the *Letter of Peter to Philip*,[10] the *Apocalypse of Peter*,[11] the *Kerygma Petri*,[12] and the *Acts of Peter*.[13] But while this literature consistently takes Peter as a guarantor of apostolic authority and paints him in positive terms, he remains theologically elusive, in part because he is used to authorize conflicting theological positions. For example, *2 Peter*, an early second-century letter, claims Peter's explicit support of apostolic authority by calling upon the readers to remember "the commandment of the Lord and Savior through your apostles" (*2 Pet* 3:1–2). It also invokes Peter's authority against certain interpretations of Paul that the unknown author of the letter opposed (see *2 Pet* 3:14–17). While Irenaeus uses Peter as a witness to the physical reality of Jesus' incarnation,[14] the *Apocalypse of Peter* has him receive a revelation from the Savior that rejects the incarnation and affirms that Jesus only *seemed* to have a body. In the *Gospel of Peter*, which was ascribed to him, Peter appears only once in the extant fragment, but in a crucial role. After Mary of Magdala and other unnamed women meet the angel at the tomb and flee in fear, Peter along with Andrew and Levi go out fishing. The manuscript cuts off here and what happens is lost, but it is highly likely that what followed was an account of the first resurrection appearance of Jesus. Also, other than the *Gospel of Mary*, this is the only gospel that associates Peter and Andrew with Levi—all as witnesses to the resurrection—and Mary of Magdala is the only other disciple to appear by name. This grouping may provide a key to Levi's prominent role in the *Gospel of Mary*: there may have been a widespread tradition that these four had special post-resurrection experiences.

After the second century, Peter continued to have a long and illustrious afterlife in legend, art, and ecclesiastical politics as the preeminent apostle of Christian faith, the co-founder of the Roman church, and the apostolic guarantor for papal authority.[15] In the *Gospel of Mary*, however, none of this is apparent. Peter appears solely in his role as ignorant hothead. His challenge to Mary presents him as a jealous man who cannot see past the weakness of the flesh to discern spiritual truth.

## Mary of Magdala

The earliest Christian literature, including the gospels that came to reside in the New Testament, portrays Mary of Magdala as a prominent Jewish disciple of Jesus of Nazareth.[16] Her epithet "Magdalene" probably indicates that she came from the town of Magdala (Migdal), located on the west shore of the Sea of Galilee (Lake Gennesaret), just north of the city of Tiberias.[17] Along with many other women, she accompanied Jesus throughout his ministry.[18] She was present at his crucifixion[19] and burial,[20] and was a witness to the empty tomb.[21] Among the earliest surviving Christian art is a portrait of Mary Magdalene with other women bringing spices to anoint Jesus at the tomb.[22] Early Christian gospel traditions generally accord Mary of Magdala a prominent position among the followers of Jesus, especially among the women followers, as is attested by the frequent practice of placing Mary's name first in the lists of women who followed Jesus.[23] She is one of the main speakers in several first and second-century texts recording dialogues of Jesus with his disciples after the resurrection.[24] Indeed, she is portrayed as the first or among the first privileged to see and speak with the risen Lord.[25] In the *Gospel of John*, the risen Jesus gives her special teaching and commissions her to announce the good news of the resurrection to the other disciples. She obeys, and is thus the first to proclaim the resurrection. [26] Although she is never specifically called an apostle, she fills the role and later tradition will herald her as "the apostle to the apostles."[27] The strength of this literary tradition, attested as it is in multiple independent witnesses, makes it possible to suggest that historically Mary may have been a prophetic visionary and leader within some sector of the early Christian movement after the death of Jesus.[28] This much may be said of Mary of Magdala with a high degree of historical probability.

The *Gospel of Luke* does provide two additional details, but both have been questioned by scholars. *Luke* 8:2 identifies Mary as the one "from whom seven demons had gone out," but it is the only independent source to do so. [29] Although it does not explicitly say that Jesus himself cast out the demons, he was well known as an exorcist— however moderns may understand that practice—and it is probable that *Luke* intends readers to think that he healed Mary.[30] In addition, *Luke* 8:3 mentions that Mary Magdalene was of independent means and supported Jesus out of her own resources, as did other Galilean women like Joanna the wife of Chuza, Herod's steward. But this piece of information also is found only in *Luke*, and it may very well have been retrojected back into the early period from a later time when Christianity was supported by wealthy patrons.[31] If it is historical, however, it indicates that certain women had significant resources at their own disposal and, more particularly, that Mary was Jesus' patron.

Scholars have been suspicious of these two bits of data, not only because they are given only in *Luke*, but also because they fit into *Luke*'s tendency to reduce the status of Mary Magdalene and indeed of women in general to subordinate roles, especially in comparison with the enhanced roles of Peter and "the twelve." *Luke* 8:1–3 is a good example.[32] This short passage describes the male disciples only as "the twelve" but readers will come to learn in the *Acts of the Apostles* that this group has preeminent responsibility for the preaching of the gospel and the founding of the church. The women disciples in contrast are described as recipients of healing and financial supporters, a description that has frequently been interpreted to indicate women's "natural" weakness and to limit women's roles to rendering financial support or material service that leaves men free to preach the gospel.[33] Even though she has been healed, the story of Mary's possession effectively portrays her as unclean and susceptible to demonic influence. It is hard not to read these two details in *Luke*'s description of Mary as an attempt to conceal her prominence rather than as a report of historical facts.

Since the eighteenth century, discoveries of unknown early

Christian literature from Egypt have greatly enhanced our knowledge of how Mary was portrayed in the first centuries of Christian beginnings.[34] Chief among them was a find of enormous significance near the village of Nag Hammadi in middle Egypt.[35] In 1945, a peasant had serendipitously uncovered a clay jar containing fourth-century papyrus books, including several which develop the early portrait of Mary as a prominent disciple of Jesus. These include the *Gospel of Thomas, First Apocalypse of James, Dialogue of the Savior, Sophia of Jesus Christ*, and the *Gospel of Philip*.[36] Another important work is *Pistis Sophia*, inscribed in a fourth-century parchment codex that had already come to light in the eighteenth century.[37] It contains an extensive revelation dialogue between Jesus and his disciples, among whom Mary figures prominently. To these, we must of course add the *Gospel of Mary* from the Berlin Codex.[38]

These works often portray Mary as one of the interlocutors in dialogues of Jesus with his disciples. In the *Gospel of Thomas*, for example, Mary questions Jesus and is one of only five disciples specifically named (logion 21). The disciples usually ask Jesus questions as a group, but two women, Mary and Salome, are singled out by name, each asking a single question. The only other named disciples are Thomas, Peter, and Matthew. The second-century work, *First Apocalypse of James*, suggests that James should turn to Mary and the other women for instruction. The passage is difficult because the manuscript is badly damaged, and a small hole is located precisely in the middle of the sentence about Mary. Antti Marjanen has restored the passage so that it reads as follows (with the restorations in square brackets). The Lord tells James: "'When you speak these words of [per]ception, be persuaded by the [word of] Salome and Mary [and Martha and Ars]inoe.'"[39] This mysterious command tells us nothing about what it is James can expect to learn from the women, but even this brief mention of Mary shows a high regard for her spiritual understanding, along with that of three other women disciples.

In another second-century writing, *Dialogue of the Savior*, Mary is named along with Judas Thomas and Matthew in the course of an extended dialogue between Jesus and his disciples. She speaks frequently and indeed she acts as a representative of the disciples as a group, addressing several questions to the Savior. She thus appears as a prominent disciple and is the only woman named.[40] Moreover, in response to a particularly insightful question, the Lord says of her, "'You make clear the abundance of the revealer!'" (*DSav* 140:17–19).

At another point after Mary has spoken, the narrator confirms, "She uttered this as a woman who had understood completely" (*DSav* 139:11–13). These statements make it clear that Mary is to be counted among the disciples who fully comprehended the Lord's teaching (*DSav* 142:11–13).

The *Sophia of Jesus Christ*, also from the second century, gives Mary a clear role as one of the seven women and twelve men gathered to hear the Savior after the resurrection, but before his ascension.[41] Of these only five are named and speak, including Mary.[42] At the end of his discourse, he tells them, "I have given you authority over all things as children of light," and they go forth in joy to preach the gospel (*SoJsChrNHC* III 119:4–6; BG 126:12–15). Mary is included among those special disciples to whom Jesus entrusted his most elevated teaching, and she is commissioned along with the other disciples to preach the gospel.

In the third-century text *Pistis Sophia*, Mary again appears to be preeminent among the disciples, especially in the first three of the four books.[43] She asks more questions than all the rest of the disciples together, and the Savior acknowledges that: "You are she whose heart is more directed to the Kingdom of Heaven than all your brothers."[44] Indeed, Mary steps in when the other disciples are in despair and intercedes with the Savior for them.[45] Her complete spiritual comprehension is repeatedly stressed.

All of these works contain extensive dialogues between Jesus and his disciples, and Mary is an active and vocal participant. She speaks frequently and often is praised for her insight. Other narratives contain little dialogue but still portray Mary as a prominent disciple. In the *Gospel of Philip*, for example, Mary Magdalene is explicitly mentioned as one of three Marys: "There were three who always walked with the Lord: Mary his mother and her sister and (the) Magdalene, the one who was called his companion. For Mary is his sister and his mother and his companion" (*GPhil* 59:6–11). This formulation is intriguing for at first it distinguishes three distinct Marys: Jesus' mother, her sister (i.e., his aunt),[46] and his companion, who is explicitly identified as the Magdalene.[47] Yet the next sentence suggests that there is only a single Mary, one who is his mother, his sister, *and* his companion. The *Gospel of Phillip* wants its readers to see that these figures are more than literal, historical characters.[48] "Truth did not come into the world naked," says the author, "but it came in types and images. (The world) will not receive (the truth) in any other way."[49] Mary is the image of a greater spiritual truth. How should we understand this passage? Of what truth is Mary the image? Scholars have made a number of suggestions, based in large part on a later passage where Mary is mentioned again. Unfortunately this section of the work is damaged. With the reconstruction again in square brackets, it reads:

> As for Wisdom who is called "the barren," she is the mother [of the] angels and the companion of the S[avior. Ma]ria the Mag[da]lene — (she is the one) the S[avior loved] more than [all] the disciples [and he] used to kiss her on her [mouth of]ten. The rest of [the disciples …]. They said to him, "Why do you love her more than us?" The Savior replied; he said to them, "Why do I not love you like her? If a blind man and one who sees are both in the dark, they do not differ from each other. When the light comes, then the one who sees will see the light, and the one who is blind will remain in the dark" (*GPhil* 63:33–64:9).[50]

This passage presents several intriguing puzzles, but it also points toward some possible solutions: Why is Wisdom called "barren" if she is the mother of angels? Is Mary Magdalene identified with Wisdom here? Is that why the Savior loved her more than the other disciples? Does kissing mean that Mary and the Savior had a sexual relationship or was it a spiritual one? What does the Savior's parable mean in response to the disciple's question?

It seems that several ideas have been combined: Heavenly Wisdom is the mother of the powers that rule the cosmos; because of their evil, her fruit is "barren." But the heavenly Sophia became fruitful when she become the companion of the Savior through the Holy Spirit (see *GPhil* 59:30–60:1). Mary Magdalene, too, is the companion of the Savior because he loved her more than the rest of the disciples. If Mary is understood as Wisdom, that explains how she is at once mother, sister, and companion. She is the mother of the angels, his spiritual sister (since the son does not have children but siblings), and his female counterpart.

The next sentence provides a second interpretation. As in the *Gospel of Mary*, the male disciples are jealous and without understanding. The *Gospel of Phillip* again offers literal images—kissing and jealousy—in order to interpret them spiritually. Kissing here apparently refers to the intimate reception of spiritual teaching, for not only does the Lord suggest that the male disciples should seek to be loved by him in the same way, but he also says: "And had the word gone out from that (heavenly) place, it would be nourished from the mouth and it would become perfect. For it is by a kiss that the perfect conceive and give birth. For this reason we also kiss one another. We receive conception from the grace which is in one another" (*GPhil* 58:34–59:6). This explains yet again how Mary is at once mother (for she conceives and gives birth to spiritual things through the kiss), his spiritual sister, and companion. This portrayal affirms the special relationship of Mary Magdalene to Jesus based on her spiritual perfection.

Yet at the same time that Mary Magdalene is lauded in these works, there are signs that she is becoming a center around which controversy swirls. We know that the portrayal of Mary Magdalene as an exemplary disciple was not always linked to a positive symbolization of the feminine or a positive view of women generally.[51] Even texts that emphasized her prominence could portray her as a controversial figure. For example, the author of the second-century *Dialogue of the Savior* praises Mary "as a woman who had understood completely" (139:12–15). But in the same work, women are categorically associated with sexuality:

> The Lord said, "Pray in the place where there is no woman."
> Matthew said, "'Pray in the place where there is [no woman],'
> he tells us, meaning 'Destroy the works of womanhood,' not because there is any other [manner of birth], but because they will cease [giving birth]."
> Mary said, "They will never be obliterated" (*DSav* 144:15–22).

Usually scholars interpret Mary's response as a confirmation of the Savior's command to "destroy the works of womanhood" by ascetic renunciation of reproduction, here clearly symboled solely by the feminine. As Antti Marjanen has argued, this use of female gendered language to condemn the material world, sexuality, and death hardly works to promote the status of women.[52] I have registered many a difference of opinion with colleagues about this passage, because it seems to me that Mary's response can also be read as resistance: the works of womanhood will never be obliterated. Ann Brock agrees, arguing from a different passage:

> In one enigmatic section of the *Dialogue of the Savior* the Lord explains, "Whatever is from the truth does not die; whatever is from woman dies" (59). Taken by itself such a statement sounds misogynistic. However, in the very next line of dialogue, when Mary asks why then she has come to this place (60), the Lord responds, "<you have come> to reveal the greatness of the revealer." In other words, her purpose is not to procreate—what comes from procreation dies. She is instead to be part of revealing the revealer. The Lord's statement to her therefore diametrically opposes claims such as those in the pastoral epistles which contend "Salvation does not accrue to women because they bear resemblance to Christ, but rather because they bear children" *(1 Tim 2:15)*.[53]

At any rate, we must be careful not to appropriate these works uncritically as feminist resources simply on the basis of a positive portrayal of Mary, for they can also employ feminine imagery that denigrates femaleness.

The final saying in the *Gospel of Thomas*, probably tacked onto the end of the work by a later scribe, explicitly challenges the presence of Mary and the status of all women in the Christian community.

> Simon Peter said to them, "Let Mary leave us, for women are not worthy of life." Jesus said, "I myself shall lead her in order to make her male, so that she too may become a living spirit resembling you males. For every woman who will make herself male will enter the kingdom of heaven" (*GThom* 114).

Peter clearly wishes to exclude Mary simply on the basis of her being a woman, but Jesus defends Mary's spiritual status against the attack by suggesting that her womanhood is not a permanent impediment to salvation. In a symbol system where "female" codes body, sexuality, and materiality, and "male" codes mind and spirit, to "become male" means that women are expected to transcend their naturally lower material natures and become spiritual beings. Whether this was achieved through ascetic practice, ritual transformation, or a mythic return to an androgynous Adamic state is unclear. [54] But in any case, Jesus' reply destabilizes the categorical fixity of gender: women are not simply women; they are potentially men. Sex and gender cease to be as self-evident as Peter would have it.[55] And yet Jesus' statement at best only moderates Peter's categorical sexism: women *as women* are apparently not worthy of life; they need to become male.

In the later third-century work, *Pistis Sophia*, Peter and Mary are again seen in conflict. Mary is the single most outspoken disciple in this work, and she wants to offer her interpretation of what has been said, but she complains, "I am afraid of Peter for he threatens me and he hates our race" (*PiSo* II. 71:2). The Lord defends Mary—rather weakly in my opinion—by affirming that no power can prevent anyone who is filled with the Spirit of light from interpreting the things that are being said. But this response, too, is less than ideal for women. Although Mary has clearly accused Peter of misogyny, the Savior's response does not condemn him, but simply explains that anyone who is "filled with the Spirit of light"—man or woman—has the capacity and the responsibility to speak. The point is that sex and gender are irrelevant to spiritual development. Moreover, while the *Pistis Sophia* recognizes the superiority of Mary's spiritual understanding, it relegates the tasks of preaching the gospels solely to the male disciples.[56]

The figure of Mary in the *Gospel of Mary* belongs to this tradition which portrays her as a prominent disciple, but more than any other early Christian text it presents an unflinchingly favorable portrait of her as a woman leader among the disciples. *The Gospel of Mary* is ascribed to Mary and indeed she is the most prominent character in it. [57] Although she is referred to only as "Mary," scholars have generally identified this figure with Mary Magdalene.[58] The *Gospel of Mary* portrays her as the ideal disciple and apostle. She is the only one who does not fear for her life at the departure of the Lord. The Savior himself praises her for her unwavering steadfastness. She is favored with a special vision of Jesus and receives advanced teaching about the fate of the soul and salvation. She comforts and instructs the other disciples, turning their attention toward the teaching of Jesus and toward the divine Good. While her teaching does not go unchallenged, in the end both the truth of her teachings and her authority to teach the male disciples are affirmed. She is portrayed as a prophetic visionary and as a leader among the disciples.

But this portrait of Mary is not the only one, as we all know. In

Western European art and literature, Mary Magdalene is most often portrayed as a repentant prostitute, the Christian model of female sexuality redeemed. She stands prominently with two other figures: Eve, the temptress whose sin brought all of humanity under the judgment of death and all women into just subjugation and obedience, and Mary, the virgin mother whose impossible sexuality both idealizes and frustrates the desires of real women. Together they have formed the three-legged base upon which normative Christian models of female identity are balanced.

Where did this portrait of Mary Magdalene as a repentant whore come from? Contrary to popular Western tradition, Mary Magdalene was never a prostitute.[59] Eastern Orthodox traditions have never portrayed her as one. She appears in the *Gospel of Mary* in a role closer to her actual position in early Christian history: an early and important disciple of Jesus and a leader in the early Christian movement. As with most of the other disciples, the very meagerness of what was known about Mary's life served only to fire the imaginations of later Christians, who elaborated her history in story and art according to their spiritual needs and political aims.[60]

In contrast to the prominent role she plays in the early literature we have just discussed, the early church fathers whose writings later become the basis for orthodoxy largely ignore Mary Magdalene. When they do mention her, however, they present her in a consistently favorable light.[61] She is usually mentioned to support points they are trying to make about the reality of the physical resurrection[62] or the nature of the soul.[63] Her name comes up most frequently in connection with the resurrected Jesus' enigmatic statement to her: "Do not touch me, for I have not yet ascended to the Father" (*John* 20:17). The fathers were concerned to counter any implication in this passage that Jesus' resurrection might not have been physical.[64] Their concern was not unfounded, since the passage belongs to the earliest appearance narratives which were based on visionary experiences, not on encounters with a resuscitated corpse.[65] No criticism was directed at Mary Magdalene for Jesus' reticence about letting Mary touch him. Indeed Tertullian praised Mary because she approached Jesus to touch him "out of love, not from curiosity, nor with Thomas' incredulity."[66] In Tertullian's mind, the issue was simply that it was too early for touching; the resurrection had to be completed by Jesus' ascent.[67]

Despite their respect for her as a witness to the resurrection, the early church fathers seem to have had three problems with the gospel stories of Mary Magdalene, especially with the resurrection appearance in the *Gospel of John*:

1. Jesus' command not to touch him could be considered proof that his resurrection was not physical.
2. Since Mary was alone when she saw the Lord, her testimony could be questioned.
3. The fact that Jesus appeared to her first, gave her private teachings, and then sent her to instruct the other disciples seemed to elevate her status above the other disciples and give a woman authority to teach the male apostles.

Yet despite these issues, on the rare occasions when Mary of Magdala was discussed by the early church fathers, the image of her was largely positive.

From the fourth century onward, however, the tone began to shift. Later fathers had the same difficulty with her portrait in the gospels, but the answers they devised to address these problems resulted in a very new and different portrait of Mary Magdalene. They increasingly tended to explain Jesus' command not to touch him by arguing that Mary, unlike Thomas, was not worthy of touching the resurrected Lord because she lacked a full understanding of the resurrection and hence lacked true faith.[68] She was sent to the male apostles, it was argued, not to proclaim the good news of the resurrection, but so that her weakness could be supplemented by their strength.[69]

By conflating the account of the *Gospel of John* with that of the *Gospel of Matthew* 28:9, which tells of an appearance to at least two women, Origen had already argued that Mary was not *alone* in seeing the risen Lord.[70] The effect was to de-emphasize Mary's status as the *first* witness to the resurrection by making her only one member of a group.[71] It was nonetheless appropriate, the fathers began to argue, that a woman be the first to receive the redemption offered by Jesus through his resurrection, because it was after all—at least in their interpretation of the *Genesis* story [72]—a woman who had first brought sin into the world.[73] We begin to see references to Mary Magdalene as the second Eve, the woman whose faith in the resurrected Jesus overcame the offenses of first Eve.[74]

That Mary was reported to have received private instruction from the risen Jesus was a more difficult problem. By the end of the second century, she had become closely associated with an interpretation of Jesus' teachings very different from what the church fathers were developing. The *Gospel of Mary* clearly presents such teachings, and both the content and the title of the work associate these "heretical" views with Mary. Discrediting her may therefore have been in part a strategy of the church fathers to counter the interpretation of Jesus being spread in works like the *Gospel of Mary*.[75]

Silence, it turned out, was not an effective strategy, since it left the imaginative field open to others. So starting in the fourth century, Christian theologians in the Latin West[76] began to construct an alternative story.[77] The first move was to associate Mary Magdalene with the unnamed sinner who anointed Jesus' feet in *Luke* 7:36–50. Further confusion resulted by conflating the account in *John* 12:1–8, in which Mary of Bethany anoints Jesus, with the anointing by the unnamed woman in the Lukan account. From this point, identifying Mary of Magdala with Mary of Bethany was but a short step. At the end of the sixth century, Pope Gregory the Great gave a sermon in which he not only identified these figures, but drew the moral conclusion that would dominate the imagination of the West for centuries to come:

> She whom Luke calls the sinful woman, whom John calls Mary, we believe to be the Mary from whom seven devils were ejected according to Mark. And what did these seven devils signify, if not all the vices? . . . It is clear, brothers, that the woman previously used the unguent to perfume her flesh in forbidden acts. What she therefore displayed more scandalously, she was now offering to God in a more praiseworthy manner. She had coveted with earthly eyes, but now through penitence these are consumed with tears. She displayed her hair to set off her face, but now her hair dries her tears. She had spoken proud things with her mouth, but in kissing the Lord's feet, she now planted her mouth on the Redeemer's feet. For every delight, therefore, she had had in herself, she now immolated herself. She turned the mass of her crimes to virtues, in order to serve God entirely in penance, for as much as she had wrongly held God in contempt.[78]

Once these initial identifications were secure, Mary Magdalene could be associated with every unnamed sinful woman in the gospels, including the adulteress in *John* 8:1–11 and the Syrophoenician woman with her five and more "husbands" in *John* 4:7–30. Mary the apostle and teacher had become Mary the repentant whore.

This portrait of Mary as a prostitute and adulteress explained not only why she was unworthy to touch Jesus' resurrected body, it also reinforced the view that women were to be seen primarily in terms of their sexuality not their spiritual character. Thus for the fathers this fiction solved two problems at once by undermining both the teachings associated with Mary and women's capacity to take on leadership roles. She still maintained a prominent place in the tradition, but her radical heritage had been tamed or erased.

The overall picture sketched above accurately reflects the issues at stake and the positions that the church fathers took on those issues. To be sure, it is fairly difficult to keep all the Marys straight—Mary Magdalene, Mary the mother of Jesus, Mary of Bethany, Mary the wife of Clopas (Jesus' aunt),[79] Mary the mother of James the younger and Joses[80] (or Joseph[81]), the "other" Mary[82]; nevertheless it is notable that the Eastern Churches never confused any of these Marys with unnamed prostitutes or adulteresses. Though it is not possible to judge the minds and motives of the church fathers—since the processes of theological tradition are highly complex and often not fully apparent even to those involved—the results of their efforts are clear. Their erroneous portrait of Mary undergirded a particular set of theological perspectives on the physical resurrection and the male prerogatives of church authority. While they accepted Mary as an important witness to the resurrection, they nonetheless firmly shaped their reading of the gospels to fit the sexist prejudice that women are naturally inferior to men and should not hold positions of authority over them.

They also fell into the patriarchal trap of defining women primarily by their sexual roles and their relations to men, as virgins, wives and mothers, widows, or prostitutes. Since the symbolic field of the virgin and mother was already held by another Mary, and our Mary was not known to have been married or widowed, that left only the prostitute option available. I think it is safe to say that if Mary Magdalene had not been figured in this role, some other character would necessarily have been invented to play it. Its symbolic significance was too great to ignore.

It is true that from early on the possibility had existed that Mary

Magdalene might emerge from the speculative fray as Jesus' wife and lover. The *Gospel of Philip* said that Jesus used to kiss her often, and in the *Gospel of Mary* Peter affirmed that Jesus loved her more than other women. The third-century church father Hippolytus also used erotic imagery to allegorize the *Song of Songs* into an intimate relationship of the Church to Christ by treating Mary of Magdala as the Church-Bride and Jesus as the Savior-Bridegroom.[83] Of course, the rise of celibacy to a position of central importance in determining Christian authority structures put an official damper on these kinds of speculations. Still, the notion of an erotic relationship between Jesus and Mary Magdalene has surfaced at odd moments throughout Western history and is still capable of arousing a good deal of public ire.[84]

Yet the role of the repentant prostitute is symbolically appealing in its own right, and not just because the other options were closed off. It has proven itself to be a much more evocative figure than that of Mary as Jesus' wife or lover. The image of Mary as the redeemed sinner has nourished a deep empathy that resonates with our human imperfection, frailty, and mortality. A fallen redeemer figure has enormous power to redeem.[85] She holds out the possibility that purity and wholeness are never closed off; that redemption is always a possibility at hand. Despite the appropriation of sinful female sexuality for patriarchal aims, her rich tradition in story and art attests to the redemptive power of the repentant sinner.

And indeed Mary Magdalene has been a figure of importance not just for patriarchy, where too often Gregory's praise of a woman who "immolated herself" in order to burn out "every delight she had had in herself" has resulted in untold anguish, physical abuse, and self-destruction. Nonetheless, women are not only victims, but like all people are agents of their own lives, and so women have often interpreted her in ways that were unanticipated and no doubt not entirely welcomed. From the second to the twenty–first century, women prophets and preachers have continued to appeal to her to legitimate their own leadership roles.[86]

The stubborn and inflexible fact is that both women and men in Western society lack the option of an unambiguous symbolic tradition to draw upon. It was no one single factor, but the confluence of historical tradition with various theological problems, patriarchal prejudices, and human affections that converged to result in the complex portrait of Mary Magdalene as a repentant prostitute and preacher.

The portrait was sustained over the centuries and flourished because of even more complex motives and aims.

In the end, two basic portraits of Mary Magdalene developed, each with many variations: one stressed her roles as a prominent disciple of Jesus, a visionary, and a spiritual teacher; the other painted her as a repentant prostitute whom Jesus forgave, a latter-day Eve turned from her sinful ways.[87] While both portraits have legendary aspects, only the first has any claim to historical truth. The portrait of Mary as a repentant prostitute is pure fiction with no historical foundation whatsoever. The historical Mary of Magdala was a prominent Jewish follower of Jesus, a visionary, and a leading apostle.

## Chapter 14

# The History of Christianity

Until now every treatment of the *Gospel of Mary* has characterized it as a work belonging to the second-century heresy called Gnosticism.[1] But there was no religion in antiquity called Gnosticism. Scholars invented the term in the process of categorizing the variety of early Christian heresies. As we said above, they divided the earliest types into two groups: Jewish Christianity and Gnosticism. Jewish Christianity is characterized by too much or too positive an appropriation of "Judaism"; Gnosticism by too little "Judaism" or too negative an attitude toward it.[2] Orthodoxy is just right, rejecting "Jewish error" but claiming the heritage of Scripture for its own. This typology establishes the "correct" relationship to Jewish Scripture and tradition as the single most important factor in defining normative Christian identity. These types, however, can be established only by hindsight, and even then they are not real entities, but only academic constructs. In other words, all the texts and persons grouped under these categories did exist in antiquity, but they never understood themselves to be Gnostics or Jewish Christians, let alone heretics. Calling them Gnostics is simply a shorthand method for labeling them as heretics while maintaining the appearance of impartiality. It disguises the degree to which normative interests have pervaded supposedly objective and disinterested scholarship. I never call the *Gospel of Mary* a Gnostic text because there was no such thing as Gnosticism.[3]

It is true that all early Christians argued for the truth of their own theology and practice over against competing claims, but if we start out by dividing these groups into winners and losers, orthodoxy and heresy, it becomes impossible to see how early Christianity was really shaped. As I said above, this procedure obscures the complex dynamics of early Christian theology-making because it tends to treat all the "orthodox" texts primarily in terms of their similarities to each other and their differences from heresy, a procedure that obscures the real diversity of the New Testament literature and the processes by which the Nicene Creed and the canon were shaped. So, too, the enormous theological variety of the literature classified as Gnostic gets harmonized into an overly simplified and distorting monolithic ideology. This procedure makes it appear that all Gnostic texts say more or less the same thing, and permits their theology to be explained primarily in terms of how it deviates from the orthodox norm.

On the other hand, when historians set aside the anachronistic classification of early Christian literature into orthodox and heretical forms, analyzing both the similarities and the differences among the extant remains, then a much more complex picture emerges. It becomes possible to consider afresh what was at stake in how Christians formulated their beliefs and practices, and we come to see more clearly the dynamics of their interactions and the nature of the debates in which they were engaged. Eliminating these anachronistic terms of theological hindsight fosters a fundamental rethinking of the formation of early Christianity. Contemporary Christians may gain new insights and resources for reflecting on what it means to be a Christian in a pluralistic world, and for addressing the pressing need to rethink the relationship of Christianity to Judaism, Islam, and other religious traditions in order to meet the demands for social well-being and justice.

We can begin by considering how the master story of Christianity has been constructed.

Although Jesus and his earliest followers lived in the first century, Christianity as we know it was forged in the second to fourth centuries. These are the centuries in which creed and canon were shaped, in which the idea of the New Testament as a collection of books came into being, in which creedal statements gradually came into use as gauges of correct belief. First-century Christians had no New Testament or Nicene Creed. For most observers this well-known fact has not seemed problematic; and since early Christians wrote and distributed these works, the New Testament texts and early creeds are indeed important primary source materials for the reconstruction of the history of early Christianity. Yet so fundamental are creed and canon to informing our very definition of what Christianity is, that it is almost impossible to imagine what Christianity was like without them. As a result, the period of Christian beginnings has almost unavoidably been read from hindsight through the lenses of later canon and creed. But if we can remove these lenses, the story of Christian beginnings may sound quite different from the way it has generally been told, as Elaine Pagels' groundbreaking book, *The Gnostic Gospels*, demonstrates.

Here is where the recent discovery of early Christian writings from Egypt is so utterly crucial. These writings are of inestimable importance in drawing aside the curtain of later perspectives behind which Christian beginnings lie, and exposing the vitality and diversity of early Christian life and reflection. They demonstrate that reading the story of Christian origins backwards through the lenses of canon and creed has given an account of the formation of only one kind of Christianity, and even that only partially. The fuller picture lets us see more clearly how the later Christianity of the New Testament and the Nicene Creed arose out of many different possibilities through experimentation, compromise, and very often conflict. The Nicene Creed emphasized that salvation came through the virgin birth, death, resurrection, and exaltation of Jesus, but some forms of Christianity focused almost solely on Jesus' teaching and did not even mention these doctrines. Some of them rejected the idea of a benevolent God requiring blood atonement for sin, seeing Jesus instead as the living messenger of reconciliation and spiritual truth.

Much of early Christian history has been a matter of adding details or making minor corrections to the basic plot provided by those who won for themselves the title of orthodoxy. With the discoveries of new primary texts, we have firsthand testimony from perspectives other than those of the orthodox writers who won. These texts retrieved from the dry sands of Egypt are allowing scholars to paint a much fuller picture of Christian beginnings and to approach the familiar stories and teachings with fresh perspectives.

We are only beginning to understand how radically the new texts will affect our reading of early Christian history and, indeed, of ancient Mediterranean religion more generally. What is already clear, however, is that the study of this period is potentially fruitful for reflection about many contemporary concerns. The Mediterranean world in which Christianity appeared was in a period of rapid social change and religious experimentation. Traditional values and ways of life were being challenged and reshaped through contact with others; the family, gender roles, and sexuality were being redefined; local resistance to Roman rule often took religious form—whether by outright rebellion as in the Jewish revolts in Palestine, or more covertly by turning a crucified criminal named Jesus into an heroic symbol of resistance to worldly power and tyranny. It was a time in which a new "cult" called Christianity moved from the margins of society to become the official religion of the Roman empire. Such a period offers much to think about and a rich supply of material to think with.

The beginning is often portrayed as the ideal to which Christianity should aspire and conform. Here Jesus spoke to his disciples and the gospel was preached in truth. Here the churches were formed in the power of the Spirit and Christians lived in unity and love with one another. The mission was clear, and strong faith was forged in the fires of persecution.

But what happens if we tell the story differently? What if the beginning was a time of grappling and experimentation? What if the meaning of the gospel was not clear and Christians struggled to understand who Jesus was and what his violent death might mean? What if there were not unity and certainty at the beginning but Christians differed in their views and experiences and sometimes came into conflict and division? What if the earliest Christians don't model for us a fixed and certain path, but instead call us to emulate their struggles to make Christianity in our day? What might beginnings tell us then?

The first step in answering these questions is to scrutinize the version of early Christian history that has dominated contemporary perspectives. Unless we first understand what this history looks like, we will continue to use it uncritically and read the new material through old lenses of hindsight without recognizing the consequent distortion. Inevitably, an old wineskin filled with new wine will burst.

To appreciate the potential impact of recent discoveries, it is necessary to review the most widespread view of early Christian beginnings, what I shall call "the master story." The German historian Walther Bauer proposed that despite the seeming variety of historical narratives, the master story always presupposes the following elements:

1. Jesus reveals the pure doctrine to his apostles, partly before his death, and partly in the forty days before his ascension.
2. After Jesus' final departure, the apostles apportion the world among themselves, and each takes the unadulterated gospel to the land which has been allotted him.
3. Even after the death of the disciples the gospel branches out further. But now obstacles to it spring up within Christianity itself. The devil cannot resist sowing weeds in the divine wheat field—and he is successful at it. True Christians blinded by him abandon the pure doctrine. This development takes place in the following sequence: unbelief, right belief, wrong belief. There is scarcely the faintest notion anywhere that unbelief might be changed directly into what the church calls false belief.[4]

This master story asserts that an unbroken chain stretching from Jesus to the apostles and on to their successors in the church—elders, ministers, priests, and bishops—guaranteed the unity and uniformity of Christian belief and practice. This chain links modern Christianity securely with its historical origins in the life and deeds of its founder, Jesus the Christ. The correct form of this belief and practice is called "orthodoxy." It is inscribed in the New Testament canon and the Nicene creed, and enacted in such ritual performances as baptism, the Lord's supper or Eucharist meal, and ordination.

The narratives of the canonical gospels form the basis for this linear history. *Luke-Acts* in particular connects the ministry of Jesus with the foundation of the church through the sending of the Holy Spirit following Jesus' ascension. *Luke's* story of Christian beginnings was consolidated and extended by the fourth-century theologian Eusebius. He wrote the first comprehensive history of the church, alleging that Christianity in its original unity, purity, and power had survived the attacks of Satan from both within (heresy) and without (persecution) in order to triumph finally in the conversion of the Roman emperor Constantine to Christianity. Constantine not only ended the persecutions, he became the patron of Christianity and attempted to arbitrate Christian disputes. It was he who convened the Council of Nicaea, which formulated the Creed that became the basic form of Christian confession and to a large degree defined orthodoxy at the beginning of the fourth century.

While the plot of the master story presents a powerful and compelling—if problematic— paradigm for religious belief and practice, it is poor history. First of all, the story is incomplete and noticeably slanted. The roles of women, for example, are almost completely submerged from view. In the master story, the male Jesus selects male disciples who pass on tradition to male bishops. Yet we know that in the early centuries and throughout Christian history, women played prominent roles as apostles, teachers, preachers, and prophets. Moreover, the use of normative terms like "orthodoxy" and "heresy" immediately designates who were the winners and losers, but in practice "heresy" can only be identified by hindsight, instituting the norms of a later age as the standard for the early period. Hence the logic of the story is circular: the New Testament and the Nicene Creed define orthodox Christianity, not only in the fourth century and beyond, but anachronistically in the previous centuries as well.

One consequence of the triumph of Nicene orthodoxy was that the viewpoints of other Christians were largely lost, surviving only in documents denouncing them. Until now. The clearest contribution of the recent discoveries is in providing a wealth of primary works that illustrate the plural character of early Christianity and offer alternative voices. They disclose a much more diverse Christianity than we had ever suspected; for the master story presents only two kinds of Christians: true Christians (the orthodox) and false Christians (the heretics). We now know that the real situation was much more complex. Not stark contrasts, but multiple levels of intersection and disjuncture best define the situation.

In the end, the master story of the early church and scholars' neat division of earliest Christianity into well-defined types are oversimplifications that misrepresent the experience of early Christians. The early churches were diverse communities in which difficult choices were made, compromises formed, and persuasion exerted. Early Christians intensely debated such basic issues as the content and meaning of Jesus' teachings, the nature of salvation, the value of prophetic authority, the roles of women and slaves, and competing visions of ideal community. The New Testament and the Nicene Creed were not the starting points but the end products of debate and dispute, the result of experience and experimentation. As the new materials from Egypt demonstrate, the master story of Christian origins is not an impartial account of historical reality, but a construction representing the practices and viewpoints of some Christians, but not all. And just as the master story functioned to authorize the particular theology and practices of what later came to be orthodoxy, the invention of Gnosticism and Jewish Christianity by modern scholars continues that process in our own time.

If then we set this master story to one side, and with it the categories of orthodoxy and heresy as well as Gnosticism and Jewish Christianity, it becomes possible to read both the new works and familiar texts with new eyes. A few examples will help illustrate this point.

If we look at the earliest Christian works to survive, the letters of Paul, we see ample evidence of controversy within the earliest churches over the meaning of Jesus, the relationship of the Christ fellowships to Jewish law, women's roles, church organization and authority, to name but a few issues. The *Letter to the Galatians* notably illustrates the heated character of debates over whether Gentile men who have received salvation in Christ must undergo circumcision, and whether Christian communities should adhere to purity distinctions in their table fellowship. Rather than framing these issues as battles between true Christians and heretics (Judaizers), we should recognize Paul's letter as but one side of a story about early followers of Jesus working out what it means to be a Christian in a world where Jews and Gentiles are sharing meals together. No wonder that when people clashed over what it meant to accept Jesus as the Christ, the discussion grew heated. Some Christians held to the sincere conviction that accepting the gospel meant following the whole law of God. It was not an unreasonable position, but it was not the direction most communities would eventually take.

Similarly, the differences among New Testament books are perfectly understandable once we accept that the norm of early Christianity was theological diversity, not consensus. For example, one learns virtually nothing about the life and teachings of Jesus by reading Paul's letters or the *Book of Revelation*. Paul is interested primarily in Christ's death and resurrection, and offers little about Jesus' life and teachings, while *Revelation* offers a cosmic Christ ruling in heaven but says little about the significance of the death and resurrection so crucial to Paul's theology. Or imagine what would happen if a Christian belonging to a community which knew only the *Gospel of Matthew* were to travel and encounter a community of Christians who had only Paul's letters. What discussions they would have had! In *Matthew*, Jesus says that he has come to fulfill every jot and tittle of the law; he chastises anyone who ignores any part of it, no matter how trivial.[5] Paul's *Letter to the Galatians*, on the other hand, teaches people that they do not need to follow the laws of circumcision and ritual purity for "no one shall be justified by works of the law."[6] What a debate they might have had about the role of the Mosaic law in Christian practice! Now imagine an even more complicated scenario— one which we could not have imagined before the discovery of the new texts—where a Christian who knows only the *Gospel of Mary* enters the conversation. This work rejects any law but Jesus' teaching, seeing excessive external regulation as a bar to the preaching and reception of the gospel.

But while these examples help us imagine the situation more accurately, they are misleading insofar as they imply that believers got their information about the content of Christian teaching and practice from written texts. As we noted earlier, most people in the ancient Mediterranean world did not read or write. People heard about Christianity primarily through preaching and teaching; they practiced Christianity primarily through prayer, singing, and table fellowship. At what point and how often the reading of texts would have been a part of Christian worship or instruction is unclear, but it is clear that the domination of the Bible in our own print culture is an entirely inaccurate model for imagining early Christian life.

Nonetheless the picture is accurate to the degree that it suggests that Christian communities had access to a considerable variety of materials and produced diverse versions of Christian thought and practice. We know that churches in different geographical areas had different written texts and oral traditions, so we cannot assume that all churches used or even knew about the same texts. Certainly they did not have a collection called the New Testament, nor did they all agree on what texts should be considered authoritative. For many, Scripture meant the Jewish Scriptures, now read as Christian texts.

Moreover, we can see the interests of later Christians at work in the formation of the early written works. The *Gospel of Mark* originally ended at 16:8 with the flight of the astonished women disciples from the empty tomb. The editorial process by which verses 9-20 were later added in order to domesticate Mark's unsettling conclusion says something about the attitude of early Christians toward their texts: the life of the community took priority over the fixity of literary works.

The multiformity of early Christianity becomes even more evident when we remove our canonical spectacles. All historians recognize that since the earliest churches lacked a New Testament, limiting the construction of early Christianity to the information given in the New Testament cannot give us the whole story. Historians have to take account of all those materials that are Christian, whether or not they came to reside in the canon, and even if they later were understood to be heretical.

Many of the works early Christians possessed—such as the *Gospel of the Hebrews* or the *Gospel of Barnabas*—remain lost to us. Others have surfaced among the discoveries from Egypt. Some of these, like the *Gospel of Truth*, were known to us only because their titles had been mentioned in surviving works. Others, such as the *Gospel of Mary* and the *Treatise on the Resurrection*, were complete surprises. These new materials let us see more of the complexity and abundance of early Christian thought. For example, despite the enormous variety of the early Christian literature that eventually came to reside in the New Testament collection, all the New Testament texts conform to one perspective: that the death and resurrection of Jesus and his coming at the end of time are central to salvation. The Nicene creed emphasizes this point by making the death, resurrection, and second coming, along with the virgin birth, the central points that a Christian must affirm about Jesus:

> "I believe in ... one Lord Jesus Christ ... who for us and for our salvation came down from heaven, and was incarnate by the Holy Ghost of the Virgin Mary, and was made man. And was crucified also for us under Pontius Pilate; He suffered and was buried. And the third day he rose again according to the Scriptures; and ascended into heaven ... "[7]

In view of the centrality of this position, it is astonishing to learn that some early Christian communities didn't think Jesus' death had any saving value at all, and who were not looking for his return. What kind of Christians were these?

Among the newly discovered texts are several that emphasize the importance of Jesus' teaching for salvation—in contrast to the Nicene Creed which did not ask believers to affirm anything about the content of Jesus' teaching, or even that Jesus was a teacher. One of these is the *Gospel of Mary*. Two others are the *Gospel of Thomas* and the *Gospel of Truth*.

The *Gospel of Thomas* is an early collection of Jesus' sayings. It employs some dialogue, but in general lacks any kind of story line. It contains no account of Jesus' birth, his death, or resurrection. It does, however, refer to "the living Jesus," perhaps as a way of acknowledging his resurrection as well as his continuing presence. In the *Gospel of Thomas*, the focus of salvation clearly falls not on Jesus, but on his teaching: "Whoever finds the interpretation of these sayings will not experience death."[8] Indeed Jesus cautions the disciples not to follow a leader, but to look inside themselves for the kingdom.[9] Jesus is not portrayed here as the messiah, Christ, Lord, Son of Man, or Son of God. Saying 55 alludes to his death, but never suggests that his suffering could lead to salvation for others. Rather Jesus is presented in terms most similar to Jewish Wisdom speculation.

In Jewish tradition, Wisdom is described as the co-creator and first born of God,[10] as the light, the bringer of life and salvation,[11] as a teacher,[12] and as the designer and controller of history.[13] She comes down to humanity in a variety of guises to offer her wisdom, but is rejected.[14] Hidden even from the birds of the air, the place of Wisdom is known only to God.[15] Similarly, in the *Gospel of Thomas*, Jesus comes to humanity in the flesh, but finds everyone intoxicated with the world.[16] He is portrayed as the light found in all creation,[17] the drink that transforms and discloses what is hidden to revelation.[18] His teaching gives life; it reveals what is hidden in creation yet beyond human ability to perceive.[19] The *Gospel of Thomas* is meant to encourage people to seek the kingdom of God within themselves, to uncover the hidden wisdom of God in creation, and to reject worldly pursuits that lead one away from God. Those who do will find life and never taste death. Above all, it is Jesus' teaching that leads people to enlightenment and salvation.

The *Gospel of Truth* was written in the second century by the theologian Valentinus.[20] He was both a poet and a systematic thinker, and this theological treatise shows the complexity of his thought as well as his poetic use of language. He interpreted Jesus, the Logos or Word of God, as the revelation of God in the world. The need for revelation, according to Valentinus, resulted from God's utter transcendence.[21] Because of his radical "otherness," he actually appears to be absent; this seeming absence means that the world is ignorant of him. Since evil and suffering are by definition the absence of God, knowing God overcomes evil. Jesus was sent to reveal the Father,[22] to be the presence of God in the world. He brings salvation as the teacher of divine knowledge.[23]

While the *Gospel of Truth* acknowledges that Jesus was persecuted and suffered on the cross,[24] it interprets the crucifixion as the publication of his teaching.[25] Jesus, the Word, was nailed like a public notice upon a wooden pole, the cross. In order to give a spiritual meaning to the cross, the *Gospel of Truth* interprets the wooden cross as a type of the *Genesis* tree of life, and Jesus as the incarnate Word,[26] a kind of book of revelation. The revelation of Jesus brings about a restoration to unity[27] with the Father by eliminating the deficiencies of ignorance and destroying all the defects of suffering. It brings about authentic existence and awakens people from their nightmare-like state.[28] The Spirit reveals the Son, and the Son's speech brings about the return to the Father,[29] eliminating error and showing the way like a shepherd. The return to the Father does not come about through an apocalyptic catastrophe; rather it is described as a gentle attraction, a fragrance and merciful ointment. Souls are said to participate in the Father "by means of kisses." The work states explicitly that it is wrong to think of God as harsh or wrathful; rather he is without evil, imperturbable, sweet, and all-knowing.[30] The final goal of salvation is rest in the Father.[31]

In the *Gospel of Truth*, we meet with many elements common to New Testament portrayals of Jesus, such as the incarnation, crucifixion, and the image of Jesus as the Word; but all these elements are interpreted very differently. People do not need to be saved from sin, but from error, anguish, and terror. Jesus is incarnate, he suffers and dies, but his suffering and death are not saving in themselves. As in the *Gospel of Mary*, one is redeemed *from* suffering not *by* suffering. Jesus' ordeal is only an example of the general human condition associated with the body and the antagonism wrought by malicious error in the face of the truth. Jesus became a human being not in order to suffer as an atoning sacrifice for human sin, but to bring the revelation of saving truth. In a theology like this one, martyrdom can be seen as a rational and even necessary alternative to denying Christ, but at the same time there is no enthusiasm for it, since martyrdom does not itself bring salvation. Suffering and death belong to the nature of the perishable body. From the *Gospel of Truth*'s perspective, God does not desire human suffering; in his compassion he wants to save people from it.

Anyone who is acquainted with the New Testament gospels will find much that seems familiar in these three new gospels, for they all imbibed from the same pool of early Christian tradition. Their authors drew on similar traditions, but shaped them along different lines, due no doubt in part to the different backgrounds, needs, and experiences of their diverse Christian communities. They all affirmed Jesus as savior, but how they understood salvation differed.

Despite the considerable debate and tension among Christians during the first two centuries, early Christian theology and practice were fairly fluid affairs in this period. By the third century, lines hardened as it became increasingly clear that theological views had direct consequences for some very pressing issues. Two new texts dating from the third century, the *Apocalypse of Peter* and the *Testimony of Truth*, address some of these issues from perspectives that are new to us.

Like the other rediscovered texts we have discussed, the *Apocalypse of Peter* rejects the saving value of Jesus' death on the cross, but it does so vehemently, calling cross theology an evil "error." It charges that:

> they cleave to the name of a dead man, thinking that they will become pure. But they will become greatly defiled and they will fall into a name of error, and into the hand of an evil, cunning man and a manifold dogma and they will be ruled heretically (*ApocPet* 74:13–21).

It is not clear what the "name of error" refers to nor who is to be identified as the "evil, cunning man" (perhaps Paul?). But the references to "manifold dogma" and being "ruled heretically" clearly demonstrate that one issue at stake in cross theology was authority. The *Apocalypse of Peter* rejects the position that the legitimacy to rule others was grounded in the dogma of the crucifixion.

Another issue was that the rejection of Jesus' death as a saving event had direct consequences for attitudes toward martyrdom. The *Testimony of Truth* claims:

But when they are "perfected" with a martyr's death, this is the thought that they have within them: "If we deliver our-selves over to death for the sake of the Name we will be saved." These matters are not settled in this way (*TestTruth* 34:1–7).

In an age of increased persecution, the rejection of martyrdom was no doubt an issue over which feelings ran very high. Moreover, rejection of the saving character of Jesus' death and resurrection meant that baptism, the central rite of entry into the Christian community, could not be understood as a reenactment of Christ's death and resurrection as it had been for Paul.[32] Instead, the *Testimony of Truth* argues:

There are some who, upon entering the faith, receive a bap-tism on the ground that they have it as a hope of salvation... But the Son of Man did not baptize any of his disciples... If those who are baptized were headed for life, the world would become empty ... But the baptism of truth is something else; it is by renunciation of the world that it is found (*TestTruth* 69:7–24).

Rejecting the idea that being immersed in water is sufficient for salva-tion, these Christians interpreted baptism allegorically to signify renunciation of the world and reorientation toward God.

The *Apocalypse of Peter* and *Testimony of Truth* oppose the theo-logical centrality of Jesus' crucifixion, a basic element of what would become Nicene orthodoxy. For orthodoxy, the authority of the apos-tles was based on their being witnesses to the death and resurrection. That authority was then thought to be passed on through ordination, and thus the basis for the hierarchical organization of the church was laid. The apostles were considered to be the guarantors of the true teaching of the church, and male bishops claimed to be their sole legit-imate successors. This male model of discipleship also provided (and often continues to provide) a rationale for the exclusion of women from leadership roles, ignoring the presence of women disciples throughout Jesus' ministry, at the crucifixion, and as the first witnesses to the resurrection. The theological emphasis on the saving nature of the bodily incarnation, suffering, and death of Jesus was tied directly to an ethics of sin and judgment, as well as a model for martyrdom. All of these elements of Nicene orthodoxy had already been contested by other strains of early Christianity that instead offered teaching on the basis of unmediated revelation and illumination. They emphasized the importance of inner spirituality and an ethics of internal purity, freedom, and resistance to injustice. Authority within the community was based on spiritual achievement, maturity, and prophetic inspiration. These Christians emphatically denied that a good God would desire the suffering and death of his son or his followers.

The struggle to understand the meaning of Jesus on the cross continues to be a living issue for Christians. There are some people who would basically agree with the views of these rediscovered texts, that the figure of Jesus on the cross is incompatible with their belief in the goodness of God. And yet the scandalous image of God suffering on the cross has functioned for many to confer meaningfulness and redemptive power to the human experience of suffering. The issue in today's world is complex, for there are cases where the symbolism of the cross has justified a variety of forms of abuse, including anti-Judaism; it has supported continued suffering rather than empowered people to struggle against injustice. The Catholic liberation theologian Elisabeth Schüssler Fiorenza argues that if Christians are to keep the cross, the redemptive power of this symbol has to lie in its capacity to lead people to solidarity with the poor and the suffering, to stand in the hope of the resurrection. The early Christian debate over the meaning of Jesus on the cross goes to the heart of these and other vital issues. In the end, Christians and others may or may not think that Nicene theologians were right in their rejection of the views illuminated by the new texts. But either way, examining these controversies makes it possible to gain a much richer grasp of the meaning of Christian teachings.

The central challenge, facing anyone interested in the full history of Christianity, is to comprehend the meaning of these new materials in their own right. So powerful is the later Christian tradition, that it is all but impossible to read these new materials without automatically and unreflectively placing them into the old structure of the master story, assuming the normative status of the later canon and creed and reading these new materials as deviant. The perspective of the master story is fundamentally ingrained not only in Christian theology, but also in the imagination of historians. It is extremely difficult to think our way out of imagining that early Christians had a New Testament, or that Jesus established and authorized the religion of the Nicene Creed. The standards of orthodoxy and heresy, the appeal to Christian origins for authorization, and the normative status of canon and creed, all continue to exert an enormous amount of influence, even among scholars. But the new works from the Egyptian desert are proving to be very helpful. They allow us to see the degree to which the master story of Christian origins is not a naively "literal" and impartial factual account, and they are helping us construct a more complete narrative that will reflect the particular interests and perspectives of diverse Christians engaged in experimentation, compromise, collaboration, and synthesis.

What will this new story look like? The final answer to this question lies somewhere in the future. We are only beginning to construct the pieces of a fuller and more accurate narrative of Christian beginnings. At this point I can only say that it will be a story of diverse groups of people engaged in the difficult business of working out what it means to be a Christian in a world of rapid social change, increased inter-cultural contact, and dominated overall by Roman imperial power. The story will talk about the issues that concerned the first Christians, their differences of opinion, the debates they had, and the solutions they devised, both successes and failures. It will portray some of them as pretty radical social experimenters, and others as more willing to compromise with the values of the dominant culture. It will talk about the kind of communities they formed, about the utopian ideals of a loving God they nourished, and the burning desire for justice and for revenge that moved their imaginations.

By this point, it should be clear that the terms "orthodoxy" and "heresy" or "Gnosticism" and "Jewish Christianity" do not belong to impartial historical description. They were developed to identify the winners and losers in inner-Christian debate. Within this bifurcating frame, the new texts are relegated to the side that lost out, and therefore people might wrongly conclude that these views had no further place in Christian history after the establishment of Nicene orthodoxy in the fourth century. This conclusion would, however, be misleading and incomplete.

Despite the fact that many of these views were decried as "heretical," they have had a lasting influence. The positions of the "heresies" were only partially rejected. The portrayal of Jesus as a teacher of divine wisdom, the power of his words and deeds to transform lives, the understanding of his crucifixion as a call to overcome ignorance and suffering, the resurrection as a triumph over unjust domination, the authority of the prophetic spirit, the continued enactment of women's leadership and theology-making despite continued opposition, the insistence that baptism must be more than a magical rite of cleansing, the body as a site of resistance to worldly values, the paving of a mystical path to God through knowledge and love—all these ideas and practices were maintained inside of Christianity, and indeed they continue to evoke devotion and controversy down to the present day. It would indeed be impossible to imagine Christianity without them. The new discoveries perhaps allow us better to imagine Christianity with them.

## The Gospel of Mary

We can now return to our earlier question: Is the *Gospel of Mary* gnostic? From the first publication of the *Gospel of Mary*, its gnostic character was assumed.[33]  Some scholars early on argued that the controversy in the *Gospel of Mary* represented an historical situation of conflict between gnostic and orthodox Christians. Perkins, for example, suggested that Mary represents the gnostic position, while Peter represents the orthodox.[34] These views continue to be very much alive in studies of the *Gospel of Mary*, and most have presupposed that a gnostic myth[35] or typical gnostic themes[36] lie behind the work.

One way scholars have supported this position is by comparing the teaching of the *Gospel of Mary* with standard interpretations of the New Testament,[37] thereby anachronistically setting up a contemporary understanding of orthodox Christianity against which the *Gospel of Mary* fails. Having assumed in advance that the *Gospel of Mary* is heretical, scholars only had to ask what kind of heresy it was. At this point, they turned to descriptions of Gnosticism that scholars had constructed out of an enormously varied group of materials whose only real common denominator was that they showed too few "Jewish" elements or too negative an attitude toward "Judaism." They drew heavily upon early church polemics to construct a unified picture of Gnostic heresy, reproducing the arguments of polemicists like Irenaeus of Lyon. The heretics, he claimed, rejected the God of the Hebrew Bible as the true God and creator of the cosmos. Against what he saw as the clear evidence of Scripture, they denied the divine goodness of both the creator and the creation. Moreover, they undermined salvation by denying that Jesus had had a physical body, and that believers would rise physically from the dead even as Jesus had. They actually allowed women to preach and preside over the Eucharist and presumptuously claimed that only a spiritual elite would be "saved by nature" due to their heavenly origin; salvation came not by faith in Christ but through knowledge revealed only to them. In Irenaeus' view, such positions were arrogant as well as erroneous. In general, the polemicists objected that these beliefs implied that humanity did not need a savior, and that the moral efforts of instruction, purification, and good works were unnecessary. It was false belief, they claimed, that led the heretics to reject the authority of the legitimate successors of the apostles—the bishops and the priests of the true Church. This kind of theology, they claimed, could lead only to amoral or immoral practices, whether ascetic or libertine. Increasingly, however, scholars are coming to recognize the biased perspectives of these denunciations. The new texts from Egypt have been central to rethinking the history of early Christianity, in part because they show no evidence of the immorality or elitism described by the polemicists.[38]

It is equally difficult to reconcile the *Gospel of Mary* with the typical scholarly construction of Gnosticism. It promotes neither immorality nor elitism, but rather argues for the necessity of purification from evil and implies that all persons are spiritual by nature. Some themes in the work that have been identified as "Gnostic," such as the rise of the soul as release from matter or the distinction between inner and outer, are commonplaces of ancient philosophy. Nor are the most characteristic themes ascribed to Gnosticism, such as the distinction between a lower demiurgic creator and a higher transcendent Deity, present in the *Gospel of Mary*. It does clearly argue that the resurrection is spiritual, not physical, and affirms that women can serve as teachers and preachers, but these themes are not sufficient to characterize the *Gospel of Mary* as Gnostic. Clearly what marks the text as Gnostic in the eyes of theologically-minded historians is the *Gospel of Mary*'s lack of any strong ties to Jewish tradition; it is rather, as I have argued, primarily a product of Gentile Christians.

To be sure, its position on women's leadership is no doubt a factor in its being labeled heresy. Yet the nature of the resurrection and the legitimacy of women's leadership—as well as notions about the rise of the soul as release from matter, salvation as an inner process of turning toward God, and a Christology that either rejects or simply does not include the notion of Christ as judge—are all ideas that early Christians experimented with in their theology-making. The fact that the views of the *Gospel of Mary* did not prevail does not mean that they were regarded as non-Christian in their own day. Rather the conflict between the disciples in the *Gospel of Mary* shows all the markers of intra-Christian conflict in which proponents of different views cannot yet appeal to such fixed norms as the New Testament canon or the Nicene Creed.

Scholars have long felt that the conflict between Peter and Mary is the key to determining where to fit the *Gospel of Mary* into the story of early Christianity. Although Andrew attacks Mary and Levi defends her, both play only supporting roles in what is predominantly a conflict between Mary and Peter. It was Peter who in the first place had asked Mary to speak, and she responds only to him in defending herself. This scene has roots deep in a tradition of the two apostles in competition with one another. The chronological and geographical spread of the tradition about Mary and Peter in conflict did not follow a single trajectory, but was widely dispersed. Anne Brock has traced the seeds of this conflict in the earliest Christian literature, noting that Peter and Mary are the only two of Jesus' immediate followers reported to have received individual resurrection appearances; otherwise all appearances are to groups of Jesus' followers. Moreover, different works identify either Peter or Mary as the first to receive an appearance, putting them in competition for that preeminent status.[39] In *1 Cor* 15:3–5, Paul confers the honor upon Peter, but in the *Gospel of John* Mary is the first to see and speak with the risen Lord and the first commissioned to proclaim the good news of the resurrection (*John* 20:11–18).[40] Brock further observes that works that magnify Peter's status tend to reduce Mary Magdalene's role (for example, in the *Gospel of Luke*), while texts in which Mary Magdalene plays an important role, especially as witness to the resurrection, accord Peter a significantly less prominent status (for example, *John* 20). She further suggests that the overt competition between Mary and Peter in such later works as the *Gospel of Mary* and the *Gospel of Thomas* continues this early and widespread tradition.[41] Moreover, the stories of Peter and Mary seem to be connected to disputes over women's authority. Mary texts offer a strong basis for legitimating women's leadership, while texts where Peter is figured as the apostolic authority consistently do not present arguments supporting the role of female leaders; rather the role of women is effectively modeled in women's absence, silence or submission.[42]

Brock's study helps explain why the competition between the two was both pervasive and heated. Already in Paul's letters, a strong link had been forged between receiving a resurrection appearance, appointment as an apostle, and authority for the content of his gospel.[43] This powerful conjunction led early Christian groups to appeal to specific apostles to substantiate and authorize their teachings and practices. Certainly this is the case for the *Gospel of Mary*; it demonstrates unequivocally that Mary had become a figure to whom some Christians appealed in order to defend and promote their views of the meaning of Jesus' teachings, the basis for leadership, and the roles of women.

The repeated concern over the Savior's demand that the disciples preach the gospel gives these topics a special emphasis in the *Gospel of Mary*. The dialogues explore at length the closely related issues of who has understood the gospel and who has the authority to preach. The *Gospel of Mary* was written at a time when the answers to these questions were not yet settled. Since no one could appeal to a fixed canon or creed, the *Gospel of Mary* resolves the issue by contrasting Mary's character with that of Peter. The charges that he and Andrew make against her illustrate what was at stake: the content of the Savior's teaching, the right of women to instruct men, and the criteria to be used to judge apostolic authority. Any hesitation about Mary's status and the truth of the *Gospel of Mary*'s teaching is swept away by Levi's defense. The Savior knew her completely and loved her more than the other disciples, even the men, because she had understood and appropriated his teachings and attained a stability of character that the other disciples lacked. Because of her steadfastness, he had granted her special revelation. The message is clear: only those apostles who have attained the same level of spiritual development as Mary can be trusted to teach the true gospel.

Other scholars have suggested that more may be read into the conflict between Mary and Peter than I have found. Mary Thompson, for example, suggests that "It is difficult, if not dangerous, to read these gospels with too literal an interpretation, but the continuing presence of conflict between Peter and Mary of Magdala is pervasive and gives rise at least to the suspicion that there was such a conflict in the early churches and the disciples of Mary of Magdala may well have been in serious conflict with the disciples of Peter."[44] While intriguing, the suggestion is difficult, as she notes. The tradition is too widespread to limit the conflict to only two groups.

More frequently, Peter and Mary are taken as representatives of orthodox and Gnostic forms of Christianity.[45] This position assumes that the *Gospel of Mary* is Gnostic, and because Mary is the apostolic guarantor of that teaching, she becomes a representative of

Gnosticism. The seeming persuasiveness of this position stems only from the power of hindsight. Gazing back at the second century from the position of the twenty-first century, we know that the teaching of the *Gospel of Mary* lost out in the battle for theological hegemony. We know, too, that Peter became the preeminent representative of orthodoxy. Knowing all this makes it nearly impossible *not* to read the conflict between Mary and Peter as one between heretical and orthodox forms of Christianity. But no one in the second century would have seen it that way because they could not have known what we know. What matters at this point is not whether Gnosticism ever existed, but whether the conflict among the apostles in the *Gospel of Mary* can be taken as an intentional conflict of orthodox versus gnostic disciples. The answer to that question is no. In framing the problem as a conflict between orthodox and heretical Christians, we miss the historical significance of the work's own rhetoric of conflict and the complex dynamics of early Christian social and theological formation.

The *Gospel of Mary* frames the conflict in terms of preaching the gospel and the character of the apostles, but these concerns can be obscured when our reading becomes entangled in the substance and rhetoric of later controversies, when hindsight leads us to imagine that the conflict was about issues that only arose later. For example, some scholars have suggested that the real conflict in the *Gospel of Mary* was over whether authority should be grounded in apostolic succession or prophetic experience. Elaine Pagels has argued that the controversy among the disciples reflects the tension between later priests and bishops who claimed authority based on seeing themselves as the successors of the immediate followers of Jesus—represented in the text by Peter and Andrew—and those who thought authority should be based on spiritual gifts, especially prophetic experience—represented by Mary Magdalene.[46] Indeed "Gnostics," she says, "recognized three sources of revelation apart from the common tradition mediated through the apostles": from secret apostolic tradition, from visions, and from within oneself, through direct spiritual experience and inspiration.[47] All three apply to the *Gospel of Mary*.[48]

In my own work, I too have argued that Mary's vision took place after the resurrection, in which case this revelation would potentially be in competition with transmission of the public ministry since its content augmented or even altered Jesus' public teaching.[49] I had assumed that the account of her vision began with the statement, "I saw the Lord in a vision, and I said to him, 'Lord, today I saw you in a vision,'" and continued through Mary's account of the final rise of the soul to rest. Judith Hartenstein argues, however, that Mary is reporting on a vision she had had during the ministry of the historical Jesus and a conversation with him later the same day about the vision. In this case, she argues, the *Gospel of Mary* is "no reference for continuing revelation through visions."[50] Instead, she insists, the topic of the vision was brought up only as a starting point for the discussion of how visions take place. This point is confirmed, she continues, by the fact that Peter objects only to the idea of Mary's having received special teaching in private, not to her having received it through visions.[51]

I think Hartenstein's point is wonderfully insightful. It solves the problem of Mary's use of the perfect tense with the present ("I *saw* you in a vision *today*"), and the oddness of discussing the visionary experience within the vision itself.[52] It still leaves the problem of the oddity of having a vision of Jesus and then seeing the earthly Jesus later on the same day, but here Hartenstein points to the transfiguration in *Matt* 17:1-13.[53] If Mary's vision took place during the pre-resurrection ministry of Jesus, it could imply that she saw him as he truly was in all his glory and therefore understood his divine nature already during his public ministry.[54] That would also make sense of the Savior's response to Mary: "Blessed are you for not wavering at the sight of me" (*GosMary* 7:3). At any rate, as Hartenstein points out, Mary's vision and her stability point toward her worthiness to receive special teaching from Jesus.[55] The issue is not whether teaching relies upon the historical Jesus or upon continuing visions;[56] that conflict belongs to a later time. In the *Gospel of Mary*, all the Savior's teaching is given in a post-resurrection vision so the conflict between Peter and Mary has to be based on something else. Only Mary's teaching and her role as beloved disciple is challenged. That points to Mary as herself the focus of the conflict.

One final suggestion scholars have proposed is that the conflict pits the twelve against all comers. Hartenstein notes, again perceptively, that the *Gospel of Mary*'s choice of characters sets two of the twelve (Peter and Andrew) over against two who did not number among the twelve (Mary and Levi).[57] That choice might indicate that the *Gospel of Mary*'s author is directing an all-but-explicit polemic against locating apostolic authority solely with twelve male disciples. Yet as we've already noted, Mary's status as an apostle is not in question and therefore doesn't need to be defended.[58] The issue arises for modern scholars only by assuming hegemonic notions associating apostleship with men only. Indeed early studies of the *Gospel of Mary* assumed that Mary was not an apostle,[59] but Helmut Koester has shown that limiting the appellation "apostle" to a small group of male disciples (especially the twelve) was only one way in which the term was used in the first two centuries of Christianity.[60] Bernadette Brooten, for example, has demonstrated that Paul used the term "apostle" of a woman, Junia, in *Rom* 16:7.[61] The work of Ann Brock on the figures of Peter and Mary in early Christian tradition further supports the view that apostolic authority was not limited to the twelve in early tradition.[62] She argues that the tradition of the twelve and the connection with Peter was first formulated in the *Gospel of Luke*, but only slowly became a widespread paradigm. The competition between Peter and Mary, on the other hand, had its roots in the pre-Pauline and pre-gospel tradition. Mary's role in the *Gospel of Mary* presumes that she was regarded by the readers as an apostle—that is, as one of those who received the Savior's commission to go forth and preach the gospel.[63] It would seem that the *Gospel of Mary* reflects a time and place at which the exclusive tradition of the twelve was not fixed.

Indeed, our concerns about whether women were numbered among the apostles, tied as it to contemporary arguments for or against women's ordination, was simply not an issue to such a community, although the *Gospel of Mary* is concerned to protect the right of women to preach and teach against opposition such as Peter's. The controversy between Mary and Peter is not about who is an apostle—indeed the term is never used—but about who has understood and appropriated the teachings of the Savior. The question at issue is who is able to preach the gospel. The *Gospel of Mary* is quite clear that neither following Jesus, nor encountering the risen Lord, nor receiving his teaching and commission—nor for that matter all three together—is sufficient. All the disciples received teaching and commission, but only Mary is figured as a model disciple. Only Levi defends her. By portraying the other disciples, especially Andrew and Peter, as divisive and uncomprehending even after the resurrection, and by contrasting them with the steadfastness of Mary, the *Gospel of Mary* clearly questions apostolic witness alone as a sufficient basis for preaching the gospel.

As was noted above, the choice of these two characters was no accident. Early traditions that Mary saw the risen Lord and was an important follower of Jesus no doubt weighed heavily in casting her to play a similar role in the *Gospel of Mary*. Peter, too, was a good candidate for his role. It is important to remember that while Peter eventually became central to the patriarchal hierarchy of the church, in the early period his character was more fluid.[64] The *Gospel of Mary* did not choose him because he was already associated with a developed position on apostolic authority, but because he was known to be impulsive, uncomprehending, and fearful. In the *Gospel of Mary* Peter is portrayed as a jealous and contentious character, who cannot see beyond his own male pride and who clearly has not achieved inner stability and peace. He represents the folly of naively trusting the witness of the apostles in order to understand Jesus' teaching. And Mary, not yet tendentiously transformed into a repentant prostitute, is consistently represented as a faithful disciple.

The portrait of Mary Magdalene in the *Gospel of Mary* offers an alternative to apostolic witness as the sole source of authority. Although she too knew the historical Jesus, was a witness to the resurrection, and received instruction from the Savior, these experiences are not what set her apart from the others. Rather it is her exemplary discipleship. She doesn't falter when the Savior departs, but steps into his place, comforting, strengthening, and instructing the others. The superior spiritual comprehension and maturity demonstrated in her calm behavior and especially in her prophetic experience form the basis for her legitimate exercise of authority in instructing the other disciples. She does not teach in her own name, but passes on the words of the Savior, calming the disciples and turning their hearts toward the Good. This portrayal constitutes an explicit argument that the sure source of truth and authority can be confirmed only by the character of the disciple.

I would argue that the contrasting portrayal of the disciples in the *Gospel of Mary* is not aimed against the twelve, nor to support Gnostics against orthodox, nor visionaries against apostolic witnesses. The problem being addressed is rather that of criteria: The *Gospel of Mary* was written at a time when the truth of Christian teaching could not be settled by appeal to a commonly accepted rule of faith or canon of gospel literature, let alone an established leadership. The *Gospel of Mary* framed the issue as a matter of character: Who can be relied upon to preach the gospel? The argument for the truth of its teaching is based on a contrast between Mary's character and Peter's. Peter represents the error of assuming that simply having heard the teaching of Jesus is enough to ensure that one has actually understood it.

Andrew, as Peter's brother, seems to be guilty by association. Mary, on the other hand, is consistently represented as the faithful disciple. To read more into the controversy would anachronistically assume a fixity of theological positions and hierarchical practices that did not yet exist.

Framing the issue as one of character places the *Gospel of Mary* firmly in the context of early Christian practice, where the standard method to distinguish true prophets or teachers from false ones was by examining their character and behavior. Today we distinguish quite sharply between teachers and prophets, but in antiquity the line between them was much more blurred. Since all truth was understood to be divinely inspired, Christian prophets played a variety of leadership roles—prophesying and speaking in tongues, offering prayer, providing guidance, interpreting scripture, and teaching—and clear distinctions were not always made among these functions and their accompanying roles of leadership. For example, in the late first-century work *The Teaching of the Twelve Apostles* (commonly called the *Didache*), the earliest Christian work on church order, the prophet not only provides instruction, but also performs the eucharist and leads prayer.[65] In particular, teaching was connected with the gift of prophetic inspiration. Even where the role of teacher had become formalized, it was still connected with prophetic inspiration.[66] *1 Timothy*, for example, indicates that the roles of public reading of scripture, preaching, and teaching were conferred at once by prophetic utterance and the laying on of hands by a council of elders (*1 Tim* 4:13–14).[67] In the third century, Tertullian provides a description of a woman prophet in his congregation:

> We have now amongst us a sister whose lot it has been to be favored with sundry gifts of revelation, which she experiences in the Spirit by ecstatic vision amidst the sacred rites of the Lord's day in the church: she converses with angels and sometimes even with the Lord; she both sees and hears mysterious communications; some hearts she understands, and she distributes remedies to those who are in need. Whether it be in the reading of Scriptures, or in the chanting of psalms, or in the preaching of sermons, or in the offering up of prayers, in all these religious services matter and opportunity are afforded to her of seeing visions. It may possibly have happened to us, while this sister of ours was rapt in the Spirit, that we had discoursed in some ineffable way about the soul.

After the people are dismissed at the conclusion of the sacred services, she is in the regular habit of reporting to us whatever things she may have seen in vision (for all her communications are examined with the most scrupulous care in order that their truth may be probed). "Amongst other things," says she, "there has been shown to me a soul in bodily shape, and a spirit has been in the habit of appearing to me; not, however, a void and empty illusion, but such as would offer itself to be even grasped by the hand, soft and transparent and of an ethereal color, and in form resembling that of a human being in every respect." This was her vision, and for her witness there was God, as well as the apostle (Paul) who most assuredly foretold that there were to be "spiritual gifts" in the church.[68]

This unnamed woman prophet was clearly respected; she functioned not only as a visionary, but also acted as a counselor and healer.

In the *Gospel of Mary*, it is Mary Magdalene who plays the role of the prophetic teacher.[69] Not only does she have a vision of the Lord,[70] but she assumes the roles of comforter and teacher to the other disciples, admonishing them to be resolute. She turns their hearts toward the "Good" so that they begin to discuss the words of the Savior. She steps into the Savior's roles as the mediator of saving wisdom. The authority she exercises is not that of judge or ruler, but spiritual guide and instructor.

Because of the widespread belief in antiquity that the gods spoke through human vessels, prophets potentially had enormous power to direct people's lives, political events, and public opinion. Diviners and oracles were consulted by senates, kings, and emperors, who yet sometimes forbade inquiry into politically sensitive areas, such as the emperor's health.[71] Since prophecy represented a dramatic claim to authority, both for the prophet and for the message, serious issues of power were at stake in distinguishing true from false prophets. In the culture of early Christianity, if people were to accept that Mary's teaching came from a true vision of the Savior, her authority and teaching would be unquestioned. The problem was how to determine if it was an authentic vision. From a Christian perspective, the issue was theoretically simple: True prophets were inspired by divine agency; false prophets were inspired by the Devil and his demons.[72] In practice, distinguishing the two was trickier.

The problem was that it wasn't possible to tell on formal grounds.

The ideal way to assess a prophet's inspiration was to see whether his or her prophecy came true. But often this was impossible, either because the prophecy did not entail a future prediction or because it was too soon to tell. A more serviceable criterion focused on the moral character and behavior of the prophet. As Justin put it, prophetic vision is possible only for those "as shall live justly, purified by righteousness, and by every other virtue."[73] The eminently practical *Teaching of the Twelve Apostles* suggested that "the false prophet and the true prophet can be known from their behavior."[74] If a prophet stays one or two days, he or she is a true prophet; if three days, a false prophet. If a prophet in a trance orders a meal for himself or demands money, he is a false prophet.[75] And so on. Such precautions were no doubt necessary, since it was possible for con artists to prey upon the goodwill of Christian charity, as well as on people's credulity.[76]

The widespread assumption that the prophet needed to be morally spotless and spiritually mature in order to be a channel for the divine Spirit also provided material for intra-Christian polemics. A common way to disparage opponents was to slander their moral character. Accusing heretics of moral depravity was meant not only to portray them as hypocrites, but also to prove that they were vessels not of the Holy Spirit but of demons.[77] One particularly clear example is Tertullian's condemnation of the prophet Philumene. After twice calling her a "virgin" and affirming that she had a "vigorous spirit," he then dismisses her completely with the unsubstantiated charge that later she "became an enormous prostitute," thereby closing the entire discussion on a note of indisputable moral finality.[78] Tertullian can make this charge seem plausible because he associates her "erroneous" teachings with penetration by evil spirits and, hence, sexual pollution.[79] This example of sexual condemnation could easily be multiplied.[80]

In the case of women who prophesied, judgment about moral character depended heavily on their conformity to established social gender roles: that meant fulfilling their roles as wives and mothers, and keeping silence in church assemblies.[81] In such matters as speaking, preaching, teaching, and praying aloud before the whole community, women's sexual status was often evaluated differently from men's. The ancient sources, whether by Christians or other Mediterranean groups, often explicitly note the sexual status of women in discussing their prophetic experience, while analogous observations about men prophets are rare. Moreover, this attention consistently follows a clear pattern: When women's prophetic status is positively valued, their sexual purity is emphasized by pointing out that they were virgins, chaste widows, or devoted wives.[82] But in cases where the writer opposes a woman, her sexual status becomes an explicit basis for condemnation.[83]

There are good warrants for supposing that at least some women prophets rejected marriage, possibly following Paul's advice that it is better not to marry, for "the unmarried woman or virgin is anxious about the affairs of the Lord, how to be holy in body and spirit; but the married woman is anxious about worldly affairs, how to please her husband. I say this for your own benefit, not to lay any restraint upon you, but to promote good order and to secure your undivided devotion to the Lord" (*1 Cor* 7:34–35). It is notable that in his corresponding advice to men, Paul does not mention anything about them being "holy in body and spirit," only that they be anxious "to please the Lord" (*1 Cor* 7: 32–33). One aim of the opposition to women's public leadership apparently involved "restoring" women to their roles as wives and mothers. It is no coincidence that *1 Timothy* links its condemnation of women's public speech with a call for women to bear children in order to ensure their salvation:

> Let a woman learn in silence with all submissiveness. I permit no woman to teach or to have authority over men; she is to keep silent. For Adam was formed first, then Eve; and Adam was not deceived, but the woman was deceived and became a transgressor. Yet woman will be saved through bearing children, if she continues in faith and love and holiness, with modesty (*1 Tim* 2:11–15).

It is a double bind: for their prophecy to be considered authentic, women need to give up its public practice. The ambiguity and tension we witness in many of the sources—both those supporting and those opposed to public roles for women prophets—reflect the contradictions of this dilemma.

The practical consequences of this invidious criterion can be seen by again comparing Tertullian's views with those of the *Gospel of Mary*. Their differing attitudes toward the body are directly tied to valuations of the gender roles inherent in traditional Mediterranean patriarchy. For Tertullian, these are based in nature; for the *Gospel of Mary*, they are illusory. Their attitudes towards the role of women as prophets correspond to these perspectives. In the *Gospel of Mary*, Mary takes on the role of the Savior at his departure, engaging in public instruction of the other disciples. In Tertullian, a woman prophet had no right to speak during the public community gathering. Instead her visions were examined by male elders after the "people" had left. It was up to the men to determine the authenticity and truth of her revelations. Her experience might be highly valued, but her role as a public leader was not.[84]

A second criterion often employed to distinguish a true from a false prophet was whether or not the content of a prophetic message was found to be palatable—that is, whether it conformed to one's own interpretation of Scripture and tradition. The *Teaching of the Twelve Apostles*, for example, states: "Whoever comes and teaches you all these things which have been said, receive him. But if the teacher himself is perverted and teaches another doctrine to destroy these things, do not listen to him, but if his teaching be for the increase of righteousness and knowledge of the Lord, receive him as the Lord" (*Did* 11:1). The "things" which have been taught include only basic ethical instruction, as well as information about how to practice baptism, fasting, prayer, and the eucharist; a specific rule of faith is not given. By the third century, however, Tertullian argued that the Devil sought to corrupt the orderly discipline of the church by inspiring prophecy that differed from the rule of faith.[85] It was necessary for the leaders of the congregation, therefore, to examine the prophet's words with scrupulous care in order to probe their truth.[86] This approach is very effective if you have an established rule of faith ready to hand as Tertullian did. In the early period, of course, there was no widely established consensus on the meaning of Jesus' teachings, the proper interpretation of the Hebrew Scriptures, or the practices and beliefs that ensured salvation. Or even what salvation was: was it the resurrection of the body or the ascent of the soul to God? In such a context, invoking an appeal to the true faith was more of a rhetorical move than anything else. Appealing to conformity pointed quite anxiously to the spectral absence of a normative standard against which prophecy could be measured. In effect, then, the question about the truth of prophecy takes us right into the middle of debates over the meaning of Jesus' teaching, the interpretation of scripture, community organization, and leadership.

As tradition became more fixed and authority increasingly centered in a connected, hierarchical leadership, opposition to such works as the *Gospel of Mary* would have become easier.[87] Already by the end of the second century, Irenaeus was arguing that the testimony of the four public gospels[88] showed up the deceit of those who claimed to have received private post-resurrection teaching from Jesus before his ascent.[89] Such an argument as Irenaeus' would be persuasive only to those who accepted the four gospels as normative for Christian faith, but in his day Irenaeus could expect it to be taken seriously by many Christian groups. Even more critical, the establishment of the Nicene Creed as the rule of faith at the beginning of the fourth century provided a clear standard by which such texts as the *Gospel of Mary* would certainly be found wanting. The importance of prophecy declined as inspired teaching came more and more to be viewed merely as a supplement to the full truth already available in the normative teaching and practice of the church. But as we have repeatedly emphasized, at the time the *Gospel of Mary* was written, Christianity had no common creed, canon, or leadership structure. Attempts to distinguish true from false prophecy on the basis of content alone could only lead deeper into tangled debates about the meaning of Jesus' teachings and the location of God's guiding presence in the community.

Both the charges against Mary and Levi's defense of her belong to this early period. Andrew and Peter charge her with teachings that are "different" and challenge her authority to teach because she is a woman. There is no express attempt to denigrate her sexuality—an interesting point given the later fabrication of her as a prostitute. Levi's defense of her appeals solely to her relationship with the Savior, and the author uses the controversy with Peter solely to establish her character. Neither her detractors nor her supporters appeal to apostolic succession, to a limited canon of gospels, or a rule of faith; evidently these institutions had not yet been established.

That situation provides an important clue to dating the composition of the *Gospel of Mary*. Since the oldest surviving manuscripts, represented by the two Greek fragments, date to the early third century, the work must have been written by that time at the very latest. The only external, partially datable event referred to in the *Gospel of Mary* is the death of Jesus, which scholars generally place at about 32 CE on the basis of the claims in other gospels that Pontius Pilate ordered his execution. That sets the date of the *Gospel of Mary* sometime between 32 and 325 CE. Because no known, datable author cites the *Gospel of Mary* or mentions it by name, we cannot further narrow the date. It does appear, however, that our author was familiar with traditions found in the *Gospel of John* and perhaps the letters of Paul. If so, that would put the gospel sometime after 90 or 100 CE. Further narrowing of the date depends upon how historians assess where its contents fit in the general history of early Christianity.

That determination is crucial, but it is also the trickiest of all the factors used in determining the date of a work because of its circularity. The dating of a work depends on how the historian constructs history, but since history is constructed from the sources, the two processes necessarily effect each other. In the case of the *Gospel of Mary*, most scholars have dated the work to the late second century because they understand its theology to be a late development of Gnosticism. But the issues it addresses and the way in which it presents those issues fit best in an early second-century context. The controversy over women's roles, the appeal to one apostle over against others, and the discussion about the meaning of Jesus' teaching, his death, and resurrection are all issues that we know were being hotly debated at this time. Because the *Gospel of Mary* defends the validity of Mary's revelation on the basis of her character, not by appeal to a fixed apostolic succession, a limited canon, or a rule of faith, it was probably written before these had been fully developed and were widely accepted. Given these factors, it would seem best to date the *Gospel of Mary* to the first half of the second century.

Although only fragments survive, they prove that the *Gospel of Mary* was circulated and read in Egypt over a period of at least three centuries, from the time of its composition in the second century until the copy made in the fifth-century Berlin Codex. Indeed, it may have been composed in Egypt, but Syria is also a possibility; we cannot be certain.

Finally, we must face the question of authorship. The work is titled after Mary; given that Mary Magdalene was a prophetic visionary and teacher, is it possible that the teachings of the *Gospel of Mary* actually come from her? I think not, primarily because it is too difficult to imagine that Mary, a Jew, could have developed teachings so removed from any basis in Jewish theological tradition. It is far more plausible that the teachings of the *Gospel of Mary* developed among Christians whose thought world was shaped by popular philosophy steeped in the ideas of Platonism and Stoicism. The gospel was ascribed to Mary in order to claim apostolic authority for its teachings, much as the other gospel literature of the first and second centuries came to be ascribed to apostles or their followers. The actual author remains unknown to us.

On the other hand, the theology of the *Gospel of Mary* may well have been informed by women's theology-making. Until its discovery, we knew of no gospel ascribed to a woman and calling upon her to guarantee the credibility and authority of the work. To be sure, early literature frequently mentioned women disciples as important inter-locutors and sources of tradition. In addition to Mary Magdalene, these chiefly included Mary the mother of Jesus, Salome, Martha, and Arsinoe,[90] and the *Sophia of Jesus Christ* also maintains a tradition of seven women disciples in addition to twelve male disciples as repre-sentatives of the apostolic tradition. Some scholars have even sug-gested that the *Gospel of Mary* was written by a woman.[91] Though we cannot know this for certain, it is plausible because women were fol-lowers of Jesus from the beginning of his ministry and they continued to play important roles in early Christian groups, and we do know of women authors in antiquity.[92] Given the ubiquitous presence of women throughout Christianity, we have to assume that women as well as men passed on and interpreted Christian tradition, and that their voices as well as those of men found their places within the liter-ary tradition of the gospels. Even if the *Gospel of Mary* was not com-posed by a woman, it probably does contain women's theology. I suggest this possibility primarily because of the close resonance of the *Gospel of Mary* with the theology of the Corinthian women prophets,[93] the Montanist oracles of women prophets, and Perpetua's prison diary. If we put these quite varied theologies side by side it is possible to dis-cern shared views about teaching and practice:

> Theological reflection is centered on the experience of the person of the risen Christ more than the crucified Savior.[94] Jesus was understood primarily as a teacher and mediator of wisdom rather than as ruler or judge.

> Direct access to God is possible for all through the Spirit. The possession of the Spirit is available to anyone. Those who are more spiritually advanced give what they have freely to all without claim to a fixed hierarchical ordering of power. An ethics of freedom and spiritual development is emphasized over one of order and control.

> Identity as a Christian is constructed apart from gender roles, sex, and childbearing (with or without actually abandoning

these roles). Gender itself as a "natural" category is contested in the face of the power of God's Spirit at work in the community and the world.

The unity, power, and perfection of the Spirit are present in Christian community now, not only in some future time.

These elements may not be unique to women's religious thought or always result in women's leadership, but as a constellation they point toward one type of theologizing that was meaningful to some early Christian women, that had a place for women's legitimate exercise of prophetic leadership, and to whose construction women contributed. Focusing on these concerns enables us to discern important contributions of women to early Christian theology and practice, and to discuss some aspects of early Christian women's spiritual lives: their exercise of leadership, their ideals, their attraction to Christianity, and what gave meaning to their self-identity as Christians.

Peter's challenge represents an issue that was being hotly debated in early Christian circles: the legitimacy of women's leadership. The *Gospel of Mary* makes a forceful argument that authority and leadership roles should be based upon a person's spiritual maturity, regardless of whether that person is a man or a woman, and it affirms unambiguously that women were among the authentic followers of Jesus. We know from other sources as well that in many places women were early and important leaders in the Christian movements.[95] It is indeed impossible to understand the shrill condemnations of women's public speech found in texts like *1 Timothy* unless they were in fact prominent. We know many of their names and functions: Mary of Magdala, Joanna, Susanna, and "many others" who were immediate followers of Jesus[96]; the apostles Junia[97] and Priscilla[98]; Prisca,[99] Nympha,[100] and Lydia,[101] the heads of house churches; the deaconess Phoebe[102]; Mary,[103] a worker; and numerous women prophets, including those at Corinth,[104] Philips' daughters,[105] Ammia of Philadelphia,[106] Philumene,[107] and the visionary martyr Perpetua.[108] And surely there were many others. In the following centuries, women continued to make important contributions to Christianity in a variety of leadership roles.[109]

Yet in every century, from the first to the twenty-first, women's leadership has been opposed.[110] The attempts of some of their fellow Christians to exclude them from roles as prophets, teachers, and preachers must have been a bone of contention, even as it is today.

Yet because these opponents largely succeeded in dominating Christian theology and practice, the surviving literature gives very little information about the responses of women leaders and their supporters. Until now. The *Gospel of Mary* gives us new and precious information about how another side of the debate sounded. It argues that women's leadership is valid when based on unwavering faith, spiritual understanding, moral strength, and a commitment to further the gospel and help others—the same qualifications as those required for men's leadership. Those who oppose this kind of leadership do so out of false pride, jealousy, lack of understanding, spiritual immaturity, and contentiousness.

Mary as a woman is therefore crucial to the *Gospel of Mary*'s treatment of women's roles, but her sex-gender is also crucial to emphasizing its *theological* teaching about the body and salvation. For the *Gospel of Mary*, the body is not the true self. Even as God is non-gendered, immaterial and transcendent, so too is the true human self.[111] The Savior tells his disciples that they get sick and die "because you love what deceives you" (*GMary* 3:7-8). Peter sees only that Mary is a woman, not that she is a spiritually mature disciple. He apparently "loves" the status his male sex-gender gives him, and that leads to pride and jealousy. Levi's correction of Peter helps the reader to see one of the primary ways in which people are deceived by the body: it can seem to determine a person's character and spiritual qualities.

The *Gospel of Mary* develops Mary's role as a visionary and leading female disciple for its own ends: to legitimize its interpretation of Jesus' teaching, to support its theology more generally, and to argue for leadership based on spiritual maturity—not solely on apostolic transmission and never on sex-gender distinctions, rooted as they are in the perishable world. According to the *Gospel of Mary*, merely hearing or seeing Jesus, before or after the resurrection, was not enough to ensure that the gospel was preached in truth. It was precisely the traditions of Mary as a woman, an exemplary disciple, a witness to the ministry of Jesus, a visionary of the glorified Jesus, and someone traditionally in contest with Peter, that made her the only figure who could play all the roles required to convey the messages and meaning of the *Gospel of Mary*. It was these characteristics that made her a figure around which controversy was sure to swirl.

## Conclusion

When Jesus died, he did not leave behind him an established church with a clear organizational structure. The patriarchal and hierarchical leadership of the church developed only slowly over time and out of a wide variety of possibilities. Early Christians experimented with a variety of formal arrangements, from relatively unstructured charismatic organizations to more fixed hierarchical orders. In some congregations, leadership was shared among men and women according to the movement of the Spirit in inspiring gifts of prophecy, teaching, healing, administration, and service.[112] Others were headed by elders, bishops, deacons, and widows.[113] Some had formal offices; others meted out duties according to capacity and inclination in a discipleship of equals. In many, women and slaves were important leaders; others resisted this reversal of the dominant social order and worked to exclude them. The *Gospel of Mary* was written at a time when it was not yet clear which direction church organization would take.

From at least the time of Paul, Christian churches had stressed the presence of the Spirit within the churches, and the manifestation of spiritual gifts among all believers. They assumed that Jesus intended to generate a movement that would spread his teaching to all nations. The *Gospel of Mary* traces its own spiritual legacy to the early Christian tradition that Jesus had commissioned his disciples to preach the gospel. The dialogues among the disciples are framed in order to explore the meaning of Jesus' admonition to preach the gospel. What is the content of that gospel? Who has understood it and who has the authority to preach it? What insures that the true path to salvation is being taught? The *Gospel of Mary* takes very clear positions on each of these issues, but the controversy that erupts among the disciples also shows that the author of the *Gospel of Mary* was fully aware that not all Christians agreed with its views.

Increasingly the tide would turn toward favoring a patriarchal, hierarchical authority. It was the predominant form by which power was exercised in the Roman world, and it afforded at once more stability and more respectability than charismatically organized groups, which stern Roman sensibilities apparently found radical and disorderly. In the early fourth century, when the Roman emperor Constantine first legalized Christianity by issuing an edict of toleration,[114] he recognized a group of male bishops as the established leadership of the church, and in doing so sanctioned a power structure that would govern Christianity for centuries to come. But Constantine only gave systematic order and imperial approval to what was largely already in place. For by the second century, bishops had begun to base their claim to be the legitimate leaders of the church on apostolic succession, claiming to trace their authority through a direct line to Jesus' immediate male followers, who were styled as the great apostolic founders of Christianity. This succession of past witnesses, it was argued, ensured the truth of the Church's teaching and guaranteed the salvation of believers.

The *Gospel of Mary* directly challenges the validity of such claims, and offers instead a vision of Christian community in which authority is based not solely or even primarily upon a succession of past witnesses, but upon understanding and appropriating the gospel. Authority is vested not in a male hierarchy, but in the leadership of men and women who have attained strength of character and spiritual maturity. Prophetic speech and visions are given a place of primacy as the manifestation of spiritual understanding and the source of sound teaching. Christian community constituted a new humanity, in the image of the true Human within, in which the superficial distinctions of the flesh lacked any spiritual significance. Women as well as men could assume leadership roles on the basis of their spiritual development. The *Gospel of Mary* rejects any view of God as divine ruler and judge and, hence, repudiates those as proper roles for Christian leadership. The true model for leadership is the Savior, the teacher and mediator of divine wisdom and salvation who cautions his disciples against laying down fixed laws and rules that will come to enslave them.

According to the master story of Christian origins, Jesus passed down the true teaching to his male disciples during his lifetime. They, as witnesses to the resurrection, were commissioned to go out and spread this teaching to the ends of the earth; and only later was that true apostolic teaching corrupted by Satan, who sowed the weeds of heresy in the apostolic fields. According to the *Gospel of Mary*, however, the weeds were sown by the apostles themselves. Men like Peter and Andrew misunderstood the Savior's teaching and sowed discord within the community. According to the master story, the full doctrine of Christianity was fixed by Jesus and passed on in the doctrines of the Church. The *Gospel of Mary* instead suggests that the story of the gospel is unfinished. Christian doctrine and practice are not fixed dogmas that one can only accept or reject; rather Christians are required to step into the story and work together to shape the meaning of the gospel in their own time. Because human passions and love of the world incline people to error, discerning the truth requires effort, and it insists that communities of faith take responsibility for how they appropriate tradition in a world too often ruled by powers of injustice and domination.

For centuries, the master story has shaped people's imagination of the first Christian centuries; it has provided a myth of origins which casts the early Church as a place where true, uniform, and unadulterated Christianity triumphed. This story has again and again fueled the fires of reformers who appeal to it to legitimize changes in Christianity as it encountered very different conditions and cultural settings around the world. Historians, however, have come more and more to understand the *Gospel of Mary*'s portrait—despite its imaginary elaborations—as in a number of respects more historically accurate than that of the master story. The earliest Christian texts we have don't portray a harmonious and unified Church of spiritual perfection, but communities working through issues of conflict and difference. The *Gospel of Mary* also makes it quite clear that the appeal to particular kinds of apostolic authority is a theological stance, not an historical judgment. It is unlikely that twelve male disciples, each with the identical understanding of Jesus' teaching, went out and started the movements that would eventually become the religion of Christianity. We know too much about the influential activities of other figures, not least of whom are Paul, Jesus' brother James, and Mary Magdalene, to think that. The ancient texts from Egypt show that early Christians were not of one mind—even about so crucial an issue as whether the cross and physical resurrection of Jesus were important for salvation or not. The *Gospel of Mary* and other works argue energetically that the appropriation of Jesus' teachings points the way to true discipleship and salvation.

The historical importance of the *Gospel of Mary* lies in letting us see the contours of some crucial debates over the authority of apostolic tradition, prophetic experience, and women's leadership. We are in a better position to judge what was at stake in the road Christianity followed by walking a way down one of the paths that has been little trodden.

# Notes

## Chapter one

1. See the summary in Till and Schenke, *Die Gnostischen Schriften*, 1–2.

2. See, for example, Koester, "Writing and the Spirit"; "Written Gospels or Oral Traditions?"

3. See Markschies, "Lehrer, Schüler, Schule," 98.

4. These letters are contained in the New Testament canon, and include *Romans, 1* and *2 Corinthians, Galatians, Philippians, 1 Thessalonians,* and *Philemon.* It is possible, although widely disputed, that Paul wrote *2 Thessalonians, Ephesians* and *Colossians* as well. The others letters attributed to him (*Hebrews, 1* and *2 Timothy,* and *Titus*) are pseudonymous.

5. See *Galatians* where this issue is a topic of considerable controversy.

6. See *1 Cor* 11–14.

7. See Schmidt, "Ein vorirenaeisches gnostisches Originalwerk," 839.

8. An English translation of these works can be found in Robinson and Smith, *NHLE.*

9. Schmidt, "Ein vorirenaeisches gnostisches Originalwerk," 839.

10. See *Die alten Petrusakten*, 2.

11. Or perhaps eight? Hans-Martin Schenke has suggested that the roll from which the first pages of the Berlin codex were cut would have been a standard length if we were to reckon that two additional (uninscribed) pages had been at the beginning of the codex. See Schenke, "Bemerkungen," 315–16; Robinson, "Codicological Analysis," 40. At any rate, only six *inscribed* pages are missing; any additional pages would have been blank.

12. Schmidt clearly mentions the cover in his announcement of the find: "Das manuskript lag noch in dem Originaldeckel aus Leder und Papyrus, wie überhaupt das Ganze in einem unversehrten Zustande gefunden sein musste." ["The manuscript yet lay in the original cover made out of leather and papyrus, so that the whole must have been found in an undamaged condition."] ("Ein vorirenaeisches gnostisches Originalwerk," 839.) Nothing is said about the cover in Till's publication, however, and it seems to have been misplaced. Myriam Krutzsch and Günter Poethke, curators at the Egyptian Museum in Berlin, recently found a leather cover, whose size and date fit the Berlin Codex; they have suggested this cover belongs to the Berlin Codex (see "Der Einband des koptisch-gnostischen Kodex Papyrus Berolinensis 8502").

13. This disorder may account for the fact that not only the first six pages were lost, but also four additional pages in the middle of the work (pp. 11–14). It is easy to imagine how the top pages would be removed, perhaps in hopes of an independent sale, but the reason for extracting pp. 11–14 is less clear, unless in the jumble they had come to follow p. 6. Thus whoever took the pages, took the top five leaves (ten pages).

14. "Ein vorirenaeisches gnostisches Originalwerk," 839. Because the pages were out of order, Schmidt at first mistakenly thought that *GMary* was part of another work, *ApJohn*. Once the confusion got straightened out, it became clear that *GMary* was a work in its own right.

15. Till and Schenke, *Die gnostischen Schriften*, 1.

16. Till and Schenke, *Die gnostischen Schriften*, 1.

17. Till and Schenke, *Die gnostischen Schriften*, 1.

18. Roberts, "463. The Gospel of Mary."

19. Till and Schenke, *Die gnostischen Schriften*, 24–25.

20. Till and Schenke, *Die gnostischen Schriften*, 2.

21. In 1972, Schenke published an up-dated version (see Till and Schenke, *Die gnostischen Schriften*). Pasquier (*L'Évangile selon Marie*) and George MacRae ("The Gospel of Mary") have offered new readings of difficult passages. See the summary of Schenke, "Carl Schmidt und der Papyrus Berolinensis 8502."

22. See Lührmann, "Die griechischen Fragmente."

23. Parsons, "3525. Gospel of Mary."

## Chapter three

1. Compare *Matt* 28:16–20; *Mark* 16:14–20; *Luke* 24:44–52; *Acts* 1:6–8; *John* 20:17–18.

2. See also the discussion of Hartenstein, *Die Zweite Lehre*, 127–60.

3. *Matt* 28:9–10, 16–20; *Mark* 16:9–20; *Luke* 24:13–53; *Acts* 1:2–9; *John* 20:11–21:23. For other post-resurrection dialogues, see Perkins, *The Gnostic Dialogue*.

4. *Luke* 24:25–27, 32, 45–47.

5. *Matt* 28:18–20; *Mark* 16:15–18; *Luke* 24:44–49; *Acts* 1:8.

6. See Perkins, *The Gnostic Dialogue*, 25–72, esp. 30–32. Perkins classifies the genre of *GMary* as a post-resurrection dialogue (see *The Gnostic Dialogue*, 25–36, 133–37).

7. See Koester, *Ancient Christian Gospels*, 21–22.

8. See Perkins, *The Gnostic Dialogue*. The *Gospel of Mary* has also been categorized as a "discourse" (Puech and Blatz, "The Gospel of Mary," 391) and an apocalypse (see J. Collins, "Introduction"; Fallon, "The Gnostic Apocalypses"). According to Pheme Perkins, "…the revelation dialogue seems to have been as characteristic of Christian Gnostics as the Gospel was of orthodox Christians" (*The Gnostic Dialogue*, 26). Here she is following the line of argument suggested by James Robinson (Perkins cites Robinson "On the Gattung of Mark (and John)," in *The Gnostic Dialogue*, 26, n.3) and Helmut Koester that certain distinct genre of early Christian literature developed to express distinct Christological tendencies (see Koester in Robinson and Koester, *Trajectories*, 158–204). From their perspective, the narrative gospel was always based on the kerygma of the crucified and risen Lord; the sayings gospel, on the other hand, as exemplified by *GThom*, was catalyzed as a genre by "the view that the kingdom is uniquely present in Jesus' eschatological preaching and that eternal wisdom about man's true self is disclosed in his words. The gnostic proclivity of this concept needs no further elaboration" (Koester in Robinson and Koester, *Trajectories*, 186). Furthermore, according to Koester, the features of the framework of the revelation discourse, such as one sees in the *ApJohn*'s account of a luminous appearance to the disciple John, "cannot be derived from the resurrection appearances of the canonical gospels, even though a number of gnostic revelations admittedly have been influenced by the canonical Easter stories" (Koester in Robinson and Koester, *Trajectories*, 195. In his founda-

tional work, *Ancient Christian Gospels*, Koester further develops this thesis that sayings collections and dialogue gospels generally precede narrative gospels). While accepting the existence of the dialogue genre, two studies have recently criticized this general theory regarding the relationship between genre and Christology. Martina Janßen has noted the wide diversity of content, form, and function of dialogues in ancient literature, and argued that the evidence does not support tying a "gnostic" theological content to this genre ("Mystagogus Gnosticus?"). On the contrary, she suggests that the so-called "gnostic revelation dialogue" is an artificial construct that distorts interpretation, especially by over-simplification of the diversity among the texts so classified. In short, she problematizes the connection between dialogue form and heretical "gnostic" theological content. Judith Hartenstein (*Die zweite Lehre*) takes a different tack by examining the frame narratives of the revelation dialogues, isolating a sub-type of appearance dialogue. She concludes that it is the frame narrative's relating a post-resurrection appearance of Jesus to his disciples that consistently marks a clear Christian element in these texts and provides a clear connection to the New Testament gospels. In short, she argues that such appearance frameworks show a dependence upon the narrative gospels, while the content of the dialogues can be quite diverse in both origin and content. It is precisely the genre of the work that gives it its Christian (as opposed to gnostic) character. Although in the end, Hartenstein supports the view that the *GMary* is a gnostic work, that is not because of the genre, but because of the content of Jesus' and Mary's teachings.

9. *GMary* 4:2, 5–7.

10. *AgHer* 5, Preface (*ANF* I, 526). All translations are adapted from this edition.

11. *AgHer* 5.1 (*ANF* I, 526; trans. adapted).

12. Irenaeus' understanding of creation and what it means to be human differs significantly from *GMary*. He argues that one does not have to leave the body in order to see God. The body is itself the locus of divine revelation and simultaneously the subject of divine salvation. It is in the body that humanity receives the Spirit and is restored to likeness to God. The presence of Spirit is not a future event; it is "dwelling in us, rendering us spiritual even now, and the mortal is swallowed up by immortality." Irenaeus assures us that this "does not take place by a casting away of the flesh, but by the importation of the Spirit" (*AgHer* 5.8 in *ANF* I, 533; adapted). For further discussion, see King, "Hearing, Seeing, and Knowing God."

13. *GMary* 4:3–5.

14. *GMary* 4:9–10.

15. A point noted in conversation. For further discussion, see below p. 56.

16. *Gal* 1:11–12.

17. *Rev* 1:1.

## Chapter four

1. For further discussion, see King, *What is Gnosticism?*

2. See Wilson, "The New Testament."

3. First published in English in 1978, now in the third edition by James M. Robinson and Richard Smith.

4. Edited by Hedrick and Mirecki and published in 1999.

5. Edited by Hans-Martin Schenke and published in 2001.

6. *GMary* 10:2.

7. See *Phaedo* 64c–65d.

8. Plato uses the famous Greek word play that the body (*sôma*) is a prison (*sêma*). See, for example, *Phaedrus* 250c.

9. On the nature of death, see *Phaedo* 64c.

10. See *Phaedo* 64e–65c.

11. See *Timaeus*, especially 27d–29d.

12. See *Theaetetus* 176a.

13. *Theaetetus* 176e–177a; cited from Hamilton and Cairns, *Collected Dialogues*, 881.

14. *Theaetetus* 176a–c; cited from Hamilton and Cairns, *Collected Dialogues*, 881.

15. *Theaetetus* 176e–177a; cited from Hamilton and Cairns, *Collected Dialogues*, 881.

16. *Theaetetus* 176e–177a; cited from Hamilton and Cairns, *Collected Dialogues*, 881.

17. See *Timaeus* 90e–92c.

18. See *Phaedo* 107c–d.

19. The following is based on Nussbaum, "The Stoics on the Extirpation of the Passions," *Apeiron* 29 (1987), 129–77, see also Cicero, *Tusculan Disputations*, IV.22 (in Graver, *Cicero on the Emotions*, 46–47; see also her notes, 93–94).

20. Nussbaum, "Extirpation of the Passions," 158–59.

21. For an introductory discussion of literacy, see Yaghjian, "Ancient Reading."

22. For other examples of the so-called "Platonic underground," see Dillon, *The Middle Platonists*, 384–96.

23. See *Mark* 4:9 and parallels. See also the forthcoming dissertation of Anne-Marit Enroth-Voitila, "'Whoever has ears, let that one hear.'" A tradition- and redaction-critical Analysis of the Hearing Formula in Early Christianity."

24. The terms "natural, molded, or created" indicate the totality of all existing material things. Compare *GPhil* 63:18–19; see Pasquier, *L'Évangile selon Marie*, 50; Tardieu, *Écrits gnostiques*, 226.

25. Compare *GPhil* 53:14–23; *OrigWorld* 127:3–5.

26. See Dillon, *The Middle Platonists*, 128.

27. *Academica Posteriora* I,27 (Rackham, *Cicero*, 439).

28. *1 Cor* 7:31.

29. *Mark* 13:31.

30. *2 Pet* 1:5–7.

31. *2 Pet* 1:9.

32. See *2 Pet* 2.

## Chapter five

1. See also Pasquier, *L'Évangile selon Marie*, 53.

2. See *Phaedo* 65b; cited from Hamilton and Cairns, *Collected Dialogues*, 48.

3. See *Phaedo* 65b–c. These ideas of Plato received considerable attention and elaboration in the centuries which followed. Increasingly, true knowledge came to be associated with knowledge of the immaterial realm of Being (God), and knowledge of the sensible world was disparaged as a lower concern fit only for people without higher intellectual and spiritual sensibilities. While economic and class interests are definitely at work in this formulation, the appropriation of the disparagement of matter in the *Gospel of Mary* is shaped less by upper class derogation of manual labor than by a deep sensitivity to the connection of suffering and death with the physical body.

4. See especially *Timaeus* 27d–29d.

5. Pasquier suggests that suffering arises directly from "the nature of adultery," that is, the mixing of the spiritual and material natures: "The adulterous union with matter provokes suffering because it is contrary to nature" (*L'Évangile selon Marie*, 54).

6. Compare *GPhil* 67:9–11.

7. Trans. Wesley W. Isenberg, *NHLE*, 175.

8. In arguing (correctly in my opinion) that this saying has been misinterpreted by scholars, Svartvik paraphrases his own interpretation as follows: "In other words, in reply to the questioners who complain about the disciples' breach of the tradition, Jesus rebukes them: —Why are you slandering them? Why are you insinuating that they do not keep the Law? Remember that giving vent to slander is even a graver sin than breach of your expansive interpretation of the purity laws! Indeed, *a person is defiled not so much by what goes into the mouth as by what comes out of the mouth*" (*Mark and Mission*, 409).

9. In conversation (Nashville, November, 2000).

10. Many New Testament scholars regard these verses as a later interpolation into Paul's letter, in part because of his appeal to the law and in part because the manuscript tradition is unstable here, placing these verses sometimes at *I Cor* 14:33b and sometimes after. But Wire argues to the contrary that Paul's letter has been leading up to this injunction (see *The Corinthian Women Prophets*, 152–58).

11. For the appeal to "nature" to support women's subordination, see *1 Cor* 11:2–16, esp. v. 14.

12. See Tardieu, *Écrits Gnostiques*, 229.

## Chapter six

1. This notion may very well be connected to ancient philosophical speculation that the true nature of humanity is divine.

2. *L'Évangile selon Marie*, 62.

3. Plato clearly imagined the form of Man as a male image, not gender inclusive as does the *Gospel of Mary*.

4. *Parmenides* 130c.

5. Similar language appears in *Eph* 4:13 (εἰς ἄνδρα τέλειον) and *Col* 1:28 (ἄνθρωπον τέλειον), but in both cases most English translations obscure the similarity to *GMary* by translating "perfect" as "mature" (see, for example, NRSV).

6. Schröter sees this application of the phrase "Son of Man" to humanity not just to Jesus, as a "democratizing" of the concept (see "Zur Menschensohnvorstellung," 186–87).

7. This inclusive translation should not obscure the fact that the usage of the masculine to refer to humanity as a whole is not accidental or incidental. This usage clearly reflects the values of Mediterranean culture, where the male represents what is perfect, powerful, and transcendent (see for example Philo, *Questions and Answers on Genesis* 4:15: "The soul has, as it were, a dwelling partly in men's quarters, partly women's quarters. Now for the men there is a place where properly dwell the masculine thoughts (that are) wise, sound, just, prudent, pious, filled with freedom and boldness, and akin to wisdom. And the women's quarters are a place where womanly opinions go about and dwell, being followers of the female sex. And the female sex is irrational and akin to the bestial passions, fear, sorrow, pleasure, and desire, from which ensue incurable weaknesses and indescribable diseases" (trans. Marcus; *Philo Supplement* 1, 288).

## Chapter seven

1. The Greek version reads: "*Once* when the Lord appeared to me in a vision," implying that he may have appeared on more than one occasion.

2. See Williams, *The Immovable Race.*

3. Variations of this saying are also attested in Clement of Alexandria (*Who is the Rich Man who will be Saved?* 17:1; *Stromateis* IV,6:33), Justin Martyr (*Dialogue with Trypho* 6:2), Macarius (*Homily* 43:3), and others.

4. See *Matt* 6:21; *Luke* 12:34.

5. For a fuller exposition of this issue, see King, "Prophetic Power and Women's Authority."

6. In taking this position, Tertullian is close to the Stoics who regarded the soul as material.

7. Some manuscripts read "Paul" instead of "people" (see Waszink, *Tertulliani,* text, p. 12, note 15).

8. See, for example, *De anima* 36.4 where he states that Eve's soul was more complete than Adam's.

9. This view is shared by many Platonists of this period. For example, in *The Face on the Moon,* one of Plutarch's characters argues that a human being is tripartite: body, soul, and mind. The body derives from the earth, the soul from the moon, and the mind from the sun. At death, in various stages, each returns to that from which it came (*On the Face of the Moon* 28). Plutarch writes: "Most people rightly hold a person to be composite, but wrongly hold him to be composed of only two parts. The reason is that they suppose mind to be somehow part of soul, thus erring no less than those who believe soul to be part of body, for in the same degree as soul is superior to body, so is mind better and more divine than soul. The result of soul and body commingled is the irrational or the effective factor, whereas of mind and soul the conjunction produces reason; and of these the former is the source of pleasure and pain, the latter of virtue and vice" (*On the Face of the Moon* 28; trans. Cherniss and Helmbold, 197).

10. See *De anima* 40.

11. Here Tertullian departs from the views of Soranus and the Stoics. He argues strongly against their views on the fate of the soul after death and that sense perception is fallible. He also argues against the Platonic views on metempsychosis since they endanger his view that the flesh is resurrected.

12. See *De anima* 41.3–4.

13. See *De anima* 41.4

14. Text in Waszink, *Tertulliani,* 62. Compare Cicero: "When, therefore, the soul has been withdrawn by sleep from contact with sensual ties, then does it recall the past, comprehend the present, and foresee the future. For though the sleeping body then lies as if it were dead, yet the soul is alive and strong, and will be much more so after death when it is wholly free of the body" (*De divinatione* I.30.63 in Falconer, *Cicero,* 295). This perspective is actually closer to that of *GMary* than to Tertullian insofar as it presupposes that the soul is permanently separated from the body at death. For a fuller discussion of Tertullian on ecstasy, see Nasrallah, "'An Ecstasy of Folly.'"

15. *De anima* 47. Compare Cicero on the views of Posidonius, *De divinatione,* I, 30 (64).

16. See *De anima* 6:3.

17. Text and trans. in Heine, *Montanist Oracles,* 68, 69, with modification; I

have changed the pronouns in this translation from the masculine used by Tertullian to plural pronouns since Tertullian clearly believes that both men and women are capable of prophecy; see *De anima* 9:4. See also the study of Tabbernee, *Montanist Inscriptions and Testamonia*, which includes important attestations to women leaders among the Montanists. For discussion of the Montanist women prophets and office-holders, see Jensen, *God's Self-Confident Daughters*, 133–82; Eisen, *Women Officeholders in Early Christianity*.

18. And among non-Christians; see, for example, Cicero, *De divinatione* I.30.63.

19. Justin here presupposes a tripartite division of body, soul, and spirit. The mind, it would seem, is the ruling portion of the soul. He holds with Tertullian in arguing that the body itself will be saved (see Tertullian, *On the Resurrection*), but not due to its own nature. It was created and therefore exists only because of God's will (see *Dialogue with Trypho* 5). The soul itself is neither immortal nor unbegotten, unlike the spirit which animates it (*Dialogue with Trypho* 6). In this schema, reason is essential to knowledge of God and to obtaining salvation by the exercise of one's God-given capacity for free will (see *Dialogue with Trypho* 141).

20. Cited by Tardieu, *L'Écrit gnostiques*, 232.

21. "'Blessed are you for not wavering at seeing me. For where the mind is, there is the treasure'" (*GMary* 7:3–4).

22. Compare Seneca (*Natural Questions* I, pref. 11–13), who considers the mind to be the divine part of humanity, but says it can roam the divine heavens only when it "retains very little of the body, only if it has worn away all sordidness and, unencumbered and light, flashes forth, satisfied with little. When the mind contacts those regions it is nurtured, grows, and returns to its origin just as though freed from its chains. As proof of its divinity it has this: divine things cause it pleasure, and it dwells among them not as being alien things but things of its own nature. Serenely it looks upon the rising and setting of the stars and the diverse orbits of bodies precisely balanced with one another . . . Here, finally, the mind learns what it long sought: here it begins to know god" (trans. Corcoran, *Seneca*).

## Chapter eight

1. This speculation is based on the fact that Darkness is the first of the seven Powers of Wrath.

2. The word eternal is not quite correct here, since the *Gospel of Mary* understands the final resting place of the soul to be beyond time and eternity.

3. As Pasquier points out, three terms structure the dialogue of the third Power with the soul: ignorance, domination, and judgment. These three form the basis of the Power's illegitimate domination over entrapped souls. See Pasquier, *L'Évangile selon Marie*, 89–92.

4. See Pasquier, *L'Évangile selon Marie*, 80–83; Michel Tardieu, *Écrits Gnostiques*, 290–92. Concerning the origin of their names, see Pasquier, 80–86; Tardieu, 234.

5. The Greek and Coptic texts show minor variation in sense here. The Greek reads: "the [due] measure of the time of the aeon" (PRyl), while the Coptic reads: "the time of the due measure of the aeon" (BG).

6. Compare *DSav* 141:3–9.

7. Published by Louis Robert, "Trois oracles de la Théosophie et unprophètie d'Apollon" (cited from MacMullen, *Paganism in the Roman Empire*, 13).

8. See, for example, the discussion of Culianu, "Ascension"; Colpe, "Jenseits

(Jenseitsvorstellungen)"; "Jenseitsfahrt I (Himmelfahrt)"; "Jenseitsreise (Reise durch das Jenseits"); Casadio, "Gnostische Wege zur Unsterblichkeit"; A. Y. Collins, "The Seven Heavens"; Segal, "Heavenly Ascent."

9. See, for example, *1 Enoch* 70–71.

10. An especially rich source of such material is found in the *Books of Jeu*, especially book 2, and *The Chaldaean Oracles*.

11. Koester and Pagels have suggested that the rise of the soul at the beginning of *DSav* presupposes a baptismal setting (see *NHLE*, 245).

12. See especially *Zostrianos*, *Three Steles of Seth*, and *Allogenes*.

13. See, for example, the theurgic rites implied by the Chaldean Oracles (see Ruth Majercik, *Chaldaean Oracles*).

14. Trans. W. Scott, *Hermetica*, 129 (modified).

15. In addition to *ApocPaul*, see, for example, *DSav* 120:1–124:22; *Three Steles of Seth*, *Allogenes*, *Zostrianos*, *2 Apocryphon of James* 32:28–36:13; Irenaeus, *AgHer* 1.21:5; Epiphanius, *Panarion* 26.13:2; 36.3:1–6; *PiSo* 286:9–291:23.

16. *Domination and the Arts of Resistance*, 198–99. My emphasis in the last paragraph.

17. J. Scott, *Domination and the Arts of Resistance*, 124.

18. Cited in J. Scott, *Domination and the Arts of Resistance*, 124.

19. See J. Scott's discussion, *Domination and the Arts of Resistance*, 103–7.

20. See also the discussion of Wink, *Cracking the Gnostic Code*, which does not treat the *Gospel of Mary* but does consider how the Powers may have been understood in antiquity in terms of social criticism.

## Chapter nine

1. The Coptic here reads ϩⲏⲧ ("heart") while the Greek reads νοῦς ("mind").

2. Schenke suggests that the Coptic term for "greet" might also have included a kiss of greeting (see Till and Schenke, *Die gnostischen Schriften*, 338; also Mohri, *Maria Magdalena*, 262).

3. I use the term "apostle" here (a term which does not appear in the work itself) to refer to those who received the commission from the Savior to go forth and preach. It is basically synonymous with "disciple" since *GMary* does not distinguish between the two, and indeed neither term appears in the work at all to describe the Savior's dialogue partners. All those who receive teaching are also given the commission to preach. There is no evidence here of a special group like "the twelve."

4. Indeed the seeming contradiction between Peter's affectionate request and his challenging response have led some scholars to suggest that the text has been secondarily edited (see the summary of Mohri, *Maria Magdalena*, 266–67).

5. This supposition is based not merely on the expression of conflict within the text's dialogue, but on widespread external evidence from other sources that the issues raised here were widely under debate in this period. See, for example, Perkins, *The Gnostic Dialogue*, 73.

6. I am thinking here of the philosopher Hypatia who was murdered by Christians; and Philomene may be a Christian example as well (see the discussion of Jensen, *God's Self-Confident Daughters*, 194–222).

7. See *AgHer* 3.3:1

8. See *AgHer* 3.2:1.

9. In the *Gospel of Mary*, this self is referred to as "the child of true Humanity" or "the perfect Human."

10. This position is developed further in King, "Prophetic Power and Women's Authority."

## Chapter ten

1. A post-resurrection dialogue setting is also widely attested outside the canonical materials in second and third century tradition, for example in *ApJohn, BkThom, SoJsChr, 1ApocJas,* or *ApocPet.* For a full discussion, see Perkins, *The Gnostic Dialogue.* There are important other dialogues as well, although without a post-resurrection setting, for example, *DSav.* The latter is especially important as a generic parallel to *GMary,* for it contains not only dialogue but also a reference to the ascent of the soul.

2. A famous account of the early research on the historical Jesus may be found in Schweitzer, *The Quest for the Historical Jesus.*

3. For a fuller history of New Testament gospel scholarship, see Koester, *Ancient Christian Gospels.*

4. Koester, "Written Gospels or Oral Tradition?" 297.

5. Irenaeus, *AgHer* 3.2.1, citing *1 Cor* 2:6.

6. These changes can be readily seen by comparing the texts side by side (see Funk, *New Gospel Parallels*). In addition, the authors of *Matthew* and *Luke* also drew upon another (lost) collection of Jesus materials that scholars have dubbed *Q* (from the German term "Quelle," which means "source"). A reconstruction of this lost work can be found in Miller, *The Complete Gospels* or Kloppenborg, *Q Parallels.* To learn more about *Q,* see Mack, *The Lost Gospel.*

7. Sometimes changes were made to clarify shifts in theology (see examples in Ehrman, *The Orthodox Corruption of Scripture*).

8. Wilson, "The New Testament," 242.

9. Wilson, "The New Testament," 240.

10. See the discussion of Vorster, "The Protevangelium of James and Intertextuality," 268–69.

11. Although the gospels of *Mark* and *Luke* are not ascribed to one of the known apostles, later tradition claims that Peter was the ultimate source of *Mark* (Papias, cited in Eusebius, *HistEccl* 3.39.15), and Luke is associated with Paul (see *2 Tim* 4:11). Several New Testament letters ascribed to Paul are considered to be pseudonymous (e.g., *Hebrews, 1* and *2 Timothy, Titus*).

12. So, too, they may have made associations unknown to us, whether to unfamiliar literary works or oral traditions and practices.

13. Wilson, "The New Testament," 239; Schröter sees no literary dependence of this passage on the New Testament gospels, but rather suggests that the situation of the farewell is common and presupposed by the *Gospel of Mary* ("Zur Menschensohnvorstellung," 181, n. 6).

14. This passage appears only in some manuscripts (see Metzger, *A Textual Commentary on the Greek New Testament,* 160).

15. Examples can be found in *1 Pet* 5:14; *Rom* 1:7; *1 Cor* 1:3.

16. The only exception to the post-resurrection setting is one occurrence (out of four) in the *Gospel of John* during the farewell discourse of Jesus to his disciples before his death (*John* 14:27).

17. Because of the unusual use of "my," historical critical approaches have taken Jesus' greeting in *John* 14:27 to be a direct literary parallel to the second saying in the *Gospel of Mary,* "Acquire my peace within yourselves!" But they don't explain why the *Gospel of Mary* would cite the *Gospel of John* or what effect that intertextual reference might have had on readers (see Wilson and MacRae, "The Gospel of Mary," 458; Pasquier, *L'Évangile selon Marie,* 57). Tardieu calls it a "johannisme," and comments: "*Paix* désigne ici la dimension intérieure du salut" (*Écrits gnostiques,* 228).

18. See Crossan, *Four Other Gospels*, 32–33.

19. The admonition to follow may also point toward the soul's journey described later by Mary, but in the extant text there is no indication that the soul is meant to follow the path of the Savior in the ascent.

20. *Ancient Christian Gospels*, 186.

21. See also a version of the "seek and find" aphorism in *DSav* 126:6–17; 129:14–16, and the discussion of Koester, *Ancient Christian Gospels*, 176–77.

22. Koester lists the *Gospel of Thomas*, *Dialogue of the Savior*, and *Apocryphon of James* as examples of this kind of Christology (see *Ancient Christian Gospels*, 263–67); to these we may add the *Gospel of Mary*.

23. *Ancient Christian Gospels*, 264–65; see also the discussion of DeConick, *Seek to See Him*.

24. See Pasquier, *L'Évangile selon Marie*, 62.

25. Cf. *Mark* 8:35; *John* 12:25, 15:20.

26. Although not a quotation from Jesus, this treatment of the disciples' fear of death thematically reflects Jesus' admonition not to fear those who can kill the body, but those who can harm the soul (*Q* 12:4–7; *Luke* 12:4–7; *Matt* 10:28).

27. *AgHer* 3.1.1 (*ANF*, 414).

28. This is no doubt due in part to the designation of the text as late (that is, not of value for the historical Jesus or the origins of Christianity), derivative (that is, dependent upon the New Testament), and "Gnostic" (that is, heretical). Indeed the first author to devote a study to the question of the relationship of the *Gospel of Mary* to canonical texts considered its Christian character itself to be a question, devoting four pages (out of eight) to the question of whether or not the underlying base text was non-Christian (see Wilson, "The New Testament," esp. 237–40).

29. See "The Gospel of Mary" (in Miller, *The Complete Gospels*) and "The Gospel of Mary Magdalene" (in Schüssler Fiorenza, *Searching the Scriptures*).

30. "How," Koester asks, "can we know when written documents are the source for such quotation and allusions?" The answer he gives is redaction criticism: "Whenever one observes words or phrases that derive from the author or redactor of a gospel writing, the existence of a written source must be assumed" (Koester, "Written Gospels or Oral Tradition?" 297).

31. It may also be noted that some scholars continue to pursue aspects of source criticism under the rubric of intertextuality. A case in point is the work of Dennis MacDonald in *The Homeric Epics and the Gospel of Mark*. There he offers criteria of "accessibility, analogy, density, order, distinctiveness, and interpretability" to determine whether the author of the *Gospel of Mark* intentionally alluded to Homeric epic. The criterion of accessibility assesses whether the author had access to the source; analogy asks whether other works are imitating this same model; density determines the volume of the parallels between two works; distinctiveness notes rarities that are "flags for readers to compare the imitating texts with their models"; and interpretability refers to whether knowing a source helps the reader make sense of the text (8–9). Where MacDonald's work moves from source criticism to intertextuality lies in considering intelligibility from the reader's perspective, and in inquiring about the function of such intertextuality (in this case, suggesting that the author of *Mark* used allusions to Homer in order to present Jesus as superior to the ancient Homeric heroes). This issue of function is sometimes considered through another historical-critical method, redaction criticism, which considers how an editor has changed his sources in order to express his own theological tendencies. That MacDonald retains many of the assumptions of historical critical methods is demonstrated in his conclusions: that "the primary

cultural context of the Gospel (is) in Greek religious tradition, not in Judaism" and that dependence upon classical poetry undermines the historical veracity of many scenes in the *Gospel of Mark* (189–90). My use of intertextuality in contrast would suggest that history is always interpreted out of the cultural resources at hand; questions of fact and fiction are not settled by intertextual reference. As Kristeva famously puts it, "any text is constructed as a mosaic of quotation; any text is the absorption and transformation of another" (*Desire in Language*, 66).

32. Koester, "Written Gospels or Oral Tradition?" 297.

33. See Crossan, *In Fragments*, 37–54.

34. This passage appears only in some manuscripts (see Metzger, *A Textual Commentary on the Greek New Testament*, 160).

## Chapter eleven

1. *L'Évangile selon Marie*, 14–17.

2. *Rom* 1:18–32.

3. See Johnson Hodge, "'If Sons, Then Heirs.'"

4. *Rom* 7:4–6.

5. *Gal* 2:16.

6. Another case of possible misunderstanding is found in *DSav* 135:16–136:5 where, as result of Jesus' teaching, the disciples "concluded that it is useless to regard wickedness." That this statement does not dismiss evil is shown by an interchange between Judas and Jesus that follows later in the work: "[Judas] said, 'Tell me, Lord, what the beginning of the path is.' He said, 'Love and goodness. For if one of these existed among the governors, wickedness would never have come into existence'" (*NHLE*, 73–74).

7. For Paul, see *Gal* 5:16–26.

8. This discussion of ethics relies upon the superbly thoughtful work of O'Connor, "On Doing Religious Ethics."

9. A modified quote from John Cobb, cited in O'Connor, "On Doing Religious Ethics," 85.

10. *The Gnostic Gospels*, esp. 70–101.

11. See, for example, *Acts* 8:3 which explicitly states that both men and women were being put in prison.

12. Cited from *NHLE*, 436, with modifications.

## Chapter twelve

1. Schaberg, *The Resurrection of Mary Magdalene*, 184, 236,

2. Comments made in discussion at the Universal Truth Center Women's Retreat, October, 2000.

3. So, for example, Origen, an early third century theologian from Alexandria in Egypt, works hard to dispel this impression (*Commentary on John* 6.37; 10.21); see also Irenaeus, *AgHer* 5.31.

4. *Eumenides* 103 and *Aeneid* 6.450–58. See De Conick, "Blessed are Those Who Have Not Seen," 392–393.

5. See Hock, "Homer in Greco-Roman Education."

6. Bultmann, *The Gospel of John*, 681–97, esp. 688.

## Chapter thirteen

1. The references follow the only published edition of this work, by Hedrick and Mirecki, *The Gospel of the Savior*, even though Emmel has recently suggested a reordering of the pages of this work ("The Recently Published Gospel of the Savior").

2. For more on Andrew, see Peterson, *Andrew*; MacDonald, "Andrew (person)."

3. The best treatment of Peter is by Perkins, *Peter*; see also Brown et al., *Peter in the New Testament*; Donfried, "Peter (person)"; Grappe, *Image de Pierre*.

4. Cephas (the underlying Aramaic means "stone"); Peter (a Greek name derived from *petros*, meaning "stone"); Simon was probably his given Hebrew name.

5. Notably Perkins, *Peter*, 156–59, an otherwise excellent study of the early traditions about Peter.

6. The Revised Standard Version diplomatically translates the Greek *hypokrisei* as "insincerity" instead of "hypocrisy."

7. See the discussion of Kessler, *Peter as the First Witness*.

8. Donfried offers numerous examples of *Luke*'s rehabilitation of Peter (see *ABD* V, 258–59).

9. See Miller, *The Complete Gospels*, 393–401.

10. See *NHLE*, 431–37.

11. See *NHLE*, 372–78.

12. See Schneemelcher, *New Testament Apocrypha*, II, 34–41.

13. See Schneemelcher, *New Testament Apocrypha*, II, 271–321. See also the *Acts of Peter and the Twelve Apostles* (*NHLE*, 287–94) and the *Act of Peter* from the Berlin Codex (*NHLE*, 528–31).

14. See *AgHer* 3.13.2: "How could Peter, to whom the Lord gave the testimony that flesh and blood had not revealed this to him but heaven, have been in ignorance?" referring to *Matt* 16:17.

15. See the discussion of Kessler, *Peter as the First Witness*, 197–207; Perkins, *Peter*, 168–81.

16. See especially Ricci, *Mary Magdalene*, 51–161; De Boer, *Mary Magdalene*, 18–57; Collins, "Mary (person)"; D'Angelo, "Reconstructing 'Real' Women"; Schaberg, *The Resurrection of Mary Magdalene*, 204–99.

17. See Schaberg's account of visiting the present location in "Thinking Back through the Magdalene" and a revised version in *The Resurrection of Mary Magdalene*, 47–63. See also Strange, "Magdala"; De Boer, *Mary Magdalene*, 21–31, who traces the history of the city to understand Mary's background; and Ricci, *Mary Magdalene*, 130–31.

18. See *Mark* 15:40–41; *Matt* 27:55–56; *Luke* 8:1–3; *John* 19:25; *GPhil* 59:6–9(?).

19. *Mark* 15:40–41; *John* 19:25. She was also said to be present at the entombment in *Mark* 15:47 and *Matt* 27:61.

20. The presence of women at the tomb, and indeed the entire empty tomb story, has been questioned by modern scholars (see e.g., Crossan, *The Historical Jesus*, 354–416; *The Birth of Christianity*, 550–62). The Jesus Seminar found it plausible that women witnessed the crucifixion (see Funk, *The Acts of Jesus*, 157–158, 264, 362–63, 437–39). Schaberg argues that it is plausible that Mary Magdalene did indeed observe the crucifixion and followed to see where Jesus' body was buried (see *The Resurrection of Mary Magdalene*, 276–91).

21. *Mark* 16:1–8; *Matt* 28:1–7; *Luke* 24:1–10; *John* 20:1, 11–13. *GPet* 12:50–13:57 also gives Mary of Magdala a preeminent place as the first witness to the empty tomb, although the material about Mary may be a secondary addition (see Crossan, *The Cross that Spoke*, 285–86; see Schaberg's critique, *The Resurrection of Mary Magdalene*, 238–53). The Jesus Seminar holds that "Mary was among the early witnesses to the resurrection of Jesus" (Funk, *The Acts of Jesus*, 479).

22. See Milburn, *Early Christian Art*, 12; Haskins, *Mary Magdalen*, 58–63.

23. For example, *Mark* 15:40–41, 47; 16:1; *Matt* 27:55–56, 61; 28:1; *Luke* 8:1–3; 24:10; *GPet* 12:50–51; *Manichaean Psalmbook* 192:21–22 and 194:19; but not *John* 19:25 or the *1ApJas* 40:25–26

24. *GThom; GMary; SoJsChr; DSav; PiSo.*

25. *Matt* 28:9–10; *John* 20:14–18; *Mark* 16:9; *Apostolic Constitutions* 5.3.14.

26. *John* 20:17. In *Mark* 16:7 and *Matt* 28:7, angels commission Mary and the other women to carry the news of the resurrection.

27. See Schüssler Fiorenza, "Apostle to the Apostles."

28. So, for example, Funk and the Jesus Seminar, *The Acts of Jesus*, 479. Schaberg appropriately criticizes my summary there as giving too little emphasis to the controversy over how to portray Mary already present in the gospels (*The Resurrection of Mary Magdalene*, 234–38). I hope that the treatment of the controversy between Mary and Peter that follows in my discussion here will have rectified that deficiency.

29. *Mark* 16:9 is generally considered to be dependent upon the Lukan account, and hence it does not provide independent evidence.

30. It was interpreted this way by *Mark* 16:9.

31. See *Luke* 8:1–3; see also Haskins, *Mary Magdalen*, 14. Schaberg concludes: "Schottroff is right, in my opinion, to judge that Luke's 'idea that wealthy women were close to Jesus does not originate from otherwise lost traditions of the Jesus movement but from later experiences of the young church in the cities of the Roman Empire outside Palestine, which Luke projects back into Jesus' time' (see *Acts* 16:14–15; 17:4, 12)" (*The Resurrection of Mary Magdalene*, 265).

32. Other examples include Luke's larger program to restrict the apostolic mission to men, for example in limiting the selection of a replacement for Judas to men (*Acts* 1:15–26). Even when women appear in powerful roles, as Priscilla (*Acts* 18:18, 26) or the daughters of Philip who prophesy (*Acts* 21:9), they always appear with husbands and fathers.

33. Ricci (*Mary Magdalene*, 41) notes that this patronage has often been interpreted in terms of women's enabling function; she cites R. P. Baden, for example, "who, to define the role of the women, observes that while the Lord 'did not want women to preach his doctrine... (since) the fragility of their nature and the modesty of their sex' would not allow this, he nevertheless left them to take care of the men's material needs in order to leave them free to proclaim the good news." Schaberg suggests that this tradition is not historical, citing Luise Schottroff: "While the women's 'service' may have originally indicated a powerful leadership position, it is most often read as casting them in the roles of financial supporters or servants caring for the physical needs of the men, confining them in private rather than public roles" (*The Resurrection of Mary Magdalene*, 265).

34. The portraits of Mary Magdalene in this literature are thoroughly discussed and evaluated in Bovon, "Mary Magdalene's Pascal Privilege" and Marjanen, *The Woman Jesus Loved*; see also Schmid, *Maria Magdalena*; and the judicious study of Mohri, *Marie Magdalena*.

35. For the story of the find, see Robinson, "From Cliff to Cairo."

36. For an English translation of these works, see *NHLE*.

37. This codex was purchased in 1772 by A. Askew, the London physician after whom it was named (Codex Askewianus). Its date of discovery and specific provenance are unknown. The Coptic text and English translation may be found in Schmidt and MacDermot, *Pistis Sophia*.

38. Additional material on Mary is found in the *Manichaean Psalmbook* (see Coyle, "Mary Magdalene in Manichaeism?"; Marjanen, *The Woman Jesus Loved*,

203–15), but these works belong to the religion of Manichaeism and will not be discussed here.

39. *1ApJas* 40:22–26.

40. See *DSav* 126:17; 131:19; 134:25 (?); 134:25; 137:3; 139:8; 140:14, 19, 23; 141:12; 142:20; 143:6; 144:5, 22; 146:1.

41. There should be no surprise that a tradition developed about a group of women disciples, given the testimony of the gospels (see *Mark* 15:40–41; *Matt* 27:55–56; *Luke* 8:1–3; 23:49, 55; 24:10). Ricci concludes that *Luke* 8:1–3 "provides the information that a group of women followed Jesus constantly on his traveling since the beginning of his public activity in the land of Galilee. A circle of women: Mary Magdalene, Johanna, Susanna and many others; they set out with him, leaving home, family, relations, their village, their everyday life, and stayed with him, listening, speaking, traveling, offering goods and services, living with him, in short, and in the end followed him to the cross, where they, the only faithful witnesses, were to see him die" (*Mary Magdalene*, 53).

42. *SoJsChrNHC* III 98:10; 114:9; BG 90:1; 117:13.

43. In addition to Mary Magdalene, Jesus' mother also appears in these works (see Brock, "Setting the Record Straight.")

44. *PiSo* 26:17–20; see also 199:20–200:3; 232:26–233:2; 328:18–19; 339:8–9.

45. *PiSo* 218:10–219:2.

46. Some have suggested emending the text to read "his sister" instead of "her sister."

47. This grouping is similar to the list of women at the foot of the cross in *John* 19:25: "Meanwhile, standing near the cross of Jesus were his mother, and his mother's sister, Mary the wife of Clopas, and Mary Magdalene."

48. Scholars are divided over how to understand the phrase that Mary is his sister, his mother, and his companion. Some read it to say merely that Mary Magdalene was one of three Marys who accompanied Jesus, while others see the three as one figure (see the discussion of Marjanen, *The Woman Jesus Loved*, 160, including nn. 57 and 58). Marjanen concludes, "She is to be seen as a mythical figure who actually belongs to the transcendent realm but who manifests herself in the women accompanying the earthly Jesus" (161). The syntax of the Coptic seems to support the latter view, as does the general theological tendency of *GPhil*.

49. *GPhil* 67.9–12; Layton and Isenberg, "The Gospel of Philip," 174–75.

50. Alternatively, lines 63:30–34 could be reconstructed to read: "Wisdom, who is called 'the barren,' is the mother [of an]gels and [the] companion of the s[avior, Ma]ria the Mag[da]lene" (see Layton and Isenberg, "*Gospel According to Philip*," 166–67). In this case, the text would identify Sophia (Wisdom) with Mary Magdalene as the companion of the Savior. Schenke has argued persuasively against this reading, however, by noting that even though Sophia becomes the heavenly companion of the Savior, Sophia is barren because she is the mother of the archontic rulers of the lower world. Nonetheless, he notes that when this passage about Wisdom is read next to the passage where Jesus kisses Mary Magdalene, it allows the reading that Mary Magdalene is the heavenly syzygos (companion) of the Savior (see Schenke, *Das Phillipus-evangelium*, 336). As Layton and Isenberg note (op. cit. 166–67), the lacuna in line 63:36 where the Savior kisses Mary can also be restored in various ways: "on her mouth" or "her feet" or "her cheek" or "her forehead." The reading "mouth" is preferred here because of the reference to kissing on the mouth found at *GPhil* 58:34–59:4; the other readings, however, are also possible.

51. See *The Woman Jesus Loved*, esp. 189–90.

52. *The Woman Jesus Loved*, 189–190. In cases like these, Marjanen argues that the mere presence of Mary is not meant to engage the general question of women's leadership. In contrast, see Petersen, *'Zerstört die Werke der Wieblichkeit!'*.

53. Brock, "Mary Sees and Reveals."

54. See Meyer, "Making Mary Male" and "Gospel of Thomas Logion 114 Revisited"; Buckley, "An Interpretation of Logion 114"; McGuire, "Women, Gender and Gnosis."

55. See Castelli, "'I Will Make Mary Male'."

56. *PiSo* 201:21–25; 296:10–12.

57. *GMary* 10:15. Mary's name appears repeatedly; see *GMary* 5:4, 9; 6:1, 3; 9:30; 10:5.

58. From the first publication of the Berlin manuscript by Till, the assumption has been that the Mary of *GMary* is Mary Magdalene (see Till and Schenke, *Die gnostischen Schriften*, 26; also Pasquier, *L'Évangile selon Marie*, 6; Bovon, "Mary Magdalene's Pascal Privilege," 147–57; Tardieu, *Écrits gnostiques*, 20, 225; Schmid, *Maria Magdalena*, 93 n.9, 101 n. 29; Atwood, *Mary Magdalene*, 186–96; De Boer, *Mary Magdalene*, 81; Marjanen, *The Woman Jesus Loved*, 94–95, n. 2; Petersen, *'Zerstört die Werke der Weiblichkeit!'*, 94; Schaberg, *The Resurrection of Mary Magdalene*, 126–27; et al. This conclusion has been questioned by Lucchesi ("Évangile selon Marie") and especially Shoemaker ("A Case of Mistaken Identity?"), who argue that the figure of Mary is better understood as Jesus' mother. Rebuttals to these positions are found in Marjanen, *The Woman Jesus Loved*, 94–95 n. 2; Marjanen, "The Mother of Jesus or the Magdalene?"; and King, "Why all the Controversy?" Much of the discussion has centered around the portrayal of Mary in a later work, called *Pistis Sophia*, rather than in *GMary* (see especially Schmidt, *Gnostischen Schriften*, 453–54, 597; Shoemaker, "Rethinking the Gnostic Mary"; and see especially the excellent discussion of Brock, "Setting the Record Straight"). The discussion focuses around three main issues: 1) the form of the name; 2) the relationship to portrayals of the Marys in the New Testament gospels; and 3) the portrayal of gender (see especially Petersen *'Zerstört die Werke der Weiblichkeit,'* 104). Based on these three points, I would argue that the portrait of Mary in *GMary* is more closely allied to the historical Mary Magdalene than to Jesus' mother or to the sister of Martha (see "Why all the Controversy?").

The scholarly discussion has been very useful, however, for pointing out the tendency of the tradition toward conflating the various Mary figures, a fact that should incline us to see these Marys as literary portraits, not historical figures. In every case, the first question is not "which Mary?" but "How is Mary being portrayed, what roles is she given, and what issues are at stake?" In the end, Western tradition distinguishes between Mary Magdalene and Mary the mother based largely on the portrayal of their sexuality: the repentant whore and the virgin mother—although in the end, both are used to promote the tradition of celibacy.

59. See Schaberg, "How Mary Magdalene became a Whore." This fact has long been recognized by Western scholars (see the overview of research in Ricci, *Mary Magdalene*, 30–40; De Boer, *Mary Magdalene*, 9–16), and Eastern tradition never portrayed Mary Magdalene as a prostitute.

60. For the story of her later mythic and legendary exploits, including those as a preacher and teacher, see Malvern, *Venus in Sackcloth*; Haskins, *Mary Magdalen*; Jansen, "Maria Magdalena: *Apostolorum Apostola*."

61. See Corley, "'Noli me tangere'"; Haskins, *Mary Magdalene*, 58–67, 90.

Price has argued that the tendency to diminish Mary's role as the first, and perhaps only, witness is already evidenced in the New Testament gospels and Paul (see "Mary Magdalene: Gnostic Apostle?").

62. See, for example, Origen, *Against Celsus* 2.70.

63. See Tertullian, *De Anima* 25.8. He uses the report that Mary was possessed by seven demons to support his view (that a child possesses soul from the moment of conception) by showing that it is possible for one person to have two souls (that is, the soul of the mother and the soul of the child).

64. See, for example, Irenaeus, *AgHer* 5.31; Origen, *Commentary on John* 6.37; 10.21.

65. See Robinson, "Jesus from Easter to Valentinus."

66. *Against Praxeas* 25.

67. See Origen, *Commentary on John* 6.37; 10.21.

68. For example, Ambrose, *On the Christian Faith*, 4.2; Jerome, *To Pammachius Against John of Jerusalem* 35; Jerome, *To Marcella* 59.4; Augustine, *Sermon* 244.3.

69. Ambrose (see Haskins, *Mary Magdalene*, 93).

70. Origen, *Against Celsus* 2.70.

71. Price has suggested that this strategy was already intended by the gospel authors of *Matthew* and *Luke*. Moreover, he suggests that all four of the gospels diminish her prominence by making the appearance to her only one of a series (see "Mary Magdalene: Gnostic Apostle?").

72. For two alternative readings, see Trible, "A Love Story Gone Awry," and King, "*The Book of Norea*."

73. See, for example, Gregory of Nyssa, *Contra Eunomium* 3.10; Augustine, *Sermon* 232.2.

74. See Ambrose, *Of the Holy Spirit* 3.11.

75. Or those in the *DSav, SoJsChr*, or *PiSo*.

76. The Eastern churches never made this error, and therefore never developed a portrait of Mary Magdalene as a prostitute. She is honored as an important witness to the resurrection.

77. See Lagrange, "Jésus a-t-il été oint plusieurs fois et par plusieurs femmes?"; Holzmeister, "Die Magdalenenfrage."

78. Gregory, *Homily* 33 (quoted from Haskins, *Mary Magdalen*, 96).

79. *John* 19:25.

80. *Mark* 15:40, 47.

81. *Matt* 27:56.

82. *Matt* 27:61; 28:1.

83. See Hippolytus, *Commentary on the Song of Songs*; and the discussion of Haskins, *Mary Magdalen*, 63–67.

84. Most recently of course it was popularized in the opera "Jesus Christ Superstar," and in the suggestion of marriage that appeared in Jesus' dream life in the film "The Last Temptation of Christ." This supposedly scandalous movie simply repeats in cinematic form the pervasive and completely unoriginal theme of Western Christianity that female sexuality is the greatest temptation men have to overcome (or control). But, as the reaction to "The Last Temptation" shows, any portrayal of Jesus as a fully human sexual person is still capable of arousing a good deal of critical public response.

85. A point brought home to me by Robert Funk in conversation.

86. See, for example, Jansen, "Maria Magdalena: *Apostolorum Apostola*."

87. There are cases in the Medieval period when these two portraits were combined. See Jansen, "Maria Magdalena: *Apostolorum Apostola.*"

## Chapter fourteen

1. For a more detailed elaboration of the position given in the paragraph, see King, *What is Gnosticism?* esp. 1–54.

2. I put the term Judaism in quote marks here to signal an acknowledgement of the gap between the Christian construction of "Judaism" and an historical description of Jewish beliefs and practices. For more on this issue, see King, *What is Gnosticism?* 40–47.

3. Some specialists are now beginning to restrict the term Gnosticism to one group: Sethians (see King, *What is Gnosticism?* chapter 6). The *Gospel of Mary* does not belong to this group.

4. Walter Bauer, *Orthodoxy and Heresy*, xxiii.

5. Cf. *Matt* 5:17–18

6. *Gal* 2:16

7. It is important to note, too, that the creed was never intended to be a full statement of Christian belief. Rather it was formulated as a hedge against heresy. For every affirmation of the creed, there was at least one corresponding alternative perspective that the bishops wanted to refute.

8. *GThom* 1.

9. *GThom* 3.

10. *Prov* 8:22–31; *Ecclesiasticus* 1:4.

11. *Wis* 7:25–28; *Prov* 8:32–36.

12. *Prov* 1:20–22; 8:1–11.

13. *Wis* 10:1 ff.

14. *Prov* 1:20–33.

15. *Job* 28:21–28.

16. *GThom* 28, 38.

17. *GThom* 77.

18. *GThom* 108.

19. *GThom* 5, 6, 17, 18.

20. Some scholars dispute whether Valentinus wrote the *Gospel of Truth*, at least in its current form (see Mortley, "The Name of the Father"), but most agree that he is the author (see the arguments of van Unnik, "The 'Gospel of Truth' and the New Testament"; Wilson, "Valentinianism and the Gospel of Truth," 133–41).

21. *GTruth* 18:2–11.

22. *GTruth* 18:11–21.

23. *GTruth* 19:18–27.

24. *GTruth* 18:21–31.

25. *GTruth* 20:12–21:2.

26. See *GTruth* 23:18–24:9.

27. *GTruth* 24:9–27:7.

28. *GThom* 27:2–30:16.

29. *GTruth* 30:16–33:32.

30. *GTruth* 42:4–10.

31. *GTruth* 40:23–43:24.

32. See *Rom* 6:1–11.

33. See Till and Schenke, *Die gnostischen Schriften*, 26–32.

34. Perkins, *The Gnostic Dialogue*, 136, 141. She suggested that "the picture of Mary in *Gospel of Mary* was formulated in association with a Gnostic sayings tradition" (135).

35. See, for example, Pasquier, *L'Evangile selon Marie*, 5–7; Hartenstein, *Die zweite Lehre*, 137.

36. Petersen, *'Zerstört die Werke der Wieblichkeit!'*, 60–61. She determines the *Gospel of Mary* to have non-Christian, gnostic content, primarily by: 1) marking out "typical Gnostic themes" (e.g., the rise of the soul as release from matter; the contrast between the inner and the outer, so that peace and salvation come from within a person and not from without; the Son of Man is not the judge of the end-time, but the true Human in humanity), and 2) comparison with the New Testament.

37. See Wilson, "The New Testament," 240.

38. Attempts by scholars to characterize the essential features of Gnosticism, such as we see for example in the now-classic work of Hans Jonas ("Delimitation of the Gnostic Phenomenon"; *Gnosis und spätantiker Geist*; *The Gnostic Religion*), are less self-evident than they used to be, given the variety of the literature from the Egyptian discoveries. Already in 1961, Carsten Colpe had shown that "the gnostic redeemer myth" was itself an artificial and inaccurate scholarly construction (*Die religionsgeschichtliche Schule*). More recently, Michael Williams has demonstrated the inadequacy of typological definitions of Gnosticism to characterize accurately the variety of materials grouped under this rubric (*Rethinking "Gnosticism"*). It is increasingly apparent that the reification of the (normative) rhetorical category of Gnosticism into a monolithic historical entity is untenable. The bifurcating frame of orthodoxy and heresy (here represented as orthodoxy versus Gnosticism) does not do justice to the theological or sociological diversity of early Christianity. Appeal to a "Gnostic redeemer myth" or "typical Gnostic themes" is no longer sufficient to determine the social or theological setting of a work like the *Gospel of Mary*. For further discussion, see King, *What is Gnosticism?*.

39. See Brock, *Mary Magdalene*.

40. This competition is still a live issue, especially for Catholics who base papal authority on the preeminence of Peter as the first witness to the resurrection, as well as others who wish to exclude women from ministry. Peter Kessler, for example, says that it is possible that Mary Magdalene was the first eyewitness of the resurrection, but he contrasts her status with Peter by arguing that "the role of Peter is an official, enduring, public leadership, whereas the leadership of Mary Magdalene is more intimate and temporally prior, but not something of which we have any indication of continuity" (*Peter as the First Witness*, 200–201). He argues that "Peter's witness was not merely a moment of seeing (witnessing of) the risen Lord, but a permanent ministry of proclaiming (witnessing to the gospel that Jesus is alive and is Lord). Such a rediscovery of the Easter context of Peter's primacy, by placing it in its proper context, may help to emphasize the credibility and the profundity of that ministry" (*Peter as the First Witness*, 203). Clearly what is at stake here are challenges to the exclusion of women from leadership in ministry.

41. See Brock, *Mary Magdalene*, especially 101–4.

42. Paraphrasing Brock, *Mary Magdalene*, 173.

43. See Funk, *The Acts of Jesus*, 458. Wilhelm Bousset notes in *Kyrios Christos*, 156, that Paul mentions his vision only when he needs to support his authority.

44. Thompson, *Mary of Magdala*, 117. Earlier she had argued that the conflict between Peter and Mary in *GThom* 114 "probably reflects something of the situation of the churches at the time of the writing of this gospel. Peter was a leader in

competition with Mary of Magdala or followers of Peter were in competition with followers of Mary" (100).

45. See, for example, Till and Schenke, *Die gnostischen Schriften*, 26). See also Price, "Mary Magdalene: Gnostic Apostle?"; Maish, *Between Contempt and Veneration*, 26–27; Grappe, *Image du Pierre*, 202–5; Hartenstein, *Die zweite Lehre*.

46. See Pagels, *The Gnostic Gospels*, 13–14.

47. Pagels, "Visions, Appearance, and Apostolic Authority," 426–27. Andrew and Peter, Pagels notes, look "to past events, suspicious of those who 'see the Lord' in vision," while Mary "claims to experience his continuing presence" (*The Gnostic Gospels*, 13–14). Pagels has further argued that: "From these [Gnostic] accounts we observe, *first,* that the authority and commission of the disciples (or 'apostles') depends not on the witness to the resurrection for which ecclesiastical Christians revere them, but on special visions and revelations that go beyond orthodox tradition. *Second*, the accounts define that authoritative circle in different ways... Despite their differences these texts [*Apocalypse of Paul, Letter of Peter to Philip, Dialogue of the Savior*] seem to agree—against ecclesiastical tradition— that belonging to the original circle of disciples (or 'apostles') matters less than receiving new and continuing visions" ("Visions, Appearances, and Apostolic Authority," 422). For Pagels, the *Gospel of Mary* represents the most extreme of these works insofar as "the disciples consent to receive this revelation from Mary, acknowledging that her direct contact with the Lord through visions surpasses their own" ("Visions, Appearance, and Apostolic Authority," 425).

48. This position regarding the sources of revelation, Pagels argues, correlates with a "devaluation of the apostles' original witness," and resulted in a strong response from ecclesiastical Christianity in legitimizing "a hierarchy of persons through whose authority in teaching and discipline all others must approach God" (Pagels, "Visions, Appearances, and Apostolic Authority," 425, 430).

49. See King, "Prophetic Power and Women's Authority."

50. Hartenstein, *Die zweite Lehre*, 130 and see note 14, contra Pagels, Pasquier, King, Marjanen; on p. 153, n. 141, she adds a reference to Petersen.

51. Hartenstein, *Die zweite Lehre*, 153.

52. See King, "Prophetic Power and Women's Authority," 24.

53. See also Marjanen's discussion of transfiguration material in other works (*The Woman Jesus Loved*, 166–67).

54. Perkins had earlier made this point in passing, in a comparison with *Apocalypse of Peter*; see *The Gnostic Dialogue*, 133.

55. Hartenstein, *Die zweite Lehre*, 154.

56. It should be said that Hartenstein does consider the *Gospel of Mary* to be a Gnostic work, and she understands the contrasting portrayal of the disciples in terms of orthodox versus gnostic teaching. Here Peter and Andrew represent orthodoxy; Mary and Levi, Gnosticism. Those who teach a gnostic understanding of the Savior's teaching are the true apostles, according to the *Gospel of Mary*.

57. Hartenstein, *Die zweite Lehre*, 130–32. This point assumes that Levi is not identified with Matthew at this stage of tradition.

58. See Hartenstein, *Die zweite Lehre*, 150. She argues that Mary's response to Peter and Andrew indicates that neither of them is willing to go so far as to suggest that she is lying. The effect of Mary's reply is rather to sharpen the point that Peter (and the other disciples—and readers) must either accept everything Mary has said or fundamentally deny that she is a disciple. Already by causing a rift among the disciples, Peter shows himself to be the guilty one.

59. In the first edition of the Berlin Codex, Walter Till argued that Mary plays

the main role in the second half of the work where her teaching is the main topic, but that she played little or no role in the first part of the work, the Savior's appearance and dialogue with his disciples. Indeed, he suggested that these two parts were originally independent works, and that the scene where Mary comforts the distraught disciples at the end of part one was added to link the two otherwise completely unrelated works (see Till and Schenke, *Die gnostischen Schriften*, 26). Till clearly does not count Mary as one of the apostles, but states rather that the *Gospel of Mary* "elevates her over the apostles." Till of course published this work before knowing the Nag Hammadi texts in which Mary is reckoned among the disciples/apostles in a variety of works classified as revelation dialogues (such as *DSav, SoJsChr, 1 ApocJas*), but he does note the corresponding portrait of Mary in *PiSo*. Nonetheless, he does not treat Mary as an apostle. Pheme Perkins classifies the *Gospel of Mary* among "the non-apostles." (The chapter title is: "Those Whom Jesus Loves: The Non-Apostles.") She wrongly translates 10:10, saying that Mary "is called 'the one whom the Savior loved more than the apostles because of her gnosis.'" She then concludes: "She clearly represented the Gnostic claim to a truth greater than that contained in the apostolic tradition" (*The Gnostic Dialogue*, 134).

60. See Koester, "La Tradition apostolique."

61. See Brooten, "'Junia ... Outstanding among the Apostles'." For a long time scholars emended the name of the woman apostle, Junia, mentioned by Paul in *Rom* 16:7, to a man's name "Junias," assuming that it must be an error since women could not be apostles. The manuscript tradition is clear, however, that Junia is the name of a woman whom Paul says is "outstanding among the apostles," and many English Bible translations are now being updated to correct this error.

62. See Brock, *Mary Magdalene*, 1–18, 169–70; "What's in a Name?"

63. So, too, in *Sophia of Jesus Christ*, the Savior commissions his disciples (12 men and 7 women), and at the end of the work they begin to preach the gospel.

64. For an excellent and more extensive discussion of Peter, see R. Brown et al., *Peter in the New Testament*.

65. See *Did* 9–10.

66. See *Did* 11.

67. Ash argues that prophecy was appropriated by the episcopate at the expense of women's prophetic leadership ("The Decline of Ecstatic Prophecy"; see also Schüssler Fiorenza, *In Memory of Her*, 294–309). This view is opposed by Robeck, *Prophecy in Carthage*, 203–5.

68. *De anima* 9:4 (cited from Wire, *Corinthian Women Prophets*, 264, slightly modified).

69. It is of note that the post-resurrection appearance of the Savior to the disciples does not have the same status as Mary's visionary experience. In other situations, such an appearance could well be conceived as prophetic.

70. The Greek text reads *en horamati* ("in a vision").

71. For a fuller discussion, see Potter, *Prophets and Emperors*.

72. Tertullian argued, for example, that the human soul is the same as the human spirit, but is to be distinguished from the spirit of God and the spirits sent by Satan. Using King Saul as an example, he notes that a spirit can be good or evil (*De anima* 11).

73. *Dialogue with Trypho* 4 (text in Otto, 18).

74. I love this little text exactly for this practicality. It tells us, for example, "If

you can bear the whole yoke of the Lord, you will be perfect, but if you cannot, then do what you can" (*Did* 6:2; trans. Lake, 319).

75. *Did* 12; see also 10:7; 13; 15:1–2.

76. See, for example, the exposures by Hippolytus, *Refutations,* or the amusing portrait of a charlatan by the Roman author Lucius, called *Alexander the Quack Prophet.*

77. A good example is the condemnation of "Jezebel" in *Rev* 2:20–23; see Räisänen, "The Nicolaitans."

78. Tertullian, *Prescription against Heresies,* chapters 6 and 30.

79. We learn, by the way, that Philomene's prophecies had been collected and written down by a male disciple. She was apparently a significant enough threat to warrant condemnation.

80. For example, Priscilla's virginity is called into question by Apollonius (Eusebius, *HistEccl* 5:18); the Asian woman prophet noted by Cyprian is accused of seducing a deacon (Cyprian, *Epistle* 74:10). Note, too, that the male heretic Marcus was also accused of seducing women (Irenaeus, *AgHer* 1.13.1–4).

81. For example, Tertullian, in his refutation of Marcion, writes: "Similarly, when (Paul) prescribes silence for women in the church, that none should deviate merely to speak out of ambition—although he already shows that they have the right of prophesying when he imposes a veil upon women prophets—he is taking from the law (the view) that women be subject to authority" (*Against Marcion,* 5.8; text in Semler, 347–48).

The issue of conformity to the teachings of the churches was invoked as well in these debates, but this point was rather rhetorical in the first and second centuries since the rule of faith had not yet been clearly established. The issue of conformity thus pointed quite anxiously to the spectral absence of a normative standard against which prophecy could be measured. In practice, then, questions about the truth of prophecy take us right into the middle of debates over the meaning of Jesus' teaching, interpretation of scripture, community organization, and leadership. *GMary* is fully engaged in these debates, as I have shown elsewhere (see "The Gospel of Mary Magdalene" in *Searching the Scriptures,* 621–25).

82. For example, Diodorus of Sicily writes of the Delphic oracle: "It is said that in ancient times virgins delivered the oracles because virgins have their natural innocence intact and are in the same case as Artemis; for indeed virgins were alleged to be well suited to guard the secrecy of disclosures made by oracles. In more recent times, however, people say that Echecrates the Thessalian, enamoured of her because of her beauty, carried her away with him and violated her; and that the Delphians because of this deplorable occurrence passed a law that in future a virgin would no longer prophesy but that an elderly woman of fifty should declare the oracles and that she should be dressed in the costume of a virgin, as a sort of reminder of the prophetess of olden times" (*The Library of History* 16.26.26; cited from Wire, *Corinthian Women Prophets,* 253). For additional examples, see the examples in Wire: Ovid, *Metamorphoses* 14.129–46,151–53; *The Confession and Prayer of Asenath;* Plutarch, *The Oracles at Delphi* 405CD; Plutarch, *Lives: Numa* 5 and 8; Pausanias, *Description of Greece* II.24.1; Philo, *On the Contemplative Life.*

83. As is common with witchcraft accusations against both men and women, the charges here are raised because their conservative opponents feel they have overstepped acceptable boundaries by advocating changes in established relations and practices. Ideology that attempts to relegate women to areas separate from politics can here be used against them in a kind of circular social logic.

While women's presence was the normal practice in Christian worship, Karen Torjesen has argued that a woman exercising public leadership could be open to charges of immorality (see *When Women were Priests*, 143–49).

84. See, for example, *De anima* 9.4.

85. *On Monogamy*, 2.3 (text in Mattei, 136).

86. See *De anima* 9.4 (text in Waszink, 11).

87. Epiphanius, for example, can base his arguments against the Montanists by appeal to Scripture in a way that would not have been possible in the first and early second centuries.

88. See *AgHer* 3.2.1.

89. See *AgHer* 1.30.14.

90. For example, *GThom* (Salome); *1ApocJas* (Martha, Salome, and Arsinoe); *PiSo* (Mary the mother, Martha, and Salome).

91. See the discussion of Morard, "Une Évangile écrit par une femme?"

92. See Cole, "Could Greek Women Read and Write?"; Kraemer, "Women's Authorship"; Rowlandson, *Women and Society*, 299–312.

93. Based on the reconstruction of Wire, *Corinthian Woman Prophets*.

94. Interestingly enough, this is true even in the case of the martyr Perpetua. One might expect her to identify with the suffering Christ, but it is the risen Christ she encounters in her vision, and it is victory she experiences in her combat in the arena, not passive endurance in the face of suffering.

95. The list of works being produced on this topic is burgeoning. The best and most foundational work is still Schüssler Fiorenza's ground-breaking work, *In Memory of Her*.

96. See *Luke* 8:1–3.

97. See *Rom* 16:7; Brooten, "Junia."

98. See *Acts* 18:26–27.

99. See *1 Cor* 16:19; *Rom* 16:3.

100. *Col* 4:15.

101. See *Acts* 16:14–15.

102. See *Rom* 16:1.

103. See *Rom* 16:6.

104. See *1 Cor* 11:2–16; Wire, *The Corinthian Women Prophets*.

105. See *Acts* 21:8–9.

106. See Eusebius, *HistEccl* 5.17.2–3.

107. See Eusebius, *HistEccl* 5.13.2; Tertullian, *Prescription against Heresies*, chapters 6 and 30; Jensen, *God's Self-Confident Daughters*, 373–426.

108. See *The Martyrdom of Perpetua*.

109. See the examples given in Kienzle and Walker, *Women Prophets and Preachers*.

110. See King, "Afterword."

111. In the *Gospel of Mary*, this self is referred to as "the child of humanity" or "the perfect Human."

112. See, for example, *1 Cor* 12–14.

113. See, for example, *1 Tim* 3–5.

114. The questions of whether, when and where it had been illegal to be a Christian are matters requiring considerable nuance. In the early centuries, Christianity was not always precisely illegal, but neither was it condoned. Much depended upon local attitudes and the personal views of the current Roman emperor. It was only in the third century that two systematic attempts to wipe Christianity out were made. The importance of Constantine's edict is that it ended state persecution of Christians as such.

# Terms & Sources

*Against Heresies*, see Irenaeus

**androgyny** The state of possessing both male and female characteristics.

*Apocryphon of John* A revelation from Christ to his disciple John after the resurrection. Dated to the mid-second century CE, this work is an important treatise on early Christian views of theology, creation, and salvation. A copy was included in the Berlin Codex, and three additional copies were recovered from the find near Nag Hammadi in 1945.

*Apocalypse of Paul* A first person account of Paul's ascension through the heavens (see *2 Cor* 12:2–4), probably written in the second century. The only existing copy was found near Nag Hammadi in 1945.

*Apocalypse of Peter* A post-resurrection dialogue between Peter and the Savior in which the Savior reveals the true meaning of the crucifixion and arrest of Jesus. It polemicizes against the "bishops and deacons" of the church who wrongly believe in the physical resurrection and the value of martyrdom. It probably dates to the early third century. The only existing copy was found near Nag Hammadi in 1945.

**apocalyptic** A theological perspective that through an act of divine intervention the present world is about to be destroyed and replaced with a new and better world in which God's justice prevails.

**Augustine** Early Christian theologian and bishop of Hippo in North Africa (396–430 CE). He exerted enormous influence on the development of orthodox Christianity in the Latin West.

**beatitudes** Literary or oral formulations that confer good fortune on the recipient. They usually begin with the expression "Congratulations to" (more traditionally translated as "Blessed is").

*Book of Thomas the Contender* A revelation dialogue between the resurrected Jesus and his twin brother Judas Thomas. Its tone and content are dominated by the condemnation of sexual intercourse and attachment to the flesh. Possibly composed in Syria (ca. 225 CE), the only existing copy was found near Nag Hammadi in 1945.

**canon** A closed collection or list of authoritative books accepted as holy scripture. The canon was determined for Roman Catholics at the Council of Trent in 1546 CE; it has never been determined for Protestants, except by common consent and the action of some individual denominations.

*Dialogue of the Savior* The report of a dialogue between the Savior and his disciples, including Judas, Mary, and Matthew. It was probably composed in the second century CE. The only existing copy is in a badly damaged manuscript found near Nag Hammadi in 1945.

**Didache** An early Christian compendium of instruction, also known as the *Teachings of the Twelve Apostles*. The final form of the *Didache*, which was discovered in 1875, dates from the early second century, but its main sections go back to the first century.

**Eusebius** Theologian and bishop of Caesarea in ca. 314. He was the author of the first extensive *History of the Church*, tracing the origins of Christianity from the first century up to the conversion of the Roman Emperor Constantine to Christianity. He attended the Council of Nicaea in 325 CE.

***First Apocalypse of James*** A second-century revelation dialogue between the Lord and his brother, James. Although the only surviving manuscript, discovered near Nag Hammadi in 1945, is badly damaged, it is clear that the work contains advice to James about how to overcome the attacks of the hostile powers that rule the world and try to keep him from ascending.

***Gospel of the Nazarenes*** An expanded vision of the *Gospel of Matthew* preserved in quotations and allusions in early Christian writings and in marginal notations found in a number of medieval manuscripts. It is evidently a translation of the Greek *Gospel of Matthew* into Aramaic or Syriac. The earliest surviving reference is a quotation in Hegesippus around 180 CE. It probably comes from western Syria.

***Gospel of Peter*** An account of the death and resurrection of Jesus, probably dating to the end of the first century CE. A fragmentary copy of an eighth to ninth century Greek manuscript was discovered in the nineteenth century in upper Egypt.

***Gospel of Philip*** A compilation of diverse materials, including teachings of and about Christ, dogmatic pronouncements, parables and allegories, and statements about early Christian sacraments of baptism and a rite called "the bridal chamber." The theological views of the work fit with those of the disciples of Valentinus, and the work may be dated to the late second or early third centuries. The only existing copy was found near Nag Hammadi in 1945.

***Gospel of the Savior*** A fragmentary second-century gospel, contained in a papyrus manuscript that was written sometime in the fourth to seventh centuries. The surviving portion of the text recounts a dialogue between Jesus and his disciples set shortly before the crucifixion. It was first published in 1999.

***Gospel of Thomas*** A collection of sayings and parables of Jesus from the first or second centuries CE. Although three Greek fragments were recovered from Oxyrhynchus, the only complete copy was found near Nag Hammadi in 1945 written in the Coptic language.

***Gospel of Truth*** A treatise or sermon giving a figurative interpretation of the significance of Christ for salvation. It was probably composed by the theologian and poet Valentinus, who was born in Egypt and taught in Rome in the mid-second century CE. Two copies (one very fragmentary) were found near Nag Hammadi in 1945.

***History of the Church***, see Eusebius.

**Irenaeus** Born in Smyrna in Asia Minor, he was a theologian who studied and taught in Rome and probably later became the bishop of Lyon (ca.

115-202 CE). Among his writings is a polemical work titled *Against Heresies* (ca. 180) that described and refuted the views of Christians he opposed.

**lacuna** A gap in a manuscript caused by damage or deterioration.

***Letter of Peter to Philip*** A narrative that begins with a letter telling Philip to gather with the other apostles on the Mount of Olives where they receive an appearance and revelation from the risen Christ. The only existing copy was found near Nag Hammadi in Egypt. It was probably composed in the second century CE.

**Nag Hammadi** The town in Egypt near which a discovery of ancient papyrus books was made in 1945.

**Nicene Creed** A formulation of Christian dogma made in 325 CE at the Council of Nicaea, a gathering of male bishops called and headed by the Roman Emperor Constantine to resolve problems of internal controversy in the Church.

***On the Origin of the World*** A philosophical treatise and account of the creation of the world. It retells the creation story of *Genesis* from a perspective which assumes the creator God is ignorant and wicked. A complete copy of the work was found near Nag Hammadi in 1945. It probably dates to the second or early third centuries CE.

**original sin** The theological doctrine, articulated by Augustine of Hippo, that the male seed was vitiated through the sin of Adam and Eve (pride). Sin left humanity in a state in which people are unable to obey God's commandments and hence are in need of God's undeserved grace in order to obtain salvation.

**Oxyrhynchus** An ancient village in Egypt where numerous papyri have been discovered, including the fragments of early Christian gospels.

***Pistis Sophia*** An extensive revelation dialogue between the Savior and his disciples set after the resurrection in which Mary Magdalene plays a leading role. The only existing copy is contained in a fourth century parchment book called the Askew Codex, which was discovered in the eighteenth century. It was probably composed in the third century CE.

***Q (Synoptic Sayings Source)*** *Q* stands for the German word *Quelle*, which means source. Q is a source on which the *Matthew* and the *Luke* draw.

***Sophia of Jesus Christ*** One of the works found near Nag Hammadi in 1945, it contains a second century revelation discourse from the risen Savior to his twelve male and five female disciples. It is a Christianized version of another treatise found near Nag Hammadi, titled *Eugnostos the Blessed*.

***Synoptic Sayings Source***, see *Q*.

***Teaching of the Twelve Apostles***, see *Didache*.

**Tertullian** African theologian of the second and third centuries CE who lived in Carthage. In addition to his apologetic and moral-disciplinary works, his extensive writings include polemical works written against the views of other Christians he opposed, in particular Valentinus and Marcion. He was later condemned as a heretic himself for his support of Montanism, a prophetic movement that arose in second century Phrygia.

***Wisdom of Solomon*** A collection of wisdom materials attributed to Solomon, but written in Greek in the first century BCE, probably in Alexandria, Egypt.

# Works Cited

Ash, James L. "The Decline of Ecstatic Prophecy in the Early Church."
*Theological Studies* 37 (1976), 227–52.

Atwood, Richard *Mary Magdalene in the New Testament Gospels and Early
Tradition*. European University Studies Series XXIII Theology 457. Bern:
Peter Lang, 1993.

Bauer, Walther *Orthodoxy and Heresy in Earliest Christianity*. 2nd ed.
Philadelphia: Fortress Press, 1971.

Bousset, Wilhelm *Kyrios Christos. A History of the Belief in Christ from the
Beginnings of Christianity to Irenaeus*. Trans. John E. Seeley. Nashville:
Abingdon Press, 1970.

Bovon, François "Mary Magdalene's Paschal Privilege." Pp. 147–57 in *New
Testament Traditions and Apocryphal Narratives*. Allison Park, PA:
Pickwick Publications, 1995.

Brock, Ann Graham *Mary Magdalene. The First Apostle: The Struggle for
Authority*. Harvard Theological Studies 51. Cambridge: Harvard
University Press, 2002.

——"Mary Sees and Reveals: An Analysis of the Speeches in Dialogue of
the Savior (NHC III,5)." Unpublished paper.

——"Setting the Record Straight—The Politics of Identification: Mary
Magdalene and Mary the Mother in *Pistis Sophia*." Pp. 43–52 in *Which
Mary? Marys in the Early Christian Tradition*. Ed. F. Stanley Jones. SBL
Symposium Series 20. Atlanta: Society of Biblical Literature, 2002.

——"What's in a Name? The Competition for Authority in Early Christian
Texts." Vol. 1, pp. 106–24 in *Society of Biblical Literature Seminar Papers*.
Atlanta: Scholars Press, 1998.

Brooten, Bernadette "Junia…Outstanding Among the Apostles." Pp. 453–71
in *Women Priests: A Catholic Commentary on the Vatican Declaration*.
New York: Paulist Press, 1977.

Brown, Raymond E., Karl P. Donfried, and John Reumann (eds.) *Peter in the
New Testament. A Collaborative Assessment by Protestant and Roman
Catholic Scholars*. Minneapolis: Augsburg, and New York: Paulist Press,
1973.

Buckley, Jorunn Jacobsen "An Interpretation of Logion 114 in The Gospel
of Thomas." *Novum Testamentum* 27 (1985), 245–72.

Bultmann, Rudolph *The Gospel of John. A Commentary*. Philadelphia:
Westminster, 1971.

Casadio, Giovanni "Gnostische Wege zur Unsterblichkeit." Pp. 203–54 in *Auferstehung und Unsterblichkeit*. Ed. Erik Hornung and Tilo Schabert. Eranos n.F. 1. Münich: Wilhelm Fink Verlag, 1993.

Castelli, Elizabeth "'I Will Make Mary Male': Pieties of the Body and Gender Transformation of Christian Women in Late Antiquity." Pp. 29–49 in *Body Guards. The Cultural Politics of Gender Ambiguity*. Ed. Julia Epstein and Kristina Straub. New York: Routledge, 1991.

Cherniss, Harold and William C. Helmbold (ed. and trans.) *Plutarch, Moralia*. Loeb Classical Library vol. 12. Cambridge, MA: Harvard University Press, 1957.

Cole, Susan G. "Could Greek Women Read and Write?" Pp. 219–24 in *Reflections of Women in Antiquity*. Ed. Helen P. Foley. New York: Gordon & Breach, 1981.

Collins, Adela Yarbro "The Seven Heavens in Jewish and Christian Apocalypses." Pp. 59–91 in *Death, Ecstasy and Other Worldly Journeys*. Ed. John J. Collins and Michael Fishbane. Albany: SUNY, 1995.

Collins, John J. "Introduction: Towards the Morphology of a Genre." Pp. 1–20 in *Apocalypse. The Morphology of a Genre*. Ed. John J. Collins. *Semeia* 14 (1979).

Collins, Raymond F. "Mary (person)." *ABD* 4 (1992), 579–81.

Colpe, Carsten *Die religionsgeschichtliche Schule: Darstellung und Kritik ihres Bildes vom gnostischen Erlösermythus*. Forschungen zur Religion und Literatur des Alten und Neuen Testamentes N.F. 60. Göttingen: Vandenhoeck & Ruprecht, 1961.

———"Jenseits (Jenseitsvorstellungen)." Pp. 246–407 in *Reallexikon für Antike und Christentum*. Vol. 17. Ed. Ernst Dassmann. Stuttgart: Anton Hiersmann, 2000.

———"Jenseitsfahrt I (Himmelfahrt)." Pp. 407–66 in *Reallexikon für Antike und Christentum*. Vol. 17. Ed. Ernst Dassmann. Stuttgart: Anton Hiersmann, 2000.

———"Jenseitsreise (Reise durch das Jenseits)." Pp. 490–543 in *Reallexikon für Antike und Christentum*. Vol. 17. Ed. Ernst Dassmann. Stuttgart: Anton Hiersmann, 2000.

Corcoran, Thomas H. (ed. and trans.) *Seneca. Natural Questions*. Loeb Classical Library. Cambridge: Harvard University Press, 1971.

Corley, Kathleen "'Noli me tangere.' Mary Magdalene in the Patristic Literature." Major Paper Submitted in partial fulfillment of the PhD Program in New Testament at the Claremont Graduate School, 1984.

Coyle, J. Kevin "Mary Magdalene in Manichaeism?" *Museon* 104 (1991), 39–55.

Crossan, John Dominic *The Birth of Christianity. Discovering What Happened in the Years Immediately after the Execution of Jesus*. San Francisco: Harper Collins, 1998.

———*The Cross that Spoke: The Origins of the Passion Narrative*. San Francisco: Harper and Row, 1988.

———*Four Other Gospels. Shadows on the Contours of Canon*. Minneapolis: Winston Press, 1985.

———*The Historical Jesus. The Life of a Mediterranean Jewish Peasant.* San Francisco: Harper Collins, 1991.

———*In Fragments. The Aphorisms of Jesus.* San Francisco: Harper and Row, 1983.

Culianu, Ioan Petru "Ascension." Pp. 107–16 in *Death, Afterlife and the Soul.* Ed. Lawrence E. Sullivan. New York: Macmillan, 1989.

D'Angelo, Mary Rose "Reconstructing 'Real' Women from Gospel Literature. The Case of Mary Magdalene." Pp. 105–28 in *Women and Christian Origins.* Ed. Ross Shepard Kraemer and Mary Rose D'Angelo. New York and Oxford: Oxford University Press, 1999.

De Boer, Esther *Mary Magdalene. Beyond the Myth.* Harrisburg, PA: Trinity Press International, 1997.

De Conick, April D. "'Blessed are Those who Have Not Seen' (Jn 20:29): Johannine Dramatization of an Early Christian Discourse." Pp. 381–98 in *The Nag Hammadi Library after Fifty Years. Proceedings of the 1995 Society of Biblical Literature Commemoration.* Ed. John D. Turner and Anne McGuire. Nag Hammadi and Manichaean Studies 44. Leiden: E. J. Brill, 1997.

———*Seek to See Him. Ascent and Vision Mysticism in the Gospel of Thomas.* Leiden: E. J. Brill, 1996.

Dillon, John *The Middle Platonists. A Study of Platonism 80 B.C. to A.D. 220.* London: Duckworth, 1977.

Donfried, Karl P. "Peter." *ABD* 5 (1992), 251–63.

Ehrman, Bart D. *The Orthodox Corruption of Scripture. The Effect of Early Christological Controversies on the Text of the New Testament.* Oxford: Oxford University Press, 1993.

Eisen, Ute E. *Women Officeholders in Early Christianity. Epigraphical and Literary Studies.* Collegeville, MN: The Liturgical Press, 2000.

Emmel, Stephen "The Recently Published *Gospel of the Savior* ('Unbekanntes Berliner Evangelium'): Righting the Order of Pages and Events." *Harvard Theological Review* 95.1 (2002), 45–72.

Falconer, William Armistead (ed. and trans.) *Cicero.* Vol. XX. Loeb Classical Library. Cambridge, MA: Harvard University Press, 1979.

Fallon, Francis "The Gnostic Apocalypses." Pp. 123–58 in *Apocalypse. The Morphology of a Genre.* Ed. John J. Collins. *Semeia* 14 (1979).

Funk, Robert W. *New Gospel Parallels.* 2 vols. Foundations and Facets: New Testament. Philadelphia: Fortress Press, 1985.

Funk, Robert W. and the Jesus Seminar *The Acts of Jesus. The Search for the Authentic Deeds of Jesus.* San Francisco: Harper Collins, 1998.

Grappe, Christian *Images de Pierre aux deux premiers siècles.* Étude d'histoire et de philosophie religieuses. Paris: Presses Universitaires de France, 1995.

Graver, Margaret (trans. and commentary) *Cicero on the Emotions. Tusculan Disputations 3 and 4.* Chicago: University of Chicago Press, 2002.

Hamilton, Edith and Huntington Cairns (ed.) *The Collected Dialogues of Plato including the Letters.* Bollingen Series LXXI. Princeton: Princeton University Press, 1961.

Hartenstein, Judith *Die zweite Lehre. Erscheinungen des Auferstandenen als Rahmenerzählung frühchristlicher Dialoge.* Texte und Untersuchungen. Berlin: Akademie Verlag, 1998.

Haskins, Susan *Mary Magdalen. Myth and Metaphor.* New York, San Diego, and London: Harcourt Brace & Co., 1993.

Hedrick, Charles W. and Paul A. Mirecki *The Gospel of the Savior. A New Ancient Gospel.* California Classical Library. Santa Rosa, CA: Polebridge Press, 1999.

Heine, Ronald E. *The Montanist Oracles and Testimonia.* North American Patristic Society Patristic Monograph Series 14. Macon, GA: Mercer University Press, 1989.

Hock Ronald F. "Homer in Greco–Roman Education." Pp. 56–77 in *Mimesis and Intertextuality in Antiquity and Christianity.* Ed. Dennis R. MacDonald. Studies in Antiquity and Christianity. Harrisburg, PA: Trinity Press, 2001.

Holzmeister, Urban "Die Magdalenenfrage in der kirchlichen Überlieferung." *Zeitschrfit für Katholische Theologie* 46 (1922), 402–22, 556–84.

Jansen, Katherine Ludwig "Maria Magdalena: *Apostolorum Apostola.*" Pp. 57–96 in *Women Preachers and Prophets through Two Millennia of Christianity.* Ed. Beverly Mayne Kienzle and Pamela J. Walker. Berkeley: University of California Press, 1998.

Janßen, Martina "Mystagogus Gnosticus? Zur Gattung der 'gnostischen Gespräche des Auferstandenen'." Pp. 21–260 in *Studien zur Gnosis.* Ed. Gerd Lüdemann. Arbeiten zur Religion und Geschichte des Urchristentums. Frankfurt am Main: Peter Lang, 1999.

Jensen, Anne *God's Self–Confident Daughters. Early Christianity and the Liberation of Women.* Louisville, KY: Westminster John Knox Press, 1996.

Johnson Hodge, Caroline E. "'If Sons, Then Heirs': A Study of Kinship and Ethnicity in Paul's Letters." Ph.D. Dissertation. Providence, R.I.: Brown University, 2002.

Jonas, Hans "Delimitation of the Gnostic Phenomenon—Typological and Historical." Pp. 90–108 in *Le Origini Dello Gnosticismo.* Ed. Ugo Bianchi. Numen supplement 12. Leiden: E. J. Brill, 1967.

——*Gnosis und spätantiker Geist. I. Die mythologische Gnosis.* 3rd ed. Göttingen: Vandenhoek & Ruprecht, 1964.

——*The Gnostic Religion. The Message of the Alien God and the Beginnings of Christianity.* 2nd ed. Boston: Beacon Press, 1958.

Kessler, William Thomas *Peter as the First Witness of the Risen Lord: An Historical and Theological Investigation.* Tesi Gregorianan, Serie Teologia 37. Gregorian University Press, 1998.

Kienzle, Beverly Mayne and Pamela Walker (ed.) *Women Preachers and Prophets through Two Millenia of Christianity.* Berkeley: University of California Press, 1998.

King, Karen L. "Afterword. Voices of the Spirit: Exercising Power, Embracing Responsibility." Pp. 21–41 in *Women Preachers and Prophets through Two Millennia of Christianity.* Ed. Beverly Mayne Kienzle and Pamela J. Walker. Berkeley: University of California Press, 1998.

————"The Book of Norea titled *Hypostasis of the Archons.*" Pp. 66–85 in
*Searching the Scriptures. Vol. 2 A Feminist Commentary.* Ed. Elisabeth
Schüssler Fiorenza. New York: Crossroad, 1994.

————"The Gospel of Mary." Pp. 357–66 in *The Complete Gospels.*
*Annotated Scholars Version.* Ed. Robert J. Miller. Rev. and ex. edition.
Sonoma, CA: Polebridge Press, 1994.

———— "The Gospel of Mary Magdalene." Pp. 601–34 in *Searching the
Scriptures. Vol. 2. A Feminist Commentary.* Ed. Elisabeth Schüssler
Fiorenza. New York: Crossroad, 1994.

————"Hearing, Seeing, and Knowing God. *Allogenes* and the *Gospel of
Mary.*" Forthcoming in *Crossing Boundaries and Removing Barriers in
Early Christian Studies. Essays in Honor of François Bovon on His
Sixty–Fifth Birthday.* Ed. Ann Graham Brock, David W. Pao, and David
Warren. Leiden: E. J. Brill, 2003.

———— "Prophetic Power and Women's Authority: the Case of the Gospel of
Mary Magdalene." Pp. 21–41 in *Women Preachers and Prophets through
Two Millennia of Christianity.* Ed. Beverly Mayne Kienzle and Pamela J.
Walker. Berkeley and Los Angeles: University of California Press, 1998.

———— "The Rise of the Soul: Justice and Transcendence in the *Gospel of
Mary.*" Pp. 425–42 in *Walk in the Ways of Wisdom. Essays in Honor of
Elisabeth Schüssler Fiorenza.* Ed. Shelly Matthews, Cynthia Briggs
Kittredge, and Melanie Johnson–DeBaufre. Harrisburg, Pennsylvania:
Trinity Press International, 2003.

————*What is Gnosticism?* Cambridge, MA: Harvard University Press, 2003.

————"Why all the Controversy? Mary in the *Gospel of* Mary." Pp. 53–74 in
*Which Mary? The Marys of Early Christian Tradition.* Ed. F. Stanley Jones.
SBL Symposium Series 20. Atlanta: Society of Biblical Literature, 2002.

Kloppenborg, John S. *Q Parallels. Synopsis, Critical Notes, and Concordance.*
Sonoma, CA: Polebridge Press, 1988.

Koester, Helmut *Ancient Christian Gospels: Their History and Development.*
Philadelphia: Trinity Press and London: SCM Press Ltd, 1990.

————"La Tradition apostolique et les origines du Gnosticisme." *Revue de
Théologie et de Philosophie* 119 (1987), 1–16.

————"Writings and the Spirit: Authority and Politics in Ancient
Christianity." *Harvard Theological Review* 84.4 (1991), 353–72.

————"Written Gospels or Oral Tradition?" *Journal of Biblical Literature*
113.2 (1994), 293–97.

Kraemer, Ross Shepard "Women's Authorship of Jewish and Christian
Literature in the Greco–Roman Period." Pp. 221–42 in *Jewish Women in
Hellenistic Literature.* Ed. Amy–Jill Levine. Septuagint and Cognate
Studies. Atlanta: Scholars Press, 1991.

Kristeva, Julia *Desire in Language: A Semiotic Approach to Literature and
Art.* New York: Columbia University Press, 1980.

Krutzsch, Myriam and Günter Poethke "Der Einband des koptisch–
gnostischen Kodex Papyrus Berolinensis 8502." Pp. 37–40 in *Forschungen
und Berichte. Staatliche Museen zu Berlin, Hauptstadt der DDR. Band 24
Archäologische Beiträge.* Berlin: Akademie Verlag, 1984.

Labriolle, Pierre de (ed.) *Tertullien. De praescriptione haereticorum.* Paris: Librairie Alphonse Picard et Fils, 1907.

Lagrange, Marie–Joseph "Jésus a–t–il été oint plusieurs fois et par plusieurs femmes?" *Revue biblique* 9 (1912), 504–32.

Lake, Kirsopp (ed. and trans.) "The Didache, or The Teaching of the Twelve Apostles." Vol. 1, pp. 308–33 in *Apostolic Fathers.* Loeb Classical Library. Cambridge, MA; Harvard University Press, 1977.

Lamb, W. R. M. (ed. and trans.) *Plato. Alcibiades.* Loeb Classical Library. Cambridge, MA: Harvard University Press, 1927.

Layton, Bentley and Wesley Isenberg (text and trans.) "The Gospel of Philip." Pp. 131–217 in *Nag Hammadi Codex II, 2–7.* Vol. 1. Ed. Bentley Layton. Nag Hammadi Studies XX. Leiden: E. J. Brill, 1989.

Lucchesi, E. "Évangile selon Marie ou Évangile selon Marie–Madeleine?" *Analecta Bollandiana* 103 (1985), 366.

Lührmann, Dieter "Die griechischen Fragmente des Mariaevangeliums POxy 3525 und PRyl 463." *Novum Testamentum* 30.4 (1988), 321–38.

MacDermot, Violet and Carl Schmidt *Pistis Sophia.* Nag Hammadi Studies IX. Leiden: E. J. Brill, 1978.

MacDonald, Dennis R. "Andrew (person)." *ABD* 1 (1992), 242–44.

———*The Homeric Epics and the Gospel of Mark.* New Haven and London: Yale University Press, 2000.

Mack, Burton L. *The Lost Gospel. The Book of Q and Christian Origins.* San Francisco: Harper Collins, 1993.

MacMullen, Ramsey *Paganism in the Roman Empire.* New Haven and London: Yale University Press, 1981.

MacRae, George M. (ed.) and Robert McL. Wilson (trans.) "The Gospel of Mary." Pp. 524–27 in *The Nag Hammadi Library in English.* Ed. James M. Robinson and Richard Smith. 3rd ed. San Francisco: Harper and Row, 1988.

Maisch, Ingrid *Between Contempt and Veneration: Mary Magdalene, The Image of a Woman through the Centuries.* Collegeville, MI: Liturgical Press, 1998.

Majercik, Ruth *The Chaldean Oracles: Text, Translation, and Commentary.* Ph.D. dissertation. University of California, Santa Barbara, 1982.

Malvern, Marjorie *Venus in Sackcloth. The Magdalene's Origins and Metamorphoses.* Carbondale and Edwardsville: Southern Illinois University Press, 1975.

Marcus, Ralph (ed. and trans.) *Philo Supplement* 1. Loeb Classical Library. Cambridge, MA: Harvard University Press, 1953.

Marjanen, Antti *The Woman Jesus Loved. Mary Magdalene in the Nag Hammadi Library and Related Documents.* Nag Hammadi and Manichaean Studies XL. Leiden: E. J. Brill, 1996.

———"The Mother of Jesus or the Magdalene? The Identity of Mary in the So–Called Gnostic Christian Texts." Pp. 31–41 in *Which Mary? Marys in the Early Christian Tradition.* Ed. F. Stanley Jones. SBL Symposium Series 20. Atlanta: Society of Biblical Literature, 2002.

Markschies, Christoph "Lehrer, Schüler, Schule: Zur Bedeutung einer

Institution für das antike Christentum." Pp. 97–120 in *Religiöse Vereine in der römischen Antike. Untersuchungen zu Organisation, Ritual und Raumordnung.* Ed. Ulrike Egelhaaf–Gaiser and Alfred Schäfer. Tübingen: Mohr Siebeck, 2002.

Mattei, Paul (ed.) *Tertullien. La Mariage unique (De monogamia).* Sources Chrétiennes 343. Paris: Les Éditions du Cerf, 1988.

McGuire, Anne "Women, Gender and Gnosis in Gnostic Texts and Traditions." Pp. 257–99 in *Women and Christian Origins.* Ed. Ross Shepard Kraemer and Mary Rose D'Angelo. New York and Oxford: Oxford University Press, 1999.

Metzger, Bruce M. *A Textual Commentary on the Greek New Testament.* 2nd ed. Stuttgart: Deutsche Bibelgesellschaft, 1994.

Meyer, Marvin W. "Making Mary Male: The Categories 'Male' and 'Female' in the Gospel of Thomas." *New Testament Studies* 31 (1985), 554–70.

———"*Gospel of Thomas* Logion 114 Revisited." Pp. 101–11 in *For the Children, Perfect Instruction. Studies in Honor of Hans–Martin Schenke on the Occasion of the Berliner Arbeitskreis für koptisch–gnostische Schriften's Thirtieth Year.* Ed. Hans–Gebhard Bethge, Stephen Emmel, Karen L. King, and Imke Schletterer. Nag Hammadi and Manichaean Studies XLIV. Leiden: E. J. Brill, 2002.

Milburn, Robert *Early Christian Art and Architecture.* Berkeley and Los Angeles: University of California Press, 1988.

Miller, Robert J. (ed.) *The Complete Gospels.* Sonoma, CA: Polebridge Press, 1992.

Mohri, Erika *Maria Magdalena: Frauenbilder in Evangelientexten des 1. bis 3. Jahrhunderts.* Marburger theologische Studien 63. Marburg: Elwert, 2000.

Morard, Françoise "L'*Évangile de Marie*, Un Messsage ascétique?" *Apocrypha* 12 (2001), 155–71.

———"Une Évangile ecrit par une femme?" *Bulletin de Centre Protestant d'Etudes* 49.2–3 (May, 1997), 27–34.

Mortley, Raoul "'The Name of the Father is the Son' (Gospel of Truth 38)." Pp. 239–52 in *Neoplatonism and Gnosticism.* Ed. Richard T. Wallis and Jay Bregman. Studies in Neoplatonism: Ancient and Modern 6. Albany, NY: SUNY Press, 1992.

Nasrallah, Laura S. *'An Ecstasy of Folly': Rhetorical Strategies in the Early Christian Debate over Prophecy.* Th.D. dissertation. Harvard University, 2001.

Nussbaum, Martha "The Stoics on the Extirpation of the Passions." *Apeiron* 20 (1987), 129–77.

O'Connor, June "On Doing Religious Ethics." *Journal of Religious Ethics* 7.1 (1979), 81–96.

Otto, Io. Car. Th. eques de (ed.) *Iustini Philosophi et Martyris. Operis.* Vol. 1.2. Jena: Libraria Hermanni Dufft, 1877.

Pagels, Elaine H. *Beyond Belief. The Secret Gospel of Thomas.* New York: Random House, 2003.

———*The Gnostic Gospels.* New York: Random House, 1979.

————"Visions, Appearance, and Apostolic Authority: Gnostic and Orthodox Traditions." Pp. 415–30 in *Gnosis. Festschrift für Hans Jonas.* Ed. Barbara Aland. Göttingen: Vandenhoeck and Ruprecht, 1978.

Parsons, P. J. "3525. Gospel of Mary." Pp. 12–14 in *The Oxyrhynchus Papyri* vol. 50. Graeco–Roman Memoirs, No. 70. London: Egypt Exploration Society, 1983.

Pasquier, Anne *L'Évangile selon Marie.* Bibliothèque copte de Nag Hammadi, Section "Textes" 10. Québec: Les Presses de Université Laval, 1983.

Perkins, Pheme *The Gnostic Dialogue. The Early Church and the Crisis of Gnosticism.* Studies in Contemporary Biblical and Theological Problems. New York: Paulist Press, 1980.

————"Mary, Gospel of" *ABD* 4 (1992), 583–84.

————*Peter. Apostle for the Whole Church.* Studies on Personalities of the New Testament. Columbia, South Carolina: University of South Carolina Press, 1994.

Petersen, Peter M. *Andrew, Brother of Simon Peter, His History and His Legends.* Novum Testamentum Supplement 1. Leiden: E. J. Brill, 1958.

Petersen, Silke *'Zerstört die Werke der Wieblichkeit!' Maria Magdalena, Salome und andere Jüngerinnen Jesu in christlich–gnostischen Schriften.* Nag Hammadi and Manichaean Studies 48. Leiden: Brill, 1999.

Potter, David *Prophets and Emperors. Human and Divine Authority from Augustus to Theodosius.* Cambridge, MA: Harvard University Press, 1994.

Price, Robert M. "Mary Magdalene: Gnostic Apostle?" *Grail* 6.2 (1990), 54–76.

Puech, Henri–Charles and Beate Blatz "The Gospel of Mary." Pp. 391–95 in *New Testament Apocrypha. Vol 1 Gospels and Related Writings.* Rev. ed. Wilhelm Schneemelcher. Trans. R. McL. Wilson. Cambridge: James Clark and Co.; Louisville, KY: Westminster/John Knox Press, 1991.

Rackham, H. (ed. and trans.) *Cicero.* Vol. XIX. Loeb Classical Library. Cambridge, MA: Harvard University Press, 1979.

Räisänen, Heikki "The Nicolaitans: Apoc. 2; Acta 6." Pp. 1602–44 in *Aufstieg und Niedergang der römischen Welt.* Vol. 26.2, part 2: Principate. Berlin and New York: Walter de Gruyter, 1995.

Ricci, Carla *Mary Magdalene and Many Others. Women who followed Jesus.* Trans. Paul Burns. Minneapolis: Fortress Press, 1994.

Robeck, Cecil M., Jr. *Prophecy in Carthage. Perpetua, Tertullian and Cyprian.* Cleveland, OH: Pilgrim Press, 1992.

Roberts, C. H. "463. The Gospel of Mary." Vol. III, pp. 18–23 in *Catalogue of the Greek Papyri in the John Rylands Library* III. Manchester: University Press, 1938

Robinson, James M. "Codicological Analysis of Nag Hammadi Codices V and VI and Papyrus Berolinensis 8502." Pp. 9–45 in *Nag Hammadi Codices V, 2–5 and VI with Papyrus Berolinensus 8502, 1 and 4.* Ed. Douglas M. Parrott. Nag Hammadi Studies XI. Leiden: E.J. Brill, 1979.

————"From Cliff to Cairo. The Story of the Discoverers and Middlemen of the Nag Hammadi Codices." Pp. 21–58 in *Colloque international sur les*

*Textes de Nag Hammadi (Québec, 22–25 août 1978)*. Ed. Bernard Barc.
Bibliothéque copte de Nag Hammadi section Études 1. Québec and
Louvain: Les Presses de l'Université Laval and Éditions Peeter, 1981.

———"Jesus From Easter to Valentinus (or to the Apostles' Creed)."
*Journal of Biblical Literature* 101.1 (1982), 5–37.

———"On the Codicology of the Nag Hammadi Codices." Pp. 15–31 in
*Les Textes de Nag Hammadi*. Ed. J.–É. Menard. NHS 7. Leiden: E. J.
Brill, 1975.

Robinson, James M. and Helmut Koester *Trajectories through Early
Christianity*. Philadelphia: Fortress Press, 1971.

Robinson, James M. and Richard Smith (ed.) *The Nag Hammadi Library in
English*. 3ʳᵈ ed. San Francisco: Harper and Row, 1988.

Rowlandson, Jane (ed.) *Women and Society in Greek and Roman Egypt. A
Sourcebook*. Cambridge: Cambridge University Press, 1998.

Schaberg, Jane "How Mary Magdalene Became a Whore." *Bible Review* 8.5
(1992), 30–37, 51–52.

———*The Resurrection of Mary Magdalene. Legends, Apocrypha, and the
Christian Testament*. New York and London: Continuum, 2002.

———"Thinking Back through the Magdalene," *Continuum* 1.2 (1991),
71–90.

Schenke, Hans–Martin "Bemerkungen zum koptischen Papyrus Berolinensis
8502." Pp. 315–22 in *Festschrift zum 150 jährigen Bestehen des Berliner
Ägyptischen Museums*. Mitteilungen aus der Ägyptischen Sammlung 8.
Berlin: Akademie Verlag, 1974.

———"Carl Schmidt und der Papyrus Berolinensis 8502." Pp. 71–88 in
*Carl–Schmidt–Kolloquium an der Martin–Luther–Universität 1988*.
Martin–Luther–Universität Halle–Wittenberg Wissenschaftliche Beiträge
1190/23. Halle (Saale), 1990.

———*Das Matthäus–Evangelium im mittelägyptischen Dialekt des Koptischen
(Codex Schoyen)*. Oslo: Hermes, 2001.

———*Das Philippus–Evangelium (Nag–Hammadi–Codex II,3). Neu her-
augegeben, übersetzt und erklärt*. Texte und Untersuchungen 143. Berlin:
Akademie Verlag, 1997.

Schmid, Renate *Maria Magdalena in gnostischen Schriften*. München:
Arbeitsgemeinschaft für Religions– und Weltanschauungsfragen, 1990.

Schmidt, Carl *Die alten Petrusakten im Zusammenhang der apokryphen
Apostellitteratur nebst einem neuentdeckten Fragment untersucht*. Texte
und Untersuchungen 24/1 n.F. 9/1. Leipzig, 1903.

———"Ein vorirenäisches gnostisches Originalwerk im koptischer Sprache."
Pp. 839–47 in *Sitzungsberichte der preussischen Akademie der
Wissenschaften zu Berlin, phil.–hist. Kl*. Vol. 36. Berlin: Verlag der
Akademie der Wissenschaften, 1896.

Schmidt, Carl (text edition) and Violet MacDermot (translation and notes)
*The Books of Jeu and the Untitled Text in the Bruce Codex*. Nag Hammadi
Studies 13. Leiden: E. J. Brill, 1978.

———*Pistis Sophia*. Nag Hammadi Studies 9. Leiden: E. J. Brill, 1978.

Schneemelcher Wilhelm (ed.) *New Testament Apocrypha*. 2 vols. Rev. ed.

Trans. R. McL. Wilson. Cambridge: James Clark and Co.; Louisville, KY: Westminster/John Knox Press, 1991–1992.

Schröter, Jens "Zur Menschensohnvorstellung im Evangelium nach Maria." Pp. 178–88 in *Ägypten und Nubien in spätantiker und christlicher Zeit. Akten des 6. Internationalen Koptologenkongresses Münster, 20.–26. Juli 1996. Band 2: Schrifttum, Sprache und Gedankenwelt.* Ed. Stephen Emmel, Martin Krause, Siegfried G. Richter, Sofia Schaten. Wiesbaden: Reichert Verlag, 1999.

Schüssler Fiorenza, Elisabeth *In Memory of Her. A Feminist Theological Reconstruction of Christian Origins.* New York: Crossroad, 1985.

———"Mary Magdalene: Apostle to the Apostles." *Union Theological Seminary Journal* (April 1975), 22–24.

Schweitzer, Albert *The Quest of the Historical Jesus.* Minneapolis: Fortress Press, 2001.

Scott, James C. *Domination and the Arts of Resistance. Hidden Transcripts.* New Haven and London: Yale University Press, 1990.

Scott, Walter *Hermetica. The Ancient Greek and Latin Writings which Contain Religious or Philosophic Teaching Ascribed to Hermes Trismegistus.* Boston: Shambhala, 1985.

Segal, Alan F. "Heavenly Ascent in Hellenistic Judaism, Early Christianity and their Environment." Pp. 1333–94 in *Aufsteig und Niedergang der römischen Welt* II. Principat 23.2. Berlin and New York: Walter de Gruyter, 1980.

Semler, Ioh. Salomo (ed.) *Q. Septimii Florentis Tertulliani Opera.* Vol. 1. Magdeburg: John Christian Hendel, 1827.

Shoemaker, Stephen J. "A Case of Mistaken Identity? Naming the Gnostic Mary." Pp. 5–30 in *Which Mary? Marys in the Early Christian Tradition.* Ed. F. Stanley Jones. SBL Symposium Series 20. Atlanta: Society of Biblical Literature, 2002.

———"Rethinking the 'Gnostic Mary': Mary of Nazareth and Mary of Magdala in Early Christian Tradition." *Journal of Early Christian Studies* 9.4 (2001), 555–95.

Smith, Terrence V. *Petrine Controversies in Early Christianity: Attitudes towards Peter in Christian Writings of the first two Centuries.* Tübingen: Mohr, 1985.

Strange, James F. "Magdala." *ABD* 4 (1992), 463–64.

Svartvik, Jesper *Mark and Mission. Mk 7:1–23 in its Narrative and Historical Contexts.* Stockholm: Almquist & Wiksell International, 2000.

Tabbernee, William *Montanist Inscriptions and Testamonia. Epigraphic Sources Illustrating the History of Montanism.* Patristic Monograph Series 16. Macon, GA: Mercer Press, 1997.

Tardieu, Michel *Écrits Gnostiques. Codex de Berlin.* Sources Gnostiques et Manichéennes. Paris: Les Éditions du Cerf, 1984.

Thompson, Mary R. *Mary of Magdala.* New York/Mahwah, N. J.: Paulist Press, 1995.

Till, Walter C. "Die Berliner gnostische Handschrift." *Europäischer Wissenschafts–Dienst* 4 (1944), 19–21.

———"Die Gnosis in Ägypten." *La parola del passato* 12 (1949), 230–49.

Till, Walter C. and Hans–Martin Schenke, *Die gnostischen Schriften des koptischen Papyrus Berolinensis 8502.* 2nd ed. Texte und Untersuchungen 60. Berlin: Akademie Verlag, 1972.

Torjesen, Karen Jo *When Women Were Priests. Women's Leadership in the Early Church and the Scandal of their Subordination in the Rise of Christianity.* San Francisco: Harper and Row, 1993.

Trible, Phyllis "A Love Story Gone Awry." Pp. 72–143 in *God and the Rhetoric of Sexuality.* Philadelphia: Fortress Press, 1978.

Van Unnik, Willem Cornelius "The 'Gospel of Truth' and the New Testament." Pp. 79–129 in *The Jung Codex: A Newly Recovered Gnostic Papyrus.* Ed. Frank L. Cross. London: A. R. Mowbray, 1955.

Vorster, Willem S. "The Protevangelium of James and Intertextuality." Pp. 262–75 in *Text and Testimony. Essays on New Testament and Apocryphal Literature in Honour of A. F. J. Kiljn.* Ed. T. Baarda, A. Hilhorst, G. P. Luttikhuizen, and A. S. van der Woude. Kampen: J. H. Kok, 1988.

Waszink, J. H. *Tertulliani De anima.* Amsterdam: J. M Meulenhoff, 1947.

Williams, Frank (trans.) *The Panarion of Epiphanius of Salamis.* 2 vols. Nag Hammadi Studies 35; Nag Hammadi and Manichaean Studies 36. Leiden: E. J. Brill, 1987 and 1994.

Williams, Michael A. *The Immovable Race. A Gnostic Designation and the Theme of Stability in Late Antiquity.* Nag Hammadi Studies 21. Leiden: E. J. Brill, 1985.

———*Rethinking "Gnosticism": An Argument for Dismantling a Dubious Category.* Princeton, NJ: Princeton University Press, 1996.

Wilson, Robert McL. *Gnosis and the New Testament.* Philadelphia: Fortress Press, 1968.

———"The New Testament in the Gnostic Gospel of Mary." *New Testament Studies* 3 (1956/1957), 236–43.

———"Valentinianism and the Gospel of Truth." Pp. 133–41 in *The Rediscovery of Gnosticism: Proceedings of the International Conference on Gnosticism at Yale, New Haven, Connecticut, March 28–31, 1978.* Vol. 1 *The School of Valentinus.* Ed. Bentley Layton. Studies in the History of Religions XLI. Leiden: E. J. Brill, 1981.

Wilson, Robert McL. and George W. MacRae, "The Gospel of Mary." Pp. 453–71 in *Nag Hammadi Codices V, 2–5 and VI with Papyrus Berolinensis 8502, 1 and 4.* Ed. Douglas M. Parrott. Nag Hammadi Studies XI. Leiden: E. J. Brill, 1979.

Wink, Walter *Cracking the Gnostic Code. The Powers in Gnosticism.* Society of Biblical Literature Monograph Series 46. Atlanta, GA: Scholars Press, 1993.

Wire, Antoinette Clark "I Corinthians." Pp. 153–95 in *Searching the Scriptures. Vol. 2 A Feminist Commentary.* Ed. Elisabeth Schüssler Fiorenza. New York: Crossroad, 1994.

———*The Corinthian Women Prophets. A Reconstruction through Paul's Rhetoric.* Minneapolis, MN: Fortress Press, 1990.

Yaghjian, Lucretia B. "Ancient Reading." Pp. 206–30 in *The Social Sciences and New Testament Interpretation.* Ed. Richard Rohrbaugh. Peabody, MA: Hendrickson, 1996.

# Index of Citations